THE STAR TSAR

by

John Guy Collick

Banjo and Alexandra Book One

Published by John Guy Collick

ISBN: 978-0-9954673-5-4

Cover photography by Alexey Mikhailov
Model: Miroslava Bronnikova

In memory of Wendy and Richard.

We've inspected the sky
inside and outside.
No gods or angels
were found.
Vladimir Mayakovksy. The Flying Proletariat, 1925

A hundred icons scattered in the snow, churned up with blood and soot - all dead, all useless.

The Theotokos of St Theodore
The Virgin of Kazan
Mandylion
Christ Pantokrator.

They drifted by like leaves on a river, their annealed faces full of laughing contempt as Grishka stumbled, weeping, away from the train.

An officer strode ahead towards the trees. What was his name? Prince Vasyutin. As arrogant as all the rest. So arrogant that he waded through the snow picking off the fleeing soldiers with his Mausers, one in each hand, shooting the poor bastards in the back of the head as if he was hunting pheasants.

Leaving them for her so she'll feed on their corpses first and give him time to escape. He won't turn around and shoot me because he doesn't want to see her break free.

A blast of sound – a cracked bell as an iron fist hit the inside of a steel prison. And again. And again. The last one brought Grishka to his knees, the snow swallowing his thighs. *Burrow under it like a rabbit and she won't find you.*

Vasyutin stopped at the edge of the trees and turned around. Grishka waited for the bastard to murder him too but instead the prince gazed past, frowning like someone trying to make out a friend's face in a crowd.

She's right behind me. Burning eyes waiting to bore out my soul as she peels my face off with her dagger teeth.

But the White officer's expression wasn't that of a man standing before Hell, so Grishka risked a glance over his shoulder.

He laughed. He actually laughed. The armoured train, all six hundred tons, lay neatly on its side in the drifts next to the track, like an amber necklace dropped from a girl's throat. Ruptured valves shrieked steam that rolled over the track in waves and melted the banked snow. Shapes sprawled in the slush around the wreck.

The world rang again, and a dome appeared in the wall of the middle carriage – the one the priests had hung with icons, garlanding the house-sized cylinder with seraphs, saints and Christ himself. A crack appeared in the glitter-stretched steel. Claws worked through the rent and forced it wider. The last of the gold faces fell away. Grishka managed to stand.

Don't look into her eyes.

Instead he turned to Prince Vasyutin just as the officer put a Mauser to his own temple and blew his head open in a bright spray.

He wasn't running away. The last one was for himself.

Grishka floundered towards the trees. Tearing metal. He didn't need to look - he knew exactly what was happening. She'd rip open her cage and leap into the sky, riding her iron mortar, burning with hunger for the flesh of Russian men. She'd smell him out, under the snow, under the dark pines, wherever he hid. And yet he kept running until he was among the trees.

A shape howled across the sky and he glimpsed red eyes, writhing hair, the crucible in which she'd grind his bones – and then nothing, just endless grey clouds.

The demon let me live. I'm saved, I'm free.

But through the forest more icons floated towards him. These were the size of men and rolled through the snow on wheels - staring eyes and skull grins in golden light. And between them, walking on their hind legs, came her spider children - idiot faces filled with monstrous hunger.

CHAPTER ONE

Ikayungri, Siberia, May 1923.

B anjo woke up with rust down the back of his neck and the same curse with which he'd greeted every dawn for the past eight months. *Ernie Featherington and the basket trick - idiotic little fucker.* A year and a half ago, in Vladivostok, a drunken doughboy from the *USS Sibley* told his moronic friend that one of the brothels had a Japanese madam offering said basket trick for two dollars and the fool had staggered into the night with all his savings in his fist and dribble on his chin. Banjo knew that fantasy always outstripped reality. From what he'd heard all a man could expect from the basket trick were concentric lacerations around his bollocks and splinters up his arse. But Ernie wasn't having any of it and so Banjo's stupid sense of duty forced him after the lad as he lurched three miles through the mud and rain up the hill to the whorehouse.

They passed mansions where drunk colonels from the Hernia Brigade staggered through waltzes with White heiresses under cracked chandeliers - desperately begging each Princess Katerina or Empress Anastasia for a kiss and a grope in exchange for the liberation of Mother Russia, and Banjo knew some of those distraught vampires would say yes. Nothing like desperation to fire up the organs. Anyone with half a brain would be on the next steamer to Yokohama or Shanghai but these poor orchids had their roots too deep in this rotten soil to tear themselves away.

Tasha's was in the sludge-coated warren behind the Armenian Church where the lads from the Royal Hampshires had stowed their bicycles. Banjo handed his charge over and settled down in a corner of the makeshift bar with half a bottle of vodka. In two days he'd be back in the engine room of the *Karagöz*, heading for Japan with another couple of hundred refugees rich enough to pay Waza the Turk for passage. He'd say farewell to the mad shit once they'd docked - he knew the Japanese were always looking for good engineers. The Reds would roll up sooner or later and he'd no intention of being here when they did.

Tasha had persuaded a couple of sailors to steal a piano from one of the abandoned hotels overlooking the bay and an American rating began cranking out *Sewer Rat Stomp*. A lieutenant from the Royal Sussex promptly drew his revolver and put a bullet through the keyboard because it was 'damnable jungle music not fit for British ears'. That kicked off the grandfather of all bar fights. Banjo ran upstairs to rescue Ernie but some cowardly bastard blackjacked him on the landing and he woke up to find himself rattling to and fro on the floor of a rail car heading west, surrounded by glittery-eyed Czech soldiers and a deranged Japanese officer who shot himself in the head on the third night.

By the time he'd located a bunch of lads from the Hampshires it was clear they weren't going to turn the train around just for him. When a valve on the locomotive ruptured he fixed it, thinking that would stop him being press-ganged into the ranks, but it only made things worse. The allies were delivering fifty Austin armoured cars to some military depot in the middle of nowhere and now he was second mate to the mad Glaswegian in charge. Fine - hand them over and back to Vladivostok. Except the train wasn't going that way, and two weeks later the place was swarming with Reds, his fellow travellers were all dead or missing, and Banjo had gone to ground.

He crept to the end of the abandoned boiler he'd made his home for the last five months. The depot had turned out to be a huge ironworks and factory complex sprawled across the foothills of the Yablonoi Mountains. When winter hit he'd burrowed himself a nest at the back of a furnace room to stay alive but after the Bolsheviks swarmed the place he retreated to one of the outlying warehouses, a collapsing hulk of rust and girders.

It was spring now. He had until autumn to make his escape before the snows came. Even that was wildly optimistic. The arrangement he had with the poor buggers the enemy had forced to be their engineers wasn't going to keep him alive for much longer. All the White mechanics had vanished as soon as the Soviets turned up, leaving the local peasants to service the forges and the machines. The dozy sods hadn't a clue about anything more complex than a hinge and so he sneaked around at night fixing things in exchange for scraps and silence. One even told Banjo his name - Epifan - or maybe that just meant 'fuck off demon'. Perhaps they thought he was some kind of local spirit who brought them luck. Fat load of good that would do him.

This new lot were a right shower - crisp and purposeful in their uniforms, draping red flags over everything and holding committee meetings into the wee hours. He'd seen huddles of grubby Ivans and Olgas bent over pamphlets while some windbag declaimed about the wonders of communism with a finger pointed at heaven. Banjo had even spotted a squadron of Cossacks who'd realised which way the wind blew and thrown their lot in with the new order. He guessed the war was over and the Reds were just mopping up, chasing out any Japanese or Whites who'd decided to try their hands at banditry once they realised they were never getting their palaces back.

He crept out onto the factory floor, rolled up in oily sacking just in case any of the guards finally decided to visit the abandoned engine room and he had to play dead. That forced a chuckle. *I'm a corpse already, filled with nothing but dirt and shit.* Dusty light slanted across the vault, picking out fragments - a stack of rusted wheels, crumbling shells of machinery, heaps of chains with links as big as his head. Through a collapsed section of the north wall he saw the edge of the pine forest. Someone had left an icon by the breach to ward off the devils that lived in the woods and mountain passes.

It was so tempting to wander into that endless wasteland, but what would be the point? He'd grab a few days of freedom at most and then be eaten by bears or run out of food and have to slink back to beg crusts from Epifan and his dim-witted chums. Pain lanced through his guts and he shambled off across the hall in search of dinner.

Banjo slunk through halls filled with rust and shadows, and engine sheds whose tracks had dissolved into red grit like troughs of dried blood. Once in a while he passed gangways sloping down to double doors. They led to a labyrinth of forges and workshops underneath the ironworks. He'd never explored the cellars and as far as he knew everyone avoided them - first the Whites and now the Reds. He'd toyed with the idea of finding another entrance, thinking it would be safer to hole up underground, but something about the corroded chains wrapped around the handles warned him away. There were other things in this place, part-glimpsed among the machinery - silhouettes, glints of glass and copper, twitching shadows. Or maybe it was just the hunger, fear and loneliness making him hallucinate.

No options left. Staying here would kill him. He couldn't go west. He'd either have to try to retrace his steps back to Vladivostok and stow away on a ship bound for Japan or China, or head south to Mongolia. If he tarted himself up a bit and pretended to be deaf, dumb and bonkers, he might pass muster as a holy fool. They liked holy fools here, or they did until the Mad Monk started rogering the Tsarina. *You're as barmy as Rasputin himself if you think you'll get ten yards.* But if he didn't come up with an idea fast it was death from starvation and the cold, or those Reds would find him and hang him from a tree by his bollocks if he was lucky. Banjo had seen what they did to the enemies of the people and hanging was the least of it.

Night fell as he approached the centre of the works. Despite this being the arse-end of beyond the Russians had built a truly enormous city of foundries and workshops spreading out like a fan from the sharp-lit point of the station to the dead cold sweep of the outer perimeter touching the northern forest. God only knew why. Perhaps they'd planned it as a depot and factory complex for the entire east - but this wasn't even on the trans-Siberian railway. From what he could tell Banjo was marooned on some pissy little branch line out of Chita, which lay another four hundred miles to the south.

He shook the thoughts out of his head and picked up a length of pipe to use as a weapon, keeping to the shadows and hoping his stench didn't go too far before him. A balcony ran around the inside of the next shed so he climbed up out of sight and scouted through a gap in the crumbling brickwork. It was going to be a cloudless night with a three-quarter moon. No chance of thieving from the soldiers. Although they were an ill-disciplined and drunken lot in the evenings, grown complacent with victory, he still couldn't risk it under clear skies.

To the southwest, beyond the dark shells of more factory buildings and engine sheds, he saw the main camp in and around the scrabble of huts that made up the town of Ikayungri. Light spilled into the streets from open doorways and tent awnings, and soldiers walked back and forth along the rutted pathways, some leading their horses to forage. He heard the bright hiss of trains in the distance. It sounded like one had just arrived, bringing more fanatics from Moscow or Petrograd with their shining caps, prophetic literature and Mausers. He fought a wild urge to walk up to the station and ask for a first-class ticket. *Single to Chapel Allerton, Leeds, Yorkshire, England, and keep the change Comrade.* A wave of exhaustion and sadness flooded through him as he clambered down into his shadow hell.

Every night the peasant mechanics left the parts they couldn't fix at one of four locations. If the machines were too big to move Epifan scribbled chalk marks on the floor to guide him. It only took Banjo a few moments to locate the tiny arrow, then the next. They led him to three Maxim guns, all jammed or broken. Someone had already had a go at repairing the first but clearly hadn't a clue. It was wrecked beyond repair. He found a clutch of filthy tools wrapped up in sacking inside a disused furnace and set to.

He cannibalised the broken gun to fix the others. It was simple enough, but hunger made it hard to concentrate and his hands trembled. It was cold in this night-warren, but he sweated with the effort. Someone was watching him. He guessed it was the peasants, trying to figure out what he was doing. He toyed with the idea of taking a gun back to the lair for defence, but that would break trust and, besides, he had no ammunition. Banjo hunted for a wrench. The stupid bastards hadn't left him one. *How in the realm of fuck-buggery am I supposed to mend a Maxim without a wrench?* He had a spare in his nest - stolen in the early days. Fetching it would lose an hour, but he reckoned he still had time to get the machines working before sunrise.

Banjo returned to where the chalk arrows started and found another sack with half a loaf of bread, a mouldy sausage and a bottle of what passed for vodka in these parts. Good old Epifan - he'd done himself proud tonight. Once Banjo had finished the job he might even risk creeping onto the roof to read his book by moonlight. When he arrived back at the deserted hall he was so wrapped up in anticipation that he almost didn't notice the creatures stumbling across the rubble-littered floor towards the hole in the north wall.

"We heard The Hammer weeping in the night."

Viktor cornered Alexandra in the train corridor and steadied himself against the lurch of the carriage by clutching at her coat. She supposed the idiot couldn't help himself but she pushed his hand away and vowed to break his nose if he ever scrabbled at her with his opium-stained fingers like that again.

What did he expect her to do? *We all weep in the night. The whole country cries itself to sleep.* But that didn't ease the guilt. *I've got to try harder with The Hammer - how can I cure his pain?* Her broken dolls, all of them - the singer, the poet and the soldier.

"How's Ekaterina?"

Viktor's eyes were black dots in watery circles the colour of rotten sandalwood.

"A bad night, such a bad night," the man gave a sigh and pressed the back of his hand against his forehead. She guessed he'd spent most of it dispensing 'medicines' to his sister and himself. "But what to do? What to do?"

"How much did you give her?"

"Enough."

"How much is left?"

"Enough."

Alexandra detached herself from Viktor's clutches, polished her glasses on her greatcoat lapel and glanced out of the window.

The train curved along the tracks towards the outskirts of Ikayungri. The morning fog blanked out most of the landscape but where the sun burned off the mist she made out the charcoal scribble of the forest and the outline of the mountains beyond. Her heart skipped to the sound of the wheels. *There's powerful White science buried in this wilderness.* She'd dig it out with her own hands and turn it over to the people so they could forge a future for everyone. And it was so vast. She'd assumed Ikayungri was nothing more than a supply depot the White army had concealed north of the trans-Siberian line, yet as the warehouses, factories and forges coalesced among the earthbound clouds, she realised she was looking at a whole city of industry and engineering.

Perhaps the wild exaggerations of the driver and his comrades weren't fantasy after all. In the drunken aftermath of Ekaterina's performance to the Red Guard in Krasnoyarsk the crew had told her of the mighty Tsarist armoured trains that still prowled the eastern forests. Far bigger than the Czech Legion's fearsome *Orlik*, they were powered by engines as huge as cities and spired with gun turrets upon gun turrets. Thanks to the sorcery of Rasputin several had been built in Hell itself and were crewed by fallen angels. Now the enemies of the revolution had fled they slept somewhere in that endless wilderness, curled up in the ash and clinker nest of Tugarin the earth dragon, waiting to be tamed again. *You're still there aren't you, mad old Efrosinya Nikolayevna? Reeking of piss and camphor. Terrifying me with your folk tales and monsters until father sent you packing and burned your nightmares out with magnesium.*

A hand trailed across her cheek. Ekaterina - shawl held tight across her shoulders and hair bound into a single plait that reached the back of her knees. Sleepiness and the drugs made the actress's face gaunt and her kohl-rimmed eyes seemed to fill half her skull, turning her into an exquisite dream of death.

"Why would he come here?"

To run away from you.

The singer shuddered as the shadow of an abandoned foundry slid past.

"He's gone mad. Pavel has gone mad. Why else would he come to the ends of the Earth among all this machinery and fire? This is the land of Vrubel's demon."

Viktor took his sister's hand.

"We'll be there soon. You must prepare yourself. They will want the great Comrade Rusanov to sing for them, you know they will. Please rest."

Alexandra swore under her breath.

"You didn't tell them we were coming, did you?"

Viktor shifted his feet uneasily and shrugged before leading Ekaterina to her cabin.

Anyone with half a brain knew the reason Pavel had abandoned his job as director of the Proletkult Theatre *October Dreams* and set off for Siberia in an Agit-Propaganda train was because he'd fallen in love with another actress and didn't have the courage to face Ekaterina. Mind you who could blame him for running away? Ekaterina was the cousin of Iron Felix himself, architect of the Extraordinary Commission for Combating Counter-Revolution. How else did Viktor get away with pouring his tinctures into himself and his sister every night? A jilted singer wouldn't usually warrant an expedition across the entire country to track down her betrayer, yet Iron Felix had but to raise his hand and it was so. But if that idiot Viktor had telegraphed ahead to trumpet the arrival of the Siren of the Revolution, her ex-lover would be well out of sight by the time they arrived. *God, Pavel, I really do hope you're far away. Ekaterina's got to give up this insane quest. Surely when Viktor's medicines run out we'll have to turn back.*

The actress's voice drifted along the corridor, a mournful lament she didn't recognise. Throughout their journey Ekaterina had sung to the soldiers and the crew with the generosity of her art that made her famous. They were the old songs they'd listened to in the trenches. As a commissar she was obliged to remind her friend to lead the audiences in the new ones too - *Boldly Comrades Keep in Step* and *Varshavianka*, but the cry always went up for the ancient favourites as they travelled further east, and they were so beautiful Alexandra hadn't the heart to tell her off. *My broken dolls - take what happiness you can.*

And right on cue a shadow moved at the end of the corridor. The Hammer stared back at her through the grainy air. As ever, he wore his cavalry uniform - blue jacket, red trousers and black leather boots immaculately polished so they gave off their own dark light. He had a photograph face - fixed and grey as he stared down the horrors that broke over him in endless night-tides.

Alexandra smiled and saluted. The Hammer didn't respond. She could tell by the man's eyes it'd be a few days before the soldier returned to her. At least like this he wouldn't harm anyone. He was too busy fighting monsters on abandoned battlefields thousands of miles away.

Any hope that their arrival at Ikayungri would be a muted affair vanished as they pulled into the station. Alexandra was momentarily distracted by the sight of an armoured train being loaded with ammunition, a chain of soldiers passing shells up to one of the domed green-steel turrets. On an adjacent track cavalrymen guided horses into a support wagon. They paused, yanked off their caps and cheered as the locomotive from Krasnoyarsk hissed to a stop. More cries came from the platform and as the smoke cleared she saw groups of men and women in various uniforms crowding towards them. She could have cheerfully hit Viktor when the man gave her yet another 'what to do?' shrug before leading Ekaterina to the top of the steps. She was wearing her army greatcoat, belt and Cossack sabre and when she emerged into the morning a great cheer went up.

"Comrade Rusanov, Comrade Rusanov, sing for us!"

One private began *Oleg the Wise* basso profundo and others joined in. When Ekaterina responded by singing the chorus the roar of approval drowned out the singers.

God help us, this is ridiculous.

An officer struggled through the mass, berating the soldiers on either side as they shuffled open a path, alternately shame-faced and grinning. The newcomer invited Ekaterina to climb down. Alexandra joined them and the man gave them both a crisp salute. He was scrawny and nervous with a face that looked like it'd been worked out of dark brown clay by a clumsy child and he seemed to be looking for someone who wasn't there. Alexandra allowed him a minute of this all-too-familiar pantomime before introducing herself.

"I am Commissar Lobachevsky of the People's Commissariat for Education. I'm in charge of the expedition searching for the Agit-Train *A Bolshevik Forever!*" Even then it took another thirty seconds for the ignorant shit to grasp the fact that he'd have to deal with a woman. He gave her another confused salute.

"Comrade Commissar. I am Assistant Commander Yohzin, at your service. It's a great honour to welcome the great Comrade Rusanov to our camp. We've prepared your quarters."

"We don't need quarters, we'll billet with the rest."

"Impossible." One glare and he reined in the spluttering. "But Comrade Commissar, all the men voted to provide the best lodgings for the Siren of the Revolution - a house, with a stove, and beds."

Alexandra couldn't be bothered to argue so she gestured for him to lead the way instead. Yohzin wriggled with pleasure. The crowd parted and he guided them down from the platform and into a network of muddy streets that curled around the outside of the factories like a breakwater.

The village had long been overtaken by warehouses, lumber yards and coal heaps. An Austin armoured car rattled past, the crack from its exhaust echoing against the brick walls that towered over wooden huts. Alexandra gawped at the abandoned complex, struggling again to understand how and why the Whites had built this here in the middle of the wilderness.

Yohzin took them to a requisitioned Ataman's cabin. Rich light spilled out between the planking, bringing with it the fragrance of stoves and a samovar. Alexandra was about to follow the others when the aide pulled her to one side and whispered that the commander wanted a word.

The officer escorted her to an engine yard. They climbed up iron steps to a cluster of wooden offices bolted onto a locomotive assembly shed like limpets on a dreadnought's hull. Alexandra could hear the grinding rumble of furnaces and machinery through the stone wall and feel the vibrations under her boots as she ascended.

Two desks faced each other across bare boards with an unlit stove between them. A sharp-faced officer with lizard eyes and a broom moustache pored over a ledger. He had a pipe in his mouth and as he drew meticulous lines with a steel ruler the smoke curled around his head. Alexandra put him at about fifty. The man stood up and gave her a salute and an easy grin.

"Comrade Commissar. Commander Aminev at your service. We are deeply honoured to welcome you and Comrade Rusanov to this shit hole."

Alexandra saluted back and presented her letters. Aminev waved her to a spare chair while he read. The commander finished with a grunt and passed the documents to Yohzin.

"The Agit-Train *A Bolshevik Forever!* arrived a month ago."

"The players are here?"

Aminev shook his head.

"They left after a fortnight."

Viktor and his stupid telegrams. As suspected, the moment Pavel had learned Ekaterina was on the way he'd fled.

"Where to?"

Yohzin looked up at his commanding officer with big round eyes, folded the letters and gave them back to Alexandra with a trembling hand. Iron Felix's signature had that effect on people.

"No idea," Aminev perched himself on the edge of his desk. "God knows why they came here in the first place. Fifty actors and actresses on a train garlanded like an Easter cheesecake turned up one morning with no protection, just pamphlets, stage props and film cameras. We assumed they were on their way east and diverted to avoid bandits on the trans-Siberian. I offered to lend them a wagon-load of cavalry and a machine-gun to escort them back to Chita where they'd be safe, but the day before the planned departure they vanished."

"Vanished?"

Aminev shrugged and lifted his hands.

"Thirty branch lines spiral out from here into the mountains and the forest. They could be anywhere."

"Did you search for them?"

Aminev and his aide exchanged looks. Alexandra caught a flash of irritation in the commander's eyes.

"To be honest, Comrade Commissar, I'd more important things on my mind. Even though the enemy's defeated there are still gangs of White scum given over to banditry in this godforsaken land. I only have enough men to protect the works, not to go out on extended expeditions looking for actors. All our resources are directed into understanding what we have here, something I hope the People's Commissariat for Education can help with."

"A secret armoured train factory."

"So it seems. But why here? There's no strategic value in this wilderness. Why so big?"

Yohzin piped up.

"We didn't realise how important the Agit-Train was. If Iron Felix himself..."

Commander Aminev held up his hand and his assistant suddenly became very interested in the notebook on his desk.

"I sent some riders along the most likely routes, but they found nothing. Your friends are on their way to Vladivostok or lost in the mountains. I suggest you look to the east or wait for them to come slinking back here. We'll give you what limited help we can."

"I ask for no more," answered Alexandra, inventing a whole swathe of excruciating punishments for spoilt actors in her head.

"In the meantime, perhaps Comrade Commissar could organise the nurse's detail," said Yohzin. "The health of the men is of concern to Comrade Commander and the women lack guidance..." he tailed off at Alexandra's expression, looking to Aminev who grinned back at him. The officer tapped the letter with the stem of his pipe.

"Comrade Commissar's orders are pretty clear to me."

Yohzin turned red and stared down at his desk, scribbling furiously in a ledger.

"Although," the commander tamped down a fresh wad of tobacco. "Would Comrade Rusanov sing for the troops? This place unsettles them. Joy rather than endless discipline and punishment may lift their spirits. The Agit-Train put on a play but nobody understood what the hell it was about."

"Of course - and I'm also happy to give a lecture to our comrades on the future of scientific communism."

Yohzin stifled a cough and Aminev smiled.

"What a wonderful idea."

CHAPTER TWO

Banjo slipped behind a stack of rotten railway sleepers and hunched down, hoping the rags and the half-light would make him look like a heap of sacking to anyone glancing his way. *You knew this day would come.* But it still left him feeling sick. The Reds were finally taking over the outlying factories. No choice but to flee or try his luck in the cellars. It'd have to be the forest. Underground he'd be even more trapped.

But these newcomers didn't look like soldiers or peasant engineers. They shuffled along in baggy robes, hauling what appeared to be a strange pram, like fat, unkempt nannies taking their bairns for a Sunday stroll through Roundhay Park. Banjo counted four figures, one at each corner, and he realised they weren't actually pulling anything. The machine trundled along by itself on three large bicycle wheels, jouncing over the uneven factory floor.

It resembled a glass-sided cabinet full of glowing water, with spiky metal arms sticking out from the casing. Was that the silhouette of a torso outlined in the grainy liquid? *Jesus Christ.* A medical specimen perhaps - something wretched, deformed and drowned in formaldehyde from *Dr Aether's Emporium of Marvels and Grotesques* on Scarborough pier. But what were four Russian peasants doing with it in the middle of nowhere?

With only moonlight falling through gaps in the roof it was

impossible to make out anything about the box's escort. They moved in a silent lope, not speaking a word. One of them bent down to throw the icon aside and something in the way the hands moved made Banjo shuffle back on his bottom until he fetched up against the wall, breathing hard. The last figure paused at the breach and turned its head in his direction. The hooded face was in shadow and told Banjo nothing. He managed not to whimper, hoping it was just scanning the hall one last time. The group squeezed through the gap and made its way across the yard outside.

While fear and fascination slugged it out in his skull Banjo hauled himself up and scuttled through the shadows to the hole, keeping close to the wall so he could scrunch down into a heap of rubbish if anyone decided to come back for another shufti. *You're acting like a fucking idiot. The clock's ticking.* He needed to find a wrench and get back to fix the machine guns before sun-up if he was going to keep in with Epifan and his mates, otherwise the buggers were bound to turn him in.

And yet there was something about the intruders that pulled him on, especially that ambulatory cabinet. As he watched, it swivelled towards the north and increased speed, its companions trotting to keep up. They crossed the moonlit yard on the other side of the wall. Beyond it a lead-coloured grass slope rose towards the woods, shivering in the moonlight. The forest looked like a breaking wave of shadow pouring down from the mountains.

One of the walkers reached up and pulled back its hood. Chalk-white skin, though Banjo still couldn't tell if it was a man or a woman. It ran ahead, crouching down as if scouting a path to the woods before turning to face the others. Its shadow unrolled across the grass in the moonlight. Four arms - the second pair sprouting from its armpits. *A Great White Ape from Mars. I've finally gone raving mad.*

The group disappeared into the trees, leaving Banjo clutching the jagged brickwork to keep himself from falling over or running screaming one last time through the furnaces and forges of this iron asylum. It had to be a hallucination, had to be. For the last year and a half of hunger and misery, fear and loneliness, he'd buried himself in the one book he always carried with him, scouring out his misery with visions of romantic adventure on another world, and it was finally making him see things. *John Carter fought with the Great White Apes on Barsoom, and now there's one down here in this arse-end of a Russian nowhere. Rubbish, just listen to yourself. He didn't have four arms, it was just the shadow of a piece of machinery or sacking he'd nicked.* Banjo looked at the trees, then up at the mountain peaks. Through a snow dusted saddle between two ridges he saw another, far vaster mountain, its upper peak a tin-coloured shard under the moon. An orange light shimmered near its summit.

The Maxims, you fool. He ran back to his den, fully expecting to see a four-armed monster squeezing through the crack in the masonry each time he glanced behind. Nothing re-appeared so he stashed the food Epifan had left for him and grabbed the wrench.

It was a mirage, an illusion brought on by endless grinding fear, like the visions madmen saw in the trenches. Banjo cursed himself - he'd always been distracted by mysteries and wonders, like a child. And here of all places. *Stargazing, head in the clouds. Reading that tripe again, filling your head with nonsense.* Mother's voice echoed in his head. Even so he picked up the copy of *A Princess of Mars* he'd kept with him since Gallipoli. *Is that where you came from?* He riffled through the pages. A couple had come loose and he coaxed them back in. *The creatures were about ten or fifteen feet tall, standing erect, and had, like the green Martians, an intermediary set of arms or legs, midway between their upper and lower limbs.* Was he going mad and giving life to characters from a bloody Edgar Rice Burroughs' novel?

Banjo downed a swig of the horse-piss vodka to marshal his nerves and set off for the workshops - creeping through the shadows in case any more creatures decided to pay him a visit. This time he followed the route that kept him well away from the chained doors to the cellars. That lost him an hour, but his imagination filled the basement with more horrors waiting to burst the locks and chew his head off.

He found the machine guns again and worked frantically to mend them. The darkness was already fading and he kept making stupid mistakes, struggling to coax the smaller parts into place with trembling hands. He was just about to re-attach the armoured plate to the second Maxim when he heard voices. Without thinking he ran behind a heap of broken machinery only to realise he'd left the wrench hanging from a bolt. Banjo hesitated, gathering his courage to rush out and snatch it back before he was spotted, but it was too late. If he moved now the bastards would have him.

Six soldiers and two peasants came into the room. Banjo recognised Epifan - a heavy-set bearded man with an expression like a screwed-up sock. He stopped when he saw the part-assembled guns and his shoulders slumped. The Russian didn't speak but the realisation of his betrayal screamed out from every grimy crease in his face and clothes. One of the guards had the insignia of a section commander on the arm of his grubby tunic. He yelled something at the engineers but Epifan ignored the orders. Instead he eased the wrench clear of the gun and held it in his hand, turning it this way and that. He glanced towards the machines where Banjo was hiding and for a second the Englishman swore their eyes met. Anyone with any sense would turn him in to atone for their failure to fix the Maxims. Instead Epifan turned back to the wrench in his hand. Perhaps he was going to use it as a weapon.

No such luck. The commander hit him and pointed at the machine guns once more. Banjo reckoned they'd found the workers away from their posts, assumed they were slacking and brought them here to finish the job. The beet-faced officer carried on ranting, belting Epifan across the face and shoulders. The peasant just stood there in silence. *Go on - brain the bastard. What's the matter with you?* But Banjo knew it would be suicidal. The other engineer snatched his own cap from his head and fell to his knees, begging the guards. *Please Comrade. Epifan can't work if you beat him senseless.* The commander kicked him over and stalked out. The remainder of the squad perched on crates to watch the engineers struggle with the guns.

Maybe once Banjo might have taken them on. Even now, half-starved and mad with visions, he'd still have a chance but what good would that do? Killing six Reds would just bring the rest of them down on him. All he could do was hope the bastards would get bored and wander off, giving him time to make it to the door and return to his lair.

The last hours of the night crawled on but the guards showed no intention of leaving. He tried to send psychic instructions on how to mend the Maxims to Epifan and his mate but it was clear they hadn't a clue. They bumbled back and forth, struggling to fix the guns and Banjo saw the hope leaching out of them minute by minute. A couple of times a fierce urge swept over him - to run out and throw himself into the repairs or surrender to the watchmen and beg for death. But fear and sense kept him hidden.

The section commander returned. The engineers got to their feet. The officer took one look at the broken Maxims, unholstered his Mauser and shot Epifan through the eye before pistol-whipping the other peasant. Despite himself Banjo let out a muffled cry, clamping his fingers over his mouth, but the soggy blows and howls of the victim drowned out the sound. Even so, one of the guards glanced his way. Banjo just managed to control his loathing and fury. He pulled himself further into the gloom and thankfully they didn't spot him. The Red bastard holstered his gun, smoothed his hair back with both hands like a man composing himself after a dance, and gestured for the surviving engineer to be dragged away, his boots leaving two bloody trails in the concrete dust.

Banjo waited half an hour before creeping out. If only he could take one of those Maxims and find a belt for it, he'd make those sadistic cunts suffer before they hung him upside down from a beam or fed him into a furnace. But it was a stupid fantasy and even Epifan's remaining eye seemed to laugh at him for his pitiful desperation. No use robbing the corpse of clothes or any food the man might have stuffed into his pockets. That would definitely alert the Reds. He picked up the wrench just as returning voices echoed outside, and made his solitary way back to the outer warehouses.

He sat for an hour in the rusted cocoon of his boiler, staring at the landscapes marked in corroded curves up the opposite wall - maps of wars past and yet to come scribbled out in crystallised blood. His only friend in this brick and iron hell was dead. If the other engineer was in on the deal he'd know that Banjo had broken trust. So, no food or drink anymore. He'd always known it'd end up like this - try to escape or die here. He needed a plan but was so tired and leached of all hope by exhaustion and hunger. A spear of watery light fell from a crumbling rivet hole above his head. Without thinking he opened *A Princess of Mars* and began to read, only pausing occasionally to wipe away the drops with his thumb.

Ekaterina's joy and languid despondency bore no relation to the day or hour but were marked out in tiny spoons, some filled with cocaine, some with black opium. It was illegal of course, but she was the famous Comrade Rusanov, Siren of the Revolution, and dwelt in a separate reality. Her emotional calendar was just as different - wild happiness, lethargy, fury and hungry curiosity for the wonders of humanity's rebirth rarely coincided with what was happening around her. It was only when she sang, danced and acted that the hyperactive sensuality of her sphere intersected the broken world.

Except now. It took a good quarter of an hour for the news to fully sink in but when she realised her lover Pavel had fled once more in the Agit-Train she shrieked solidly for ten minutes, Viktor hysterically begging her to stop before she ruined her voice. A group of worried soldiers gathered at the entrance to the Ataman's cottage but The Hammer planted himself in the doorway and the Georgian's expression sent them slinking away. By the time Ekaterina had calmed down enough to shout actual words she'd managed to break a bed, kick a hole in the rotten wall and almost throw the samovar through the window. While Viktor sat on the floor cuddling the battered kettle and weeping, Alexandra snatched at the actress's wrists and, despite her face being sprayed with oaths she hadn't heard since the trenches, manoeuvred her friend onto the one still-unbroken divan.

"Ekaterina, give up this quest. Give up Pavel. He's not worthy of you," she shook the woman's arms, trying to catch her gaze which was abyss-eyed and full of hell. Alexandra had done this many times before - that night they'd defended the theatre against the marauding Cossacks and Ekaterina had gone berserk with bloodlust at the news of her father's death. In these moments something in Alexandra's voice and touch had the power to calm the singer, who fought for breath like a drowning swimmer. At last she clamped her mouth tight and nodded fiercely.

"You are Ekaterina Leonovna Rusanov, the brightest star in the Proletkult universe. You don't need anyone else."

"But why does he run from me?"

"Because he's lost. Look at this vast wilderness, tainted by our enemies. We can't bring the new science and order here overnight, as hard as we may strive, and the tormented land fights back in its pain and swallows up weaker people than you and I."

Ekaterina touched her cheek.

"I will find him. I will find him."

Alexandra bit her tongue and managed a smile. *Broken dolls. What happened to us all? Wild artists at the dawn of revolution - we were inseparable. War shattered our souls and Pavel used that excuse to go where his cock led him - all the way here with that witless idiot Galina.*

No-one was happier than Alexandra when the lecherous bastard set off for Siberia in the Agit-Train. It had been like a new spring for the collective and she'd assumed Ekaterina would finally see the wretched shit for what he was. But one morning the actress triumphantly handed over the orders she'd wheedled out of Iron Felix. Commissar Alexandra Lobachevsky was to accompany the renowned Comrade Rusanov with whoever else she deemed necessary to go after the Agit-Train *A Bolshevik Forever!* and return with it and its crew of actors and actresses to

Petrograd before the winter.

She heard a faint cough and turned to see Yohzin's head peeking round The Hammer.

"Is Comrade Rusanov unwell?"

"She's just tired. Perhaps it would be better if she sang tomorrow night."

"No," said Ekaterina, leaping to her feet and pushing Alexandra out of the way. "I will sing. I will sing now!"

Knowing there was nothing she could say or do, the commissar gave Viktor a weary nod. He abandoned the samovar and scrambled to his case of bottles, searching for a tincture to carry his sister through the evening. Luckily Yohzin had disappeared. Alexandra hoped The Hammer had kicked him out into the street for his insolence. When she looked outside the road was empty.

As the day faded half a dozen Cossacks cantered up to the house with a spare horse, insisting that Ekaterina ride with an escort down to one of the foundries where the troops had set up an impromptu theatre. Alexandra walked behind, smiling to herself at the ease with which her friend sat amid the guard of honour with their swords and whips. When they entered the yards, the hot wind from the forges streamed the singer's shawl sideways in rivers of sparks that strangely avoided her to hiss and die on the men's thick kaftans and sheepskin hats.

The stage was nothing more than a warehouse door set on barrels in the middle of a factory with furnaces on one side and a curving slope of sweat-faced soldiers and workers on the other. The joyful roar at their entrance nearly deafened Alexandra. Commander Aminev reached up for Ekaterina but she ignored the courtesy and jumped down beside him, placing a hand on his shoulder and gesturing to heaven. The officer winked at Alexandra, who stepped up next to the actress and turned to the crowd.

Alexandra knew the audience was there for songs and already they passed bottles and flasks back and forth, roaring their fellowship in each other's faces. Nearly all were men, though she spotted a handful of women comrades dotted here and there. She didn't grudge the crowd's attention, so kept her speech short - telling them of the future of a noble proletarian science forging new Soviets on new worlds, and they cheered and shouted with an enthusiasm that reached a crescendo as Ekaterina kissed her on the cheek, bowed and broke into *Boldly Comrades Keep in Step.*

As Alexandra watched the actress perform amid the iron shadows and annealed fires, a rare hope kicked her into a happy grin. It was like standing in an artefact of futurity - a bright engine built from genius and labour, so meticulous and good that the troops, the singer and the factory became a single mechanism. Ekaterina's hands and feet snatched the foundry's power from the air and cast it towards the wall of laughing faces piled up beside the stage. Even when the chaos set in, as the audience got drunk and roared and stamped through the songs and dances, she saw nothing more than a machine unable to contain its own joyous energy. *We shall build bigger and better engines in our new worlds, ones as big as cities to carry us all to the stars.*

A soldier fell from the second row, tumbling over his comrades to sprawl in the dirt. He got to his knees, clasped his fists together and started to yell at the ceiling. Alexandra noticed anger in Aminev's eyes so she approached the guard. He was calling on God and the saints to protect them.

"It's only old Klimov, Comrade, he's mad," shrieked a woman in the crowd, and those around her bellowed with laughter.

Irritated that the fool had broken into her dreams of science, she bunched the drunk's tunic in her fist and shook him.

"God is dead. God and his saints are dead. There is only the Revolution," Alexandra shouted, trying to be heard above the singing. The soldier grabbed her arms, eyes staring.

"Baba Yaga and her monsters. The Holy Seraphim of Sarov protect us. She lives in the forest. This is her hell, and we cast her out." He became more desperate and with a start Alexandra realised the man had pissed himself. The fingers dug deeper into her coat as she tried to pull away. "I saw her in the forest. She flies through the sky on her iron mortar and feeds on the flesh of

Russian men. This is her hell, comrade, and we cast her out."

Two soldiers hauled him to his feet.

"Take this bloody fool and toss him in the river," said Aminev. The nearest members of the audience fell silent, clearly frightened the commander would turn on them next. Judging by their expressions he was probably restraining himself for Alexandra's benefit. He pointed at the doorway with his pipe.

"Let's talk, Comrade Commissar."

As his companions dragged the weeping soldier into the night the two of them stood in the entrance to the foundry, the heat and noise streaming past them into the darkness. The commander lit his pipe, watching her sideways through the smoke.

"It's a constant battle against ignorance and superstition. It holds us back."

He gestured towards the forest and the mountains beyond.

"This is a wild realm. Hundreds of years ago the Old Believers came here in their rebellion, armed with primitive faith in ancient magic and a vengeful God. Their dreams infect the place."

"But this will be a crucible of our science and we'll burn all that nonsense away forever," said Alexandra. Standing in the rays of the furnace and surrounded by machines her visions of the future took on a fierce, exhilarating energy. Here she could truly believe they would become masters of the ages. Aminev chuckled.

"With a bit more help from Petrograd. The only engineers we have are the ones left behind by the Whites who threw themselves on our mercy. They're hopeless - stupid children. They babble endlessly of curses and demons in the woods. The enemy filled them with ghost stories to keep them in line. Some of the idiots still speak of the Good Tsar who'll save them from tyranny."

The Good Tsar. The further east she'd gone the stronger the peasant's belief in the Good Tsar - true father of the nation, kind and saintly, imprisoned in a palace somewhere, yearning to care for his people if only the cruel and corrupt bureaucrats would let him. When they'd stopped to cut wood for the train on the way to Chita an old man had come to Alexandra with trembling hands and blessed her and the Revolution - *God be with you my daughter, for you have returned the Good Tsar to us.*

"I told them the Romanovs are dead," continued Aminev. "But even if I brought Nikolai's head here and stuck it on a pole they wouldn't believe me. The idea clings no matter how many times I try to beat it out of them."

He kicked at a lump in the ground.

"How's Comrade Lenin's health? We've heard rumours."

"Counter-revolutionary propaganda. He's resting and will soon return to work."

"We hope for his swift recovery," said Aminev after a while.

Alexandra tried a reassuring smile and hoped it looked convincing in the half-light. She'd heard rumours too but hers came from an altogether more reliable source. At least they had Comrade Stalin as go-between for Lenin after his stroke. She ought to speak with him, find out the truth, but she hadn't seen Stalin since London before the war and doubted the Georgian would even remember her.

"Once we educate the people in the liberating ideals of Soviet science they'll break the chains of ignorance by themselves," she said, to change the subject.

"You think so?" asked Commander Aminev. "You're a good, noble and wise citizen, Comrade Commissar, and I admire your belief and trust in the future. Do you really believe you can chase away these demons and monsters of the forest? That they'll fade like smoke in the clear light of your bright dawn? Baba Yaga, the Crystal Mountain, Koschei the Deathless, all the spirits I heard about when I was an infant?"

"Tugarin the earth dragon," said Alexandra, despite herself.

Aminev laughed out loud.

"We must have had the same nurse."

Mad old Efrosinya Nikolayevna. No-one else could have been so unfortunate.

"They'll fade, Comrade Commander, they'll fade. And from these factories and furnaces rocket ships will rise to carry our new Soviet men and women to the stars."

The soldier conceded her a grin.

"This place is incredible and we never suspected it existed. Have a look at the engine sheds. Some of the land ironclads they designed would dwarf even the mighty *Orlik* - true rail dreadnoughts. If there's a birthplace for your dreams, this is it."

Aminev looked up at the clear sky and following his gaze the commissar saw the ships of her imagination soar above the ruin and desolation of war.

"I like it that poetry and science live together in your soul, and you have a woman's good sense, more than an old fool like me," continued the commander. "We have need of it all, but for now I want your analytical mind. I've found a mystery here that needs solving by a person of your intellect. A common soldier like myself can't comprehend what he sees but perhaps you can."

CHAPTER THREE

When the Reds first captured the factories, they'd thrown the bodies of their victims into the furnaces. Sometimes they didn't even bother shooting them. In fact, if they wanted to make a particular point, the bastards would strap their prisoner to a plank and ease him in slowly, feet-first. After things settled down they stopped burning the corpses - Banjo reckoned it was because the residue buggered up the works - and took to dragging them to the abandoned outer buildings and dropping them down wells or into any handy pits they found. Some they bothered to coat with lime, otherwise if the shaft was deep enough or covered in an iron lid they just tossed the wretches in and that was that.

Epifan ended up in a disused smelting pit with half a dozen decomposing cadavers two halls along from Banjo's hideaway. Even though their executioners had sprinkled a couple of barrels of lime around the stench still clawed at the back of Banjo's throat as he clambered down in the moonlight. The dead engineer's tunic and trousers were fine but blood had soaked the cap into a claggy mess. Luckily, he found another on the head of a rotting White infantryman and once he'd pulled the insignia off it looked more or less like an ordinary worker's.

He mumbled a half-remembered sailor's prayer over Epifan. Maybe he should get the icon the monster threw to one side - they loved their icons in this benighted land - but he didn't want to go near that hole in the wall again. Besides, it would do nothing to ease his guilt.

In the safety of the boiler he put the clothes on. Normally they'd be too small but semi-starvation had squeezed him out. He felt like that dying bear in the stinking pit of a zoo in Valparaiso - bone, hair, misery and not much else. Which led him to the problem of the beard which was halfway down his chest and, as far as he could tell, turned him into Rasputin's brother. There was no way to cut it off. He'd tried burning it away but that made him look as if he had the mange. It would have to stay. He attempted to stuff the rest of his tangled mane under the cap but it just balanced on top like a yacht on a pyramid. His only realistic option was to escape in the dead of night.

The perimeter to the west and east had patrols. Banjo always wondered why he never came across the Reds to the north but after seeing the creatures and their roving cabinet he was beginning to understand why. Even if it had been a desperate fantasy carved out of his loneliness, those woods and mountains looked all too ready to be the backdrop to delirium. If he wanted to get to the station and stow away on a train, or steal one of those fine Cossack horses, he'd have to go via the factories. He reckoned the first leg wouldn't be too hard - there were enough abandoned gantries for him to avoid the soldiers, but then he'd be in the ironworks proper. If he kept to the shadows and didn't have to talk to anyone he might make it. After that it was through Ikayungri itself to the trains. *You're utterly insane. Everywhere will be swarming with patrols and guards and even if the bastards are drunk half the time you stick out like a bloody circus clown who's spent a month rolling in shit.* But what choice did he have?

He hid *A Princess of Mars* in the lining of Epifan's tunic, stuck the remains of the piss vodka in a pocket and ate the last of his rations, a grim meal of black bread and mouldy sausage. He'd sharpened down one edge of a foot-long piece of steel and wrapped cloth around the end as a handle. Fat good it would be against a Mauser but stuffing it up his sleeve made him feel better.

He set out, refusing to look back at his home for almost half a year. His usual route brought him to the machine guns, still unfixed. So the stupid idiots hadn't found a replacement mechanic to mend them. Epifan was probably their best, more fool them. Once Banjo had been able to heft a Maxim and fire it from the hip but now he was too weak and besides, he didn't have the ammunition.

The ironworks were a long-vaulted inferno filled with furnaces, heaps of spoil and castings. *Where is everyone?* Only one of the forges was active, a couple of men stripped to the waist leaning on shovels and staring into the fire. Banjo couldn't believe his good fortune. Before anyone looked in his direction he picked up a wheelbarrow full of clinker and trundled past. It worked. Whatever they saw in the roiling flames turned them into brass and soot statues.

The archway at the end of the hall led to a vast engine assembly shed. Two part-built armoured trains sat next to each other. They had hulls of green riveted steel and turrets rising up into the gloom, their gun slots empty. *Strewth. How did the Whites lose when they had these?* For a moment he forgot where he was, the mechanic in him stunned by the precision and power slumbering in those plates, rivets and wheels. But they weren't finished - the enemy had come too quickly. *If Lenin's hordes figure out how to complete the job, God help the rest of mankind.*

And then he stood outside, above the town, with a soft wind drifting up the street to push the fires and heat back into the maelstrom behind him. The cluster of lights at the bottom of the long slope marked the station. Still no sign of the usual guards although he heard horses stabled nearby. Perhaps it would make more sense to steal a ride and head south to Mongolia. Mind you, he'd be hard put to outrun the Cossacks if they came after him.

A woman's voice drifted on the night - clear, beautiful and operatic, singing an old song that made the hairs on his neck rise, even though he couldn't understand the words. It was an achingly gorgeous lament, the kind a Martian princess might keen for her love under twin moons. *Get a grip, you pillock. No time to laik about.* Down the hill, around a corner and he found himself in front of one of the Austin armoured cars they'd brought from Vladivostok.

"Bugger me," he said without thinking. Fire that up and he'd be away in minutes.

Two soldiers stepped out from behind the vehicle and strolled towards him with guns drawn.

When Alexandra lived in London before the war she and half a dozen other Bolsheviks gave their Scotland Yard spies the slip and went down to Brighton for the day. On the Palace Pier Zoltar the Magician sat in a glass booth and told fortunes for a penny. As Alexandra was the only one who understood English she fed her friends' coppers into the machine and read out their destinies. Hers was some nonsense about a tall dark stranger taking her to the stars so she scrunched it up and tossed it into the Channel. Yet the mannequin's chipped mask and hands tapping at the crystal ball lingered in her mind, stirring up nightmares for many years afterwards.

Standing in the back of an empty engine shed in Siberia, Zoltar the Magician was the first thing that sprang into her head when Aminev pulled away the tarpaulin. The next was that the officer had found a strange medical specimen - a woman's naked torso preserved in a box of formaldehyde for male students to snigger at. The glass-sided cabinet stood on three rubber-tired wheels with thin steel spokes. Articulated arms like parts of a dentist's drill stuck out at random intervals from the lower half of the case, which looked as if it was moulded out of Bakelite reinforced with copper strips. Alexandra read the number *339* in faded script on the plastic. Oily liquid filled the inside of the iron-framed tank, staining the corpse a greasy yellow. The corpse was bald and thankfully her eyes were closed, turning her into the grotesque echo of a sleeping baby. Her forearms ended in metal and canvas sheathes curving into the bottom of the artefact. More tubes snaked from the side of her skull, neck and from underneath her breasts. Shreds of skin, peeled loose by time, decay or mishandling, floated in the preservative.

"Where on Earth did you find it?"

Aminev tapped the glass with his nail.

"In a cellar under one of the factories. There's a maze beneath our feet filled with more machinery and strange objects. This was in a locked room, covered in dust so I guess it'd been abandoned for a long time. Do you have any idea what it might be?"

"A medical specimen?"

"Here? In an ironworks?"

Alexandra looked closer. Apart from the box and tank, which appeared clumsily mass-produced, the rest of the workmanship surprised her, especially where the pipes met the body in a network of teased glass. She peered down inside as the commander held his lantern high, but the bottom of the case was filled with sediment and she could only just make out a jumble of shapes below the torso. More wires? Tubes? Machinery?

"This looks like it had power - electricity. If we find a way to open this cabinet there may be an accumulator we can recharge," she said.

"To make it do what?"

That brought Alexandra up short. The blood thundered in her ears and the shadows in the room seemed longer. She studied the woman's face. In her thirties, she guessed, and although the flesh had sunk and the ridges of her teeth were visible through her lips, she was once beautiful. *To make it do what?* This wasn't a fairground trick or a museum sample. She suspected she was in the presence of a dark, malevolent science - audacious and cruel. And there was more beneath her feet?

"What else did you find in the cellars?"

Aminev laughed and Alexandra sensed the man's unease.

"The soldiers I ordered down there said they found nothing but I think they went to the bottom of the steps, drank vodka and played cards, and then ran back up into the light. This electrical girl disturbs me, Comrade Commissar. She should mean nothing - just a ridiculous bauble from a decaying world - but something about her haunts me and the place she came from terrifies the men."

"So you haven't been underground yourself."

Alexandra heard Aminev tap out his pipe. A few moments later fresh vanilla smoke saturated the room. Aminev threw the canvas back over the machine. If he was angry or scared, he hid it well.

"If I had the time and the inclination I'd go and have a hunt around. That's a luxury I can't afford. Yet as long as this thing remains a mystery it breeds suspicion and fear, so I look to your learning and wisdom to penetrate the veil."

"I'd like to examine this more closely."

"It's not going anywhere. But now I suggest you sleep. Tomorrow morning let's meet and talk further about how we may help each other so you'll find your Agit-Train and I'll understand my electrical girl."

Alexandra walked back through the factory complex, trying to process what she'd just seen. A butchered woman in a glass case on wheels, mated with a strange mechanism whose purpose she could only guess at. That ludicrous abomination couldn't be science. There'd always been rumours that the Whites had toyed with sorcery and alchemy - desperate fantasies of a corrupt regime epitomised in the idiocy of the Tsarina and her obsession with the holy fool Rasputin.

Petrograd was full of stupid tales of wickedness told to impress those peasants incapable of understanding the truth of their material condition. She'd written some of the propaganda herself, piling lurid stories on top of each other, not for a second thinking that any of it was actually true. Unable to face sleep yet she found herself on an external gantry that looked north towards the forests and the mountains.

A monster bellowed and she jumped, grabbing at the railing to stop herself pitching over. For a second she thought the distant peaks were shouting at her. The noise turned into words. *English words. Here?* Alexandra followed the cacophony to an iron-doored hut behind the engine sheds. Four guards had chained a man upside down to a hook in the ceiling. Fresh blood spattered the floor and the windowless room reeked of sweat and shit.

When Alexandra entered, the men snapped to attention.

"Comrade Commissar, we've found a White spy trying to wreck one of the armoured cars." said the leader. The prisoner started swearing and yelling again. A soldier went to beat him but Alexandra raised her hand and he paused.

"Who are you?" she said in English.

Her comrades' mouths dropped open. She repeated herself until the man quietened down.

"Who are you, you pasty-faced shit? Fuck me, are you a woman? Jesus Christ."

Despite his scrawny half-starved look the captive was tall and broad-framed with hands like red boulders. Filthy hair and a beard soaked with blood hid his face, but two wolf-eyes glared at her from the matted shadows. Judging by the mess on the floor the guards had given him a hell of a thumping.

"I am Commissar Alexandra Lobachevsky of the People's Commissariat for Education. One last time - who are you?"

"Tars Tarkas, Jeddak of Thark, you little turd."

"These men say you're a spy and a saboteur."

That prompted more incoherent bellowing. The Englishman wriggled frantically, looking for all the world like a muddy cocoon trying to spit out a butterfly.

"How strong are these chains?" Alexandra shouted to the soldiers above the noise.

"They'd tether a locomotive but beware, Comrade Commissar, he has ferocious strength."

He also had to be the world's biggest, noisiest spy. When exhaustion eventually shut him up, she spoke in Russian to the guard behind the prisoner.

"Castrate him and then feed him slowly into a furnace, feet first."

The soldier flashed a happy grin and pulled out his knife. Alexandra watched the captive. No response, apart from a persistent grumbling from the other side of that hedge of black hair.

"He doesn't understand Russian. I doubt he's a spy. Put that away."

The guard scowled in disappointment.

"Why are you here?" she asked in English. Wary calculation replaced fury in his eyes.

"I'm a mechanic. I was press-ganged into the Hernia Brigade. They brought a load of Austins here. When you bastards chased the Whites away, I was trapped so I went into hiding."

"How did you manage to survive undetected?"

Silence. A guard lifted his rifle to brain the prisoner but Alexandra commanded him to stand down.

"Leave him to swing a little longer. No more beatings. I need him capable of answering my questions."

In the morning she told Aminev and the commander ordered the Englishman brought to his office for interrogation. Alexandra took The Hammer with her as a precaution, relieved to see him back from the terrors and nightmares of the trenches. He never fully returned, her broken soldier, but there was enough there for him to nod in agreement when she told him about the prisoner. The guards unhooked their captive but as soon as they put him right way up he made a break for it, chains flailing. The Hammer grabbed him in a bear hug. To Alexandra's dismay the two seemed equally matched, despite the Englishman being half-starved and covered in bruises. The Georgian broke the stalemate by head-butting the other man with a sound like billiard balls striking each other. The prisoner staggered to his knees and the soldiers jumped onto him in a heap. Alexandra shouted at them not to hurt him but their blows only enraged the man. In the end they chained him to a board and carried him, bellowing all the while, through the factories. When she told him he needed to calm down if he wanted to live he shouted all the louder.

In the office they hung him from a girder right way up. While Yohzin threw open the windows to clear the stench, Aminev stared at the Englishman.

"Give him water. So he's an engineer?"

The Hammer held a flask to the prisoner's lips at arm's length.

Alexandra tried again.

"Who are you?"

"Banjo."

"Banjo what?"

"Banjo Zeal-For-The-Lord Hawkridge."

"Zeal-For-The-Lord?"

"My parents were Quakers."

Alexandra didn't have time for this senseless gibberish so she told Aminev the Englishman's story about being left behind.

"If what he says is true, how's he survived for nearly a year without being found?"

Alexandra translated the question. She saw Banjo's defiance drop a notch. The man tried to conceal it but he stopped meeting his interrogator's gaze and clamped his lips shut.

"You had help, didn't you?" concluded Alexandra. No answer. She softened her voice.

"The man with the pipe is in charge. He thinks you're a deserter, a coward, a spy and a saboteur. I stand between you and a very ugly death. Have you seen what happens to traitors here?"

A flash of dark fury.

"I fixed stuff and he gave me food until you fuckers murdered him."

"Who?"

"Epifan."

Aminev summoned the head of the guards from Factory no. 3. The soldier stood mashing his hat in his hands as if he expected to be the next one to swing from the ceiling. The commander opened a ledger and ran the stem of his pipe down the entries.

"You shot Comrade Engineer Avdinon two days ago. Why?"

"He was slacking in his duties, Comrade Commander. He was supposed to repair three Maxim heavy machine guns but deserted his post. When I forced him to return he failed to fix them."

"And yet records show that up to this point every task you set him was finished with skill and efficiency. So why would he struggle with such a simple piece of maintenance?"

The guard was all but wetting himself.

"Why didn't you repair the Maxim guns?" Alexandra asked Banjo in English. The colour drained from the prisoner's face, leaving her stunned by his reaction. What could possibly scare this raging ogre? Forgetting the man's strength she stepped closer, ignoring the stench of fear and piss.

"What were the Whites doing here?" she continued. *You want to tell me, don't you? But you're too scared to say it.*

"Shenanigans. We saw a lot of priests hovering around. When I tried to find out what they were up to I was told to fuck off. The Russians who came with us from Vladivostok couldn't wait to get away."

Aminev sat on the edge of his desk and stared at the two of them through a cloud of smoke.

"So this man worked for our mechanics in exchange for food because the bastards were too stupid and too idle to do it themselves."

"We need good engineers," said Alexandra.

"I'm not that desperate."

"He can help us understand this place."

Aminev's eyes narrowed a fraction as he caught the hint. *The electrical girl.*

"Is this something interesting? *Mon dieu*, I'm bored to sobs."

Ekaterina floated in. Alexandra recognised the signs of Viktor's medicines. In her head she no doubt walked through a lotus-filled garden admiring the perfumed houris and their indolent dances.

"Comrade Rusanov this is no place for you," Aminev took her hand and kissed it. "It's too dangerous." To be fair, the man had never seen her standing on a barricade with a pair of Mausers, picking off White Cossacks one by one as they fled down Nevsky Prospekt.

"At last! A proper woman! Madame, what a vision of loveliness you present to chase away the shadows that beset me in my woeful situation," Banjo bellowed in French. Alexandra stared at him. The captive had gone from wary, cornered beast to love-struck simpleton in a second. Despite hanging from the ceiling by his thumbs he had the same dopey expression she'd seen on every soldier's face the night before as they bathed in her voice.

"Who's this silver-tongued barbarian?" Ekaterina continued in French.

"My name is Banjo, at your service fair enchantress."

"Is he talking in French?" asked Yohzin. "He must be an aristocrat. We should definitely drop him into a furnace."

"I speak French," Aminev said. His assistant mumbled an apology and took to shuffling papers back and forth across his desk.

"Comrade Commander, this man's useful to us," said Alexandra. "He's a mechanic and will know something of these factories and their purpose. I can persuade him to help."

"This brute?" piped up Yohzin again. "If we unleash him who knows what carnage he'll wreak. Torture him for information and then kill him."

"Let me be responsible," answered the commissar. "My companion The Hammer's a match for his strength and if we're humane we'll learn more than if we just use force."

"You're not going to execute such a wretched, abandoned spirit, are you, my brave soldier?" asked Ekaterina, turning to Aminev. Banjo gave a groan of forlorn desire.

"Of course not. Comrade Commissar will take charge of the prisoner and, for now, dispose of him as she sees fit." Aminev bowed to the actress before turning to the guards. "Find a room, lock him up and give our guest the key."

"I've bought you time so co-operate," Alexandra told Banjo. To his credit the Englishman didn't try to escape or attack anyone when they let him down, though as they escorted him out of the room he started singing *La Marseillaise* at full volume until Aminev called down the stairs for him to be gagged. Alexandra joined the officer out of earshot of the others.

"He may help us understand your mystery."

"How? He can't speak Russian so I don't think he was anyone's confidant. He's just another allied bandit, filled with low cunning and malevolence. Don't you think you're being too kind and trusting?" Aminev spat over the rail. "Hark at me. Comrade Rusanov had me round her little finger, old fool that I am."

"If he hid in this factory complex for almost a year, sneaking around to mend the machinery, he may have come across things concealed from our eyes. When I asked him why he didn't help the engineer he looked scared - and it would take an unusual monstrosity to frighten a man like that."

"Two days to prove himself or he joins his friend Epifan," Aminev said and went back into his office.

CHAPTER FOUR

Six Reds took Banjo down to the river and pointed rifles at him while he stripped, taking care to fold his clothes so they wouldn't find his precious book. He sluiced off the dirt, scouring the filth of nine months away with handfuls of pebbles, revelling in his rebirth as a human being despite the pain from the bruises. He'd fashioned enough of a reputation in the last twenty-four hours to keep the wary buggers at bay as he dressed and squelched his way to the cell they'd prepared. Blimey, it even had a bed, or at least the memory of one sketched out in bent iron and straw-filled sacking. They chained his feet to a ring in the wall but left his hands free. *Fair dos.* One thing years of dodging and scrounging around the world had taught him was the ability to switch off the fear once death was no longer imminent and focus on conniving a way out.

He realised he had a chance to survive in the person of that little pasty-faced lass. What did she call herself? Laxative Something-or-other? Spinstery lump of misery drowning in that baggy uniform, especially next to that beauty - the haughty princess with bedroom eyes and fingers wafting through the air like a swan's feathers. A man might choose to live just for that. In fact, all he had to do was persuade Laxative to unchain him and perhaps he'd charm himself into madam's affections. He'd have to spruce himself up first. She'd only seen him swinging back and forth over a puddle of his own blood and piss. Thank God he hadn't shat himself in front of her - starvation diet had made sure of that.

Laxative came in, planted a chair by the wall and sat down. Her fella, the big hefty lunatic with mad eyes, stood in the doorway running his thumb up and down the business edge of a Cossack sword.

"You're an engineer. You helped the peasants and in return they gave you food and drink to keep you alive. You were their kind spirit. They couldn't repair these complex machines and so you did it for them. Why didn't you say this in the beginning?"

"I saw what you bastards would do to them. Your guards shot my friend because I couldn't fix the machine guns in time."

"We need mechanics. I think I can persuade Commander Aminev to let you live. I'll convince him that you are too stupid, big and loud to be a spy and a saboteur. You help me and I'll unchain you and give you food and drink and a chance to become a man again in service to your fellow workers."

God, she was a pompous shit - all holier than thou and *I know what's good for you*, like the Quaker Elders traipsing into the parlour for a bit of plain speaking with Father. *Art thou living a goodly life in the eyes of the Lord, Thomas Hawkridge? With four brats and no work? Fuck off.*

On and on she droned. Banjo realised she was after something else as well but wasn't sure what. Best go along with it. There was a chance he might live and get the opportunity to run away. He tried to look appreciative.

"I believe all men are good - even the spies and saboteurs of our enemy," the Red was saying, her eyes magnified by those rimless glasses. She looked for all the world like an otter pretending to be human but who hadn't quite got the hang of it. Banjo couldn't tell if she was joking or not. The po-faced bint had a seriousness about her that was unnerving, as though she was peeling away his skin and having a poke around in his soul.

"If you work with me I will cure you of your false bourgeois consciousness."

"My what?"

"You must give me your word as an English gentleman not to flee or fight us."

He almost gave the game away by bursting out laughing. *The woman's an idiot.* Banjo agreed and Laxative seemed satisfied.

"Aminev has insisted that you remain chained and The Hammer will be your keeper."

"He's called The Hammer?" Banjo studied the soldier standing in the doorway. "What happened to him?"

The commissar cocked her head in her otter way as if she was seeing the Englishman in a new light.

"The Kerensky Offensive. We fought at Smorgon. He hung on the barbed wire for two days. I rescued him."

"You were in the trenches?"

As hard as he tried, he couldn't help losing it at the thought of this runty little madam waving a rifle around, cap falling over her eyes, wading through shit and mud. *Jesus Christ, Charlie Chaplin with tits.*

After he'd stopped laughing the silence dragged on long enough for a twinge of fear to spark up in his guts. He waited for her to pull out that Mauser and shoot him, or order bugalugs to twist his head off.

"Sorry."

Another whole minute trundled by before she spoke to him in a voice full of acid and broken glass.

"Did you fight in the war?"

"Me? Not really. I was on a boat at Gallipoli, then ended up in Yokohama working on a steamer taking refugees from Vladivostok to Shanghai and running supplies for White troops and their allies."

"So you're a coward as well as a moron. How did you end up here?"

Hey-ho, in for a penny...

Banjo told her about Ernie Featherington and the basket trick, drawing a diagram in the dirt when his powers of description deserted him. Laxative's ears went bright crimson.

"And that's supposed to be pleasurable?"

"To be honest the idea is better than the reality. I've never had it myself. Don't get me wrong, I'm all for a bit of variety. Her on top is fine. It gives the knees and elbows a rest. Some of these ladies of the night go for the gymnastic when they're desperate for punters. Your ones in Vladivostok were alright but I prefer the lasses in Japan. They're clean, gentle and very anxious to please and none of this swinging from the chandeliers malarkey. That princess friend of yours looks on a bit on the rambunctious side. Those hoity-toity wenches usually are."

Laxative was now completely red in the face. In fact, she looked on the verge of apoplexy. He sensed the interview wasn't going in the right direction. *Me and my big gob.*

"Comrade Rusanov is a great artist of the People's Revolution, not a whore," hissed the Russian. "And prostitution is the worst example of capitalist exploitation. Under communism all men and women are equal and worthy of respect. And love is given freely, not bought or sold."

God help the poor fucker who gets your love for free.

"Absolutely. Hurrah. So, do you think I have a chance with what's-her-face?"

Laxative gave a strangled squeak, so he decided to change the subject.

"What's your name again?"

"Commissar Alexandra Lobachevsky."

Jesus Christ.

"Got anything shorter?"

The woman sighed.

"I'll allow you to call me Alexandra."

"Alexandra eh? At least that's better than Laxative."

"Pardon?"

"So, what happens next?"

I've made a stupid mistake. He's nothing more than a crude brute - ignorant and obsessed with women. At first she'd thought there was a spark of nobility in the man but God only knew why. *The shit has*

one more chance to prove his worth and if he fails I'll execute him myself.
On her orders they dragged the prisoner to the machine guns and
Alexandra watched while he fixed them. In an hour two out of
three were mended using parts butchered from the last one.

"I should still shoot you," she told him. "Take him back and
lock him up."

She couldn't face another inane conversation with the pervert
so she and The Hammer set off in search of the captive's den.
Following the Englishman's directions they ended up in an
abandoned hall at the northern edge of the factory complex.
Through the shattered windows Alexandra could see the peaks of
the Yablonoi Mountains - titanic shards of dark glass stuck into
the earth. Despite the spring warmth the vault felt like a
mausoleum built out of marble and painted to resemble iron, rust
and brick.

It was easy to locate the hideout by the smell. Inside the
abandoned boiler Alexandra found empty bottles and crumbs, a
pile of rags and a couple of stolen tools carefully wrapped in a
scarf. She spotted a crumpled piece of paper, unfolded it and
jerked upright, banging her head on the roof and making the
metal ring. *A Bolshevik Forever! presents - Man of the Future!* A
shadow-puppet worker printed in heavy woodblock lifted
imploring hands to the stars while another held a fat capitalist by
the ankle over a meat-grinder. *Man of the Future! by Alexandra
Lobachevsky and Anton Poltzin.*

She clamped her hand over her mouth and glanced outside.
The Hammer was searching the far end of the hall by the breach
so he wouldn't see the tears spilling down her cheeks and come
running.

*Foreheads touching, bent over the desk, pouring all our dreams of
futurity into this - Tsiolkovsky's rockets, the visions of Liakide and
Krasnogorsky, and the Frenchman Jules Verne and the English socialist
H. G. Wells - iron, steam, joy and labour to fashion a prophecy of Soviet
Super Science that would fill the worker's hearts with hope after this
eternity of grief, horror and bloodshed.*

You laughed at me as you struck out most of my words with a stubby wax crayon but I didn't care because you took what was left, perfected it and placed it in the mouths of such real characters - Lena the Girl, Comrade Machine Man, World Warrior. And I didn't see it, Anton, I had no idea until you tried to kiss me, and I pushed you away. You spat in my face.

"So it's true! I know what you are. We all do. You're sick in the head, Alexandra. Why do you think father stopped you going to study at the Institute with Natasha?"

I didn't see it. I still don't.

"God," said The Hammer, a broken icon in his hand.

Alexandra quickly wiped her face, folded the playbill and put it in her pocket. She looked at the painting - a cheap copy of the Feodorovskaya *Mother of God*, probably dropped by a worker or one of the priests the Englishman claimed he'd seen.

"Where did you find it?"

The Hammer led her to a gap in the wall. Alexandra didn't see anything special so she stepped through into the yard. In the distance a low rise ended at a line of birch and pine, and beyond those she saw the mountains, their tops now lost in cloud. She turned to go back inside but stopped when she spotted marks on the ground between her feet - three wheel tracks as if someone had ridden a big tricycle towards the forest. She hunkered down and peered at the mud. It was damp to the touch and the ruts looked crisp and fresh. For a crazy moment she thought of Aminev's electrical girl. But that was a wreck. Were there others still being trundled around? By who and what for? She took out the playbill and pressed it gently against the dirt to get an impression. She told The Hammer to help search for more tracks but there was no sign in the hall and the trail outside petered out after a few yards.

Back in Banjo's cell Alexandra held up the *Man of the Future!* playbill.

"They performed it to the workers in one of the halls. I hid in the rafters to watch. It was a load of utter bollocks."

Ignorant oaf.

"How would you even understand it if you don't speak

Russian?"

"Everyone started booing and chucking things when this bloke with a silver hat who kept going 'Poop Poop' pretended to saw the priest's cock off. I think they stopped it halfway through and did a sing-song instead. Good idea, otherwise they might have got lynched."

After she'd calmed down a bit Alexandra asked Banjo about the Agit-Train.

"I spotted it leaving weeks ago, early morning, but I don't know where it went. North maybe? It's a rat's nest of branch lines out there. Why? Are you looking for them?"

Alexandra ignored the question and turned the playbill round.

"These tracks came from the hall where you were hiding. They were just outside, pointing towards the woods."

Banjo's mouth dropped open and he stared at Alexandra with real fear in his eyes.

"Great White Apes."

"What are you talking about?"

"Great White Apes from Barsoom."

More gibberish, but the man had seen something. Alexandra was just concocting a suitably lurid threat when someone thumped on the door. Viktor burst in, wild-eyed and reeking of the cheap tobacco he occasionally mixed with Ekaterina's opium.

"Alexandra, they've found *A Bolshevik Forever!* Commander Aminev's preparing an expedition to retrieve it and he's leaving now."

"Bring him," she told The Hammer, pointing at Banjo.

"It sounds like your Agit-Train," said Aminev. "The scouts didn't go further down the track but they saw a carriage and came across this on the line."

He handed a mask to Alexandra - a papier-mâché square with big round washers for eyes and a mouth of gold-painted mesh - the World Warrior from *Man of the Future!* This time she was prepared for the brief surge of sad memory. They stood next to a waiting locomotive. Steam rolled out in lazy waves from between the wheels. Troops loaded up half a dozen carriages, three carrying horses and their riders. They were followed by a flatbed with a heavy-duty crane and a second engine.

"Were the actors alive?"

"The scouts didn't see anyone, but they had more important things to think about. There's a derailed armoured train like nothing we've come across. Your English friend can help us try to salvage it."

Alexandra stared at the face of the Soviet superman from her play. Why would Pavel take his travelling theatre into the middle of nowhere and just leave it there? The only logical explanation was that they'd been ambushed by bandits and murdered. The last act of their journey was about to unfold into tragedy.

"Any ideas about my electrical girl?" asked Aminev.

"The Englishman knows something."

"Does he now? All the more reason to take him with us. You can interrogate him on the way."

He nodded at The Hammer who led a shackled Banjo by a chain towards the carriages. A couple of soldiers walked beside with rifles, leaning slightly away as if he was on fire. The mechanic wore an expression of bland interest, like a visitor wasting an afternoon in a museum because all the pubs were shut. Alexandra had to admire the man's coolness. The British set great store in their self-restraint, equating emotional constipation with virtue. During her ten years in London she'd pitied their lack of poetry and passion, but here she had to admit that Banjo's sangfroid was impressive.

"Fair princess your servant languishes in abject captivity," the man bellowed in French. One of the soldiers tripped in surprise and stumbled to his knees. He stood up, furious, and thumped Banjo in the stomach with the butt of his rifle. The prisoner said *Ooof* and sat down.

"And my torment is magnified a thousand-fold by your cruel indifference," he howled from the ground.

Alexandra spotted Ekaterina wafting across the engine yard

with Viktor scampering along behind, clutching the Gladstone bag full of 'medicines' to his chest. To Alexandra's astonishment the woman blew a kiss at the prisoner who shouted in delight.

"Is this wise?" she asked.

"Comrade Rusanov insisted. She is most persuasive," said Aminev with a wry grin. "You'll all be safe. No White filth will come near my machine guns and cavalry. Besides, if I say no I think we'll have another revolution on our hands."

He pointed at the carriages where soldiers hung out of the windows and open doors, calling for Ekaterina to sing to them. One of them had already pulled out an accordion and was squeaking out *Varshavianka*. She ignored them all and strode up to Alexandra and Aminev, her eyes the colour and size of poisoned opals. God only knew what tinctures she'd fed on this morning. Alexandra tried to hide the mask but the singer snatched it from her and held it up to the sky, tears spilling down her cheeks.

"You cannot cast me off so easily, my Pavel. All my life I've stripped away masks with these claws and yours will be no exception."

Alexandra glared at Viktor but he looked just as dislocated from the world. White powder dusted his moustache. Before anyone could stop her the actress jumped up among the laughing soldiers in the first carriage and started to sing the strangest scales Alexandra had ever heard - an opium-fuelled aria from another world that sent shivers down her spine.

"We'd better move," remarked Aminev, tapping his pipe out on a wheel. "I want to get there by tomorrow morning."

Alexandra walked over to The Hammer and Banjo.

"No more shouting and no French. The Hammer doesn't like surprises and I don't want you dead just yet."

"But she is such a Trojan woman," said Banjo. "Such a Trojan woman. You're nice too," he added. "But bleeding hell, look at her!"

Alexandra slammed the door after the fool and climbed up into the next wagon as the locomotive began to move.

Banjo sat in an empty carriage on the floor opposite The Hammer who stared at him without saying a word. He could hear the actress singing in the distance. Alexandra came in.

"Doesn't say much does he?" Banjo nodded at his guard. "So where are we off to?"

"We've found an armoured train abandoned by the Whites. Commander Aminev wants you to help us repair it."

"Another test then. And if I fail that hard-faced bastard will shoot me. Why is Madam coming with us?"

The lass looked worried, her gaze far away.

"Commander Aminev says they've found our Agit-Train."

"And everyone's dead?"

"We don't know."

Banjo tried to shuffle forwards on his bottom in an attempt to be conspiratorial but the chains didn't give an inch.

"There's monstrosity in these woods and mountains. Mad stuff. I've seen what made those tracks."

He pointed at the playbill poking out of Alexandra's coat pocket and tapped the side of his nose.

"You look after me and I'll tell you everything."

It was a stupid gamble. He was asking to be tortured, but there was an odd air to the woman behind that self-righteous sour-faced communism. The Red looked a bit too earnest and thoughtful, as though she really believed in all that equality nonsense and wasn't just intoning yet another endless, bullying liturgy of cruelty. Even so he saw no point in over-egging the conversation with more sly hints. He suddenly felt very tired and Alexandra was watching him closely. *The little cow can see right inside my head.*

"You're not helping yourself," she said. It sounded almost as if she was giving motherly advice instead of uttering threats. "If you show willing and put your skills to good use you'll be treated kindly, otherwise it'll go hard for you. What were the Tsarists doing at Ikayungri?"

"Like I told you, they kept us away. When we arrived with the Austins our chief engineer got into an argument with some White

Russian arse who confined us to the station and said we had to turn back for Vladivostok the next morning. Later that night our driver said the place was cursed by a spirit called Baba Yaga."

"Baba Yaga?" spluttered Alexandra with perfect matron scorn. Banjo sensed his bargaining chips dropping through the floor.

"What is it?"

"She's a witch from old folk tales - childish fairy stories. She lives in a house with chicken legs, feasts on the flesh of Russian men and flies around in a giant mortar. It's complete and utter nonsense, of course."

Alexandra trailed off. She seemed to be remembering something.

"What else did the driver say?" she asked after a few moments.

"Nothing much. I picked a fight with the man, as you do when you're bored. After beating each other stupid we got drunk on vodka, swore to be blood brothers and passed out in each other's arms. God knows where he is now - either dead out there in the wilderness or he escaped from Vladivostok when you lot moved in."

"This is what we fight against," said Alexandra to no-one in particular. "Superstition and ignorance drag us down. How can we show the people the light of science, of Soviet Super Science and its endless promise of tomorrow?"

Banjo hadn't a clue so he stuck with an encouraging grin. Thankfully the Red had forgotten about the tyre track on her playbill. Banjo had no desire to revisit his vision from the night Epifan died.

"Go to sleep," said Alexandra. "In the morning we'll arrive at the armoured train which you must help us salvage."

"Maybe we'll find your actor friends too."

That seemed to catch her by surprise. She favoured him with a brief smile and left the room. *Bloody hell. Her face didn't crack. That's a turn up for the books.* Banjo turned to The Hammer.

"Do you know about Baba Yaga?"

But the soldier's gaze was on other horrors, soaked in mud, shit and fear far away.

Banjo woke up as the train shuddered to a halt. A couple of Cossacks flung the door aside and The Hammer led him blinking out into the light. Further along, another squad of horsemen clattered down from a wagon, followed by soldiers carrying one of Banjo's mended Maxims. They set it up at the edge of the rail with the arc of fire to the rear. He turned to look in the other direction and felt his mouth pop open.

Bugger me, it's fucking enormous.

The railway curved across a wide valley floor, angling north towards a thick forest and the mountains beyond. An armoured train lay derailed on its side next to the tracks, but it was all completely wrong. Banjo struggled to understand what he was seeing. The White juggernaut consisted of two gun cars with a pair of turrets each. He reckoned that would amount to eight five-inch cannon in total. They truly were land dreadnoughts and each of those carriages had to be a hundred tons at least, never mind the wagons jumbled between. If that monstrosity had run off the rails it would have torn up the earth and concertinaed itself into scrap before burying itself under a mountain of soil and rock. But there was hardly any damage to the ground. It was just as if someone had picked up the train and laid it alongside the railroad like a child tidying up his toys.

Alexandra joined him.

"Did you see anything similar at the ironworks?" she asked.

"No, not as big as this, but they didn't let us anywhere near the engine sheds. What happened to it?"

"We don't know."

"Maybe Baba Yaga did it," offered Banjo with a cheery grin. Alexandra glared at him so he shut up.

Aminev and a couple of peasant engineers walked towards the train.

"They won't have a clue," Banjo said. "Are you going to let us have a gander then?"

Alexandra nodded and they started along the tracks. Banjo contrived to keep falling over until the exasperated commissar told The Hammer to remove the leg irons, taking care to remind her captive that he'd given his promise as an Englishman not to run away. The closer they got the odder the wreck, and the overall strangeness of the scene threw a silence over the valley. It grew so thick and heavy Banjo found himself struggling to think. He kicked something between the sleepers and, looking down, spotted an icon at his feet. Alexandra picked it up and studied it with a frown.

"Superstitious lot of buggers those Whites - they're all over the place," said Banjo, nodding at the painted tiles littering the ground.

"They came from there," said Alexandra pointing at the centre wagon. While the others between the two armoured carriages were more or less intact and made of wooden walls with concrete cores for armour, this was a cylinder of thick steel that looked as if an explosion had ripped it open from the inside.

"What caused that?" murmured the Red, but Banjo wasn't paying attention. He'd seen the state of the frames on the locomotive and the two land ironclads. If his life depended on him getting the train back onto the rails and operational, he was doomed. Its back was broken.

CHAPTER FIVE

"The engineers say they can't salvage this," Aminev told Alexandra. She translated for the Englishman.

"They're idiots. Dig a wide trench and fill it with logs. Chain the locomotives to each section and you can drag them one by one over the rollers like the pharaohs did when they built their pyramids, and then use your crane to tip them back onto the rails. The wheels are fine on all of them except that middle carriage. Shouldn't take more than a couple of days. You'll need to pull them backwards and forwards to line them up, so send one engine ahead and one back down the track a few hundred yards, chain them to both ends of each section and you'll be able to get it into place easily."

The commander shrugged when Alexandra told him the answer.

"Nobody else has a plan. Twenty-four hours to get the armoured wagons up and rolling or I hang him from a tree for target practice."

She relayed the message and the prisoner shot them both an idiotic grin. Alexandra was about to tell him they were serious when she heard Ekaterina shouting. She looked along the line to see the singer picking up stones and hurling them at Viktor who cowered away, yelping in pain and begging his sister to stop.

"A horse, you snivelling eunuch, I shall go to Pavel now!"

The Cossacks must have overheard her for in a second she was surrounded by a cluster of mounted riders, one of whom offered his hand so she could climb up onto his horse. Alexandra shouted for them to wait and ran up to Ekaterina who glared at her, hands on hips. No point in putting it off. Alexandra had forgotten Pavel the Lecher and their idiotic quest while she was examining the broken land dreadnought, but she couldn't ignore Ekaterina any longer. God only knew what the woman might do in a fit of jilted passion.

"Where's the Agit-Train?" she asked the squad leader.

"We found the carriage a couple of miles up the track, in the forest, Comrade Commissar."

She took Ekaterina's hands and forced the singer to look at her.

"Let me go check first. Once I'm happy it's safe, I'll send a rider back for you."

"And alert the bastard so he'll flee again with his whore?"

"No-one can outrun us, Comrade Rusanov," shouted a horseman. The others cheered in agreement.

"If Pavel is there, I will clasp him to me so he can't escape."

If Pavel is there we'd know by now. She knew full well she'd find nothing or bodies. Ekaterina kissed her on the cheek.

"Ride, Alexandra, ride."

Aminev had a better idea.

"While these lazy bastards are cutting down the trees take the first locomotive and haul the Agit-Train back here. It'll be easier to protect."

He signalled for the cavalry to go with Alexandra, who climbed up into the cabin just as they uncoupled the engine. It chugged towards the forest, passing a crowd of soldiers stripping the branches off felled trunks while the others dug Banjo's channel from the first armoured carriage to the tracks.

She still didn't know what to make of the Englishman. He acted like God's fool but his proposal sounded outrageous enough to work. *He also hinted at a second electrical girl, one that still works.* She imagined another of Aminev's cabinets creeping through the outer maze of the ironworks, the preservative liquid sloshing against the glass as its wheels rolled over the uneven concrete. *Are your eyes open? Do you see and think? What are you? Who made you and why? The answer's in the vaults under the factories. Aminev and his men are too scared to go down there, because they know it's your kingdom, Tugarin, and I bet you have a legion of those butchered corpses hiding in the darkness. I'll burn you out with magnesium. As soon as we get back I'll come after you with The Hammer.*

The locomotive drove further into the woods, the endless birch a white flicker beyond the cabin. Horsemen cantered in and out of the trees on either side.

The driver slowed to a crawl and pointed ahead. Alexandra spotted a carriage a couple of hundred yards away in the half gloom, covered in paintings and slogans. *A Bolshevik Forever!* She called to one of the horsemen to return to camp and tell Aminev. The man flashed her an odd look of relief before disappearing down the tracks. The others milled around.

"It's empty Comrade Commissar," came the shout. The driver nudged the locomotive against the wagon and while he coupled the two together Alexandra jumped down and clambered through the undergrowth. The forest floor was soft and scattered with boulders. It rose in hummocks to the north. The silence she'd notice in the valley grew heavier. She had a brief impression of endless voices straining against nothing, as if this remote wilderness had expelled all humanity and she struggled through an alien world. Idiot nerves sparked by the fear at what she might find. *A bunch of corpses. You've seen plenty of them before.*

Agit-Trains usually consisted of at least half a dozen wagons filled with printing presses, film laboratories and theatre props, as well as enough supplies to keep the artists and their escorts going for weeks. *Pavel must have taken the engine and the other cars into the mountains. Why did he leave this one here? Did he want us to find him after all?*

"Scout ahead," she called up to the soldiers. They exchanged uneasy glances, the leader looking back down the tracks as if waiting for a countermand from Aminev.

"Go on! That's an order," snapped Alexandra. "Find out if the rest of the train's further on or if there's any sign of the enemy."

The officer gave her a tight-lipped nod and sent four riders along the line. The door to the carriage stood open so Alexandra clambered inside. She paused in the shadows and sniffed. Spilled chemicals but nothing else. Even so, she drew her Mauser and cat-stepped down the passageway.

The car was thankfully empty of corpses. It had also been stripped of anything valuable. Playbills and pamphlets lay scattered over the floor along with two more masks from her play, both crushed flat. She was hardened to the memories by now and ignored them. The darkroom was full of an acid reek from shattered bottles. She spotted a negative plate in the corner and held it up against the light. A treeline with a blurred smudge in the sky above. *What's that supposed to be?*

Horses thundered up to the wagon and boots clattered in the corridor. She peered round the door, Mauser ready, and saw Ekaterina clutching at the wall to steady herself, her other hand on her heart. *Oh, for God's sake!* Behind her Viktor limped along as if his knees had been tied together.

"She wouldn't wait. I tried to stop her. The riders outside want us to go back."

"He's not here, is he?" hissed the actress. "I don't need to look, I can feel the emptiness."

She half-swooned into one of the cabins, picked up a playbill and scrunched it against her breast. Alexandra recognised that expression - she was gearing herself up for another extended bout of shrieking.

"For God's sake can't you shut her up?" she muttered in Viktor's ear.

"She kicked me," whined her brother. "Down there!"

"Give her something to make her sleep - anything."

Viktor rummaged in his pockets and Alexandra heard the clink of tiny bottles. She joined the riders at the door.

"Commander Aminev wants the Agit-Train to return to the camp," said the officer. For some reason he was having difficulty controlling his horse. It danced sideways across the uneven ground, thumping into a tree so the man cursed and struck it on the side of the head with the handle of his whip.

"Is the patrol back yet?" asked Alexandra, looking into the forest to the north where the landscape quickly dissolved into a grainy murk punctuated by white tree trunks. No sign of the scouts but she wasn't going to wait. Truth be told she'd had her fill of the search for Pavel and all the emotional drama surrounding it. She signalled for the driver to pull them back into the valley. The derailed juggernaut and its burst wagon intrigued her. The Cossacks were happy to return to camp. They thundered ahead at full gallop, leaving the train to thread its own way through the emptiness.

The soldiers had finished digging the channel between the first armoured wagon and the track and were filling it with stripped tree trunks. Alexandra noticed Banjo standing on the toppled fortress trying to direct a group of peasant engineers as they fixed chains to the anchor bars at the front of the ironclad. Cheered by the man's co-operation, Alexandra raised her hand to wave. The Englishman ignored her. Instead, he sprinted to the other end of the carriage and leaped straight into the saddle of a horse left to graze while its rider fetched logs. It took a couple of seconds for Alexandra to realise what was happening. Banjo struggled to control his mount, which reared and stumbled in circles before galloping through a crowd of shouting men towards the trees. *Bastard.* She jumped down and pelted after the runaway. Far ahead, The Hammer stepped into the path of the prisoner, lifted his Mauser and fired. Sparks flew from Banjo's hands and he hurtled over the horse's rear, thumping onto his back in a spray of churned mud.

"Stop!" yelled Alexandra as the Georgian strode forwards, aiming at the renegade's head. Surely he wasn't still alive. Yet when she got to the Englishman he was staring up at the sky, mouth working furiously. The round had torn a hole in his tunic right above the heart but there was no blood. Banjo jack-knifed into a sitting position and bellowed. Alexandra saw bright metal flare on his manacles. *They deflected the bullet into your chest so why aren't you dead, you oaf?*

"Fucking bastards. You shot the princess," the man was howling at the sky. "You shot the princess you fucking arseholes."

Princess? Alexandra instinctively looked for Ekaterina, wondering if that was who he meant. The singer stood at the Agit-Train door, very much alive, curiosity having got the better of Viktor's sleeping draught. Alexandra pressed the barrel of her own pistol against Banjo's head.

"Shut up or I'll execute you like a dog."

Banjo clamped his lips tight, went beetroot red and started to snort. Alexandra pulled open his tunic to examine the wound and a book fell out. It had a hole in the cover. To her astonishment Banjo burst into tears.

"The princess. It's all I have left in this fucking shit-hole."

Alexandra picked up the book. Banjo lunged for it but the clicking of rifle bolts from half a dozen soldiers stopped him. She shook the pages and a deformed bullet tumbled onto the grass. The cover bore the title *A Princess of Mars by Edgar Rice Burroughs.* Underneath a simple line drawing showed a creature with four arms standing under two moons. The slug had neatly decapitated the monster and burrowed two thirds of the way through the novel.

"This is your princess?" she asked. The man nodded and wiped his face on his sleeve. Alexandra riffled through the chapters.

"It's a scientific romance. You read tales of science?"

She'd dismissed the Englishman as an ignorant lout with no interest in philosophy or the wonders of futurity. What could the wild beast at her feet want with such a prophetic work?

"Keep the book if it interests you Comrade Commissar," said Aminev, pulling out his own pistol as he walked towards Banjo.

"Please wait," said Alexandra. She turned to their captive. "You gave me your word as an English gentleman."

"Do I look like an English gentleman?"

"He's going to shoot you. Why should I stop him?"

"If he kills me he'll never get those trains back onto the tracks."

She translated. Aminev stared at the armoured car. Something in his eyes scared her. She realised that in the commander's head everyone here was disposable - Banjo, the soldiers, Ekaterina and her brother.

"Very well," he said after a while. She breathed again. "He lives till sundown so he can fix the train, continued Aminev. "But he dies whether he succeeds or not. Don't tell him that."

Alexandra could do nothing but nod before turning to The Hammer.

"Secure a chain between yourself and the Englishman. Make it long enough for him to be able to work."

Banjo was looking at the book with real anguish.

"And I'll give you your princess back when you've finished," Alexandra told him. She watched him led away like a reluctant puppy. *You've condemned yourself to death, you idiot. Now I'll never know what you saw in the factory.*

"Any clues about your Agit friends?" asked Aminev, sitting on a rock to refill his pipe. The monster had fled his eyes for the moment.

"No sign of the rest of the train. It must have carried on towards the mountains. Perhaps bandits stole it."

"I doubt you'd find bandits out there. They'd be completely cut off from any supplies and with nothing to forage."

"So why the railway?"

Aminev clicked the pipe into his mouth and lit it. He pointed north with the smouldering match.

"Mines maybe. There's gold in those mountains. Perhaps that's what the Whites were after, though if they were they kept it well hidden. We didn't find any maps or surveying equipment back at the factories."

"I sent a scouting party further down the line to see if they could locate the rest of the train."

Aminev glanced at her through the smoke. *You don't like me giving orders to your men.* But he just shrugged.

"Let's see if they find anything."

Alexandra looked at the forest and the walled mountains beyond. The riders were taking their time.

"This is an incredible machine," the commander continued, nodding at the wreck "It must be twice as powerful as the *Orlik*, if not more so. Look at those guns. How did it end up like this?"

He pointed at the ruptured wagon with its shattered necklace of icons.

"An ammunition store that blew up?"

"That's wasn't an ordinary explosion. And why all the icons? Did the superstitious fools imagine they were calling down God's power? Did they think they'd defeat the Revolution with prayer and pious saints? Is there any link between this and my electrical girl?"

The temperature dropped as the light waned. Alexandra pulled her coat tighter.

"When we get back, with your permission, I want to have a look in the cellars under the factory," she said.

Aminev grunted, stood up and strolled off towards a camp-fire where half a dozen guards were passing around a sack of food. *Is that a yes or a no?* None the wiser, she returned to the Agit-Train wagon where Viktor met her at the doorway, finger on lips.

"I made her a nest - she's sleeping now. Among the memories of Pavel pleasant dreams will come."

As if. She left the actress to her addled slumber and perched herself on a case in front of the engine of the rescue train so the heat would warm her back. Banjo was yelling at the peasants and soldiers, loping up and down in irons. The Hammer occasionally gave them a tug to remind the mechanic he was still a prisoner. Alexandra had assumed she'd be needed to translate but Banjo seemed to be getting his message across with shouting and gestures. As the light waned the repair detail attached the forward armoured carriage to the front locomotive. It still had the Agit-Train wagon attached but it looked as if the weight wasn't going to make much difference. The driver opened up the valves and the chains tightened.

At first nothing happened and in the distance Alexandra saw

Aminev loading his Mauser. *Time to say goodbye to Mr Banjo Hawkridge.* Yet after three painful minutes the rail dreadnought started to inch along the log-filled trench with a bone-grinding roar of straining steel and crushed timber. Cheers broke out among the bystanders and Alexandra grinned despite herself. By the time night fell the turreted juggernaut lay alongside the track at the end of a river of shattered wood and earth. Banjo clanked up the slope.

"You'll need to refill the path with fresh logs," he told her and Aminev, who'd joined them. "I expect it's goodbye Alexandra. That fucker's going to have me shot now. I see it in his eyes."

"Tell your Scheherazade he's bought himself another night," said the commander. "Lock him inside the armoured wagon and your man can make sure he doesn't try to escape again."

Alexandra translated for Banjo and got nothing but a tired shrug in return. She watched The Hammer lead the Englishman to the fallen carriage. The prisoner climbed in through a hatch in the turret, leaving the bright scribble of the chain trailing out to bunch in the Georgian's hands. She moved closer to the camp-fire, accepted bread and a piece of sausage from the huddled soldiers, and tried to start a conversation about Soviet Super Science. Most were bored, some of them stared at her with the same hostility she'd seen at Smorgon - the sullen resentment of men shamed by women fighting on their behalf. Alexandra had no patience left for them and the scouting party still hadn't returned, so she pulled out *A Princess of Mars* and read a couple of chapters by firelight.

What is this drivel? There was no vision of a future of intellect and reason - just wild romance with no science to speak of at all - page after page of empty-headed bravado and bourgeois arrogance. The women were helpless, vapid princesses and the men, thugs. And yet something kept her turning the pages - a sense of possibility and excitement tightening her guts like a clock spring, so when she finally slept her dreams were laced with moss-covered ruins and jewelled monsters roaming beneath twin moons.

Alexandra woke to find the valley filled with mist, changing the derailed juggernaut into a watercolour horizon of blocks, guns, turrets and chains. She heard the soldiers moving through the camp, and the clink of harnesses as the Cossacks tended to their horses. From behind came the low thunder of the second locomotive easing the breakdown crane through the fog. The front engine fired up and took position halfway between the armoured wreck and the woods to make way. She assumed the singer and her brother were still asleep inside the Agit-Train carriage.

The soldiers set up a field kitchen. After helping herself to a can of tea and three chunks of grey bread she wandered down to The Hammer and gave him a piece.

"Get him up."

A few yanks on the chain and Banjo's head popped out of the nearest hatch. He snarled a couple of sleepy curses at no-one in particular before scraping a handful of condensation from the armour plating to wash his face. Alexandra tossed the food up.

"I read your book."

The Englishman gave her a wary look.

"And?"

"There's no explanation of how he gets to Mars. It just happens as if by magic."

"And?"

So much for her attempt at conversation.

"Get this armoured car back onto the track without any more treacherous idiocy and I will speak to the commander about letting you live."

"Good luck with that."

God, but the oaf was stubborn. Didn't the surly cretin realise she was trying to save his life?

Shouting broke out behind her. Alexandra turned to see a single rider gallop out of the forest - one of the Cossack scouts she'd sent ahead to look for the rest of the Agit-Train. *Where are the others?* The horse thundered into the camp, scattering men, until the cook had the wit to jump up and grab the bridle. The animal kicked backwards half a dozen times and the cavalryman fell out of the saddle. Another soldier dragged him from under the hooves. As soon as she saw the sweat and foam covering the beast's flanks, Alexandra pulled out her Mauser and scanned the treeline - nothing but the silent grey wall in the mist.

The Cossack crawled on his hands and knees towards Aminev. The man had lost his hat and his kaftan was covered in scorch marks. With a shock Alexandra saw a mass of burns on the side of his face. It was a mottled, raw mess.

"She's coming, she's coming." He grabbed the commander's boots. Aminev stared down at him with disgust.

"Fly, comrades, fly."

Aminev reached down and yanked the man to his feet. Alexandra stepped back, thrown by the sheer insanity in the soldier's eyes. A couple of guards surreptitiously crossed themselves.

"What happened?" said the commander.

"She's coming - she and her white spiders. She'll kill us all."

The officer slapped him so hard he took away most of the burnt skin in a spray of blood. The Cossack seemed not to notice.

"Where's the rest?"

"She ate them," whispered the man as if he was telling a story to a round-eyed baby. "She cooked them in a pot to feed her spider children."

He staggered back, turning to his comrades.

"Flee, flee for your lives. Baba Yaga is coming."

His forehead burst open with a crack and he sat down, gave a loud belch and sprawled sideways in the mud. Aminev stood behind him with a smoking pistol.

It's not supposed to be like this anymore. It was as if Alexandra watched a play from too far away to understand who these people were and why they did such things. *We won the war, we're beating back the famine and the epidemics, and our world is born anew in the light of Super Science. This isn't meant to happen anymore.*

She could have sworn the ground shifted under her feet. *It's Tugarin the earth dragon, laughing at my science, laughing at my dreams.*

Aminev's shouted commands snapped her out of it and the camp broke apart, soldiers falling into line, rifles pointing at the trees to the north. Four gathered up the Maxim gun and repositioned it on the flat wagon in the shadow of the crane. Another squad of Cossacks galloped towards the woods, their dead comrade left where he'd fallen. Alexandra knew they'd branded him a coward but there'd been more than fear in the man's eyes as he died. She'd recognised a desperate madness.

Baba Yaga. Why this incessant nonsense about a fairy tale hag? White renegades must have ambushed the first scouts, probably the same ones who'd taken the rest of the Agit-Train. *Ekaterina!* In the chaos Alexandra had forgotten the actress and her brother. They were still in the wagon hitched to the front of the forward locomotive which hissed away half a mile up the tracks. She sprinted towards it, ignoring Aminev's shout. The bastard driver had abandoned the engine, leaving her friends at the mercy of any attack from the woods.

She was halfway when she heard the crack of gunfire behind her. Instinctively she dived to the ground to avoid crossfire. She risked a glance at the forest. The sun had burned away most of the mist and she could see the monochrome grid of the endless birch. Still nothing so she checked the soldiers. Why the hell were they firing at the clouds - the Maxim squad hosing back and forth? Another volley and then three guards threw their guns down and ran, quickly followed by others as the first line broke into a rout. Struggling to make sense of it all, Alexandra stared into the sky.

An inverted cone hurtled over the trees towards her. A shimmering cluster of arms and legs writhed on top and burning red eyes cored through the last shreds of fog. *Baba Yaga - bursting with hatred and hunger for the flesh of Russian men.* She got to her knees, stupefied with the absurdity of the vision. *It can't be true. This is the ramblings of mad Efrosinya Nikolayevna - monstrous fantasy, not science.* The creature passed over Alexandra with a high-pitched humming that drilled through her bones. Two fireflies of white light drifted down and hit the rear locomotive. It exploded, the concussion pushing her forwards into the dirt. A fragment of boiler plate jammed into the earth next to her cheek, decorated with a streak of blood.

CHAPTER SIX

Banjo knew there was no way on God's Earth they were going to fix the armoured train. Crawling through the guts of both gun carriages confirmed the truth. Twisted girders and shorn bolts said it all - the train's spine was shattered. As soon as they tried to tip it onto the rails it would fall to pieces like a broken toy. Luckily for him the Russian mechanics were too stupid to realise, or if they did they kept it hidden, probably out of fear of that chisel-faced cunt with the pipe. Hard bastard - Banjo knew exactly how the man worked. He reminded him of Captain Spalding, all glittery-eyed and slash-mouthed, standing on a table in Vladivostok firing his Webley into the ceiling and screaming *Death to the Communists!* This Bolshevik officer was yet another lunatic who'd purged himself of any humanity his mother might have dinned into him.

When Banjo first clambered into the wreck there'd been a handful of peasant engineers aimlessly fiddling with controls and engine parts - trying anything that moved in the hope they'd make the iron titan shudder back to life. He'd attempted to give them some direction by pointing and shouting but they edged away and glowered at him from the shadows. After that he blustered about, shoving and cursing them until they gave up and crawled outside, frightened to be cooped up with this raggedy lunatic. When the last of them vanished through the hatch he sat on an upturned ammunition case and squeezed his fists together, working through his plan.

Banjo had told Alexandra and Commander Sadist that the best way to recover the wreck was to tug the derailed train up the slope and crane it onto the rails, and it looked like the scrawny runts had fallen for it. As expected the Reds had detached the locomotives, sending the first up the line and the second back down in the direction of the ironworks. Both had a decent head of steam up and it'd been easy to rig it so the chains could be slipped by one man.

So far, so good. By nightfall the Russian engineers had heaved the dreadnought over his log road until it was next to the tracks. Of course, he'd tell them it wasn't close enough and they needed to use the southern locomotive to ease it into position. If he could fix it so that the soldiers were faffing about with the crane all he had to do was make it to that train, slip the links and Bob's your uncle. Even the cavalry wouldn't catch him as he thundered back towards Ikayungri.

The north engine was his second way out. That daft painted wagon coupled to the front was a nuisance - it would make it harder to get his speed up. There'd still be a chance though, especially as those woods seemed to spook the buggers. To be fair they bothered him too, and he knew the northern line would probably just take him into a dead-end wasteland, but it was better than being tied to a tree and shot or castrated and burned alive or whatever else his captors fancied for this evening's entertainment.

But first Banjo had to get rid of the bug-eyed lunatic they'd chained him to and who followed him round, clinging onto his shackles and staring at him with that drawn expression of strained nothing - as though he was two months into passing the biggest turd in history. The Hammer was an apt name. This fucker was clearly a bone-breaker, and mired in an endless nightmare of mud, gas and guts. In normal circumstances Banjo would have given him a run for his money and probably won, but hunger had made him weak. A bit of cunning was needed for that one. If he was honest he felt sorry for the poor sod. He'd seen many like him muttering and twitching their last steps into madness in the dives, brothels and alleyways of this broken world, but if the only way to escape was to kill him he wasn't going to hang back.

At first he tried to persuade The Hammer to unshackle his hands, pantomiming how hard it was to fix anything while bound at the wrists, but the idiot just stared through him. He carried one of those broom-handled Mauser automatics like everyone else round here above the rank of private, and a horrible looking knife tucked into his belt - filthy blade and stained handle wrapped in ragged leather - a real Ripper's tool. There had to be a way of disarming the man without making it too obvious what he was plotting. In the end he reckoned he wouldn't get a chance at finishing him off until they were both on the footplate of whichever locomotive he stole. Brain the bastard with a shovel. Booting him over the side would be better, but only if he'd managed to cut the chains binding them together first.

So Banjo clambered through the cold iron tomb, figuring out his moves and pretending to be busy in case Alexandra decided to check in on him. He still couldn't work out what had happened to the armoured train. It was as if a giant had picked up the whole thing and dropped it on its side next to the rails. Apart from the ruptured middle wagon there were no signs of attack or explosions, no damage to suggest a crash. To his surprise the guns were workable, though without steam the turrets wouldn't traverse. None of the shells had exploded. They lay in untidy heaps against the wall, which was now the floor. He came across bloodstains here and there but nothing too alarming. It was starting to feel like the *Marie Celeste.*

A dull explosion made the whole train rattle. The chains tightened and yanked him forward and he cracked his head against the turret base. Roaring oaths he braced his foot against the wall and heaved back - the links went slack. Shouting and screaming poured in through the open hatch, followed by more detonations. *Artillery? In this arse-end of nowhere?* Sitting in a tin box full of live ammunition was the last place he wanted to be if the Whites were shelling the camp. He clambered outside, just as The Hammer pulled on the chains again. Banjo tumbled off the carriage and landed flat on his face in the mud.

He scrambled up into a crouch, ready to take on whoever fancied their chances - especially The Hammer. If the bastard wouldn't unlock the manacles he'd chew the bugger's hands off at the wrists. Then the universe went completely mad and all he could do was gape and squeak.

The Hammer stood a few yards away with his back to the armoured train. Banjo was used to seeing him standing motionless, facing down the devils in his head, but this was a different order of stillness altogether - as if God himself had cut a soldier-shaped hole in creation. The Red's arms hung limp by his sides, the chain puddling at his feet. A monster hovered in the sky just in front of the Russian. It resembled an inverted dunce's cap with an octopus stuffed into the top but wiping the mud out of his eyes told Banjo he was looking at some kind of machine. The cone was covered in geometric silver filigree and topped by a dark ring studded with blazing red lights. Scores of metal tentacles as thick as his own arm quivered and twitched in the freezing morning air. The thing was about twelve feet tall and Banjo could have sworn it was studying them.

It must have been satisfied with whatever it found because the contraption drifted away, moving down the railway track, floating over a scene of total carnage. The south locomotive was nothing more than a bonfire on wheels. *Fuck, fuck, fuck - that was my escape route.* Another wagon had tipped onto its side, spilling boxes and bodies down the slope. More corpses lay in puddles across the scorched ground but it looked as if most of the Reds had run away. Banjo didn't blame them. All that stopped him fleeing shrieking into the woods was his legs' sudden inability to do anything other than spasm uselessly. He spotted the Maxim he'd fixed, its muzzle driven into the dirt and a pair of disembodied arms hanging off the handles, their stumps burned black. Rifles cracked in the distance. The machine hummed southwards and the shooting increased in intensity for a few seconds before fading away.

The Hammer pulled out his Mauser and the moment broke. Banjo gathered up the chain and looped it over the man's head, putting his knee into the small of the guard's back and pulling the links tight against his throat. The automatic went off with a deafening crack as his opponent struggled to shoot his attacker. When that failed he bent forwards and Banjo felt his own feet lifting off the floor. *Jesus Christ.* He wanted to grab that gun but daren't lose his grip on the chains. He twisted harder, wondering why the bastard didn't just hurry up and choke to death like someone normal.

The muzzle appeared in the corner of his eye and he jerked his face to one side as it fired again. He could have sworn his right ear had exploded and the noise scored a line of agony along his jaw. Banjo nutted The Hammer from behind but he might as well have tried to pound a boulder into gravel with his head for all the good it did. More disarming was the utter silence of the Red as he fought for his life - not a word or sound, not even the occasional grunt of pain or effort. It would have been easier to kill a statue. After a few more abortive attempts The Hammer finally succeeded in flipping Banjo over his shoulder so the Englishman landed with a thud in the dirt.

Before his captor had a chance to regain his balance Banjo managed to whip him across the face with a loop of chain. The Russian lurched sideways, blood and teeth spraying out of his mouth. That gave the Englishman time to roll onto his hands and knees. He launched himself forwards, grabbed the man's coat lapels and head-butted him three times in rapid succession.

"Die. You. Bastard."

He'd nearly knocked himself out but at least The Hammer was dazed enough to flounder backwards, unable to aim. He lifted his gun and pointed it in the general direction of his prisoner. At the periphery of his vision Banjo saw the flying machine returning. *It's attracted to gunfire.* Having dealt with the rifles it was no doubt coming over to find out what all the fuss was about. He had a choice - go for The Hammer one last time or run and hope the lumbering bastard would miss. He turned and sprinted. A second later he heard the Mauser and threw himself into the mud.

The world detonated in a blaze of light, the ground heaving him head over heels like a flipped pancake so he ended up looking at a sky filled with roiling fire. Pebbles, soil and wet stuff dropped around him as a cloud of choking dust rolled over him in a wave. Half-stunned he eased onto his hands and knees and tugged at the chain. Just a couple of feet were left, the last links fused into a blob of cooling slag.

Unable to believe he was still alive, Banjo stood up and blundered through the smoke. He guessed the flying machine was drifting around somewhere but he wasn't going to waste time looking for it. The dust began to clear and he spotted the front locomotive sitting untouched further up the line, steam hissing from its valves. Banjo broke into a lumbering run. He couldn't stop giggling at his insane luck, despite fully expecting to be blasted out of existence any second.

As soon as the rear locomotive burst apart the soldiers scattered, cavalrymen leaping onto their horses and riding chaotically into the woods. Alexandra spotted Commander Aminev, pistol in hand, watching the creature as it span back from the shattered engine. It was impossible to make out any details - the smoke and steam from the wreckage mingled with the mist, blurring the world into an acrid mess of shapes accompanied by a cacophony of howling fire and collapsing metal. As the shape dipped down towards him Aminev rolled under a wagon. A second later the car exploded, its wood and concrete walls sailing outwards at right angles to each other.

Alexandra's fearful stupor broke. She lurched to her feet, trying to figure out how to escape. Nothing could stand up to this monster and if she hung around she'd be dead like the commander. Everyone else seemed to have run away, but as she turned to flee she spotted The Hammer standing next to the fallen train. The Georgian stared up at the creature, his face filled with a strange beatific recognition as if all the horrors he'd gazed at down the long tunnel of his madness for five years had finally left the trenches and come to join him at the end of the world. Alexandra called out but the man didn't react. The chains in his fist disappeared into a hatch in the side of the nearest turret. Banjo must still be inside. Maybe she had a chance to rescue them both, but the humming in the sky grew louder, wiping out all thoughts.

Alexandra turned and sprinted along the tracks, trying to get as far away as possible. She spotted the Agit-Train ahead. *Ekaterina and Viktor.* If The Hammer and the Englishman were doomed, she'd at least try to save her other broken dolls. Half of her realised it was beyond moronic to hide in a wheeled box covered in gaudy signs and revolutionary slogans daubed in three-foot-high red letters, but the creature hadn't attacked the Agit-Train. Instead it went straight for the troops, bypassing the carriage and its gently rumbling locomotive. Maybe it wasn't interested and they had a chance to get away. It was stupid hope but what choice did she have?

The distance looked impossible. The foot plate and coal tender were too exposed and anyway she had no idea how to drive a train. Alexandra aimed at the wagon instead and flung herself through the door, rolling into the shadows, face pressed against the floorboards, unable to believe she'd made it.

Baba Yaga.

The hag didn't come. She didn't claw her way inside, jaws snapping and red eyes hunting in the darkness for the flesh of Russian men. *She doesn't exist. Whatever that is, it's not Baba Yaga.*

The sound of Alexandra's breathing filled the universe. A face floated towards her and she nearly screamed and shot it.

Viktor.

"What is it?" he mouthed.

"We're under attack."

"I saw it fly past the wagon," he said.

She pulled herself up the wall and managed to make her way past the idiot into the next cabin. Ekaterina sat in the corner, knees up to her nose, staring at nothing with big owl eyes.

"An angel." murmured the actress.

"Whatever it is we can't stay here," Alexandra told them. "The rest of the train is wrecked and all the soldiers have fled. We can either run for the trees or try to get this locomotive moving. Any idea how to drive it?"

Viktor's expression told her it was a stupid question. Besides, a lumbering train and carnival wagon were asking to be attacked. If they ran for the woods they might stand a better chance. There was still enough smoke lingering on the battlefield to cover their escape. Alexandra knew Ekaterina could sprint, even in that dress, but her brother was a liability. On most days he found it a struggle to stay upright, let alone race half a mile across open terrain into a wood that was probably filled with more horrors.

The silence gave her enough courage to hunt for a crack in the walls or a gun slit. This was the Agit-Train's film production wagon so all the windows were boarded up but she found a skylight and popped it ajar, pulling herself off the floor to look outside. To her right the rail curved round to the south. She made out the shattered locomotive and burning carriage where Aminev had hidden. The armoured train lay on the other side, obscured by their own engine. Where was the creature? She searched what little of the sky she could see. Nothing. She didn't hear any humming either. Perhaps it had flown away, thinking itself victorious.

The shape she'd glimpsed through the smoke suggested a flying cuttlefish, but that buzzing reminded her of valves in a giant radio and it carried a weapon far more powerful than any gun she'd come across. A sudden realisation made her drop down from the hatch. *Did the Whites imprison that thing in the burst wagon? Were they going to use it against us but it fought back and clawed its way out? They believed it was a demon. Why else would they stick icons all over the train?*

It clearly wasn't a demon or some foolish peasant sorcery powering the beast so the holy trinkets failed and the monster broke free and now it was after revenge. *But what the hell is it? Not Baba Yaga The universe is ruled by science, not the frightened lies of senile nurses.* As cruel and as stupid as the Tsarists were they didn't think they'd sealed a pact with the devil, did they? Of course not. So what was the science behind this dark herald that spat fire from the sky and sang through the tree tops like a child's top?

The wagon lurched forward, throwing her down the corridor. She scrambled over to Ekaterina and put her hand over the woman's mouth, holding up the Mauser in the other. Viktor was a whimpering comma at the far end of the room, coiled around his Gladstone bag. *The creature's come back and is about to destroy us.* The carriage shuddered again and Alexandra heard the shriek of wheels turning uselessly on iron. The actress prised her hand away and reached down to roll up her skirt. She had a still, focussed look Alexandra hadn't seen in years and it momentarily threw her. *What are you doing?*

Another rumble and the noise picked up its own rhythm. Above it came the brittle *tink-tink* of the wheels hitting the joints as the train increased speed. Mad hope brought Alexandra to her feet.

"We're moving. One of the soldiers must have got to the engine and started it up," she hissed, still afraid to raise her voice. Gathering the fragments of her courage she told the others to wait and returned to the skylight. She was right. Smoke poured out of the locomotive as they thundered along, birch and pine whipping past on either side. They were in the forest and that'd give them some cover against the creature. It attacked the camp over the tops of the trees rather than coming through the woods. She tried to search the narrow strip of sky above but there was no sign. That didn't mean they were any safer. The steam would mark their position like a banner. She doubted they could outrun it and had no illusions about its ability to destroy them with its bullets of light. They'd probably just drawn more attention to themselves and even now it was hurtling after them, hungry red eyes scoring through the last of the fog. Their best hope would be to abandon the Agit-Train altogether and try to make it south on foot. For all she knew they only had seconds left.

Alexandra tried to see who was driving the engine but the smokestack was in the way. Looking north she saw an approaching bend, so she ran to the wagon door and leaned out as far as she dared, hoping she wasn't going to get her head taken off by a tree trunk. Now she could see the cabin but not the driver. She waved and shouted. A faint crack above the racket of the locomotive and the door frame splintered. She jerked back just as a second bullet punched a hole in the wall.

The fool was shooting at her in fear. A creature like that would send the bravest soldier mad which meant they were probably hurtling into the unknown in a high-speed train driven by a lunatic. She risked another peek outside and yelled as loud as possible for the man to stop but the woods plucked her words away. More shots and a splinter laid open her temple. *Stupid idiot.* Surely he'd seen Alexandra by now and realised she was a commissar and on the same side. Unless.

Banjo.

She found Ekaterina drinking from a vial. The singer wiped her mouth with the back of her hand and threw it into the corner of the room to shatter.

"Ekaterina, you know they're expensive," whimpered Viktor.

"Give me your handkerchief," said Alexandra. Ekaterina favoured her with the vaguely irritated look of a great artist disturbed in the middle of profound thoughts and handed it over.

"It's that moronic Englishman," she wrenched a strip of wood from the wall. "He keeps trying to shoot me."

Alexandra tied the silk square to the end of the stick, waited for the next turn and thrust the flag out, yelling at the top of her lungs in English for Banjo to cease firing. More rounds zipped past. *Damn the bastard to hell.* Ten bullets to a clip and she'd counted seven - though the oaf might have an unlimited supply of ammunition for all she knew. The only way she'd stop the Englishman was by making it to the driver's cabin. She'd have to climb onto the footplate somehow and then sneak round the side of the boiler. How hot did those things get? Alexandra had no idea but she guessed she'd need to be quick if she didn't want to get fried. To her dismay the end door of the carriage was nailed shut and breaking it open would take forever. No choice then - it was through that skylight and over the roof of a wagon travelling at fifty miles an hour. *You're utterly insane.* But she wasn't going to wait for the cretin to halt the train and pick them off one by one or abandon them in the middle of this wilderness.

Viktor met her in the corridor and grabbed her coat.

"She's gone," he squeaked.

"What do you mean 'gone'?"

"Up there," he pointed at the ceiling.

Alexandra dragged the man underneath the skylight, told him to get down on all fours and stepped onto his back. She pushed open the hatch as far back as she could and poked her head out. At least here there was no line of sight from the cabin.

Ekaterina walked along the roof barefoot, one hand stuck out for balance and a Mauser in the other. Despite the cab juddering from side to side, snapping branches from the trees as it hurtled through the thickest part of the forest, she moved with the precision of a ballet dancer tripping an allegro across a stage. The actress dropped out of sight and a few seconds later Alexandra heard three shots. The train's brakes slammed on and she fell off Viktor, smacking her head against the floor.

CHAPTER SEVEN

B anjo had both arms in the air like a pupil desperate to answer the next question. He stared at Ekaterina with big round eyes. Now she had a pistol in each hand, pointed at his head. She swayed slightly and Alexandra feared she might shoot the man just for fun. The commissar gently extracted one of the guns from her friend's fingers. The actress kissed her on the cheek, hitched her dress up to her waist and slotted the other into a holster strapped to her thigh.

"Sweet Jesus, I've died and gone to heaven," said Banjo in a tiny voice.

The Englishman was covered in mud and soot with a fresh cut along his jaw. Nevertheless he looked as annoyingly full of life and stupid opinions as before.

"Fairest vision," continued their captive in French. "I was saving you from the flying machine."

"No you weren't, you were running away," answered Alexandra.

"If we stay here, oh most radiant light in my firmament, it will find us. We must continue at all costs."

"We can't go north, there's nothing there except the mountains and maybe an old mine."

"Pavel lies ahead," said Ekaterina, as if that decided everything. She jumped off the train, which had clunked to a stop in a silent glade, and disappeared back to the wagon.

"She's got a gun under her skirt and no, er, no..."

"She used to rob banks in Georgia with Comrade Iosef Vissarionovich before the war."

"Who?"

"Comrade Stalin."

"Never heard of him. So she was a bandit? Bugger me."

"She liberated funds for the Revolution from the corrupt bourgeoisie."

Banjo's eyes narrowed.

"Right."

"How did you escape?"

Banjo held up his chains. The ends were melted.

"The machine blew up that constipated lunatic you set to watch over me."

Alexandra finally lost her temper.

"The Hammer used to sing and dance, and write beautiful poetry that made us weep, you cretin! He filled a room with joy and laughter. Smorgon did that to him, the filthy capitalist warmongers shattered his soul!" She jabbed a finger back down the track and shouted. "He was worth a thousand of you, you debased shit!"

My broken soldier doll - I tried, dear God, I tried to bring you back, but the barbed wire was still inside you, wrapped around your heart. She struggled to keep the tears at bay.

"Alright, alright. Keep your shirt on. Listen, let me go. I'll run away and no-one will ever know. Tell them I died in the battle. I'm no good to you. Like you said I'm a debased shit with a wrong consciousness thing and that bastard was going to have me shot anyway."

"I can't let you go," grumbled Alexandra, as much as she wanted rid of the idiot. "I need you to drive this train."

"It's simple - a piece of cake once you get used to it. I'll show you how," answered the Englishman, gesturing at the wall of dials, levers and valves. Alexandra didn't have time for this nonsense.

"Start the locomotive." She pointed the gun at Banjo's head, barely trusting herself not to pull the trigger. He made a noise like a cantankerous wolf and turned back to the controls.

"We'll go north until I'm sure we're out of range of that thing." Alexandra peered up through the branches for any sign of the creature.

"You're hoping. That flying machine looked a pretty remorseless bastard to me."

This was the first time Alexandra had paused long enough to look past her terror. Banjo's comment clicked open a door in her head and suddenly everything started to make sense. Had they been attacked by a new and powerful Tsarist weapon? Is that what they'd been fashioning in the vast workshops of Ikayungri?

"You think it's a flying machine? With a pilot inside?"

"Well what did you think it was, Baba Yaga?"

Alexandra felt her ears go red.

"Is that what the Whites were building in the factories?" she asked.

"Don't ask me."

So the rumours of Baba Yaga were just propaganda to frighten the locals away and strike fear in the hearts of the bourgeoisie's enemies. Alexandra had watched planes duelling over the battlefields - canvas and wood boxes with engines that sounded like tubercular bees. They died easily, in burning paper-kite tatters. The flyer that attacked the camp, if that was what it was, was of an order of sophistication hitherto undreamed of except in tales of Super Science. It had no wings, nor any engine she could see. How did it stay aloft, and how did the pilot propel it forwards? She racked her memory for any clues. *All the books I read sitting on the window seat opposite Natasha in Uncle's library, our legs entwined as we each lost ourselves in our own worlds. Did any of them hold a clue?*

"Your writer of scientific romances, Mr. H. G. Wells, prophesied an advanced type of aerial ship like the one that attacked us. The Asiatic hordes use it to conquer the world and drive mankind into a new primitive age."

"Did he?"

"In *The War in the Air*, remember?"

"Never read it. Wells bores me stupid. I managed a couple of paragraphs of *The Time Machine* and gave up. Another pompous arse," he paused. "No offence. My Auntie Jessie and her friend Constance went to see him give a talk to the Womens' Union once. Apparently, he had the voice of a little girl and rabbited on about Free Love for three hours."

"What's wrong with Free Love?"

Banjo's thoughts were as plain as day - *what does someone like you know about love?*

"It's fine by me. Love who or what you want - but I reckon his version involves him shagging whoever he fancies and leaving a trail of broken hearts. Free Love's fine if you're a bloke. Until everyone's equal it's not so much fun for lasses. Mr Wells's Charlie was ever a-wander. They hoofed him out of the Fabians because he kept poking it into somebody important's fifteen-year-old daughter. 'Oh! Oh! Bertie, Bertie, what are you doing?'", the Englishman started squeaking, waving his hands about in a pantomime of coy refusal. Alexandra watched open-mouthed. "'Ha, ha! Now I have you my proud beauty - let me show you my big space cannon'. I prefer my stories to be all adventurous and romantic with lots of fighting. If I want sermons I'll go to the Sally Army," he finished. "Have you still got my book?" he added as an afterthought.

The commissar couldn't credit her ears. *There's a destructive weapon beyond imagination bearing down on us and I'm having an argument about literature and love with this utter buffoon.* She handed the man his copy of *A Princess of Mars*. Banjo shot her a ferocious grin.

He drove the train onward through the forest. Alexandra sensed they were slowly rising up from the valley. The landscape on either side grew craggier, the strange hummocky terrain spattered with boulders. There was still no sign of the flying machine. She should have been relieved but hungered to see it again. Despite its destructive powers it was impressive. *That's the kind of science that'll drag us out of the mire of blood and sickness that's swilled through Mother Russia for so long.*

"What are we going to do?" asked Banjo. "We can chop trees for firewood but we've no supplies and it looks like poor foraging round here. Do we keep heading north until we reach the end of the line or have you got a plan to get us back down south?"

"Don't you want to run away anymore?"

"Where to?"

Alexandra pointed up the track.

"Commander Aminev thought there might be White mines in the mountain. He believed they held gold. I'm hoping we'll come to one."

"Won't it be abandoned?"

"Some supplies may have survived and maybe even a crystal set. Can you mend radios?"

Banjo nodded.

"Shouldn't you be looking after Madam?" he asked.

Alexandra laughed. God, but the man was transparent. She'd no intention of leaving him alone. Besides, Ekaterina and her brother would be dancing through a constellation of powders and vials by now. *Only two broken toys left, the singer and the poet, both drug addicts.* Long ago she'd learned that cajoling, pleading and threatening them with prison was a waste of time. Iron Felix's cousin could do whatever the hell she wanted. The beautiful Siren of the Revolution lived in another sphere from her mere comrades.

Her thoughts were starting to drift, lulled into an easy rhythm by the swaying engine. Keeping one eye on her captive she perched on a barrel.

"Are there lots of lasses like you in the army then?" he asked.

"Why? Are you surprised? Under communism men and women are equal."

"Wonderful. Auntie Jessie would be well chuffed. So how did you end up as a Red who reads H.G. Wells?"

That took her by surprise. *Mind your own business* was the first response that sprang to mind but she had nowhere else to go and nothing to do.

"My cousin Natasha and I loved astronomy and we devoured Verne, Wells and Tsiolkovsky together. She went to study mathematics at a university for women in Petrograd but when my turn came war broke out. My friends and I made art for the revolution - wrote poems and plays and printed them in our secret cellar in Petrograd - tales of the coming epoch, of a happy time when man and women would cast aside their shackles and forge new worlds under new suns."

Cousin Anton and I. Our foreheads touching, filled with the joy of futurity as we wrote our plays, until you tried to kiss me. You said I was mentally ill, crippled with a bourgeois disease. I didn't understand why, only that I had to get away.

"I volunteered in the Petrograd Women's Battalion and went to fight. When I came back the horror of war had broken our group apart. We'd lost that joy and spring innocence that fired our dreams and now our revolution was to be altogether darker, and crueller. I never knew it would come so soon. On the day they stormed the Winter Palace Ekaterina and I defended our theatre against the government's troops. I watched her shoot half a dozen Cossacks."

Banjo whistled.

"But our group was already broken. Pavel grew distant from Ekaterina and took others to his bed, breaking her heart even as she clung to him in desperation. Eventually he ran away on this train with another actress, abandoning the theatre they'd built together in the first days of the new world. So brother and sister turned to their opium and their cocaine. The Hammer. Well, you met The Hammer. In the end I couldn't stand it anymore. It wounded my soul to look into my friends' eyes and see the ghosts of what we once were, though we still fooled ourselves we hadn't changed. When my uncle got me a job in the People's Commissariat for Education I jumped at the chance."

And Natasha? After that night in the theatre when your brother spat in my face and told me I was sick in the head I never spoke to you again, never wrote to you or answered your letters, even after I returned from the front. I couldn't bring myself to see you. Why?

And why in God's name was she telling the man all this? It was a ridiculous confession to a brute. She might as well have told her life story to a cow. But she saw sympathy in his eyes and it threw her.

"And you?" she said.

"Not much to tell. Quaker parents. Bastard father. Miserable bitch mother. Auntie Jessie and her friend Constance kept me entertained most of the time otherwise I would have drowned myself in the Leeds-Liverpool canal. Ran away to sea. Spent ten years dodging buggery from Montevideo to Shanghai and back. Learned to be an engineer. That's it."

"No friends?"

Banjo puffed his cheeks out like a hamster and blew air at the cabin roof.

"Yokohama Bettie. She asked me to marry her but she's a bit soft that way and does it to most of her clients. Waza the Turk, when he's sober. No, come to think of it he's a bastard through and through. There was a gaucho in Argentina who I got on with, Juan de Dios, but he fell off his horse drunk, cracked his head on a rock and died." He shrugged. A thought struck him.

"You wrote plays?"

Alexandra nodded.

"You didn't write that one with the man in the silver hat who went 'Poop Poop' did you?"

He saw her expression, turned slightly pink and burst into a strange coughing fit, suddenly paying very close attention to the dials above the fire door. When he'd recovered he peered along the track.

"Jesus God Almighty."

Alexandra looked out of the other side and her heart thudded in her ears. They were entering a long valley with rocky walls that rose up to a cliff face at the base of the mountains. At the far end she could just see the tumbled-down buildings of an abandoned mine complex, but between them and the entrance lay a battlefield. The ground was pitted with craters and scorch marks and dotted with tangles of rags and skeletons - both men and horses. Another armoured train lay in a crushed heap a hundred yards from the tracks which were still remarkably intact. Banjo brought the locomotive to a halt.

"What in the name of all that's holy happened here?" he growled.

They watched the valley for an hour. No movement. Banjo spotted Viktor peering out of the wagon door and Madam had clambered onto the roof again. He'd reconciled himself to being saddled with these Reds, but what a Trojan woman, and she was wearing nothing underneath that skirt apart from a Mauser strapped to that splendid leg. Jesus Christ - the mere idea would have made Mother's head explode. Alexandra shouting for her to get down interrupted his fantasies. She wriggled back inside through the skylight and Comrade Otter told Banjo to ease the train forward. It was either stay on the edge of the forest forever or risk the open. There'd been no sign of that flying machine so he let the locomotive creep out of the shadow of the trees.

Judging by the state of the fallen this battle had happened at least a year ago. Most had been reduced to bones and scraps of uniform though the winter had mummified a few into coffee-coloured mannequins. There were only a handful intact. Most looked as if they'd been caught in explosions. This had all the signature of a prolonged artillery barrage. A few Austin armoured cars lay among the dead, their armour dented or missing.

"Look at the uniforms. They're all Tsarists," said Alexandra. "None of these are ours."

The flying machine and its ray gun. Did it do all this?

"If that thing destroyed this army then it's not a White weapon. So what is it and where does it come from? Are you sure you don't have anything like this in your secret Red laboratories in Moscow and they just haven't told you about it?"

Alexandra gave a sour laugh.

"We wouldn't turn our science to such cruelty and carnage."

Yeah, right.

Banjo thought her a naive idiot, but let it go. At first he'd found that Russians had a tendency to blurt out statements of such gormless innocence that it was hard not to believe the entire nation to be half-simple. After a while he'd realised that they waged a constant battle in their hearts between utter cynicism and romantic optimism. Still, it was a struggle not to burst out laughing every time the little tart uttered yet another ridiculously pompous aphorism. He needed to stay in the woman's good books if he was to survive.

As they grew closer to the mine complex Banjo realised the railway didn't stop at the depot. It ran between two cliffs of ramshackle buildings built into the sides of a short ravine. The gully ended at the entrance to a wide tunnel leading directly into the mountain. He engaged the brakes and let the train ease to a halt a hundred yards from the opening. Alexandra beckoned Viktor over, gave him Banjo's pistol, and said something in Russian. The man nodded nervously, wrapped both hands around the handle and pointed it at the Englishman's head. The idiot couldn't stop shaking and his eyes looked as if he was stuffed full of drugs just to help him stay upright.

"Really? Look, I won't cause any trouble." said Banjo, feeling suddenly nervous.

Alexandra ignored him.

"Why don't you get Madam to watch over me instead? That'd be nice."

The Red harridan snorted and jumped down from the cabin. Banjo shrugged. *Suit yourself. First whiff of danger and I'll disarm this dribbling git.*

They climbed a staircase that ran up the front of several buildings, all piled on top of each other like a second cliff face. The planks had shrunk and turned the colour of an elephant's hide. Banjo couldn't see anything through the dark cracks between the wood.

"How long do you think this has been here?" he asked. Surely not more than a few years and yet the pumiced walls and dusted half-light made it feel like they'd stumbled across the leavings of an ancient civilisation. Alexandra stopped on a landing and cupped her hands around her face to peer through a pane of filthy glass. She kicked open a door next to the window and stepped inside. The rooms were intact but it looked as if anything of value had been taken away or looted. Half an hour's searching yielded nothing - no food, water or radio set.

"No choice then," said Banjo. "We'll have to return through the forest and take our chances. Unless you fancy paying a visit to the Hall of the Mountain King."

"Is everything a joke to you?" snapped Alexandra.

Banjo had a think.

"No."

"Alexandra," called the actress from outside. She was shading her eyes and looking across the valley with the mild interest of a stroller observing the swans at Roundhay Park on a Sunday afternoon. They joined her and with a lurch of fear Banjo saw a night-coloured triangle hovering at the other end of the battlefield, just above the trees where the railway led back into the woods to the south.

"What's the bloody thing doing? Why doesn't it attack?"

"It's examining you, my harsh barbarian," drawled Ekaterina in French. "It has a soul of metal and sees in ways we earthbound mortals cannot possibly dream of."

Alexandra glanced over the balcony at the railway leading into the mountain.

"Could that thing follow the train inside?"

"Dunno - even if it didn't we'd still be trapped."

"What choice do we have? Stay out here and we're targets," her otter eyes narrowed. "It could just be toying with us."

"Maybe it wants us to carry on. At least it's better than standing here waiting to be picked off."

At the back of his mind grew the suspicion that the flying machine, or whoever piloted it, actually wanted them to enter the tunnel. *Is it herding us along? To what?*

They clambered down to the locomotive. Alexandra told her

chums to get inside the wagon and joined Banjo on the plate. She waved her Mauser at the controls.

"Are you really going to point that bloody thing at me all the time?"

"You broke your word. I'm not so stupid as to trust you again."

Before the commissar had a chance to react Banjo flicked the cap off her head, snatched the gun out of her hands and reversed it. Alexandra stumbled back and glared at Banjo in fury. To be fair the pompous bint had guts, as well as hair. He'd assumed she'd shaved it all off to keep the nits away but a ragged bob flopped down around her face. In fact she wasn't such a boot after all. She reminded him of the droopy lass in that painting by Burne-Jones - *King Cough-it-up and the Scullery Wench*, or whatever it was called. He gave her the Mauser.

"I could escape any time I want."

"So why don't you?"

Banjo pointed at the creature in the distance, but if he was honest, deep inside a curiosity had awakened. Here was a mystery he wanted to solve, especially one with adventure and the whiff of romance. The mines called to him like the catacombs of the ancient cities of Barsoom. Besides, he knew he wouldn't stand a cat in hell's chance out here on his own. Alexandra and the divine Ekaterina were the only people in this godforsaken shit-hole he could actually have a conversation with and if he showed willing, they might find it in their hearts to help him in the end.

"Ignorant oaf," muttered Alexandra, holstering the pistol.

Banjo had spotted a couple of sidings before the entrance and to his relief a handful of axle grease scraped from underneath the locomotive was enough to free the points. He'd no intention of driving into the mountain with his view blocked by that ludicrous circus wagon but it took a good half-hour's screaming argument in Russian between Alexandra and the actress (in which Otter Woman did the arguing and Voluptuous Goddess did the screaming) before she let them shunt the carriage off the track and uncouple it. Apparently in Ekaterina's head it was now a shrine to Lost Love. All the while the dunce cap flying machine drifted back and forth across the distant tree line like a hungry wolf working out the best way to take down its prey.

Once they were left with just the engine he fed the furnace with half a dozen planks wrenched from the walls of the decaying buildings and invited Alexandra to stand on the front plate with a hand bell to watch for any obstructions. There was now so much bad feeling between the commissar and Madam that Alexandra seemed happy to act as the locomotive's figurehead and left the singer with an order to keep an eye on the Englishman. Madam gave a contemptuous laugh, tossed her head and stared resolutely in the opposite direction to Banjo. Things were looking up already, even if he'd also have to endure her lack-wit brother who sat on the floor, sorting through his endless green vials and packets by the firelight.

"It might get a bit smelly, fair Amazon, on account of the smoke and us being in a tunnel," said Banjo. Another shake of that magnificent head. Despite himself he gave a huge grin and slipped the brake.

To his surprise they only had to endure ten minutes shrouded in blood-coloured steam before the passage opened out into a vault. He brought the engine to a halt and lit a couple of storm lanterns from the fire box. Alexandra appeared.

"This looks like some kind of warehouse mined out of the rock," she said before glancing back down the tunnel. "I don't think it's followed us but we shouldn't hang around."

"I want to scout first. No point running into a wall or off a precipice."

Banjo handed a light down before jumping from the cabin. He held up his hand to Ekaterina who took it with a smile. She'd be his ere long, no doubt about that. They'd lie on the bank of a river in Paradise and he would pillow his head between those milk white orbs while she soothed his brow with her languid palm and fed him sweetmeats and sherbet.

Alexandra was blathering at him.

"I said, there are tunnels leading off in all directions and they have rails."

Banjo walked past the engine to where a cluster of junctions sent tracks spiralling into the shadows on all sides of the cavern.

"Only this one has a wide enough gauge," he pointed. "All the rest are for carts."

He spotted a lump of rock on the ground and picked it up for a look before tossing it to Alexandra.

"Gold ore. Your Commander Bastard-features was right - this is a White gold mine. So this is what the battle was about - this mountain must be riddled with the stuff."

"Maybe they thought to use it to buy allies and weapons but who besides us would fight for it? The Japanese?"

Banjo didn't have an answer. He was too busy staring across the vault to where the main line disappeared through an immense bricked arch. He lifted his lantern and looked around. More buildings ringed the cave, tucked against the dark rock. They were in better condition than the ones outside but it was hard to look at those closed doors and black windows for long. His imagination moulded watchers out of his dream memories so he lowered the light with a shudder and trotted back to the cab, keeping his gaze on the floor.

"Pavel is in those depths," Ekaterina told him. "And I am Orpheus, set to reclaim my Eurydice from the clutches of Hades."

"If you say so."

They took up stations once more and he eased the engine into motion. Fear and adventure tumbled over each other inside his head. Going deeper into the mountain was madness but he had to admit he was impressed by the Whites' engineering. Whatever Alexandra believed about the decadent Tsarists he reckoned the communists could learn a thing or too from these workings. Sometimes they crawled through low tunnels and the air filled with choking smoke. At other times they seemed to drive along the bottom of long trenches and Banjo sensed huge structures in the shadows far above. After a while the sense of happy wonder faded as he struggled to recall any human skill capable of building this honeycomb.

They entered another cavern. Frantic ringing from ahead made him slam on the brakes and a second later Alexandra appeared alongside.

"The way's blocked."

"By what?"

The Russian stared back at him wide-eyed, the fires from the engine and lanterns dancing in her glasses. She turned without word and Banjo climbed down and followed. Twenty yards in front of the wagon he found himself looking at a massive wall made entirely of icons. Hundreds of faces shining in gold and lacquer peered down at them in pious misery, sealing their way onward.

CHAPTER EIGHT

Banjo wasn't overly fond of Russian icons. To be honest, they gave him the willies, especially as they seemed deliberately designed to glare you into terror and shame. Just think of touching the Honourable Member and they'd pour screaming out of their golden heaven to tear you to pieces. Quakers didn't have much truck with art and so his childhood had been free of pictures, apart from a copy of *And When Did You Last See Your Father?* which his parents kept in the water closet to remind him of what to do if the police ever turned up. And then there was Auntie Jessie and her friend Constance who kept sneaking him away from his parents to stare at blobs and patterns on canvas in cellars where they played ragtime and everyone slunk around like tomcats in heat.

Once he'd started sailing the seven seas he'd come across more paintings and drawings but given the company he tended to keep they ran on the same basic themes - best described as celebrating the female form rather than glowering at you with boggling eyes for even acknowledging women existed. Right now every single mournful face was focussed on him and in the darkness under this mountain he heard Old Nick filing his teeth into daggers and getting ready to feast on his bollocks.

After the first shock Alexandra didn't seem particularly over-awed. Neither did Ekaterina. No doubt they were both armoured with that Red Atheism the papers back home kept thundering about. The Russians approached the wall and Banjo forced himself to join them. There was no sign of the runty brother - probably wetting himself back on the train. Close up he noticed the thin crack outlining a door across the rails. The commissar ran her hands over the images.

"This iconostasis is new. It's been built in the last year."

The actress rested her cheek against a saint's face.

"Pavel is on the other side," she whispered.

Banjo was getting tired of this Pavel of hers. He was no doubt an etiolated fop forever striking a leg and declaiming at the skies when he wasn't buried up to the gonads in some floozy. Perhaps if and when they finally met the sod he could engineer an accident, or enough of a scandal to send Ekaterina fleeing into his hearty Yorkshire embrace. He felt a draught on his legs and looked down.

"The rails carry on under the door."

"The rest of the Agit-Train must have travelled through here, in which case this was rebuilt afterwards - a couple of weeks ago," said Alexandra. "Who by? The Whites abandoned this place last year. That battlefield outside is at least that old. So who made this?"

"And who's flying that machine?" Banjo glanced back down the tunnel but all he could make out was the engine simmering in a puddle of lamplight. If their pursuer had followed them it was being very quiet about it unless it had popped over the mountain and was waiting for them to emerge on the other side.

"I can smash the train through this wall with no problem - it's only wood, or we go back and chance a run past that thing. What do you want to do?"

He looked at the Russian, expecting to see the lass pedantically working through the options with her usual expression of earnest constipation. Instead he saw a crazy gleam in those eyes. He recognised it straight away - the hunger of a mad adventurer. Since confessing her love of H. G. Wells she'd come over all fired up. Somehow that tedious old satyr had the same effect on her as Edgar Rice Burroughs had on him. It definitely wasn't the pious gaze of all those dead saints lighting up her otter face, or the holy writings of St Marx and St Lenin. It was the same desire to journey on and find out what lay beyond, to solve a mystery of the flying machine, to chase adventure like John Carter of Virginia or, in her case, some prissy bore from one of randy Bertie's tracts. Banjo cracked his knuckles.

"What do you reckon Alexandra? Shall we give it a go?"

Ekaterina clasped her hands together in prayer.

"Please do, Alexandra. We're so close - we can't turn back now."

Alexandra pushed the door open. The draught swelled to a breeze.

This goes straight through the mountain. How the hell did they manage to bore tunnels through all this granite?

The commissar walked forward, holding up a lantern. The tracks disappeared into the gloom ahead, the tunnel opening up to form a trench with walls that lofted into darkness. Banjo stepped through and, looking behind, realised that this side of the wall was also covered in paintings of the Almighty and his saints. Ekaterina gave a gasp and took his hand, raising it so the light from his lantern spread across the assembled multitude. He caught her perfume. It was laced with the petrol scent of cocaine but he didn't care.

"What is it?"

"*The Theotokos of St Theodore*," she whispered, pointing at a very uncomfortable looking Virgin Mary with a monkey clambering up her front. *That's not supposed to be Baby Jesus, is it?* "Marvellous - *The Virgin of Kazan*, Rubilev's *Mandylion* and *Christ Pantokrator*."

Alexandra joined them like the miserable gooseberry she was and rubbed the nearest picture with her finger.

"I think they're originals. The Tsarists must have brought these treasures here to hide them from us."

"Nailing them to a wall across a railway tunnel won't do them much good," Banjo pointed out.

"The priests told us they possessed great holiness and cured the sick, thwarted demons, protected the Tsar. Stupid and ignorant - we were right to destroy them. They enticed the simple minded into mental slavery."

"Such beauty," murmured Ekaterina.

Banjo didn't see it himself but he nodded vigorously and flashed her a grin. Even so, the silent staring crowds of fierce piety bothered him.

Icons by the gap in the factory wall, icons in the burst wagon and icons here. What are they so frightened of?

Alexandra wandered up the tunnel. Reflected lamplight flared on shattered glass. She'd halted next to what looked like a discarded box. Banjo followed her but halfway along his feet stopped working and cold waves washed over him in rapid succession. A broken cabinet on bicycle wheels lay beside the tracks with half a skeleton lying amid the fragments.

"You've seen something similar to this before, haven't you? Back in the factory," said the commissar when he'd finally summoned up the courage to draw closer. "So have I but mine was dead like this one. Yours still moved, didn't it? When I showed you the print of these wheels, I saw it in your face."

Banjo nodded.

"Outside the warehouse where I had my den. There were four of them and one of these, heading for the trees."

"Four of who?"

When it turned its shadow spilled over the ground and it had a second pair of arms. Hungry, hallucinating, mind half wrapped up in visions of Burroughs' Mars. It had to be a dream.

"People."

It wasn't because he thought Alexandra would laugh at him. He felt as though there was an invisible barrier between them and an unseen world of dark perversity, an insane rot threading through this wilderness like blue veins in Stilton. If he admitted that those beings were real it would mean stepping over a threshold into a hell he couldn't return from. Flying machines were one thing - even if the science behind that hovering cone was far beyond anything he'd come across it still made sense. A pickled corpse on wheels wasn't so outré - you could rob a grave or a mortuary and cobble together something similar to make a bob or two in a grubby tent on the fringe of a fairground if you weren't too fussed about decency. But living creatures that loped along with six limbs - the Great White Apes straight out of his storybook - that was mad, and wrong, and probably blasphemous to boot. He knew he should have been joshing the little Russian as usual and that his silence betrayed more than words, but it took him all his courage relive that encounter.

Luckily Alexandra wasn't pushing any further. Instead she knelt down and peered inside the remains of the box where the bottom of the skeleton's snapped-off spine disappeared into a tangled mess of rusty wires and glass tubing as fine as hair.

"You're not saying these were actually alive?" asked Banjo. "Surely they're just specimens, like doctors practice on. The one I saw was submerged in some kind of liquid - formaldehyde perhaps - it had to be dead beforehand or it would have drowned."

"What medical students would be doing experiments out here, under a mountain?" said Alexandra.

"I dunno. Our brave new century is full of cripples now - poor bastards with their arms and legs blown off - half their guts missing and having to shit into bags. Maybe they tried to find a way to give them some kind of a life by building an electrical bath chair to help them trundle around and do stuff like ordinary people."

He was grasping wildly at anything, any explanation to stop himself crossing that hideous shadow boundary into what? What realm did these monsters dwell in? Alexandra picked up a brass lozenge from among the broken glass and read the embossed number.

"271. Commander Aminev's Electrical Girl was 339. He found it in the cellars underneath the workshops."

"You mean the Whites built hundreds of these things below our feet?"

And I lived above them for nine months. Jesus Christ. In his mind an endless procession of pickled corpses trundled along grey-bricked tunnels lit only by their glowing boxes, white-eyed with lips peeled back from skull teeth. *That's my nightmares well and truly sorted for the next five years.* At least they were now a couple of days' journey away from Ikayungri, although this wreckage suggested the monsters had roamed quite a distance from home.

"There has been cruelty beyond imagining here - science turned to evil, machines consuming man in oppressive destruction," said Alexandra. *We're off again - sermon time.* "We have to stop this. We must take what these bastard Tsarists created and turn it to good, to craft a Soviet Super Science to vanquish all war and suffering."

"Absolutely," agreed Banjo, nodding enthusiastically. A round of applause would have probably gone down the wrong way. "Good luck."

"*We* have to."

"Eh?"

He saw his own reflection duplicated in a pair of owl spectacles and realise he wore the same expression of gawping dismay as St Pancreas the Dyspeptic on the wall behind him.

"Our enemies made fantastic discoveries. They learned how to meld a human with an electric machine. They built a flying engine more powerful than an ironclad. I think we defeated them too soon before they could perfect their wickedness. Destiny vanquished their attempts to turn the tide of the Revolution. That flying weapon is piloted by one of the last Tsarists. You and I must find a way of defeating him, and then returning to Ikayungri to search the laboratories they hid underground. Then we will go to Petrograd and lay our findings before the people, engage the wisest minds and transform this...", she gestured at the skeleton, "...into the service of futurity."

The Red was pacing up and down now, beating her fist against her palm. It was all very noble and inspiring. If she carried on like this any longer Banjo would have no choice but to shoot the canting fucker and make his own escape, even if it meant he'd lose the admiration of the actress. Which reminded him, where had the fair Amazon disappeared to during this impromptu lecture? If he remembered rightly she'd drifted on ahead, down the tunnel.

Banjo jogged past Alexandra who paused mid-rant. His panic settled when he spotted the actress at the edge of the lantern light, cocking her head from side to side as if listening to the darkness. She looked up and, following her gaze, he made out narrow ledges about twenty feet up the wall on both sides, running along the trench. Dark holes punctured the rock every ten yards or so, suggesting more passageways and galleries beyond.

"I think we might have an audience," murmured Ekaterina in her sing-song voice. "Or is it just the wind fluting through this ancient underworld?"

I'm moments away from a tremendous discovery - a great new Super Science I can bring before the people, one that will wash away the misery, sickness, blood and suffering. I can taste it in the air of these stupendous vaults. Her heart thundered in her chest and fired with new purpose Alexandra told the others to return to the train. They'd break through the iconostasis and keep going until they exited the mountain or came to the end of the line.

"Good idea," said Banjo as they climbed into the cabin. He suddenly seemed very keen to get moving. "We shouldn't hang around."

Viktor was studying his reflection up close in the dials, tubes and levers. The Englishman shooed him away and set the engine in motion. It lumbered up to the wall. There was a momentary creaking sound, and the barrier gave way. Gods and martyrs flamed gold as they tumbled like autumn leaves through the darkness on either side. Perhaps she should have saved them, kept the beauty of those Rubilevs for a museum. *No, you deserve to fall into darkness, you memories of decadent oppression, of priests and madmen. I've got the future to capture. Tugarin the earth dragon can have you for his filthy lair, what's left of him.* Despite her earlier admiration Ekaterina didn't seem to care either - her head was full of Pavel. After loudly protesting that she shouldn't put herself in danger, to absolutely no effect, Banjo slowed the locomotive to let her step onto the footplate so she could take a turn at keeping watch on the tracks ahead. The breath-taking sensation of having crossed a boundary had ignited her heart as well.

"We have entered a realm of great beauty and great horror," the singer told Alexandra, brandishing her Mauser a little too close to the commissar's face for comfort. "We are about to confront the greatest trial of the new age. I sense it in my soul."

They set off again and as the train picked up speed Alexandra thought she saw shadows on the tracks scattering into the walls, but Ekaterina didn't sound the alarm so she put it down to an illusion caused by the smoke.

On this side of the iconostasis the tunnels seemed older, hacked into the rock eons ago. They entered a series of caverns that resembled natural fissures torn into the mountain by long-forgotten earthquakes. The walls were laced with as-yet untouched ore which sparkled in the lamplight, chasing the train like electricity arcing through a vast machine. *Who built this labyrinth, and with what?* The Tsarists must have erected the iconostasis as a barrier against something, as they did with the icons they left in the factory or on the burst wagon - but they also laid these tracks. When they extended the railway to fetch the gold did they stumble across a secret that had them fleeing back and sealing the passage behind them in their bourgeois superstition? What would frighten them so much?

"Take us down to a crawl. I don't want to burst out of the mountain in broad daylight into the middle of any enemies," she told Banjo.

"Aye aye, Skipper."

The Englishman slowed them to a walking pace. The radiance turned into an arch of pale sunlight. The engine eased to a halt and the commissar jumped down.

"Get ready to put it into reverse."

Alexandra would have to trust the man not to flee back into the labyrinth, but she'd seen her own hungry curiosity reflected in his eyes.

She stopped at the mine entrance, blinking in the light. A soft wind cleared the steam and she found herself gazing across a broad valley. She had to be hallucinating. The woods sloping down from the mountain behind them gave way to meadows, and tilled fields? Here - in the wilderness of Siberia? *It's inhabited - this doesn't make sense.* She could have been standing in the countryside near Tver, or Yaroslavl before the war tore the world apart and spattered it with ash and blood. *Good God is that a village?* A cluster of buildings no bigger than her little fingernail sat in the shadow of an immense cliff. Above it a vaster peak rose up into the sky. It looked oddly regular, like an eroded pyramid, flanked by the cluttered geometry of yet more mountains. The outlines made her think of a box of children's wooden blocks tipped over a nursery carpet. The train tracks at her feet curved round the edge of the forest to her right, disappearing out of sight after a mile.

The air had an odd, grainy quality, as if the entire landscape had been painted on pale blue felt. Strange optical effects magnified the sun, turning it into a huge orange ball hanging at the end of the valley, silhouetting the ragged outlines of the birch trees. She shielded her eyes from the light and the warmth on her face and the backs of her hands seemed to carry with it the weight of a thousand forgotten voices.

Banjo slapped her on the back, making her jump and swear.

"I know what this is. We've found a lost world - a timeless civilisation cut off from the rest of mankind like the Kingdom of Kor, ruled over by the undying Ayesha the Immortal, She-Who-Must-Be-Obeyed, bathing herself in the fire of immortality to preserve her eternal beauty."

"What on earth are you talking about?"

"She! Wisdom's daughter herself, you simpleton. Centuries surrounded by eunuchs and effeminate degenerates, endlessly waiting for her true love, Kallikrates, to be reborn," he jabbed a thumb at his own chest. "How she will be pining for a real hero to clasp her to his manly bosom and melt that cold heart of hers with his passionate caresses!"

He broke off when he saw his companion's expression.

"Good God lass, don't tell me you've never read any H. Rider Haggard either."

"Can you please stop talking drivel, just for once, and concentrate on the matter in hand? This isn't one of your wretched fantasies."

"Bloody hell but you're hard work. You really should cheer up. Adventuring's supposed to be fun, not a fucking Sunday School outing."

Alexandra couldn't be bothered to argue.

"We need to find out who lives in that village. We'll scout along the tracks. Leave Ekaterina and Viktor with the engine."

She knew it was stupid but the urge to learn the truth behind those wonders drove her on. By rights they should have come here with an army, though the carnage around the old mine suggested that wouldn't have been enough.

They returned to the train where she took the actress's wrists in her hands until the singer finally looked her in the eye and promised to wait with Viktor until Alexandra and Banjo had scouted down the track to make sure it was safe. Short of tying Ekaterina to the locomotive there wasn't a lot else she could do. The Siren of the Revolution was drifting into one of her bouts of post-narcotic languor and Alexandra hoped it would be enough to keep her out of harm for the moment. With any luck the dwellers in that distant village hadn't spotted their arrival and she wanted it to stay that way. Knowing Ekaterina she'd be into the main square and trying to chivvy the inhabitants into a chorus of *Boldly Comrades Keep in Step!* given half a chance. That would guarantee a lynching for all of them. It was unlikely that the Revolution had bypassed the Whites and found its way here. She still remembered that old fool blessing her for returning the Good Tsar to his people, and that'd been four hundred miles back west. *Our new worker's paradise is stretched so extremely thin over the thousands of leagues between Tomsk and Vladivostok.*

Against her better judgement she handed Banjo a gun and together they sidled out into the sunshine, heading for the edge of the woods so they could keep hidden among the trees. She made sure the Englishman walked in front and got ready to shoot the fool if he tried anything. As soon as they left the track the rich scents of soil and forest thudded into her, borne between the birch and pine by a heavy silence. As she took a few steps deeper, her boots sinking into cadmium moss, she sensed a brooding, primal life - intense and unending. It was uncanny for there was no birdsong or rustling of branches, only the occasional distant crack of a falling bough. Despite herself she caught a fragment of Efrosinya Nikolayevna's mad lullaby in the shadows of her memories *"Tili Tili Bom. He walks - he is coming - he is closer. Tili Tili Bom. Here as well, his dark soul in the earth itself. Tugarin sleeping."*

Alexandra felt herself losing any sense of time and season. On the other side of the mountain it was April, with the lands still cut raw by the last of the winter frosts, but here it was as if someone had gathered a hundred warm summer evenings from long ago and poured them over the valley. Through the leaves she saw the strange amber sun smeared just above the horizon, and the pale angular shapes of the mountains tinted blue in the watery sky.

The railway entered the woods a little further on. The heaps of cut timber on either side of the clearing were already threaded with thick undergrowth. Blades of yellow and grey fungus as large as dinner plates burst through the soggy bark. Moss bubbled up between the sleepers, reaching the tops of the rails themselves in places. Did that mean the line was old or that the damp warmth beneath that turgid sun speeded up the forest's hectic life? *Everything's too rich and ripe.* The deep colours, bright flowers and fungi spoke of a desperate fertility before the rot took hold.

Banjo gave a grunt of surprise and started to run. At first Alexandra thought he was making a break for it and drew a bead on him with her Mauser. She was about to shout out for the man to stop but then she also spotted the Agit-Train half a mile ahead, its bright carriages almost hidden by the gloom.

"Looks abandoned. Not a soul, just like the one near the wreck," Banjo told her when she caught up. The Englishman climbed into the cabin to check the engine while Alexandra made her way through the five cars. This time they hadn't been looted. The passageways and cargo rooms were still full of props, supplies and costumes. The last wagon contained a printing press with stacks of bound paper, already curling and mould-spotted. Half a dozen posters for *Man of the Future!* dangled from a washing line strung from corner to corner. Where was Pavel and the others? Everything looked in its place and there wasn't any sign of damage or fighting.

"There were fifty people on board, not including the train crew," she told Banjo once she'd finished her search. "They must have gone ahead to the village."

"I reckon they were captured and taken somewhere, otherwise why not just drive this into town and say hello, save yourself the walk?" he gestured at the controls. "The engine's fine, I could have her running in a couple of hours."

I've got to talk to Ekaterina first. As soon as she learns that the rest of the Agit-Train is here she'll be looking for trouble with a Mauser in each fist. They walked back along the track towards the mine entrance. As they reached the edge of the woods Banjo held up his hand.

"Listen."

Alexandra recognised the heavy asthmatic thud of a steam train powering up.

"The buggers are running away and leaving us!"

They sprinted out of the trees just in time to see their own locomotive shudder forwards twenty yards out of the tunnel entrance. It screeched to a stop in a shower of sparks, wheels spinning backwards. A second later they bit and the engine reversed towards the mountain. Above the roar of the pistons Alexandra heard two gunshots ring out.

CHAPTER NINE

Alexandra found Ekaterina standing on the footplate with a gun in her hand, peering down the tunnel. Blood smeared the metal at her feet. Her eyes were black stones in white rings, staring down whatever horrors she alone could see. Banjo pushed past her and shut down the locomotive.

"Viktor went mad, babbling about God. He tried to drive the train back into the mountain. I shot him but he was quick and in all that smoke and steam I couldn't aim properly."

"You shot your own brother?" This was insane, even for her.

"I only blew a small hole in him."

Alexandra translated for Banjo's benefit.

"So that's why the arse was nosing around the instruments back there. He was trying to figure out how to drive the train."

"Wait here and keep an eye on Ekaterina," said Alexandra, taking a lantern.

"My pleasure," answered the Englishman with a big grin.

Alexandra ran into the tunnel. She knew the light gave her position away if Viktor had his own pistol and decided to take pot shots at her but she'd chance it. The man must be bleeding badly - a trail of blood crossed the sleepers. She called out but the mountain swallowed her voice. Banjo had switched off the engine and as the noise of the locomotive subsided she heard footsteps fading into the distance. *I ought to leave you to the darkness, you pathetic wretch,* she thought and immediately regretted it. Why hadn't she cared for him and his sister more? How had it got to the stage where Ekaterina would actually fire a gun point blank at Viktor? It wasn't until she'd seen her friend round-eyed and snarling after her fugitive sibling that she'd realised how far the woman had fallen. Her acting and singing, the drugs and the absurd theatricality - half believed, half scathing satire on the dead bourgeois world - it had hidden the true extent of her growing madness.

She slowed to a walk, fearing to trip. Glancing behind she saw with a shock that the exit was a tiny arch of brightness around the silhouette of the locomotive. The tunnel turned, closing off the last of the daylight. Alexandra stopped. The radiance from the lantern illuminated a patch at her feet and glanced off the walls, but above she sensed a void. She guessed this was one of the natural caverns they'd passed through on their journey, creeping along a trench the Whites, or someone, had cut into the floor. In that vast space it was as if she was the final human at the end of the world and the only other creatures left were the ancient titans that bore this mountain on their backs, staring down at her with granite eyes filled with implacable hatred. Her legs started to tremble as she tried to push her heart back into place, ready to give up and flee back to that strange valley with its amber sun - anywhere where there was light and people.

The sound of dislodged stones - *Viktor*. The idiot wasn't that far ahead after all. Alexandra ran forward and saw that both sides of the gully were punctuated with the entrances to more roofless passages. Another noise. This time it came from the second opening on the left. She entered. The lantern picked out lumps of ore on the floor, mixed with an odd yellow-green mineral she didn't recognise. The hacked walls were threaded with more of these crystals, scribbling out their unearthly texts in long, ragged veins. *So the Tsarists started to mine here as well, before whatever they found sent the fools back to the other side of the iconostasis.* She'd have to return here with the best geologists from Petrograd, use the latest scientific instruments to prospect these curious treasures.

A shriek of terror and pain from the darkness and she almost dropped her lantern. For a second Alexandra stood paralysed, all her fears pouring in hordes through the shadows until she forced herself to draw her Mauser and sprint towards the sound. The stupid fool must have met with some accident, cracked his head or fallen into a ravine as he blundered about in this maze. *Hysterical idiot.*

She rounded a corner and came to a circular pit about twenty yards in diameter with a narrow path corkscrewing down into blackness. She saw a light halfway along the second spiral below and realised she was looking at a knot of three figures scurrying into the depths, picked out by a faint blue glow coming from a sphere carried on the end of a metal pole. One had slung a body over its shoulder. Viktor, looking for all the world like a broken doll. Either he'd succumbed to his wound or his abductors had knocked him out, or worse. She aimed her gun, ready to call for them to halt and release her friend.

They must have sensed her because they paused and the last one turned around to lope slowly up the ramp. It stopped and looked up at her while the others hurried on. Alexandra stumbled back, whimpering, until she thudded into the granite wall behind her. White-grey skin, eyes like black tears of oil and four arms. *Four arms.* What did the mad Cossack say? *She ate them all, she cooked them in a pot to feed her spider children.* As the creature broke into a heavy run Alexandra staggered away, dropping the lantern. She raced into the darkness turning and turning again, only realising on the fifth corner that the original passageway had been straight and she'd lost herself deep inside the mountain with God only knew what on her heels.

Right, now's my chance with Madam.

Banjo watched Alexandra scamper off into the mountain after the singer's half-wit brother. He toyed with the idea of following but decided to let the two Russians slug it out between themselves. Happy to be finally alone with the fair one, he turned just in time to see the coal shovel swinging for his head. He dropped to his knees, feeling the edge of the blade scrape the top his scalp before it hit the controls with a colossal *spang*. Ekaterina tossed it to the floor and aimed her pistol at his face.

"Take me to Pavel."

Bloody hell, really?

He never fought women on principle and had no intention of starting now. Besides, there was a fine line between magnificently spirited and dangerously barmy and the actress was hopping back and forth across it several times a minute. If she'd shot her brother, she'd just as cheerfully blow his head off if the mood took her. He wearily stuck his hands up.

"I don't know where he is." An idea popped into his mind. "We found the rest of the train but there was no-one there."

Get her on her own where she can see how the cruel sod abandoned her - that'll make her a bit more malleable. He realised he wasn't the world's greatest expert on how the fair sex thought but it sounded plausible enough. It might also distract her from killing him. At the mention of the theatre train her eyes went all white-circled again, not a good sign, but she gestured at him to climb out of the cab, handing down Viktor's forgotten Gladstone bag. She followed and together they left the tunnel and headed for the woods.

It was a ridiculous plan but fortune favoured the brave. No matter how pretty this valley it was still a dead end. Steep cliffs ringed it on all sides. No point hanging around. With the other two out of sight all he had to do was worm his way into Ekaterina's affections, make some plausible excuse about the need for a quick escape and drive the train back through the mountain. He remembered enough of the journey to realise that, with a decent head of steam, he could be across the battlefield and into the woods before anything inside the mines could stop him, apart from the flying machine. Whoever controlled it had let him live the first time and if it wanted to destroy them why hadn't it followed through the tunnels or flown over the top? With any luck it had buzzed off in search of more Reds to drop bombs on. A mad dash for freedom was better than loitering in this silent wood with its disturbingly over-coloured plants and heavy scent of perfumed rot.

The actress seemed quite oblivious to their strange surroundings, ambling along the tracks and humming to herself. Once in a while she'd poke him in the back with the Mauser or urge him to hurry up as if he was a lazy pug who needed the exercise. That changed as soon as the abandoned train hove into view. Forgetting him completely she cried out and sprinted ahead.

He found her weeping on the floor of the costume wagon, surrounded by dresses. She bunched the silks in both hands and held them up to him.

"These were mine. He gave them to that bitch Galina, so she could soil them with her body, dance on stages to mock me."

"A right bastard, eh?"

"Cretin! Fool! What do you know? You don't understand him, none of you do. You don't see that Pavel is capable of great art, great beauty. His soul spans the world but she has planted a sickness within it."

She ripped an elegant skirt in half and sobbed into the crumpled rags. Sensing that whatever he said was likely to be wrong and may even result in a shooting, Banjo decided to leave her to it and crept back to the engine to give it another once over. Fifteen minutes later, after satisfying himself that everything was in full working order, he found her draped on the floor of the first carriage like a mermaid, head resting on the door frame, musing at the landscape while quietly singing. The Gladstone bag sat open beside her and three vials lay on the swollen moss between the sleepers. At least that meant she'd calmed herself and perhaps the lass's defences would be weakened by the opium. Banjo ducked out of view, spat in his palms and tried to smooth his hair and beard into some semblance of tidiness before climbing inside and sitting down at a respectful distance.

"Fair enchantress. It may be dangerous to stay here with that flying monster nearby."

Ekaterina cast a lazy glance in his direction.

"If our friends fail to return we need to think about how to escape," he continued.

She slid her gun out from under her skirt with the barrel pointing towards him.

Oh bugger.

"I may look like an enemy but believe me when I say in all sincerity that the only motive I have is my concern for the welfare of such an angel who has so utterly captured my..."

The actress wasn't even listening. Instead she stared into the forest with renewed interest. He followed her gaze. Eight men in baggy trousers, leather boots and belted white smocks stepped out from among the trees. They were hefty looking buggers - each at least six feet tall with a wedge beard and a vicious club in his fist. Banjo and Ekaterina stood up. He started cracking his knuckles, even though he knew he wouldn't stand a chance. The actress placed a hand on his arm.

"Wait."

One of the newcomers called out. Ekaterina gave a little gasp of surprise. He spoke again and she answered back. The men came closer and to Banjo's relief they seemed more relaxed.

"Friends of yours?"

"Old Believers," said Ekaterina.

Terror rode Alexandra like the Old Man of the Sea, nails digging into her temples, screaming in her ears, wicking away all thought. She ran blind and silent, bouncing from craggy wall to brittle rock face and back again. Once she swore she raced across a gulf, along a stone bridge over an infinite ocean in which all of humanity had drowned. When her feet kicked stones to plummet far down into the water the phosphorescence illuminated the faces of a hundred million dead. Somewhere another Alexandra begged her to think, to try to understand what she'd seen and what was happening so she could work out how to save herself, but her voice was swamped by the sound of the German's creeping artillery barrage, getting louder and louder as it crossed the battlefield towards her. She'd lost her gun and her lantern. How would she defend Mother Russia, her friends, herself?

Blood, mud, shit and fear.

White face with ragged holes for eyes and mouth, and six spider limbs.

You smelled the stench of formaldehyde and rotting flesh bubbling up from that spiral pit into which the monsters carried Viktor. They're all buried in there - mother, father, The Hammer and Ekaterina's brother, and at the very bottom he sits waiting, coiled in the darkness of his nest where the bright science you wrap around yourself can't protect you anymore.

She tripped and fell sprawling in the grit, cracking her head against sharp rock. Fragments of yellow crystal glowed faintly around her black cut-out hands. She wrestled with the cold air, forcing herself to breathe. The other Alexandra crept back in through the chaos of her thoughts.

There's a reason for this - for all of this - the bodies in the wheeled cabinets, the flying machine capable of destroying armoured trains, and the four-armed troglodytes dragging Viktor - is he dead or even worse, merely unconscious? - into the depths of the mountain.

Tsarist science - experiments and engineering beyond anything yet dreamed of - but the old regime was an addled pit of petit-bourgeois chaos - enervated and corrupt when matched against the possibilities of Alexandra's new age of Soviet Super Science. The aristocracy fawned after charlatans and mountebanks - Rasputin and the Tsarina locked together in their vile bestial orgies - charismatic faith and perversion writhing over each other like worms in a tin, syphilitic, rotting from within. And all the while Nikolai, last of the bastard Romanovs, rammed the people's faces so far into the dirt they were crushed against the gates of Hell and in the end had no choice but to claw their way back upwards. How had the Whites even begun to create such wonders and monsters? With who or what had they forged an unholy pact to fashion these blasphemous prodigies?

Alexandra couldn't run any further. She lay panting on the ground, trying to quieten her heart and the thundering blood in her ears so she'd hear her pursuer. *Four arms? It was wearing some type of machine harness to give it an additional set of mechanised hands. Wondrous.* But in the darkness, with the image of Viktor being carried into the depths still burning in her mind, it was a pitiful rationalisation. *I should have tried to save you, my broken poet.* Of course she should. *I'm a useless coward.* But it wasn't just the extra limbs that had sent her reeling back into the mountain night. That face - grey and smeared like a mad child's pencil scribble, slack with idiocy and feral hunger. Even a mere glimpse at a distance had been enough.

A silence deeper than any Alexandra had ever known settled around her. She'd no idea how long she'd lain there, waiting for her pursuer to start fumbling at her boots, but the creature never came and so she pulled herself to her feet and stumbled on. A plan started to form in the fragments of her mind as they clumped back together. Get Ekaterina and Banjo with their guns and the train and return to save the Viktor. Maybe it wasn't too late after all. Perhaps even the inhabitants of that village would help if they were friendly.

She'd no idea which direction she was heading in, but after what felt like hours she spotted a pale radiance ahead. Air flowed around her, smelling of rich loam mixed with rotten fruit. Moments later she tumbled down a mossy boulder-strewn slope by the edge of a turquoise stream that raced over crushed chalk and granite. Alexandra looked up at the lightning-shaped crack in the cliff - as black as scripture - and sobbed with relief. Somehow she'd survived and found her way out of the mountain. No time to rest. The creature might still be following so she turned and ran into the forest, weaving in and out of the ragged birch trunks, hoping to shake off any pursuer.

Eventually she came to a path and followed it on unsteady legs, hoping it might take her towards the rail tracks. The shadows on the moss told her the sun still hung above the horizon, but for some reason it was hard to work out which direction she was moving in. Once the sound of the brook faded all she could detect was her own breathing. Even so, with each step her courage returned, and the resolve to go back into the mines and find the wounded poet.

The path ended abruptly at a row of glass-domed buildings with copper walls. She hid awhile, waiting to catch any signs of life, but nothing moved or made a sound so she approached the first structure. The door stood ajar and inside she saw rows of trees growing from mounds of pale soil. Alexandra didn't recognise the heavy clusters of blue and yellow fruit but this was clearly some kind of greenhouse. She eased inside for a closer look. The heat fell on her like a hammer and she had the distinct feeling of thousands of tiny insects crawling over her body. She quickly stepped outside, rubbing at her clothes, face and hands. She held her fingers up to the light and thought she saw a vortex spreading over her skin. It vanished in seconds like water evaporating from a hot stone. *Fear's making me hallucinate.*

The next building looked the same but this time she didn't enter. The third hut was locked and odd shadows flickered back and forth against the crystal, cast by an internal orange light. The air hummed with science. Curiosity eclipsing fear, she crept around the corner of the nearest building and came face to face with the flying machine.

Banjo had been right, it was artificial. The inverted cone was fashioned from what appeared to be banded iron inlaid with jewels and silver wire. Red lights studded the ring at the widest part. With a shock she saw they moved like a shoal of fish, sometimes clumping together in the centre to form a buckle, sometimes spreading apart as if going on their own errands. Even the arm-thick tentacles, and she struggled to count them all, glistened as if moulded from porcelain and glass as they twitched and flicked in the dusty light. If this was an advanced type of ornithopter where did the man sit? There was no obvious cabin, window or porthole for the pilot to look out from.

If it was going to kill her Alexandra had no chance. She'd dropped her gun in the mine and besides, if the combined firepower of Aminev's men hadn't harmed it, Maxim and all, then what good would a single Mauser be? She lifted her hands into the air. Perhaps if she surrendered the aviator inside might spare her life. Nothing happened. The machine just continued to fill the world with its bone grinding hum. Her arms began to tire.

"I surrender. Show yourself."

To her surprise the engine flew away, drifting up into the sky to float above the nearest trees. She could still make out its crimson lights dancing beneath the tentacles. Was it responding to her question or something else? She heard a noise behind and turned to see a group of men, several of them holding what looked like sacks of food. Others carried clubs of polished black wood. They wore simple peasant clothes but appeared clean and too well-fed. They reminded her of aristocrats playing at being farmers - donning immaculate costumes for their sneering masquerades. But their expressions had a stolid, unyielding air, as if they'd all been carved out of mahogany.

"Comrades?"

One of them greeted her and for a second she struggled to understand what the man was saying. He spoke again and Alexandra realised she was listening to Slavonic. *Old Believers, religious exiles from the Great Cleaving seeking to escape Satan and forge a new holy realm out here under the endless sky.* Many of them had tried to fashion a home in Siberia. Most had died out or been found and absorbed back into the world, but there were rumours of isolated communities still clinging to their ancient creed. That didn't make sense. The greenhouses implied a science way beyond the grasp of modern farmers, let alone a crowd of fanatics resolutely living in the past.

"Why did the servant of the Tsar bring you here?" demanded one, who she guessed was the leader.

The Tsar?

"What is that thing?" Alexandra pointed at the flying machine above the trees.

"The Angel of the Tsar."

So it is White science. Unbelievable. And these sour old bastards staring at her with that male hostility she knew all too well? Its allies? Then why were some of the peasants looking up at the flyer with expressions of suspicion bordering on fear? She racked her brains, trying to unpick the man's words. The leader watched her with wary menace. Alexandra got the impression the man had seen uniforms before and the encounter hadn't gone well. To fools steeped in Orthodox ignorance a woman wearing one would be a hundred times worse.

"And you are the Tsar's people?"

She took the silence to mean *yes*.

"It brought me here," she lied. "I don't know why it did but I come as a friend. I have no armies or weapons. My name is Alexandra Lobachevsky." *Best miss out the 'Commissar'.*

The leader pointed at his own nose.

"Borovoi of the Wanderers. The first men before the Tsar. We are of the seven prosphora and sing in unison with special signs before God."

Alexandra hadn't a clue what he meant so she bowed in a way that she hoped appeared suitably respectful. Borovoi and his companions seemed satisfied.

"You built these?" she pointed at the buildings.

"They are the Tsar's gifts."

The peasant's bovine answers were starting to get on her nerves. No-one in their right mind would think that such knowledge came from the Romanovs. Did Borovoi mean the mythical Good Tsar, the same saintly father of the Russian people the old man thought Alexandra had liberated?

"Come with us."

"Wait."

Viktor.

"My friend is trapped inside the mountain. He was attacked and captured."

"In which case he's dead," said Borovoi. The others exchanged glances, some nodding.

"He may still be alive." *And you could have saved him if you hadn't run away.*

"He is dead, woman. Hang your head in shame as a wretched sinner before the saints and look no more for him in this world."

You know what I saw and you know what it means.

No help here then. But a dark fury welled up in her soul. These bastards were complicit in the same evil, no matter how much they cowered away from it in their superstitious stupidity. More than ever she resolved to find out who and what was creating those monstrosities. In the meantime there was nothing she could do to rescue her friend. She fell in with the group who gathered up their bags and gestured for her to come with them. Even though there was no outward threat Alexandra knew she had no choice.

Borovoi glanced up at the flying machine. The machine drifted up towards the clouds, heading across the valley in the direction of the biggest mountain. It quickly dwindled to a speck. The men walked between the buildings. Alexandra saw evidence of more machines through part-opened doors - glass and silver retorts linked by rubber tubes. What were these simple peasants doing here with their harsh medieval creed and ancient liturgy amid such futuristic science?

CHAPTER TEN

"Old Believers?" asked Banjo.

"They rebelled against the changes introduced into the church service two hundred and fifty years ago by the Patriarch Nikon and fled into the wilderness to set up their own holy communities to preserve the old ways."

He and Ekaterina walked in the centre of the group along a forest path. The peasants seemed respectful enough but swung those clubs a little too handily for his liking.

"What changes?"

"They wanted to keep the services in Slavonic, not Russian, and to bend their middle finger when making the sign of the cross, like this."

She showed him surreptitiously.

"And?"

"I think that's all. There might have been something about holy processions going clockwise instead of anti-clockwise but I don't remember."

God help us. Religious maniacs. When he was an infant Mother's one concession to affectionate parenting had been to read to him every night from Gibbon's *Decline and Fall of the Roman Empire.* Most of the time he fell asleep after three sentences, which was no doubt the intended effect, but two episodes had stuck in his mind. The first involved the salubrious antics of the Empress Theodora and her concubines, slaves, generals and horses, which had resulted in all manner of very peculiar dreams. The other was some emperor massacring an entire city because the inhabitants said the Son of God parted his hair on the left and not the right, or something like that. An entire people uprooting and sulking off thousands of miles east just so they could bend their middle fingers when genuflecting didn't surprise him at all. These glum buggers with their Hereford Bull chests and mallet hands reeked of Non-Conformism. It felt like being dragged to a Friends' Meeting all over again. Except he wasn't an innocent little boy anymore. In the intervening decades he'd turned into an utter reprobate who'd drunk, fought and whored around the world several times. And now he was strolling along in the company of a drug-taking actress who wasn't wearing any knickers. God would have a field day with the pair of them.

The Old Testament prophets marched on under the drooping boughs. They were in their element among these hectic greens, swollen tree trunks and cloying grainy air that muted all sounds. It wasn't right. Ordinary folk should find this place unnerving. He glanced to either side of the path and thought he spotted buildings in the distance through the trees, with copper verdigris walls and clear glass domes. *Greenhouses?*

They left the woods and walked across a track that spanned fields filled with a rich, dark mud. In one of them men and women worked their way along the furrows, planting seedlings with orange flowers in the shape of snake scales. A single horse snorted at the end of a plough. Apart from the railway line heading for the village, he saw no sign of modern industry.

His first impressions were right. They were a crowd of yokels wearing the mantles of latter-day Jeremiahs. Had they built that wall of icons inside the mine to block off the outside world and its corruption? Did they know anything about the wandering specimen cabinets, the four-armed men and the flying machine? He had the sudden impression of walking in a landscape painted on thin china behind whose brittle reality lurked a horde of fantastical machines and monstrosities. These bastards might be all affability and condescension now but he didn't trust them an inch.

"I know you're eager to find your Pavel," he whispered to Ekaterina. "But we need learn what these gentlemen intend. I'd advise caution."

She gave a snort of derision. To be fair she hadn't started screaming and ranting at anyone yet, and her Mauser was out of sight strapped to her thigh, but Banjo sensed she had a stratagem in her head that was probably both deranged and extremely perilous. He'd ended up carrying her bag of medicines and vowed to keep it out of her reach for as long as he could.

"If you're planning on doing anything mental it would be nice to have notice beforehand."

She ignored him and turned to the nearest peasant to ask a question. He rumbled something in return. To Banjo's ears all Russian sounded like someone trying to chew a mouthful of hot walnuts whilst drunk, but according to the actress this lot talked in medieval Russian which, surprisingly, turned out to be more than just grunting and pointing at things. She seemed unfazed by the answer. The drugs she'd ingested had coated the inside of her brain with a varnish impermeable to terror or surprise.

The leader raised his hand and the men stopped. One of them put his fingers on Banjo's shoulder. Expecting a knife in the ribs, he got ready to turn and thump the bastard on the nose when he saw the man staring upwards with an odd expression of fear and awe. Ekaterina squeaked as Banjo spotted the flying machine drifting high overhead towards the mountain above the village. He panicked, thinking it was about to swoop down and blast them out of existence. The craft continued to drift nearer to the peak. Banjo realised the crag below it was dotted with tiny holes. *There's a nest of those things?* The leader muttered something and made a sign.

"What did he say?" Banjo asked the singer.

"He called it the Tsar's angel."

So it was White science after all. The Tsarists had created machines to destroy the Reds but were defeated before they could use them. Or had they? Was that vast shard looming over the valley the last fastness where the Romanovs' mad scientists had plotted their revenge, hoping to unleash unthinkable weapons to retake Russia from the communists?

Thank god Alexandra's not here. She has Deranged Red written all over her pious mug. Banjo hoped she was still OK. Despite himself he'd started to warm to the po-faced termagant.

The flying machine disappeared among the shadows of the high peak. Banjo could have sworn the men about him relaxed. Their party set off again, leaving the fields to walk along a wide path that led to the village nestling at the foot of the mountain.

The Old Believers escorted Alexandra across a patchwork of fields to the hamlet at the foot of the cliff. They refused to answer any questions and it was obvious she was a prisoner rather than a guest. The first thing that struck her was the condition of the buildings - sturdily built with brightly painted facades in blues and greens, more like dachas than homes. Each had a garden at the front, some cultivated to grow food, others with flowers she didn't recognise. It smacked of a Potemkin village, erected to fool a stupid Tsar into thinking his peasants were well-fed and happy. The houses stood in concentric semi-circles spreading out from the precipice. Over the rooftops she saw the glistening domes of the church flush against the rock face. That wasn't so odd. The lives of these religious exiles would naturally centre on their place of worship. The commissar looked around for any signs of Pavel and the actors but the streets were empty apart from herself and her mute guides.

She expected to be taken straight to the Ataman or priest but instead they led her to a house on the edge of the settlement. Inside she found Banjo and Ekaterina sitting at a table, the Englishman shovelling spoonfuls of stew into his mouth. He'd gone beetroot red and had food in his beard and in a circle around his plate. He picked up the bowl, slurped down the last of his meal in one go, wiped his face with the back of his hand and let out a rasping belch that made the windows rattle. The singer leaned away from him with an expression of mild alarm as she nibbled a piece of black bread.

Alexandra's escorts left without a word. A couple busied themselves about a stove, gesturing for the commissar to take her place with the others. The smell of plums and meat overwhelmed the senses, clogging her thoughts in a thick ocean of hunger. When the woman placed a bowl in front of her, all rich browns and steam, she struggled to think what to do next. *I should ask questions, demand to see whoever's in charge, but that soup looks so good.*

"Get it down you lass. It's bloody marvellous," bellowed Banjo, holding out his plate for more with a terrifying grin. The woman took it and refilled it without a murmur. She had the same expression of blunt stoicism as everyone else. With her scarf wrapped tightly around her head it was impossible to guess her age.

"No Viktor then?" asked the Englishman.

Alexandra stared at her spoon, thinking furiously. *Was he alive or dead when they carried him into the pit?* She glanced at Ekaterina who had that faraway look she knew all too well. The last thing she needed was for her friend to go off on an episode at the news of her brother's capture. She caught the engineer's eye and luckily the man seemed to understand.

"I followed Viktor deep into the mountain but lost him. We'll ask these people to help us with a search party," she explained in French.

"He'll be in Moscow by now," answered the Englishman in the loud voice of someone in on a secret. God, he was a crass oaf, but the actress said nothing. Alexandra couldn't tell if she was wracked with remorse at shooting her twin, somewhere under all those endless layers of opium and cocaine. Alexandra spotted the Gladstone bag in the corner and didn't know whether to be angry or relieved. The little vials offered some measure of control over her friend.

The stew was so delicious Alexandra almost wept. Odd - it was only food after all and yet it filled her with such warmth and a strange sensation of contentment. What was in it? More drugs? Poison? Banjo gave her a grin and a wink from across the table.

"Not bad eh? Dunno what it's made from, mind."

Alexandra wondered about the blue and yellow fruit growing in the copper huts and in the gardens, and the grainy air crawling over her skin when she stepped inside one of the hothouses.

"Any word of Pavel?" she asked Ekaterina. The actress blinked, mouth pursed, and looked away with a shrug.

"She found her frocks in the Agit-Train," Banjo warned her in English. "Apparently the lecherous scallywag gave them to his other mistress so the topic's a sensitive one right now."

"That's ridiculous. Fifty rode that train. I want to find out where they are."

"We asked but all the buggers said was that they've gone to meet the Tsar. I don't know if that means..." Banjo drew a finger across his throat and made a *kkkkk* noise. A silence fell over the room and Alexandra looked up to see the man and woman glaring at him. Realising he might have overstepped the mark, Banjo mumbled something inaudible and concentrated really hard on his second helping. Alexandra wasn't going to play games.

"There were actors on the train in the woods, friends of ours. Where are they? Are they safe and well?"

"They are in the court of the Tsar," answered the woman, as if explaining to a thick child.

"Which is where?"

"Inside the mountain, of course."

The woman pointed towards the peaks above the church.

"The Tsar lives in the mountain? Can we have an audience with him?"

"That's for Father Kirill to decide," said the man in a voice that suggested the discussion had ended. The woman turned away to tend to the stove. She looked nervous all of a sudden. Alexandra translated for Banjo.

"Why do they keep going on about the Tsar? Haven't they heard you arseholes murdered him and his missus in cold blood?

And his four pretty daughters. Along with their sickly wee mite of a son. And their nanny. And their pet dog?"

Alexandra clung onto her temper with difficulty.

"A lot of the peasants out here fantasised about a mythical Tsar who wanted to protect them from the cruel landowners but couldn't because the corrupt court kept him prisoner. Some even claim our revolution has set him free so he'll return to rule them as a kindly father."

"More fool them."

Alexandra really wished the idiot would shut up. Banjo tried to catch the woman's eye for a third bowl.

Their hosts didn't look like the leavings of a country riddled with ruin, poverty and famine. She wouldn't even have described them as merely healthy. They resembled athletes stuffed into peasant garb, Greek Gods passing themselves off as mortals and not doing a very good job of it. They also looked as if they were related, as had the men who'd brought her here. That wasn't particularly surprising. In an isolated community hiding in the mountains for almost three centuries there'd be plenty of in-breeding, but that fostered degeneracy and disease. These people were closer to the fit and brave inhabitants of Alexandra's imagined futurity. She felt cheated. She'd always dreamed of the perfection of man. Scientific communism would forge an advanced race of workers in the factories of the new age. Superstitious yokels weren't supposed to have got there first.

The commissar had a thousand questions. Who was the Tsar? Who flew that machine and why did these people seem to fear it? Who'd built those greenhouses with their strange crops, which she'd probably just eaten. Overriding everything was the memory of four white man-spiders carrying Viktor into the mines. *We have to get back under that mountain to rescue him.* But it was clear the three of them were prisoners despite all this hospitality. Even if they had a Mauser hidden under the singer's skirts they wouldn't stand a chance against a village full of clubs. The only option lay in persuading this Father Kirill to let them go. Maybe she could even ask for half a dozen men as reinforcements for a rescue mission. The peasants knew what lived in the tunnels. *He is dead, woman. Seek no more for him in this world*, their leader had told her with the pious finality of the religiously deluded. Of course these bastards weren't going to help.

"What's the plan?" asked Banjo. The Englishman read her mind. She was about to answer when three of the men who'd brought her re-entered, saying they'd come from Father Kirill who would speak with them now.

"Please don't do anything stupid and let me do the talking."

"I can't understand the bloody language, can I? And besides, I'm not the one coked to the tits and seething with jealousy."

Outside the light was fading and a lazy evening rolled through the empty streets. *There's no birds, no sounds of pigs or chickens.* The cottages were picture-perfect, all assembled to the same pattern.

"This place is buggered," rumbled Banjo. "We'll be lucky to get out of here alive. They're like a bunch of wooden puppets living in dolls' houses."

They passed the innermost arc of buildings and entered the plaza in front of the church. The railway ended at a set of buffers twenty yards from the facade. The granite cliff lofted into the sky, a slab of grinding midnight offset by the last band of sunshine illuminating the peak far above their heads. Alexandra searched for the flying machine but it'd vanished. The uppermost crags were cut with shadows and faint dots that resembled cave mouths. Had it flown inside? Banjo nudged her in the ribs.

"That's not good," he nodded at three charred patches in a line next to the tracks. "I reckon they've been toasting a few backsliders."

The church looked ancient. Its domes, layered in beaten gold, butted against the stone and Alexandra realised that half of it extended into the mountain itself, either fashioned around a pre-existing cave or carved out by the patient labour of centuries.

Ekaterina pulled her shawl over her head as they entered. The commissar guessed right. A long vault stretched into the distance, filled with incense and the cloying light of hundreds of candles.

Her skin itched at the memory of the seething air inside the greenhouse. This place was designed to cow the unworthy into submission, rob them of all dignity and hope in the name of autocrats - Gods, Priests and Tsars. The jewelled iconostasis flickered judgement at the far end - another collection of angry faces created by the same artists who'd built the one in the tunnels.

A figure walked towards them down the aisle - long white beard, black robes and a face in shadow. This had to be Father Kirill. He greeted them and extended his hand. Banjo nodded and tugged his forelock, the singer ostentatiously sank to her knees and kissed the man's fingers as if she was acting out a satire for her Proletkult audiences. Alexandra did nothing. The priest looked at her with cold eyes.

"As you have seen, daughter, we have here a twofold Church - one of men, the other of angels. And since there are angels present women, when they pray, are ordered to have a covering upon their heads. Thus the wise father Origen Adamantius tells us how our pious sisters assist the saints and rejoice in the Church."

One of their peasant escorts walked forwards and threw a shawl in Alexandra's face. Banjo grumbled something and stepped between them as it fell to the floor. She ignored it. Kirill could take his twofold Church and shove it up his arse.

"Our friend became lost inside the mountains. We need to put together a search party to look for him. He may be injured."

Their host gave a bland shrug.

"The mountain is dangerous. Those mines were carved out by the second men and it is the place where they turned the gifts of the Tsar to evil. If your friend has strayed from the path in there, he is truly lost."

The second men?

"He's my brother," said Ekaterina in her *I'm about to shoot you in the face* voice. Alexandra glanced at Banjo who got the hint and moved over to position himself behind the actress just in case.

"And the creatures who live there?" asked the commissar.

"They too are lost."

This was getting nowhere.

"Fifty of my comrades rode the train we found in the woods. Where are they?"

"They are in the court of the Tsar."

Ekaterina started to bunch her skirts. Banjo clamped his hand around her wrist and the colour drained from her face.

"Who is this Tsar?" the singer asked with magnificent contempt.

"He is a holy ruler sent by God to care for us."

"You mean Nikolai Romanov?" said Alexandra.

"The one you had murdered? No."

That brought her up short.

"So you know about the Revolution and the war, how the workers and the peasants rose up against the capitalists and the international warmongers and cast off their shackles to form a union of Soviets in which all men and women are free and equal?"

"And God is dead?"

The man was toying with her and anger made Alexandra bold.

"Yes."

Father Kirill gave the grandfather of all indulgent chuckles.

"We came here at the time of the Cleaving when the Antichrist Nikon sought to spatter the holy word with the dung of common speech. We fled, but here we found the Tsar, the one true defender of the poor, the sinful and the meek, not afraid to call Christ Christ, and the Church his Church. He lifts his hand and makes the old sign of the cross," Kirill genuflected with his middle finger bent into a hook. Banjo snorted. "He protects us and nurtures us while we live here, as you see, destitute in soul and full of sin before the mercy of God and his saints."

Alexandra wasn't interested in the petty distinctions of a dead faith.

"So your descendants met a Tsar in these mountains two hundred and fifty years ago, yet you speak of him in the present, as if he's still alive."

"He is eternal," said the priest with the utter self-assurance of the completely deluded.

"May we meet him?"

"So you can shoot him too?"

Enough was enough. Alexandra clicked her fingers at Ekaterina who shook Banjo off, lifted her skirt, pulled out the Mauser and pointed it at Kirill's head.

"We are looking for our friends who came in the train abandoned in your forest. You told me they're in the court of the Tsar, by which I understand that they're inside the mountain above us. Take us to them."

"I want my Pavel," said the actress.

"But does he want you?" asked Kirill. The actress's eyes filled with tears and the muzzle wavered.

"I cannot take you now. I have no power over the Tsar but will happily petition him on your behalf and I'm sure he'll show you mercy if you come here in peace," he looked at Alexandra, "and seemly humility."

A dozen men carrying clubs stepped out of the shadows. They must have been watching the whole time. Alexandra had been an idiot to think that Father Kirill would let them get this far armed if he wasn't confident he had the upper hand. She cursed herself - she'd played her bluff and lost.

"The Revolution overthrew the tyranny of the Tsars. They were not the friends of the people."

"And so you come to overthrow us?"

He gestured at Ekaterina's gun. It was an utter miracle that she hadn't blown the charlatan's head off by now, but Alexandra could tell by her expression that she was locked away in misery, railing at the phantom of her treacherous lover as he stalked through her memories.

"You're not the first," said Father Kirill. "Others like you came here - the soldiers of the Romanovs. The Tsar told us to treat them kindly and they repaid his mercy with their dominion and cruelty, stealing from him and using his gifts to craft abominations in their mines. The Tsar sent his angel to punish them so they wouldn't return."

"You mean the flying machine?"

The priest was infuriating, lathering everything in quasi-mystical nonsense. Alexandra struggled to unpick the story. A two hundred and fifty-year old secret Tsar lived in the mountain with scientific machines far more advanced than anything yet created. The Old Believers, the first men, discovered him and he, in turn, had looked after them in their isolation. Then the Tsarists, the second men, turned up and fought a battle against the Tsar's flyer and lost. She felt her mouth fall open as realisation hit.

The Whites captured the ornithopter. They imprisoned it in the armoured train to use against us, but it escaped. But it's just a machine and wouldn't work without a pilot. Why would they need to imprison it?

Alexandra had no answers and there were more important things to think about, such as their impending deaths.

"Stay here and rest." Kirill opened his arms in welcome. "You are our guests in the sight of God and our Tsar. I will speak with him and ask him to reunite you with your missing friends."

The peasants shuffled closer and Alexandra realised the meeting was at an end. To her surprise their captors let Ekaterina holster the pistol. *They don't care if we're armed because they know it won't help us.*

CHAPTER ELEVEN

Alexandra came back from the mines looking like she'd clawed her way out of the devil's own arse. Clearly the poor lass had found horrors in the tunnels, and Viktor had met with a dreadful fate the Red didn't want to talk about in front of his sister. Banjo itched to find out what she'd seen. He had a feeling it was something to do with that skeleton in its mobile cabinet and those four-armed creatures at the factory. The Red's eyes boggled out of their sockets and her hands shook, even as she wolfed down the stew, face in the steam as if she hoped to fumigate the monsters from her head.

They were clearly prisoners and would have to sneak or fight their way out. At least this time he'd do it on a full stomach. They'd have to make a dash for the locomotive and race back through the mountains. He'd hoped that with a bit of luck it would just be him and Ekaterina - her clinging on to him in grateful, helpless passion as he drove the train into the sunset, like Dejah Thoris snuggling up to John Carter as he piloted his flyer under the moons of Mars. But now he was stuck with Comrade Otter as a bloody chaperone again. Oh well, he was developing a sneaking fondness for the woman's bone-headed pedantry.

Everywhere he looked was wrong. The village was too pretty. All the other dilapidated piles in this benighted land stank of shit and typhus and most had at least one corpse decorating the facilities thanks to war, famine and epidemics, usually the fortunate ones who hadn't been boiled in a pot for dinner. These yokels were too well fed with bright white teeth and ruddy faces, though they had the dead-eyed stares of Sunday school fanatics. Even the woman cooking dinner resembled a wrestler in a dress. Why weren't there any children or old people?

And now they stood in a church blathering la-di-da twaddle to a religious maniac in a funny hat and a long black skirt, who rumbled out portentous answers like an ox with the shits while his henchmen glowered among the tapestries. Unable to understand what anyone was talking about and with nobody bothering to translate, he amused himself by working out how many of those evil-looking bastards with clubs he could handle. Years of cunning had provided Banjo with a handy mental checklist for such situations as this. Anything suitable as a bludgeon? Those big candlesticks would do. Exits and entrances, and corners and pillars where an enemy might hide himself for an ambush? Plenty of those. And the biggest, meanest sod to tackle first? That gorilla bulging out of his tunic with the wooden stare of the town simpleton and a beard down to his waist. Easy - grab one of those oil lamps and set fire to it, kick the next ape in the balls and was that a baptismal font beside the wall? If it wasn't bolted to the floor he could brain a few with that.

Alexandra was getting more and more wound up and when Ekaterina hitched up her dress and pulled out her gun, giving him another glimpse of that magnificent arse, it looked like the conclusion of the game. He guessed they must be talking about her missing lover and the rest of the theatre troupe. Maybe they were all dead and Moses here had Pavel for tea because these bastards were cannibals. *Perhaps we had him for tea.* Banjo brightened at the thought - that'd mean the way was clear for him. He decided against favouring the woman with his most sympathetic smile just yet. For some reason it tended to induce the nervous vapours in young ladies. Feeling a bit of a spare part he turned his attention back to the iconostasis at the far end of the church. More bloody ghosts leering at him for daring to touch his tassel, all with the same constipated expression of disapproval as Mother.

Hang on.

He followed the smoke from the censers as it floated towards the roof. The vapour from the ones illuminating Jesus and the saints drifted away from the icons. He knew there was a door in that thing, it seemed a standard feature, but if a draft was blowing into the church that meant there were larger vaults beyond. *That's a way into the mountain.* He wondered if Alexandra had also spotted it, but the little communist was still in the middle of her stand-off with Moses and Ekaterina was practically foaming at the mouth. All of a sudden the tension leaked out of the air, the fair one put her gun away and the priest plaited his hands over his stomach with the same expression of smug piety Banjo had seen on every other vicar he'd ever come across. Judging by the anger on Alexandra's face they'd lost this time.

"We done? No point sitting here wasting time then. If there's adventure to be had we'd better get on with it."

"We're prisoners" said Alexandra. "Father Kirill says we must stay in the village while he petitions their Tsar on our behalf."

"Does he now?"

"The actors are inside the mountain. He's promised to take us to meet them when it's permitted."

"And Viktor?"

"Not here," muttered Alexandra. "We'll talk when we're on our own."

"Fine." Banjo tugged his forelock at Moses. "Nice meeting you."

He turned to the Red.

"Does he understand English?"

"No."

"Right, let's go back, have some more stew and plot our escape."

This time they ended up locked in a windowless one-room house at the end of a street with a crowd of guards standing outside. Banjo's immediate reaction was to kick their way out and fight the bastards, fired up with his first decent meal in ages and desperate to get out of this shithole by whatever means he could. Alexandra held him back. In the meantime Ekaterina snatched the Gladstone bag before anyone could stop her and drained three green vials, hurling them into the corner as she finished each one. She then skipped around the room humming and twirling for ten minutes before slumping down next to the samovar and falling asleep. Banjo grabbed the opportunity to have a proper chat with Alexandra.

"What happened to Viktor?"

The commissar led him away from the actress.

"He was captured by..." Alexandra stared bleakly at the wall. "By creatures."

"Creatures?"

"They must have been men, men with special clothes that made them look like..."

"...like they had four arms."

Alexandra glared at Banjo, her eyes perfect circles in the centre of those owl glasses.

"You saw them."

Banjo remembered the group creeping up to the woods and shuddered.

"Great White Apes."

"You said that before. What are you talking about?"

"On Mars, according to Edgar Rice Burroughs, all the monsters have six limbs. Tharks, Thoats, the Great White Apes..."

"What's your silly fantasy book got to do with this?"

Pompous little tart.

"I was just saying that what I saw looked like Great White Apes with an extra set of arms. They walked from the factory to the forest with one of those glass cabinets on wheels. I thought they were towing it but it moved by itself. There must be more of those things in the mines. Maybe hundreds. Perhaps it's a race of ancient monsters."

"The Morlocks," said Alexandra.

"The whats?"

"Morlocks, from H. G. Wells' *The Time Machine*."

"Oh, so when I mention my book it's bloody rubbish and when you talk about yours it's all sensible and scientific is it?"

"Wells is a prophet of the socialist future. Your writer is a bourgeois hack."

"Fuck off!"

"I'm not having an argument about scientific romances with you. This is real."

Banjo forced himself to calm down as the Russian explained what she'd found out from Father Kirill.

"So this lot have been living here for three hundred years because they think you should cock your little finger to the left when praying, instead of to the right, and they have their own Tsar who lives in the mountain and flies around in his machine. That's mad. No disrespect but how does a Russian peasant king build flying machines with heat rays?"

"Jules Verne wrote about genius rebels - Captain Nemo and Robur the Conqueror. They were anarchists and masters of science hiding away from a corrupt and tyrannical world."

"You're doing it again. Verne's another boring arse. And French."

Alexandra ignored him.

"The Whites came and befriended this Tsar to the extent that he allowed them to bring the railway here. They wanted to use his knowledge against us."

"But they fell out and he unleashed his weapons on them instead. Do you think he built those mines or did your aristos do that?"

The commissar started to pace up and down. Banjo braced himself for yet another lecture.

"There is horror and monstrosity here but also great science. Whoever this Tsar is, he must be the profoundest savant of our time - perhaps sent into exile before the Revolution by the Romanovs and their stupid counsellors who lacked the vision and understanding to realise the wisdom he possessed. Those gardens we saw, full of rich food. The peasants here, free of disease and famine. If we can persuade him to come back to us and share his knowledge with the workers we will build our new future. What wonders might we not achieve?"

"Right," said Banjo, wondering what would happen if that hatchet-faced bastard Aminev got his hands on a flying machine. He felt sorry for Alexandra and her delusions. *You fanatics are all the same. Trampling the world to shit as you run towards your daydreams like simpletons after rainbows.* "That's what the Whites tried to do and see what happened to them," he continued.

"They were cruel and stupid. Oppressors and victims of a corrupt regime. We are the new men and women. This place will be the template for a Soviet paradise. We must speak with the Tsar!"

Alexandra took her glasses off, polished them on her lapel and held them up to the light with a puzzled look on her face. She replaced them and gave Banjo the earnest expression of a Latin master who'd fooled himself into thinking his pupils would actually enjoy Tacitus if only they tried harder and stopped thinking about petticoats.

Ekaterina mumbled something and pulled herself into a sitting position. Alexandra took her hand.

"And we shall find Pavel and the others, and rescue Viktor."

This was all very noble and Banjo was certainly game for it but they were still locked inside this prison. Despite having the actress's Mauser he knew it wouldn't count for much against an angry mob of musclemen with staves. Even so, if they could escape and somehow elude their jailers there was a route into the mountain through that wall of icons.

"We can get into your Tsar's palace through the church."

Alexandra peered through the keyhole, swore, took her glasses off and looked again.

"Is there something wrong with your eyes all of a sudden?" asked Banjo. If the bugger was going blind it wouldn't help the situation, though she looked a damn sight more pleasant without spectacles.

"Six of them," said the Red. "Shooting will alert the others. If we break out of the house the noise will do the same. How good are you at stealth?"

She looked Banjo up and down and shook her head.

Bloody cheek. I hid in that factory of yours for nine months. Mind you, these zealots bore little resemblance to the weary, battered and half-drunk veterans under Aminev's command.

"I can creep," Ekaterina waved her arms like reeds in a stream. "I am the soul of darkness, a river of quiet with silver claws that I will bury in their hearts before they draw breath."

Someone tapped at the cottage door. Ekaterina's expression switched from addled to warily murderous in a second and she pulled out her gun. Banjo stuck his ear next to the hinges but couldn't hear anything else. The knock came again.

"What are they up to? They're the ones with the sodding key."

He tried the handle, fully expecting it to be locked. It swung inward.

Red lights and a mass of tentacles hovering above the street and six bodies lying in the road.

Before he could react the flying machine swooped towards him. He stumbled backwards, colliding with Alexandra so they both fell to the floor.

"Get off me you oaf," snarled the commissar, following it with a string of Russian curses. As Banjo floundered, trying to scramble to his feet, Ekaterina stepped outside. He rolled off the Bolshevik and pelted after her, ready to hurl himself at the engine before it could harm the actress. She stood in the middle of the path surrounded by their guards who lay sprawled in the dirt. The Tsar's flyer hovered in front of her, tentacles rippling as if hunting for food at the bottom of the sea. It drifted down the road, paused, came back and repeated the action.

You want us to follow. You're like a dog asking for walkies.

"Dead." Alexandra stood among the bodies. "But there's no mark that I can see."

Dead? Why was the Tsar killing off the Old Believers? Banjo realised they didn't have time to hang around or the wherewithal to find out. *The enemy of my enemy and all that.* He grabbed a couple of clubs and tossed one to the commissar.

"Come on Watson, the game's afoot." Alexandra stared at him. "Oh never mind."

Ekaterina was already tripping lightly down the path in the wake of the machine, Mauser in one hand and a knobkerrie in the other. Banjo and Alexandra ran after them. *This is a turn up for the books. Whoever's piloting that thing clearly isn't on the side of the peasants, meaning all that stuff about the wonderful Tsar and his angels is a load of tripe.*

It therefore came as no surprise when they entered the village square to find three freshly built pyres on the scorched patches by the railway buffers, each with a stake sticking out of the top.

"The bastards were going to burn us as witches," he pointed out.

"Shut up and move."

Alexandra pushed him after the machine which headed for the church with Ekaterina close behind, seemingly oblivious to the sight of her place of execution. *Too late. Me and my big mouth.* A shout, and men and women spilled out of the houses on both sides. Banjo and Alexandra sprinted for the entrance just as the singer disappeared through the door.

"We'll be trapped inside," yelled the commissar.

Bugger we will.

The flying machine roared past, aiming straight for the crowd of peasants gathered behind. They scattered. Actinic flashes stained the ground blue-white and in the silence that followed Banjo saw his shadow photographed into the grit and rock.

They thundered into the church. Ekaterina stood over the unconscious Kirill with her club lifted high, ready to pulp his face into the tiles. Alexandra grabbed her wrists and pushed her away. Banjo glanced at the priest. Apart from a cruel bruise on his temple and blood in his beard he was alive. Good, there'd been enough macabre deaths for one evening.

More yelling from outside, interrupted by a high-pitched machine wail that forced all three of them to clap their hands to their ears. Banjo hustled his companions towards the wall of icons, praying he hadn't been mistaken and they weren't just going to end up squashed into a broom cupboard. The door was sealed but a couple of heaves shattered the lock and they ended up in an altar room. A candelabra and a gold model of the church sat on a table covered in brocaded cloth and behind it a heavy curtain swayed in the half light, stirring the incense-soaked air into an endless vortex of brooding smoke. Banjo's vision started to sparkle. God only knew what they were burning in those censers but he realised that if they lingered here they'd pass out in no time and finish up strapped to those bonfires. He held his breath, tore aside the drapes and ushered Alexandra and Ekaterina through. He heaved the altar up against the iconostasis to hold back any pursuers who'd managed to get past the Tsar's flyer and followed the others.

As soon as he passed through he banged into his companions. They'd stopped, open-mouthed, on the other side. This time the officious little termagant didn't even grumble at him, mainly because the Red was too busy staring in round-eyed wonder at the tunnel stretching away from them into the mountain.

Bugger me sideways.

This was absolutely not the work of a peasant king. The granite floor and curving walls were polished to a high gloss without any marks of drilling or dynamite, as if the passageway had been moulded out of cloud-swirled glass. Every three yards a rectangular panel sat flush against the stone, glowing with a pale orange light that cast geometric patterns reflected endlessly in the mirror beneath their feet. A constant breeze syphoned along the tunnel, bringing with it the faint scent of chemicals and metal - a dance of copper, steel, iron and ammonia.

"What is this place?" breathed Alexandra.

"A tomb if we don't shape ourselves." Bitter experience had told him not to hang about when you had an outraged mob on your heels. He ran down the corridor. Luckily the two Russians had the good sense to follow.

A couple of hundred yards around the long curve they came

to a circular door swung back against the wall. It was moulded out of a metal he didn't recognise and wouldn't budge when he put his shoulder to it. They had no choice but to keep going and try to lose the Old Believers inside this ghostly labyrinth. Nothing moved and the only sound he heard was the echo of their boots, but the skin twitching on the nape of his neck told him they were being watched. The mysterious Tsar's flying machine had ushered them here. So where was it now? Had they fled from their own executions into something worse?

They emerged into an empty circular room with eight passages leading off. Banjo didn't even bother to guess - he just ran down one at random. Alexandra didn't say anything and the engineer guessed she was still tripping over herself in awe. God only knew where Ekaterina thought she'd ended up. *Bugger! We left her Gladstone bag in the cottage.* Not good. He'd seen what addicts were capable of when starved of their dosage and she was unhinged enough without a host of screaming devils to egg her on.

After half a mile they came to a second identical chamber. Another tunnel and a third atrium. He stopped and held up a finger to shush the others. Silence. No sounds of pursuit. In this polished cathedral clattering feet would carry for miles. Alexandra took the opportunity to touch one of the glowing panels.

"It's cold. Some kind of phosphorescence?"

"We must search for Pavel," declared Ekaterina.

"Well we can't go back," said Banjo. "Moses will have the three of us burnt at the stake."

"The flying machine brought us here," said Alexandra. "Kirill claimed they are the servants of the Tsar and the flyer is his angel. If that's so why did it slaughter the men and rescue us?"

"The only way we're going to find out is by talking to this Tsar himself. He must be holed up in here somewhere."

"Do you think they burned Pavel and the others?" asked Ekaterina in a tiny voice.

"The priest said he came to the Tsar's court." Alexandra stared at Banjo, her eyes full of warnings.

Right. For all we know Moses lied through his teeth and intended us to be the final three in a series of entertaining bonfires. Still, saying that out loud was no way to woo the fair maid.

They kept going. The tunnel sloped upwards but even at its steepest there were no steps. After falling flat on his face and sliding back down the incline a couple of times Banjo took his boots off and went barefoot. Alexandra did the same, but Ekaterina just skipped ahead on tip-toes, arms stuck out as if she was trying to fly. With no shoes the engineer detected a persistent thudding through the soles of his feet, as if the mountain itself had a heart.

After ages they emerged into a circular room as big as a cricket pitch. Three flying machines hung like trapped moths in a spider web of cables and wires. They looped down from a ceiling of yellow porcelain filled with pale threads that pulsed and quivered. Banjo swore and lifted his club, ready to fight. A second look told him the engines were dead or broken. Panels were missing from the closest and machine guts spilled out of the cone and lay in piles on the floor. *A repair shop.*

"Where does the man sit?" asked Alexandra.

Banjo had no idea. Even up close he couldn't see any hatch or windows where a cabin might be. The penny dropped. *There is no man. These things work by themselves.* He spotted what looked like a huge coffin on the floor with a glass lid. Inside, a fourth machine lay prone in a bath of white liquid. Faint lights flickered on the carapace and its tentacles drifted like reeds in a muddy stream. He struggled to understand what he was seeing. *I'm like a Cherokee staring down the barrel of a Gatling before it lets fly.*

"They don't have any pilots," he said.

"They're automaton," murmured the commissar.

"Eh?"

The Russian moved her hands over the glass lid as if she was standing by the sepulchre of a loved one. An unholy light shone in her eyes.

"Comrade Machine Man."

"Who?"

"In my play. Comrade Machine Man is a combination of the Soviet Worker and the science of the future. He's here, now, in this place. It's not a dream any more. It's real."

A bang and a clatter spun them round to see a dozen men armed with clubs pour into the room. Kirill stood among them, face bloodied and thunderous. He pointed a rifle at Ekaterina's heart. *Where did he get that from?* Banjo hefted his own bludgeon but he knew the three of them were outnumbered and trapped.

CHAPTER TWELVE

The voice of the Tsar filled the room, vast like an earthquake. Ekaterina screamed and clapped her hands to her ears. Banjo gave a shout and waved his club about, looking wildly around for something to hit. The brittle syllables cracked open the world, bringing with them a smoky light that flooded across the polished surfaces and trickled down the stone and metal walls. Slavonic, edged with crystal and metals and hinting at star-powered forces coiling over each other beneath blood-red skies. Afterwards the commissar struggled to remember the precise words, but she guessed it told Kirill and his men to lower their weapons and retreat to the village. In his mercy and kindness their father, the Tsar, would protect and care for the visitors as he did with the others who sought sanctuary in his home.

Mountain silence returned and Alexandra saw anger and frustration on the faces of the priest and the villagers. Not only had the Tsar killed their fellow Old Believers but now he was depriving them of their revenge. Kirill muttered to his men and they stepped back into the tunnel, glancing warily about. In a few minutes they'd gone. Banjo jogged to the entrance and peered after them.

"It drove the bastards away. What did it say?"

Alexandra called out a greeting in Slavonic but the voice didn't return.

"Still think we're dealing with a mad aristo genius?" asked the Englishman.

She'd no idea what to think. There was nothing in this room to latch onto, no frame of reference at all. Even the rock had been transformed into a cipher beyond her understanding. She'd expected the Tsar's Super Science to be an extension of what she already knew - the known wonders of creation slotted together in new and exciting ways but still recognisable. He'd have better and more sophisticated engines, more complex equations, stronger alloys and electricities, perhaps a newly discovered ray or two. Apart from the flying machine she couldn't detect meaning in any of the shapes and lights around her. All signifiers had vanished at the sound of that monstrous shouting.

Ekaterina gave a yelp of pain and sucked her finger.

"It bit me."

She pointed at the floor. Alexandra looked down to see a rivulet of milk leaking from the sarcophagus with the flyer, as precise and thin as if drawn by a mathematician. It ran down the side of the container and across the ground towards Banjo who jumped out of the way.

"What the flaming hell is that?"

Alexandra hunkered down and examined the thread. She reached out to touch it but, as she got closer, the surface changed to grey dust, seething and twisting over itself like a rope of dying maggots. She snatched her hand back and the liquid turned white again. She walked over to Ekaterina, who still had her finger in her mouth, took her friend's wrist and looked at the wound. Apart from a cluster of tiny red dots below the fingernail there was no sign of any injury.

"Are you alright?"

Ekaterina nodded.

"Is it some kind of mercury?" asked Banjo.

Alexandra shook her head. A wild idea had crept into her mind and she was trying to shake it off. *What Tsar lives for two hundred and fifty years and crafts prodigies like these?* No matter how hard she tried to get rid of the notion it ricocheted around inside her skull.

"This is not of Earth."

She jammed trembling hands into her pockets and started to pace up and down, working out her fear and wonder in footfalls, unable to credit the words she'd just uttered.

Banjo's mouth dropped open.

"What do you mean?"

"Who has ever seen science like this before?" Alexandra gestured around. "Where in the world is the genius who can make flying machines who think by themselves and rivers of milk that act with intelligence and purpose? None of this is possible. None of this should even exist," she realised she was shouting now, demanding answers of the mountain. She could see her own hunger and fear mirrored in the Englishman's eyes. *The stories Natasha and I read and loved are about to come true.* She wasn't prepared. No matter how beautiful those youthful dreams, their manifestation in reality was terrifying.

"You're talking about a creature from another world who has travelled here through etheric space?" asked Banjo in the careful voice of a psychiatrist who'd realised his patient was madder than he first thought.

Alexandra laughed at the absurdity and something in her voice made the engineer flinch. Clearly worried he now had two lunatics to deal with, the Englishman turned to the actress but Ekaterina's gaze was far away, her head twitching like a bird's as if listening to a conversation in another room.

"We go on?" said Banjo.

Alexandra followed the line of white liquid. It stopped a few yards from an arch opposite the one they'd entered through. As she approached, the tip moved again, drifting across the floor and into the tunnel. Her heart thundered in her ears.

"I think that whoever or whatever dwells in the mountain is giving us a sign in this," she said. "It wants us to follow."

"Why doesn't the bugger speak again?"

She had no idea. Maybe the voice had been produced by a machine, like a recording. The words had carried a brittle echo of gears and wires but perhaps that was how a man from the stars would sound.

"We continue."

They put their boots back on and Alexandra followed the white thread into the tunnel, with her companions close behind. The passageway angled up into the mountain. All was silent but more than ever she was convinced they were being watched.

As they travelled deeper into the mountain, following endless tunnels patch-worked with glowing panels, fear roared through Alexandra's head, swilling around her thoughts and threatening to suck them down into dark places filled with gas and blood. In the trenches at Smorgon the foul maelstrom of war had eviscerated all identity and meaning from the world. Her mind had barely survived, clutching onto the tiny, fragile promise of a reborn humanity and a science that would scour all this vileness from the Earth once and forever. And here it was - the herald of a better age carried down from the stars.

But I don't recognise any of our youthful dreams in this citadel, Natasha. Every few steps she panicked. *How can anyone comprehend this and turn it to good? Yet all these powers and prodigies have been part of the Old Believers' lives for centuries, and those creatures in the mines and Aminev's electrical girl must come from here as well. Father Kirill, with all your ignorance and contempt for me and your incense and icons - how can you exist so easily here in the shadow of futurity while I struggle to understand?*

She had to speak with this being from another world, this Star Tsar, and demand explanations. *But how will I do it? What will I say?* Would her stumbling supplication trigger an invasion? *The War of the Worlds - are you a mind vast, cool and unsympathetic? The vanguard of the coming conquest of mankind? You slew those wretches in the village with such ease.* Her vision blurred and she put her hand against the wall to steady herself.

"Alexandra, what's wrong?" Ekaterina put an arm around her shoulders.

"I, I can't..."

The commissar pulled off her glasses, trying to blink away the fear. She opened her eyes. *Wait a minute.* She replaced the spectacles and everything blurred. She removed them again and looked at Ekaterina, then at Banjo standing behind her with an expression of frustrated worry on his face.

"I'm not short-sighted anymore."

"Marvellous! Shouldn't we be getting a move on?"

"It doesn't make sense."

"Oh really, you don't say." The Englishman gave an impatient snort and strode past, following the white line which curved around the bend ahead. He stopped a few yards further on, mouth open.

"Bugger me! Take a look at this!"

Still unable to credit how bright and clear the surroundings had become, Alexandra pocketed her glasses and followed. The thread disappeared into a hollowed-out cavern filled with an unearthly garden. Ekaterina gave a cry and the commissar, looking at the hair-fine flowers and trees, finally understood they were indeed in the presence of something not of Earth.

Everything looked ink-wash and watercolour delicate as if the orchards and meadows lay underwater, bursting with the finest tendrils of sea plants in coral oceans. Blooms and lianas shivered in the grainy orange light, all deep purples, blacks and greens. They were the darkest, most hectic orchids - flowers oozing the maddest opiates to fuel Ekaterina's songs. Banjo studied a bunch of blue fruit hanging from a twisted midnight tree in the shape of a hand.

"They were growing those in the copper greenhouses," said Alexandra. "The villagers use them for food. We must have eaten them."

"Never seen anything like this before, not even in Japan or China where they scoff all manner of perversities."

Ekaterina slowly pirouetted across a patch of yellow grass that quivered around her feet, arms akimbo as if she were a clockwork doll.

"All this is of another world. Behold the lotuses of men who dwell beneath different suns."

Banjo flashed his biggest grin yet. It looked like the penny had finally dropped, even in his thick head.

"Is this it? Have we really stumbled across a creature from space?"

Alexandra took the hands of her companions.

"What are you doing?" asked the engineer.

"Comrades. This is a momentous time and it is only fitting that the most advanced and greatest society of man should be the one to speak with dwellers from other worlds. They will no doubt be far beyond Homo Sapiens in their communist wisdom so we must be brave."

"Eh? He's spent two and a half centuries talking to those canting maniacs in the village. God knows what he thinks of us. Now's not the time to start spouting a load of Red bollocks at him."

"This is important. The first meeting of the Soviets and a creature of Super Science from the stars. Please behave yourself."

Banjo snatched his hand away and jabbed a thumb at his own chest.

"You arrogant tart! Why shouldn't a citizen of His Majesty's Empire be the one to talk to it? We brought civilisation to half the world while you lot were still grubbing about in shit at the beck and call of a load of mincing inbreds."

"You can't speak to it because you don't understand Slavonic," Alexandra battled uselessly with rising fury. "I will address it and I ask that you keep quiet and a respectful distance from these vital negotiations."

"Fuck off you pompous little cow!"

"May I remind you that you are technically still my prisoner and you owe me your life."

"Oh yes? And what are you going to do about it, you turd?"

"Please! You are both giving me a headache."

"See," bellowed Banjo. "You've upset the fair one with your blather."

"Alright, alright," snapped Alexandra. *I can't believe I'm standing on the threshold of the greatest event in human history arguing with this utter moron.* Only the realisation that murder wouldn't leave the best impression on the Star Tsar stopped her from taking Ekaterina's Mauser and shooting the Englishman in the face.

"Just keep your voice down so we can at least pretend we're civilised."

Alexandra stalked ahead, wishing she'd left the man in the ironworks swinging upside down and soaked in his own piss. Ekaterina wafted along behind and Banjo took up the rear, huffing and snorting like a buffalo. She shouldn't have lost her temper with the fool. *At least you're not frightened anymore.*

Where the white thread passed through the grove it pushed apart the trees and grass to fashion a path of crystal-veined rock, compressing the garden on either side into a dark-walled forest. Through the gaps between the trunks she saw the silhouettes of blossoms and tendrils shivering in rays of smoky light, the beams patterned with dancing vortices. She remembered the crawling on her skin inside the copper greenhouse. It looked as though the air here was saturated with the same grainy motion, yet she felt nothing. *And you're no longer short sighted.* That didn't make sense. She'd needed glasses since she was fourteen but here she was, picking out the hair-fine leaves of distant, unknown blooms with her own eyes. *What's changed you? The atmosphere in here? The Old Believer's food you stupidly ate? Does everything in this realm have consciousness and powers of transformation?*

She looked at the strand of unearthly liquid. It somehow possessed intelligence like the flying sentinels though she struggled to understand how. When she'd moved to touch the surface it had dissolved into a repulsive seething mass. Best leave it to guide them onward. As heady and frightening her thoughts, she had more important things to focus on. *I'm about to meet a man from interplanetary space.* The very idea still made her dizzy but she forced herself to keep going one step at a time.

Oh to be as dislocated from reality as Ekaterina. The singer strolled along with white-circled eyes set in an expression of placid interest. It was a bizarre combination entirely suited to her surroundings. At least she wasn't demanding to be taken straight to Pavel any more. Alexandra had a horrible suspicion Kirill's men had executed the actors, as they'd planned for her and her friends, and the stories about them being admitted to the court of the Star Tsar were just cruel euphemisms.

They came to the end of the cavern and entered another tunnel. After a couple of switchbacks the walls abruptly turned a dark grey - porous and freezing to the touch.

"Pumice," she said. "This must be a volcano and we're walking through an old lava seam."

She momentarily forgot her argument with the Englishman. To his credit, anger passed through Banjo as brief as hailstorms on a summer afternoon. The engineer pointed at a machine-precise join arcing over their heads.

"It's not pumice. These walls were machined elsewhere and assembled here."

"Where?"

"Don't ask me. I've never seen anything like this before."

Staring at it produced no answers so she carried on. The turns tightened, the white line hugging the bottom of the wall.

"Right bloody maze this is," Banjo's voice echoed somewhere behind. Alexandra had rounded a bend and called out to Ekaterina and the Englishman to keep up. She waited for a few seconds but the idiot's grumbling grew fainter. *What's he doing now?* She went back and with a twist of fear saw the passageway empty. Cursing all idiots and madwomen, Alexandra ran after the others. She turned a few more corners, running faster as tunnel after tunnel revealed no sign of the engineer or actress. *But they were just behind me.*

She shouted. No answer, only the cold, grit silence seeping through the pores in the walls and floor. They'd been captured by more demon creatures with oil slick mouths and eyes. *This is a trap. What was I thinking of?* There'd be no meeting with the Star Tsar, no great reconciliation between Soviet man and the cosmos.

Alexandra forced herself to breathe and looked down. The line was still there. *Shit! Ekaterina's got the only gun but I can't stay here.* Working her way through a string of curses, including several she'd picked up from Banjo, she continued down the slope, hoping to end up back in the garden. The visitor could wait until she and the others were reunited.

Nothing - just that endless line switching to and fro as the tunnel changed direction. Come to think of it, none of this seemed familiar, and why wasn't she in the vault with its dark forest by now? *How long have I been going for? Is the passage changing configuration even as I walk through it?* She called out in Slavonic, supplicating the Star Tsar. No one answered.

Just as she was about to lose her battle with fear, the tunnel straightened for twenty paces, leading to a circular room. Alexandra stood at the entrance, looking for any life. The ash walls and floor held nothing new but high above her head the darkness thickened into a black mist. It was as if the mountain had trapped and compressed a thousand thunderstorms into a single freezing roof. Threads of hair-fine vapour curled down and dissipated in an invisible wind that sounded full of hissing ice spat out from the frozen north of an unknown world. Alexandra had the sudden vision of herself standing on a grey disk gliding over an infinite dead ocean.

Deep within that sibilant roar she heard another noise, that of a creature dragging itself over wet rock. It came from far above. She dug her nails into her palm to stop herself running howling back into the corridor and kept her gaze firmly level, watching the tip of the white thread as it approached a low bench set flush against the curving wall opposite.

The line turned into a puddle. Two lumps grew upwards, turning into feet, legs then a torso, arms and a head - a doll sitting on the bench. The commissar stumbled back. *I mustn't flee, not now, not at the final moment. But it's one of your broken dolls, plucked out of your head. The Hammer? Viktor?* A shining white mannequin sat with its hands on its knees like a wanderer resting after journeying through a desert. Its head was a smooth featureless egg but even without eyes the commissar felt it staring at her, studying her closely.

"Help me."

The Star Tsar's voice echoed around the chamber. It didn't come from the white shape sitting on the bench. Rather it filled the air, as if the roiling vortices she'd seen in the greenhouses and the forest had finally spoken. To her astonishment she managed to take a couple of steps into the room, noticing that the line still extended from the figure's left foot and disappeared into the tunnel behind. *Is it a sculpture, like a papier-mâché figurine filled with that strange milk from the sarcophagus? Is this the creature itself or another automaton through which the alien speaks?* She remembered the slithering bulk hidden high above in the black fog. *What's clinging to ceiling above me?* No matter how much she tried, she couldn't bring herself to look upwards.

"Help me. I'm dying."

The head drooped.

"Are you the Star Tsar? Did you come here two and a half centuries ago, and looked after the Old Believers - the people living in the valley outside?"

No answer. She took off her cap and stood to attention.

"I am Commissar Alexandra Sergeyevna Lobachevsky of the People's Commissariat for Education, of the United Soviet Socialist Republic. On behalf of the workers of the world I extend warm and peaceful greetings to the denizens of other planets. May we share knowledge and understanding with mutual accord and friendship." In her head she could hear Banjo snort.

"I cared for the first men, gave them the science to better themselves. The second men came, also seeking to learn. I showed them kindness but they wanted to fashion tools for slaughter. They built fortresses in the mountains and changed their slaves into machines. The third men came but it was too late. I've stayed too long and I no longer have the strength. The last survivors from the third men promised they would bring more life to me. I sent them in a ship but they have not returned. Fourth Man, I beg you to help me. There is one vessel left with enough power to make the journey."

Hearing an alien creature of Super Science speak in liturgical Slavonic was utterly bizarre. *You are the Star Tsar - the holy father*

from heaven protecting the Old Believers - those you call the first men.
It finally made sense. The second men were the Tsarists who'd
tried to steal the creature's knowledge and use it for weapons in
the war. That had led to the battle on the other side of the mines.
The Whites imprisoned the flying sentinel in an armoured train
but it clawed its way out. The third men had to be Pavel and the
other actors.

"Where are the third men now?"

"Only two survived - a male and a female. The rest were
murdered by the first. They agreed to undertake the journey for
me but they too must have perished in the void. I have one last
ship left. I beg you, take it and save me. Bring me back more life."

"Go where?"

"To the fourth world in this system."

Alexandra had to repeat the sentence very slowly in her head,
counting on her fingers like a stupid child.

"You want me to journey to Mars?"

Alright. Enough was enough. An end to the joke, this
absurdist pantomime - a satire on the dreams and fantasies of a
dying, decadent regime as fine as any *Mystery-Bouffe* by Vladimir
Vladimirovich. Any second now Pavel would leap out of the
shadows with that high, insane giggle of his and wave the
puppet's strings in her face. *A man and woman - also sent away.*

"You took Pavel and Galina from the Agit-Train *A Bolshevik
Forever!* and fired them into space, to the planet Mars. And now
you want me to go on the same trip? To bring back more 'life'?
What life?"

She looked down at the shimmering rivulet and the penny
dropped. More noises in the darkness above - rooting her to the
spot, too terrified to turn her head even a fraction for fear of what
she'd glimpse. *You are above me. I was right. This is an artificial man
speaking on your behalf.*

"Why do I have to do this? Why not send your flying machine
or this puppet?"

"They're just tools. They obey commands but are unable think
for themselves beyond the moment. I need you. On the fourth

planet there is a citadel with enough life to bring me back to strength so I can go home."

"Home? To Mars?"

"No."

"We are you from?"

"There's no time left."

"Even if you do have a space ship capable of making the trip to another planet, I can't do it. Our knowledge is nowhere near yours. We're savages compared to this. None of us understand how to pilot an etheric vessel to Mars and return. It's impossible."

The figure collapsed into a pool on the bench. It shrank and disappeared as the line withdrew into the tunnel behind her. The rustling in the vault above Alexandra increased until, unable to stand it any longer, she turned and fled, biting her tongue to stop herself crying out.

CHAPTER THIRTEEN

"**B**ugger me sideways, it's a space flyer. Look at all those rivets!"

Banjo and Ekaterina stood in a cavern. A wide tunnel led to the open air a couple of hundred yards to their left, where a storm churned its way through the clouds below. Mist and rain lashed against wet rock. They had to be close to the peak, although it didn't feel like they'd climbed that far, even with Madam running ahead up the fused tunnels, alternately screaming out for Alexandra and that bloody Pavel of hers. Now, while she slumped exhausted with her face in her hands, the Englishman gawped at the spaceship, fear temporarily brushed aside.

A long flattened tube pointed at the cave entrance, as big as a submarine with translucent bubbles peppering its surface. The front was shaped like a chisel with half a glowing egg, about three yards across, stuck to the upper bevel. The other end flared into four vertical slits that resembled radiator grills. Perhaps they were the rockets. He had no idea. This was way beyond any engineering he'd ever dreamed of, let alone come across in his travels. Summoning up his courage he placed his palm on the hull. Warm, with a slight vibration. He tasted copper and the hairs on his forearm stood up.

He longed for a look inside but there wasn't any sign of a door and his priority was finding Alexandra. One second the infuriating bint had been pomping along like a nun dragging her charges out on a Sunday school outing, all fired up with manifest destiny. The next moment she'd completely vanished. Banjo sprinted after the Red, assuming her enthusiasm for teaching a denizen of another world the virtues of communism had got the better of her. But even a deranged Bolshevik couldn't run that fast. On the fourth bend Ekaterina pointed at the floor. The white line had also disappeared.

He wouldn't leave a mate behind - especially those incapable of looking after themselves - whether it was dribbling Ernie Featherington or Comrade Constipated. For some inexplicable reason he'd grown slightly fond of the insufferable wart - though he struggled to understand why. Maybe it was their shared love of scientific romances, even if the ones she read were as dull as buggery. In the valley the thought of being alone with Ekaterina had cheered him up no end. However the loss of Alexandra as well as her two-timing beau was tearing the singer's already fragile mind to tatters, more so without any drugs to buffer her from the world. Anyway, this was a chance to prove himself. Find the Red pillock and deliver her in one piece and Old Banjo would definitely be the gallant in Madam's eyes.

Ekaterina soon scotched his fantasies of manliness. She poked a little glass bottle up her nose, inhaled and threw it away. *Where the fuck did she have that hidden?* The actress pulled her Mauser out and brandished it at the ceiling.

"The last one, Comrades, let's make it count!" she cried out in the voice of a leading lady making sure every syllable was understood at the back of the Gods.

Even as Banjo made a mental note to keep well out of the way, she gave a scream of happy recognition. Alexandra staggered into the cave, as pale as a corpse. Ekaterina hurled herself at the commissar, running her hands through the lass's hair and over her face and babbling out her joy in Russian. The Red barely seemed to recognise her. A flicker between Banjo's boots. He looked down just in time to spot the white rivulet speeding across the rock. He jumped aside. It reached the space flyer and a hatch clanged open. Lights flickered inside. He heard the hum of a dynamo powering up. Banjo turned back to the Bolshevik who sat on a fallen cylinder. She had her forearms clamped between her knees but that didn't stop her hands shaking.

"Bloody hell lass, what happened? Where did you vanish to?"

"I met the Star Tsar."

"And? What does he look like?"

Alexandra struggled to speak, half laughing, half sobbing. She looked like she was going mad as well. The actress took the commissar's fingers and knelt before her.

"Where is Pavel? Is he alive? Is he in this mountain?"

"Flown to the planet Mars."

Right - she's gone completely barmy. At least I have enough wit to understand that the books I read are made up. Now she thinks hers are real.

"Mars?" asked Ekaterina.

"Mars," answered the commissar with the same bland matter-of-fact voice as someone talking about Moscow or Ilkley. She pointed at the ceiling in case they were in any doubt as to where Mars was.

Banjo looked at the space flyer. Initial judgement aside, his experiences across the seven seas had taught him never to dismiss the babbling of lunatics lurching out of dark places.

"The Star Tsar begged me to go after Pavel."

For some reason the image of Dejah Thoris, Princess of Mars, sprawled naked over a heap of Great White Ape fur in the twin-towered city of Helium popped into Banjo's head. *Is this really happening to me?*

"In that?"

Alexandra gave Banjo a helpless look. The engineer placed his hand on the flyer hull and sneaked a glance inside, hoping the door wasn't going to thump shut and take his head with it. Geometric patches flickered across shadows and surfaces, dancing through a golden light that seemed to emanate from the grainy air itself.

"The Star Tsar is a man from etheric space who came here in

the seventeenth century - at the time of the Cleaving. He looked after the Old Believers and became their Good Tsar."

Alexandra ran her hands through her hair as if trying to convince herself she'd gone mad.

"He's ancient and dying and needs more of that to save himself," Alexandra pointed at the line. "He told me it's in his castle on Mars. He sent Pavel there but the fool hasn't returned so now it's our turn to make the journey."

Ekaterina stood up.

"Even on Mars I shall find them, tear her heart out and bind him to my soul," the singer declaimed. She lurched unsteadily towards the space flyer and clambered inside. Banjo started to panic. *She'd better not set off on her own and leave us behind.*

He was more terrified than he'd ever been in his life, standing on the edge of a gulf looking down into chaos. It wasn't because of what might happen to him on some insane space voyage. It was the choice itself, here and now, in this tempest-battered mountain. *If you turn away it'll be beyond regret. You know you won't be able to carry on living. Even if it is a lie, or a trap, or a cruel joke, it doesn't matter. It's the question that matters. Go or stay? This is the decision whereby everything you think you understand about Banjo Hawkridge will prove to be true or pitiful self delusion.*

"What do you reckon Alexandra?" he asked, trying hide the tremor in his words as he watched the lightning scribble its reflection across wet granite. "Are you game? Do we go to Mars?"

"No, no. We can't."

That pulled him up short. His companion was an arrogant shit but not a coward.

"We must return to Petrograd as soon as possible," explained the commissar. "First we'll contact Comrade Commander Aminev and tell him what's happened. This is the most momentous event in the history of humanity and we, the Union of Soviet Socialist Republics, have been chosen. It's imperative that all the workers are mobilised and come together in aid of this interplanetary being of Super Science."

The woman was babbling, sweat running down her face and

voice a-tremble. It sounded like she was reading from a speech.

"We will have a conference immediately, with the wisest savants and delegates from..."

"Are you completely fucking mad? This Star Tsar of yours is begging us to help it by flying to Mars for its cosmic medicine right now and you want to go all the way to Petrograd and call a committee meeting?"

"We can reach it in a matter of days. We'll have to fight past the villagers and use the train to return to Ikayungri but once we're back, and Commander Aminev realises the importance..."

"Commander Aminev? That murderous cunt? What do you think he'll do? Steal all these magic weapons and put a bullet through our heads to stop us telling anyone else, that's what."

Alexandra looked past him at the spaceship. Her expression was a perfect mirror of Banjo's thoughts.

"Come on Alexandra. If we don't go we'll regret it for the rest of our lives, even if that thing explodes en-route or we get eaten by monsters. It's Mars, lass! Jewelled deserts, twin moons, treasure beyond our wildest dreams, interplanetary houris with luscious bosoms and eyes brim-full of sin! And big manly blokes with strapping thews for you, if you want. And we'll be the first ones from Earth!"

"It's not that," Alexandra pointed at the hammer and sickle on her cap. "I'm a commissar. I have a duty to the USSR, to all the workers of the world. I must be the herald of this new age. That's why we've got to return to Petrograd. I can't just fly off on my own selfish adventure like the hero in your book."

"I don't think we're going to get a lot of choice."

Banjo nodded at the entrance to the cave where the flying machine now hovered. He'd no idea how it'd managed to squeeze down the tunnel. Perhaps the internal layout of this mountain changed all the time, like a puzzle moving to the whims of the space being. The engine's cluster of tentacles fanned out like the crest of an angry lizard. Three of them held black sacks. Alexandra stood up, walked towards it and said something in Russian, pointing in the general direction of what Banjo guessed was Petrograd. He had to admire the woman's guts.

"Oh for pity's sake. I'm going to Mars. Are you coming or not?" he asked.

The drone lurched, giving the Bolshevik a shove like a playground bully picking on a new bug. Banjo clenched his fists and started forwards, though he'd no idea what to do if the thing turned nasty. The Russian placed a hand on its carapace and spoke again. Halfway through her speechifying a tentacle flicked down, wrapped itself around her ankle and hoisted her into the air upside down. Banjo gave a shout of fury.

"No Banjo!" yelled Alexandra, even as the flying machine glided to the vessel's hatch. It tossed the woman inside like a porter loading up the night mail and rotated to face Banjo. Angry spider-eye lights clustered on its collar. He held his hands up.

"I'm going, I'm going."

He paused at the threshold as a final wave of utter ball-shrivelling terror passed through him. Cursing his cowardice, he climbed into the craft. Three bags drifted in on the end of oily ropes which deposited them on the floor. The tentacles retreated and the door slammed shut.

Banjo looked around. Apart from the lights and the ever-present tangerine smoke the cabin appeared featureless. The hemispheres projecting from the hull were completely transparent on the inside, giving him a clear view of the cavern walls. Ekaterina had stuck her head into one and was peering outside with inebriated curiosity. Their machine master had vanished, though the engineer heard scraping along the hull. Alexandra stood in the middle of the room, staring down at her boots with her fists behind her back and a face like a smacked arse.

Movement to his right. Banjo turned to see a low wall rise out of the floor, slanted at forty-five degrees towards the rear of the ship. It looked like a box filled with blue sand. A second later he was picked up and thrown violently into it, his face crammed into warm grit. He struggled to cry out as a heavy weight thudded across his legs. A muffled shriek came from elsewhere. It sounded like Ekaterina. He tried to force himself away from the surface but the pressure hammered him deeper into the wall. He could still breathe but even as he fought back darkness crept in at the edge of his vision.

The crush eased and Banjo floated free. He watched the indent he'd left fill with sky-coloured grain. Ekaterina drifted through the air upside down with her thistledown skirts balled about her, her eyes wide open. At first he panicked, thinking her dead, but she was watching him like a swimmer dropped into an aquarium eyeing up a strange sea creature. Alexandra bumped along the floor, an unconscious comma with blood trickling from her nose. The droplets hung in the air.

The vessel shuddered and Banjo slammed into the ground, banging his head against the metal. He sat up, holding his temples and swearing. The actress lifted herself up on one arm and looked around blinking. *Doesn't anything bother her?*

He crawled over to Alexandra. The Bolshevik was still out cold, with an ugly bruise on her forehead. Otherwise she seemed unharmed. Sensing an opportunity he decided to let the lass rest, stood up and offered his hand to Ekaterina. What woman wouldn't shrink into his arms from such peril? She ignored his grin, shooed him away, staggered over to one of the bubbles and peered out. Banjo joined her, arranging it so that her body pressed against his. He squeezed his head into the hemispherical canopy, making sure they were virtually cheek to cheek, and all thoughts of seduction vanished.

The sky outside was divided into two halves - jet black above an arcing semicircle of bright blue-white fading into darkness. A fierce sun hung in the void like a theatre spotlight. Far below, between the clouds, Banjo could see waves scintillating, as thin and delicate as spider webs annealed across an aquamarine brooch.

We have ascended into the heavens. In a space flyer. At last I am John Carter, adventurer between worlds. In the distant hallways of his thoughts he saw a boy bent over a book, sitting beside a dirty window, serenaded by the rattle of sooty rain on glass. Snapping back to the here and now, he realised the orange haze inside the Star Tsar's ship was making his eyes water so he quickly rubbed his cheeks with his palm.

He heard a noise behind them. Alexandra stood at an entrance that had opened up opposite the blue mattress, one hand clamped to her forehead and the other braced against the bulkhead. Banjo spotted another room beyond her, walled with pipes and machinery and boxes, and a corridor leading to the front of the ship. The commissar called out in Russian. No reply. Banjo joined her.

"We're flying in etheric space, far above the world," he said.

The woman limped over to the nearest window and peered outside, fingers whitening on the rim.

"We must be moving so fast that the ship's in orbit around the Earth, just as Tsiolkovsky predicted. So how do we go to Mars? I don't know how to fly this machine? Do you?" Alexandra looked puzzled and jumped up and down. "We should be floating in the air and yet we aren't. Is this real?" her eyes narrowed. "Could this be an illusion, or a dream, and we're all on Earth imprisoned in the mountain? Maybe the food we ate in the Old Believers' house was drugged."

Banjo poked the commissar's bruise.

"Ow."

"Still think you're asleep? I'm going to see if I can work out how to pilot this thing."

The next chamber felt like the inside of a machine, but the Englishman made little sense of it. Polyhedral shapes projected from the curving walls, linked by silver-branched ivy embedded in the metal. Patches of light trembled in the faint orange mist, chasing each other over the riveted hull. He hunted for any levers, dials, buttons or switches but found nothing. There wasn't even any alien script to decipher. Alexandra also drew a blank, so they carried on into the tunnel. Halfway along Banjo paused, running his gaze over the cross-section.

"What did the Star Tsar look like?"

It took a few moments for the Red to answer.

"I didn't see it, only its avatar. The white liquid formed a mannequin in the shape of a human being and it spoke to me through that but..." she paused and swallowed. "There was a black cloud over my head, covering the ceiling. I heard a movement - something dragging itself over wet rock - it was big, like a bear, or even bigger. I was too scared to look. I don't know how it clung to the roof - like a..., like a slug."

Fear aged the Russian. Her face was drawn and eyes haunted. Banjo was glad he hadn't been the first to meet the man from space.

"I didn't think this craft was built for people," he gestured at the passageway. "That blue sand box and this tunnel are shaped for your space creature."

They came to the furthest room. It was split in half by the viewing dome set into the cantilevered prow. For a horrible moment Banjo thought the cabin was open to the void. On this side the two-way glass was totally transparent without any reflections from the glowing lights dancing over every surface. A second tilted mattress made of blue sand stood opposite a shelf covered in multi-coloured circles. He watched the sea far below turn indigo as night rolled towards them.

Is that the Pacific?

He held his thumb up at arm's length and did the sums in his head.

"The Earth's dropped ten degrees. We're moving higher."

He tried to make sense of the shelf in front of him. Valves, pipes and levers he understood - proper mechanics. This looked like one of those paintings Auntie Jessie and her friend Constance had dragged him to see in that dive in Batley when he was ten - colours, splatters and shapes they told him were 'wonderfully Modern'. He poked a few at random but nothing happened. So how were they supposed to fly this bloody vessel?

"Did your Star Tsar tell you how long it was going to take to get to Mars? Or any suggestions as to how we might operate this thing?"

Alexandra shook her head.

Banjo was as familiar with the stars and planets as any sailor but had no clue about the distance to the Red Planet. *Edgar Rice Burroughs knew.* He pulled out *A Princess of Mars* and flicked through. *Here we go - Barsoom is forty-eight million miles away. Buggeration.* It'd take months, or years. How fast did this space flyer travel? His stomach rumbled. *We'll all be dead of starvation before we even start.*

Alexandra read his mind and together they headed back through the ship to find out what was in those black pouches. Ekaterina had emptied hers on the floor and was putting the contents in neat order - fruit, black bread, flasks of water and little metal tins - twelve of each. That cheered Banjo up. At least the space creature wanted to keep them alive and based on the amount of supplies they'd be able to work out the length of the journey. He checked the other sacks - just the same as the actress's but neither his nor Alexandra's had the tins.

Why's she got them and not us?

So they had food for one meal a day for twelve days, or two for six, or what? Three hearty repasts between sunup and sundown was the Yorkshire standard Banjo worked to, but that looked over-optimistic. More like a week there and a week back maximum. That wasn't so bad. He bit into a yellow fruit.

"It's madness!" shouted Alexandra.

"Keep your hat on. I thought you liked scientific romances and adventure. You're forever blathering on about Super Science and men of the future. Here you are."

"Yes, but not like this! We are destined to meet the workers of other worlds and spread out across the universe in a glorious destiny of science and praxis. There's so much to discuss, so much to learn. How can we do it here? Who is there to ask? We're prisoners shot into the void with no control over our fate yet charged with the single most important task ever undertaken by man - saving the life of a being we scarcely comprehend."

Alexandra clasped her fists behind her and paced up and down.

Oh Christ. Here we go again. Banjo left her to it and while

Ekaterina was looking the other way he surreptitiously pinched one of her tins, turned his back and pulled off the top. White powder.

Aye aye. The Star Tsar's being very accommodating.

It looked like the creature had decided to feed the actress's cocaine habit. How did it realise she even had one? Pity it didn't know about his own addiction to *Theakston's Old Peculier Ale*. God what he'd give to have a pint in his hand right now - lying in that blue sand with his feet up on Aunty Jessie's Modernist shelf, watching the stars blossom as they turned their faces away from war-torn Earth and headed off into their dreams.

He sniffed as close as he dared but there was none of the gasoline odour of cocaine. Banjo dabbed a bit on his finger and tasted - nothing. It could have been chalk for all the effect it had. He replaced the lid and slid it back amongst the others. Maybe the interplanetary being had chucked in some cosmetics as a concession to its female passengers. Alexandra had probably never worn make-up in her life. He tried to imagine her in rouge and powder and shuddered.

Realising he wasn't going to get much sense out of either of his companions, he pocketed the fruit and wandered to the front of the ship. His gob fell open. The world had vanished and he found himself peering into a void filled with stars. He guessed that on Earth the mist and smoke in the air dimmed their light but out here they were steel bright. He ambled back down the corridor and stuck his head into a bubble so he could look behind. *Fuck me.* The world was the size of a sixpence and getting visibly smaller.

On our way. Someone else is piloting this ship and we're merely passengers. How fast are we travelling? All he could sense was a slight vibration through the soles of his boots.

He returned to the bridge and looked round. *Are you another thinking machine like that flying engine?* He examined the slanting couch, poking it with his finger. The depression filled with blue sand. *This is the Star Tsar's chair - as well as that bed in the rear cabin, designed to cushion it against the sudden buffets of etheric travel. Did you fly to our world in this craft or one similar?* He tentatively planted his bottom in the grit and leaned back. The seething motion stilled - wonderfully comfortable. Here a man could rest in peace without that canting prat going on and on about workers this and bourgeois oppressors that. He closed his eyes just as a horrendous shriek echoed down the length of the rocket ship.

CHAPTER FOURTEEN

Ekaterina sat on the floor with her arms around her knees, staring into the distance. Her eyes were discs and the veins bulged on her forehead. Despite her rictus grin she hissed constantly, words pouring out of her in an incessant grinding spray. One of the tins lay on its side, powder smeared in hand prints all over the metal.

She thought it was cocaine. How could she have been so stupid?

Alexandra tried to take the woman's wrists, to force her to look into her eyes so she'd find the anchor that always seemed to calm her down, but it was like trying to prise iron bars from a cage.

Banjo charged in.

"What is it? What is it fairest one, my very delight?"

The commissar ignored him.

"Ekaterina!"

No response. Alexandra tried to pull her friend's hands free again but they were locked together. A thin trickle of blood ran down from the singer's nose.

"She's got the hopping hab-dabs," shouted the Englishman. "Do something!"

"What?"

Banjo grabbed a flask of water and tried to pour some into the singer's mouth. She smacked him with the back of hand, her arm a blur. He flew across the room, thudded into the bulkhead, slumped to his knees and held his head in his hands.

"God almighty. That hurt."

Underneath her fey theatricality Ekaterina had always been she-wolf lean. Alexandra had seen her best larger men in sabre duels but this was something else. She'd just sent a man twice her size flying across the room with a flick of her wrist. She tried to get her friend's attention again. No luck. Ekaterina carried on hissing.

"What's she saying?" Banjo limped over.

Alexandra put her ear to the woman's mouth, hoping she wouldn't get her face chewed off in a drugged fit.

"Pushkin, I think."

"Is that good or bad?"

"*Itgrowsthinthecloudsflyingbanktheeveningstarthatindeepsadnesssank*," went Ekaterina.

Banjo picked up the dropped tin.

"I don't understand." He dabbed his little finger in the residue and tasted it.

"Wait, you idiot!" The last thing Alexandra wanted was two drug addicts on the rampage. Banjo ignored her, stuck his face into the can and inhaled. He stared at the commissar with a white ring stamped around his nose. How easy would it be to stick her hand up Ekaterina's skirt and grab the Mauser before he went for her?

"Just the same. No effect. Nothing. I tried it earlier. It's just like chalk," he thrust the container at Alexandra. "Here, you have a go."

"You tried it earlier?"

"Something else must be causing this."

But what? We all ate the same food. The only difference was the Star Tsar's cocaine, or whatever it was in those tins. But it had no effect on Banjo. Despite her better judgement Alexandra took a couple of grains on her fingernail and sniffed. All it did was make her sneeze. The insufferable fool was right. It was about as potent as flour. Did it only work for the actress? Why?

Ekaterina resisted all attempts to move her. She just sat in a scrunched-up ball, spluttering Pushkin at no-one. It sounded like she was quoting her way through the entire works from memory. All they could do was watch her, wait, and hope she came down out of it soon with no lasting damage. Banjo had cleared a space around the actress and sat cross-legged opposite her. Alexandra left the engineer to his dog-like devotion, walked the length of the ship and looked out at the stars.

A heavy, exhausted sadness filled the commissar. *Did I really think I could protect The Hammer, Viktor and Ekaterina? Save them? That by calling them my broken dolls it gave me power over the death, monsters and madness that took them away? Here I am, a prisoner on an interplanetary flyer supposedly travelling to the planet Mars - a dream, Natasha, that you and I whispered together when we crept into each other's beds, all innocence and wonder. Noble and wise men and women journeying through space, forging through new realms of Super Science. Never for a second did I imagine it would be me, or that if it was, it would only be me and not the two of us together. That dream ended when Uncle told me I couldn't go with you to study mathematics and astronomy at the Institute in Petrograd.*

Alexandra recalled the quivering shadows on the dark ceiling of the Star Tsar's lair and shuddered. *I can't do this.* Ekaterina was in a drug-induced trance. Banjo was a maniac child with no self-control and a ludicrous obsession with the infantile fantasies in that book of his. *But if I'm the only one I can't give up. My dearest Natasha, if only you were here to give me the strength to see this through.* She closed her eyes and tried to tumble back through the years, just to capture the scent of her cousin's hair or hear her soft breathing in the darkness. The deep abyss of time gave her nothing.

The sun, earth and moon lay behind them now. They were speeding through the interplanetary ether and without the harsh light to swamp the sky she saw the band of the Milky Way slanting across the void - an impasto streak of orange, yellow, brown and red laid over a midnight canvas spattered with motes of glass and steel. Alexandra tried to make out the constellations but the fierce clarity of every burning spark erased any familiar patterns from the universe. Her mood started to lift, joyous excitement coalescing in her soul. *Darling cousin, out here there's no past to weigh us down - only possibility. What marvels, science and nobility await in this immense ocean?*

"She's fallen asleep at last," said Banjo standing beside her. "Why would the Star Tsar give her that powder and not us, and why does it only affect her?"

Alexandra returned to the last chamber to find Ekaterina unfolded like a flower, her eyes closed and a smile on her face. The actress looked slightly flushed, in fact better than she had done for a long time. The commissar hunkered down and gently lifted her hand. The puncture wounds on her finger had faded to clotted specs.

"If that fluid possesses intelligence then maybe it analysed her blood and discovered her addiction," said Alexandra. "It thought the cocaine and opium were part of her diet and the Star Tsar created a synthesis of both drugs just for her. Somehow it only works on Ekaterina, not us."

"It must be a hell of a concoction if it had her spouting poetry like that."

"I think the chemical unlocked the chambers of her mind, calling forth everything she's ever read or learned or heard."

Alexandra checked her friend's pulse. It was strong and rhythmic. Happy to let Ekaterina sleep, she stood up and wandered over to one of the hemispherical windows, drawn by the vision of the stars. She craned her neck to try to see Earth. Was it that blue pin-head half-buried in a cloud of light? It was impossible to gauge their speed but if their calculations were correct, and they'd been given food for a twelve-day round trip, they must be travelling more than three hundred thousand miles an hour.

"So here we are - characters in our own scientific romance on our way to the planet Mars," said Banjo. "There'll be ancient empires with noble warriors, horrible monsters and luscious women, and men, waiting for the great adventurers from Earth.

According to Edgar Rice Burroughs we'll be able to jump hundreds of yards into the air on account of the reduced gravity. That'll impress the hell out of 'em," He slapped her on the back. "We'll find a handsome captain of the guard just for you and you can communise him to your heart's content."

Alexandra was too exhausted and strung out to get angry. To her surprise, she couldn't help but laugh.

"My dear Banjo, your book is a load of primitive nonsense. There won't be any barbarian decadence or captains of the guard. Everyone knows the planet Mars is a world of Super Science ruled over by a race of savants far advanced in comparison to Earth. Theirs is a fading civilisation. They had their workers' revolution centuries ago and now dedicate themselves to the study of the universe, and to the massive feats of engineering needed to transport water in their canals from the ice caps to the arid deserts of their dying world."

"That's that short-arsed pederast Bertie Wells talking again isn't it?"

"Your dreams are the dreams of the past - heroes, villains and princesses, sword fights and sex. Don't you want to find the future? The real future?"

Banjo shrugged.

"Not sure there's a place for me in your future. I'm for a pint, a pie and a fuck. Banjo Hawkridge isn't much of a savant."

"And yet you dream of scientific romances."

"When you've spent most of your life mired in shit, blood and Quakerism you'll dream of anything."

The man was a hopeless liar.

"You do yourself a disservice. You and I are equally worthy of the future."

The stars span briefly.

The spaceship's correcting our course. What's controlling it?

Banjo had gone strangely quiet.

"The future's for everyone. I believe the workers of the world will rise and all will be equal. Mankind will enjoy the products of its labour and will turn away from the acquisition of goods and wealth and embrace this," Alexandra gestured around her. "In Russia we're taking the first steps towards a new scientific world order based on equality and labour. Soon there will be universal peace - no more dreadful wars. Don't you see?" she turned to Banjo. "The Star Tsar will be our liberator. With his help we will forge forward into new realms of Super Science. A hundred years from now our space flyers will journey between worlds as we reach out to create a socialist brotherhood of space."

"You sound like Auntie Jessie's friend Constance. She was a Theosophist and forever rabbiting on about all that Madame Blavatsky cosmic nonsense. Mind you, you're quite a persuasive bugger once you get going. I hope you're right."

Auntie Jessie's 'friend' Constance again. The question was on the tip of her tongue but she couldn't bring herself to ask it so she chose another.

"You don't think we can do it? After what you and I have found? This great task we've been given? If we save the Star Tsar's life who knows what our rewards will be."

Banjo sucked his teeth and shook his head.

"I don't think your Captain Aminev or my Captain Spalding will give much for your new world once they get their evil paws on the Star Tsar's wonderful machines. I've been around the race course too many times to have much faith in my fellow man. The vast majority haven't two thoughts to rub together. Give them food, a roof and a handful of vices and they'll trail after any jumped up nabob. Sometimes not even that. Look at all those poor bastards who bled their guts out in the mud for King and Country. So far our science has given us machine guns and mustard gas. Handing over the Star Tsar's secrets to your government or mine would be like giving a bomb to a monkey. We're not ready for this. I don't think we'll ever be ready."

He chewed the inside of his cheek and looked out at the stars.

"Apart from thee and me of course. And the princess back there."

They lapsed into silence. Alexandra remembered Aminev shooting the Cossack in the head and the fear in the eyes of his men when the commander turned away. The Englishman didn't understand. Revolution had to be absolute, at least in the beginning. The rotting monster of Imperial Russia had crawled through eight years of horror - a swilling tide of blood, shit, disease and terror - before it finally died. And even then, like one of the antediluvian creatures from the deep abyss of time, its body had lumbered on even as its brain perished. Comrade Stalin had once told her that it was only through the antiseptic, ruthless cruelty of a field surgeon would the soul of Russia breathe free beneath its vast skies. The brutality would end - of course it would - and with the Star Tsar's grateful knowledge the world would be born anew.

And yet she couldn't shake cavalryman's squalid death from her mind - his madness, *Baba Yaga is coming* - and the way his forehead popped open like a cracked egg.

She blinked. How long had she been standing here staring into space? Alexandra was exhausted and the stars had stopped speaking to her hours ago. Banjo sat in the blue couch with his feet on the shimmering lights, his fingers plaited over his chest, head nodding. The commissar made her way back to the room where Ekaterina still slept. She rolled up in her coat and drifted off only to be woken in a panic thinking the ship was breaking apart. A grinding rattle as though every rivet was working loose filled the cabin. She sat up and saw Banjo stuck in the blue mattress like a fly on paper, snoring away. Hitting the Englishman three times had no effect whatsoever. The slob didn't even stir. Alexandra gave up and staggered back to the bridge. Ahead a red star shone brighter than the others.

Mars.

She placed her hands on the inside of the glass and peered at the light.

The Star Tsar said he came from somewhere else so is Mars merely a colony? Will there be more creatures similar to him on the Red Planet? If so, why didn't they help their comrade? And what about Pavel? He'd taken this journey also - him and Galina, Ekaterina's rival. What happened to them? Did they meet with a misfortune that prevented them from returning the Star Tsar's medicine to him? *Look at us - three humans with one pistol and no idea what to do once we arrive.*

The universe held no answers so she eased herself into the blue couch by the window. It settled around her and when she pulled her feet off the floor she found that she too was stuck like a gnat in a web. A gentle trap, and with Banjo's corrugated snores a distant rumble Alexandra had no trouble falling back to sleep.

The next day she woke to find the red star swollen to a recognisable disk with two bright dots close by. *The moons of Mars.* Ekaterina sat scrunched up again, staring and chanting out an endless stream of words.

"*CanthisbestilladreamRaskolnikovthoughtoncemorehelookedcarefull yandsuspiciouslyattheunexpectedvisitor.*"

Crime and Punishment. Dostoyevsky now - she's reciting every book she's ever read.

There was white powder under her nose and Banjo looked sheepish.

"She must have got another one while we were asleep," he tried to appear cheerful. "They don't seem to be doing her any harm."

"Not doing any harm? Look at her!"

"She seems better than she did, if you discount the ravings. There's a bit of colour in those cheeks. She was a sickly-looking thing before, now she's positively strapping."

Banjo flexed his arm and poked his bicep.

"I'm feeling chipper myself and I woke up with the most glorious tumescence in the old man. I reckon it's the space fruit."

"The most glorious what?"

"I could have drilled holes in a battleship's hull with my…"

"Please, just shut up."

The commissar did a quick mental scan of her body. She did feel remarkably vigorous, considering. *The Old Believers were well nourished and healthy. The food they cultivated under the guidance of the Star Tsar must have restorative properties.* A sudden thought made her gasp.

"Not just invigorating, it's actually changed us. It cured my short-sightedness. After we ate in the village I didn't need my glasses anymore. And when Ekaterina hit you she sent you flying across the cabin. Drug addicts have phenomenal strength when they're in a fit but not that powerful."

"It's turning us into Gods."

"The new men and women of the future."

"How do we find out?" Banjo looked around. "I bet I could bend that Mauser into a knot."

He advanced on Ekaterina.

"Don't be ridiculous. It's the only weapon we've got. Wait until we get to Mars and then you can experiment to your heart's content."

The next couple of days passed pretty much the same. Ekaterina alternately chanted her way through every book she'd ever read and slept like a baby. She was oblivious to her companions so Alexandra left her alone, although she took the precaution of stowing the rest of the space being's cocaine in the front of the flyer.

As the hours measured themselves out in the flickering lights on the walls, ceiling and floor, she played endlessly through the same litany of doubts, hope and failed attempts to make sense of what was happening. Banjo wandered up and down the ship, peering intently at the surfaces. It was clear that he too was completely lost, unable to grasp the workings of this interplanetary vessel. Eventually he gave up, parked himself on the couch in the front cabin and read his book, like a voyager consulting a Baedecker Guide before he reached port.

The fourth planet grew larger and larger until it was the size of an orange.

Uncle bought you a telescope and we looked at Mars from your bedroom window at the dacha, arms around each other, trees rustling with a night breeze so deep it felt as if it came from the furthest regions of space. Finding that playbill for Man of the Future! has unlocked so much. Why now, after almost eight years silence, can't I get you out of my head? Because you should be here, dearest friend, sharing this with me, as we did the summer war broke out.

Alexandra guessed they approached along the planet's orbit so that one half lay in shadow. She remembered that when they left Earth she'd seen the faintest dusting of light as the terminator had swept in over the steppes from the Pacific. They were the lamps of Vladivostok, Harbin and countless other cities seen for the first time from space. So even at this distance from Mars she would have expected some evidence of civilisation. The brown smears should be resolving into a patchwork of farms and hydroponic plants clustered around the intersections of the mighty canals, fringed by the silver brocade of unimaginably advanced metropolises.

Something's wrong. It just looks like a bruised potato.

The ancient civilisations on this world would surely be lit by electrical or atomic power, yet the nightside of the planet was pitch black while the day was a meaningless chaos of abstract red and ochre, peppered here and there with craters like the moon.

"Where are the canals?" asked Banjo beside her, yawning and absent-mindedly scratching his testicles.

"If it's the Martian winter then maybe they've run dry. The savants believe that in summer, when the ice caps melt, they flow with water and the crops at the equator blossom so we see huge swathes of green vegetation through our telescopes. Perhaps we're approaching it at the wrong time of year." Even as she spoke it sounded all too glib. This ship and the Star Tsar had shown her that human science was still the tinkering of clothed apes on the fringes of the unknown.

"Is that a canal?" Banjo pointed at the ragged dint across the bottom half of the planet. "Looks more like an ordinary canyon to me but ye gods, it must be thousands of miles long."

Alexandra almost felt sorry for the man. Whatever outrageous fantasies were in his book wouldn't be found here.

"Is this Mars?"

She jumped. Ekaterina stood beside her. She moved with woozy languor but her eyes were bright - too bright.

"Here at last I will find my Pavel."

"How are you, fairest princess?" asked Banjo. Something in the way the actress swayed actually had him taking a few steps back, as if a tiger had appeared between them and he didn't want to alarm it.

"Translated, sublime. I remember so much."

Alexandra took the woman's hands and looked into her eyes. They tracked hers in turn and Ekaterina gave her a terrible smile. The singer's body tensed and Alexandra sensed a strength in her friend's muscles she'd never come across before. The commissar realised Ekaterina could rip her arms off in a second and bludgeon her to death with the soggy ends.

"You were in a trance, quoting endlessly from books, plays and poems."

"All the books, all the visions, all the love and every elegant conversation, murmur, poem, song, curse and blasphemy," Ekaterina plucked herself out of Alexandra's grasp. "Do you remember the winter ten years ago, when we skated on the Neva and Anton found the girl frozen under the ice? Her eyes were speckled with green - one hundred flecks in the left, ninety-five in the right. On the night of your birthday the printing press broke on the two thousand and twenty-ninth sheet of page sixteen of *Comrades Now!* at four minutes and six seconds to eleven and when you fixed it you cut your thumb, a slice half an inch long, and you bled thirty-eight droplets of your bright blood in the dust of the print shop. Poor sweet Alexandra."

The singer stroked her cheek. It was all the commissar could do not to recoil.

"My soul is a room swept clean and all the dead and dusty things that lay athwart my senses have been cast into oblivion. '*In my beloved Scottish Highlands, under a curtain of cold mists, between the sky of storms and dry sands, the grave of Ossian exists.*' The wonderful medicine of the Star Tsar has awoken me to new perceptions. My mind reaches out to the cosmos and I hear the communion of a thousand celestial beings. In here," she tapped her temple. "Constantly."

"You might want to lay off the snow for a while," said Banjo.

"And why would I do that?"

Alexandra riffled frantically through her thoughts for a suitable reply but was distracted by the vibrations under her feet getting stronger.

"Bugger me!" exclaimed the Englishman, staring out of the window. Alexandra turned and a wave of dizziness spiralled out from her heart. The bottom third of the clear bubble was filled with a red hemisphere. At the top she could see the outline of paper mountains against a thin smear of blue.

"I believe the ship is going to get ready to land," she pointed at the slanting couch. "This may protect us like the one at the back did when we left Earth."

"I hope this machine knows what it's doing," said Banjo "I don't fancy piling into Martian dirt at a thousand miles an hour. Isn't there anything we can press? We seem to be travelling awfully fast."

"We're in the hands of the Star Tsar," said Alexandra.

The engineer grumbled something incomprehensible and eased himself into the couch.

"Ekaterina, I suggest you retire to the rear compartment."

"I'm not missing this."

She lay back next to Banjo. Alexandra expected a wink and a leer but instead the man gave her the same glance of wary alarm as before. The commissar squeezed in on the other side, crammed up against the edge. The vibration increased and an orange glow tinged the bottom of the window.

"We're not going to burst into flames, are we?" asked Banjo.

CHAPTER FIFTEEN

No Helium or Zodanga then. No Dejah Thoris in nowt but her jewelled harness padding barefoot towards me across her silver-floored bedroom in the scarlet tower of Tardos Mors. Bloody hell. Mind you, it doesn't look like there'll be any of Alexandra's pompous sages either - all shiny egg heads and nary a bollock between them. If I'm going to die on the planet Mars at least it won't be from utter boredom.

Ekaterina grabbed his hand in a fierce grip. The ship shook violently, though the three of them were held fast by the blue sand. A ragged orange curtain poured up from the lower rim of the viewing bubble. The pressure built, shouldering him back into the couch. A deafening bang made him cry out. The hull shuddered and bent around him, rivets and seams creaking as if the whole vessel was about to pop apart. The rattling abruptly stopped and the craft eased into a long glide, the glow at the prow fading as they dipped into the atmosphere. Moments later they skimmed over a red desert littered with rocks and hills.

We've arrived on Mars.

Banjo slipped off the couch and managed to stagger on jelly legs to the window. Rust and sand under a pale sky threaded with fish-bone clouds so high and delicate they looked like scratches on metal. He hunted for any signs of life. Nothing, although those dark patches in the shadow side of the craters might be moss. They were travelling too fast to tell.

Clearly some intelligence directed the ship as it swooped over the dunes and tumbled scree. He stared entranced. Bugger disappointment. He'd had enough of his dreams beaten out of him over the years to know that the universe was, by and large, a foul and brutal place, and that the visions of jewelled warriors riding their six-legged Thoats across yellow and purple-lichened realms of wonder were mere fantasy in the end. This was far stranger, far more beautiful, simply because it was so very real.

Banjo struggled to grasp what had happened. He stood balanced on a little circle of red and ochre light on top of a wobbly ladder built from mad coincidence and fucked impossibility, yet each rung was just a tiny lurch upwards from last, the first one still planted in the pit of blood and shit where this had all begun. From a broken boiler in the arse end of nowhere to Mars.

I'm in my own real scientific romance, complete with a gorgeous, mad princess at my side. Even that fussy prig is playing to type. She's the swot who tags along and invents wizard gadgets to get us out of scrapes.

A few more craters flashed past, split by chasms. Far ahead, on the horizon, he saw the tip of a volcano emerging. *Holy Cow! That's above the air.*

"We must have girded a third of the planet already," said Alexandra. "I expect it's taking us to the Star Tsar's citadel."

"Why's he got his castle here? Do you think he visited all the other planets too?"

The commissar's face set in an expression of fierce wonder, her pupils flickering as she took in every rock, crag, boulder, ridge, crater and escarpment. Behind her Ekaterina sprawled across the couch, arms along the back and head slumped so she peered out from under her ragged fringe. Banjo had to admit she did an extremely good mad wife. Shame there wasn't an attic they could lock her in.

"Probably. I believe him to be a scientist sent here to study our solar system, who somehow became trapped on Earth. He didn't tell me where he came from - a distant star? But which one?"

And then they rose over a mountain range and the vessel

banked to fly along a wide valley towards a silver tower rising into the dusty sky. Alexandra gasped something in Russian and placed both hands on the window. The actress also jumped up and stalked forwards for a closer look.

"The palace of the Star Tsar," said Banjo.

"No, I don't think so," answered the commissar.

The Englishman peered through the glass. The tower, growing bigger by the second, resembled a long spear tip joined to three diamond-shaped pods resting in the sand. The penny dropped.

"My god, it's a space dreadnought."

The rocket turned their own ship into a toy pram. *It must be half a mile high at least.* They slowed dramatically, the artificial gravity buffering them from the change in velocity, and coasted past. All three craned their necks to stare up at the titan lofting far above them into the copper air. The hull was a blue-tinged mirror reflecting the surrounding landscape. No sign of a hatch or portholes. It reminded him one of those modern sculptures that had been all the rage in Paris before the war - lines and shapes and lumps by that Italian twit he'd met in Montmartre, the one who used to take his clothes off when drunk and clearly couldn't draw to save his life.

"It must be designed to fly between the stars themselves."

The Star Tsar came in that, by himself? You'd need a crew, surely. Where are they all?

"There!"

Ekaterina pointed. Half a mile away he saw a cluster of boxes in a random pile, like children's blocks knocked over in a temper. Jumbled squares of glass or crystal glittered in the sunlight. Three more vessels identical to their own sat in a neat line next to a long rectangular structure. They flew beyond the last one. The ship turned to face the buildings and settled to the ground in a cloud of dust. Banjo heard a humming and clattering from the hull outside and a shadow floated through the drifting sand towards a featureless wall of pale yellow metal.

"The flying machine," exclaimed Alexandra. "It must have come with us in a secret compartment."

"I reckon that was our pilot."

The sentinel touched the wall and an oval section detached, floating behind the artificial creature as it returned, dragging a wide pipe from the building to their ship. A clang and a freezing draught brought in the acrid scent of sulphur and rust. Tentatively Banjo peered down the vessel. The door was open onto a transparent tunnel leading into the compound.

"Why can't we go outside? Does this mean the air's poisonous?"

"Or too thin for us to breathe," said Alexandra.

Ekaterina pushed past them both and walked into the corridor before they could stop her. A few yards further on she froze, hissed and stepped back, arms arced down at her sides, fingers clawed, like an eagle about to dance a flamenco.

"Her."

A woman lay motionless on the rock halfway between their own ship and the next vessel. She sprawled on her back, head turned towards them, her dress tissued around her body. Dust covered her face and eyes.

"It's Galina," Alexandra's expression was full of hard sadness. "Pavel's lover."

"The one he chucked Ekaterina for?"

The commissar nodded.

"If she's dead then I fear he is too. She'll take it badly."

That seemed an understatement. From where Banjo stood all the actress had to do was stick her tongue out and turn blue and she'd be the spitting image of the Goddess Kali, ready to liberate a few souls, including theirs. While the two of them hovered uncertainly at a respectful distance, he tried to work out how the girl had died.

"Why's she out there? Can we go and have a look?"

"No. I think that's how she was killed. Somehow she ended up on the surface and perished from lack of oxygen. See how her eyes glitter in the light? They're frozen. These walls protect us but. .." she held her hand close to the transparent wall of the tunnel. "Feel that?"

Half an inch away it was like rubbing a block of ice with his palm. The barrier between them and outside looked thick enough. Banjo noticed soap bubble rainbows drifting sluggishly through the material. Whatever the science, it protected them from hellish cold. He shuddered. *Poor lass.* Alexandra turned away.

"We can't waste time. We have to find the Star Tsar's elixir and return to Earth as soon as possible."

He had to admire the Bolshevik's bravery when the woman walked up to Ekaterina and talked to her. Madam ignored Alexandra so she held her wrist and spoke urgently again. The singer rounded on her friend with an expression that rattled even Banjo, and went to slap her face. After his own experience of being smacked in the mouth by the tanked-up coke-fiend he fully expected the commissar to go bouncing off the walls. To his surprise Alexandra grabbed her friend's forearm in her other hand and despite Ekaterina's whole weight being behind the blow neither of them moved an inch. Banjo flexed his own arm. The muscles felt balloon tight. *It's transformed us all into super beings.*

Ekaterina turned her back on Alexandra and stalked into the building. They trailed after her and the engineer found himself tripping and stumbling along. *Low gravity, just as in Burroughs.* That cheered him up. At least the author got one thing right. A wide passageway with a jigsaw wall of brushed metal stretched into the distance. The light was as grainy as inside the flyer and full of muted blues and greys. Geometric patches of radiance fell from doorways and odd-angled windows to shatter across the surfaces but Banjo didn't spot any of the bright symbols from the control panels in their vessel. Square entrances led off into the complex on either side, ending in sealed hatches.

Now where? It was impossible to tell in the harsh algebra of this alien fortress. None of the chambers appeared to have any recognisable function and most of them were empty. Sand and rocks spread out on the floor of one, patterned like the Buddhist garden he'd seen in Kyoto. He picked up a stone. *I'm holding a piece of Mars in my hand.*

A series of deafening clangs echoed through the structure. They peered cautiously round a corner to find a door leading further in. Beyond lay a second cube - still nothing. Another clang, another open valve. Banjo wasn't sure about this at all. Whatever opened doors could just as easily shut them again and pump out the air or drop monsters through a trapdoor in the ceiling. *Mind you, it's a bit late in the day to start worrying about that.*

"Something is guiding our path," said Alexandra. She called out in Russian. No answer.

The fourth space led to a circular hall. In the middle a second chamber with glass windows formed the hub of the wheel. He looked inside - knee-high white liquid billowed like bedsheets shaken out by an invisible maid.

"We've found it. How do we get it out and back to Earth?"

They walked in opposite directions round the room but couldn't discover any way to get inside. Ekaterina stood by the entrance they'd come through and rubbed her temples.

"What's the matter?" asked Banjo.

"I don't know. Voices whispering to me. They're angry."

Alexandra tapped the window beside her with a nail and jumped back with a shout of alarm.

What in God's name?

Banjo saw the elixir pull in on itself, shrinking over the metal floor to form a column twice the height of a man. Wicked porcelain spikes bristled from its surface, all pointing towards them.

That doesn't look good.

A shadow moved past a window on the other side of the hub. He pushed himself away from the glass and stepped out into the room, ready to meet whatever approached. Alexandra spotted it too. Ekaterina pulled out her gun, but the Bolshevik waved at her to keep it hidden.

"It's not the flying machine," hissed Banjo. Perhaps it was a second Star Tsar, though it looked too small. The commissar had said the being was like a slug but bigger than a bear. This was different. Another creature - maybe one of the cabinets on wheels or its six-limbed attendants.

A man limped round the curve, clothes in tatters and hair a wild, clotted mess. The ever-present blue mist turned him into a grainy shadow but Banjo saw red eyes staring out of a sunken face. His bare feet left bloody prints on the metal and dark, treacle spots fell from his wrists. *He's tried to kill himself by chewing his hands off.*

The man gave a sad laugh and muttered something in Russian.

Oh bollocks. It's her Pavel. The bastard's alive, damn him.

A gunshot and a bullet hummed past his ear to spark against the wall beyond the newcomer.

Jesus Christ!

Alexandra shouted at Ekaterina. The singer held her Mauser in her fists, aiming at the raggedy man, although the barrel shook and tears poured down her face. Out of the corner of his eye Banjo saw the white spiked mass slamming itself repeatedly against the glass.

The gunfire triggered a defence reaction. God help us if it gets out.

Pavel lifted his hands up towards the actress - gasping with the sheer effort. Alexandra stood between the two lovers like a crucifix with arms held out to hold them apart. She spoke urgently to them both in Russian. Banjo had no idea what to do or say. *Come on love, he's clearly very sorry.* However this played out they'd have to jump the singer and get that bloody pistol off her. She didn't have that many bullets left, did she? If a single round could shatter a window they were truly fucked.

Ekaterina lowered the gun and stepped forward, saying *Pavel* over and over again, like a song. Alexandra, clearly thinking the tension had eased, let her pass and the lovers met. The actor put one hand to his face and started to sob.

"Are we good?"

"Be quiet," snapped the Bolshevik.

The engineer watched his opportunity at romance disappear as the mad theatre manager took Ekaterina's fingers in his.

"He's not having any of my grub on the way back."

The actor jerked his lover's arm upwards so the Mauser pointed at his heart. He must have hooked a thumb around the trigger but wasn't quick enough. The actress bent his wrist - Banjo heard the bones crack - and the bullet hit the nearest hub window dead centre. Even as Pavel screamed and fell to his knees clutching his shattered forearm, a white wave poured out over the two lovers.

Alexandra yelled, leaping forwards. Banjo grabbed her arm and hauled her back to the entrance, gawping in horror at the glass-spattered chaos boiling outside the inner chamber. The white fluid enveloped Pavel and he changed into a marble statue of himself. He danced a demented tarantella even as the elixir turned red and his prancing outline collapsed in on itself. Banjo turned to Ekaterina, expecting the same grotesque dissolution. Instead a smooth, man-size egg rose out of the spot where she'd stood. He heard muffled shrieking. *The poor bitch is inside.* The fluid, still mixed with Pavel's blood, raced towards them, building itself up into another wave.

"Ekaterina!" screamed Alexandra.

"Run you idiot!"

Banjo shoved Alexandra back the way they'd come. To his relief the lass sprinted ahead in loping strides, careening from wall to doorway as she struggled with Mars' gravity. Doors opened and closed without any logic, as if the fortress itself had gone insane. Banjo didn't care. Any second now that amorphous tide would clutch his feet and drag him into a foul crushing storm. He daren't look back and instead tried to glimpse its reflection in the crazy angles of the windows and rooms they hurtled through. Nothing - only endless mocking patterns of grey and blue metal and swirling air. They burst into a room with a sealed exit he hadn't come across before - a disc in the wall studded with pipes and symbols. The door behind them slammed shut and he swore he heard furious splashing on the other side. Bolts clunked and valves hissed. He swapped glances with Alexandra. Her round eyes stared at him, full of mad, terrible questions.

Oh shit. We're dead.

The circular portal swung open and beyond it lay the Martian desert.

Ekaterina had killed them all. She should have let Pavel shoot himself. Instead she'd made it look like they were attacking the elixir, provoking whatever intelligence controlled it to see them as dangerous enemies.

We failed. The first encounter between mankind and the stars had turned into a bloody farce, a dancing Grand Guignol pantomime orchestrated by their theatre of the absurd. *The Star Tsar extended his hand to us and we shat in it.*

Alexandra sank to her knees on the metal floor, waiting to die as the air emptied into the wilderness. Banjo stood with his eyes and mouth clamped shut, cheeks puffed out like an overfed squirrel. Beyond the open doorway a dust devil chased across the rubble-strewn valley.

At least I'll meet my end with the image of futurity burned in my soul. If only you were here with me, Natasha. Just one last time. I love you. She struggled to her feet so she could stagger outside and perish looking at the Star Tsar's cosmic dreadnought. Banjo opened an eye.

"Why isn't anything happening?"

The clod was right. Surely they should be dead by now, frozen and suffocated. Yet Alexandra felt no different. Banjo walked to the opening.

"Hang on. What's this?"

Alexandra joined him, curiosity briefly supplanting rage and misery. Could the atmosphere on Mars support humans after all? If so why the airlocks? Why the tunnel from the ship to the complex if it was possible to walk outside? As she got closer she noticed a rainbow shimmer.

"We're protected. There's some kind of seal in the doorway like a soap bub..."

Banjo's hand touched the light and with a muffled whoop of

surprise he hurled through the air to land a few yards away in a cloud of dust. The membrane quivered with the sound of a harp string. Alexandra instinctively held her breath. No sign of the atmosphere escaping through the breach. But the stupid Englishman had got himself killed because of his total lack of self-control and now the commissar was stuck in this place on her own.

Banjo sat up and examined his hands - front and back. He plucked at his smock. *Now what's the fool doing?* He looked odd, as if he'd just clambered fully clothed out of a river with his hair and beard plastered against his head and neck. He opened his mouth a few times, grinned, waved at Alexandra, and came bounding towards the citadel. Judging by the grotesque faces he was pulling and his gesticulations, he was trying to entice the commissar outside. Alexandra stepped forward to take a closer look at the barrier. Before she could pull back she was yanked off her feet, her body smothered in what felt like warm damp muslin. Sky and land tumbled over each other and she thudded into the rocky ground, the air driven out of her lungs by the impact. Hands that didn't know their own strength pulled her upright. Something tight and clammy clung to her skin and clothes.

"It's wonderful - a magic space caul." Banjo's voice bellowed in the centre of her skull. "It lets us see and breathe and everything." Alexandra flinched and put her fingers into his ears to block out the shouting but they pressed against a slippery plug.

"Don't rip it. You'll die."

What did Pavel murmur to Ekaterina, just before he tried to shoot himself? "I tore the veil from her eyes but the truth was too much and she perished". She bounced in the direction of their ship.

"Hey, where are you going?"

Under the fine powdered Martian soil Galina's skin shone pale blue and her pupils glittered ice. Fragments of membrane lay around her. She looked down at the girl and a sudden wave of anger washed through her.

How many women have to die so men can make their 'great art'?

"Never mind her. We've got to get back inside and rescue the princess." Banjo headed for the tunnel. There was no way in and no sign of the Star Tsar's flying machine. They searched the outside of the citadel for another entrance. Alexandra noticed that all the windows were now blank white. *Was it like that before? Surely the fluid can't have filled the entire structure, can it?* When they returned to the airlock door they found it closed. They struggled to open it again but there weren't any visible controls and no amount of pushing would budge it. Battling against fear and hopelessness Alexandra circled the fortress three more times. In the end Banjo grabbed her by the arm. For a second she didn't recognise the Englishman and had to stop herself from lashing out.

"She's gone. You heard the screams."

All my poor dolls, every single one, broken and lost because of me.

Alexandra stared around.

"I'm standing on the surface of Mars. I have come further and done more than anyone alive and yet I have failed at everything. The cosmos mocks me."

She knew her voice was trembling so she spoke as slowly and as carefully as she could, staring at the horizon, trying to locate an anchor in anything. She couldn't even bring herself to look at that idiot Banjo, she was so ashamed. "We must find a way to take the fluid back to the Star Tsar."

"Don't be daft lass, it hates us."

"How can it? It's just a thing."

"With a mind of its own and clearly on the attack. You saw how it acted when it spotted us through the window, and what it did to those loonies. It's not going to let us carry it away in buckets. Get anywhere near and we'll end up like the others."

That voice in her head - that thudding, stupid voice with its brutal, ignorant truth.

"So what do we do?"

Banjo looked across the valley towards the mighty interstellar craft.

"What do you reckon Alexandra? Fuck knows how we're going to get back to Earth as we can't get into our flyer. So what do you say we find out whether that great beauty has a hatch or doorway?"

She looked up at the vast ship, beautiful and silver. Needle prow glinted against the dark sky. Alexandra yearned to climb aboard and fly across the galaxy, to speed over ice-shattered moons and crimson oceans under double suns where antediluvian creatures clawed and tore at each other. *To stand before the beings of other stars, the legions of Super Science who have thrown off the shackles of capital and forged a true communist brotherhood of joy and praxis. And what will I say? I am a woman from Earth - a fool, a liar, murderer and wretched failure. Unwashed and vile, in a uniform still stained with the blood and shit of the trenches. Sick in the head, diseased, just as Cousin Anton said all those years ago.* She turned away from the vessel and walked towards the edge of a chasm a mile distant.

"Where are you going?"

She guessed Banjo was trailing after her like a lost dog. God, she hated the man. She turned and shoved him. The low gravity had the engineer staggering back, arms windmilling.

"What the buggery?"

"Stay away from me!" yelled Alexandra. "Stay away from me, you shit. You are everything that cripples us - lecherous, stupid, filthy and ignorant. You are the dregs of the world that keep humanity shackled in the pit amid blood and death. You hold us back from this," she pointed at the starship. "You!"

"Me?! It was your coke-snorting actors that messed all this up, not me. I egged on you when you were too much a coward. If it wasn't for me you'd be sitting in a bloody committee meeting in Petrograd like the scribbling nabob turd you are. You're all the same you Russians. One minute you act as if you're shitting Brillo pads, the next you're hopped to the eyeballs on opium and hashish and pissing on about some eternal soul. A right bunch of fucking useless cunts, the lot of you."

Alexandra picked up a rock and threw it. It bounced harmlessly off the man's chest. The Englishman looked around and spotted a boulder. He hefted it over his head and let fly. It sailed over the commissar to land a hundred yards away. Banjo staggered, lost his balance and sat down in the dirt with an oath.

"NATASHA SHOULD BE HERE, NOT YOU!" Alexandra shrieked. Unable to look at the ignorant bastard a moment longer she turned and ran sobbing for the ravine.

CHAPTER SIXTEEN

Banjo knew he should go after Alexandra. The twit had just lost all her friends and looked like she was going to chuck herself off a cliff in some ludicrous Russian act of romantic despair. But to be honest, right now, he'd be more likely to give the officious turd a helpful boot up the backside. He stomped back to the interstellar flyer, cursing the arrogant Red shit all the way. *Blaming me for fucking up the journey when it was that pair of demented theatricals who ruined everything. Bloody cheek.*

So here they were, locked outside. He wondered how long these magic suits would protect them. They weren't big enough to contain much air but somehow he managed to keep breathing, even if it felt as though someone had stuffed a wet flannel in his mouth.

The starship towered over him. Beyond it the orange haze thinned to darkness and directly above he spotted a cluster of faint stars in line with the spear tip. The fuselage wasn't the single mirror-sheened hull he'd seen when they first arrived. It was jigsawed together from geometric panels of brushed metal. Close up the reflection of the landscape faded into a chaos of cross-hatched shapes, each a different size and shape, as if the Star Tsar had crafted his flagship from some bizarre alien alphabet. He assumed the three pods contained the engines but failed to find any scorch-marks or damage to the rock where they rested on their hemispherical ends.

No-one in the citadel except that mad fluid, and no sign of any crew here. On Earth a dreadnought this size would have hundreds of sailors. Were they all dead? Asleep in that machine like King Arthur and his knights, waiting for an idiot goat-herd to find the secret entrance to their enchanted chamber? Or had the Star Tsar really sailed the endless etheric currents between the stars on his own?

Speculation was pointless. The only way he'd learn anything was by getting inside. He walked around the ship - no sign of any hatch or ladder. Far up he thought he spotted the glint of a porthole but it was hard to see. The sun, as cold and brittle as a Yorkshire autumn, hovered above a distant ridge and the light was fading, turning everything to tarnished copper. Fed up, he picked up a stone and hurled it as high as he could. Weak gravity gave it an impressive lob and it spanged off the curved hull before spinning away in a lazy arc. A slot opened up beneath the tip and a flying machine slid out.

Oh shit.

He glanced around but couldn't see the one that had piloted them from Earth. Was this the same machine? In that case surely it was on their side, even if he'd chucked a rock at it. If anything was going to open up the rocket, it would be the sentinel.

Banjo jumped up and down, waving his arms. The creature drifted down in a slow arc, shadow rippling over the hull. As it got closer its tentacles radiated out in a lizard fan. That didn't look promising - too much like a threat. He fought the urge to turn and run as it dropped in front of him.

"I want to get inside this spaceship," he said in English. No response. He tried again in French and the lights on its waist danced back and forth. *Does it understand French now? Did it pull it out of Madam's head before she was eaten by that enormous rice pudding?* He pantomimed climbing up the side of the craft, feeling a complete fool. The machine drifted forwards menacingly. He walked backwards, hands up. *The bastard does know what I want, it just won't give it to me.* It speeded up and he found himself bouncing along with no idea where he was going - to the Star Tsar's flyer? The building? Over the edge of a cliff after that Red prat?

Alexandra shouted a word in the middle of his head and the drone stopped. The commissar stood ten yards away with her arms folded and a face like Queen Victoria at the wrong time of the month. She spoke a few more words and the machine rose over their heads and floated towards the other flyer.

"It only responds to Slavonic." She didn't need to add *you total cretin*, Banjo heard it clear enough. He decided not to tell her his theory about the French.

"What did you say?" he asked.

"*Take us home.* We have a duty to return and try to help the Star Tsar, even if we've failed here. If you want to head off on your silly adventures be my guest but I'm returning. We owe it to the rest of our fellow human beings to share what we've found."

Damn the pompous git to hell but she was right.

"Calmed down a bit now, have you? I'm sorry all your friends got killed, and glad you didn't jump after them."

"Suicide is a bourgeois affectation and a total abdication of responsibility."

Oh give it a rest, for pity's sake.

"Who's Natasha again?"

Muscles bunched in the lass's cheeks and he could have sworn her eyes welled up as she stared at a spot on the ground.

"My cousin."

"The one who read Wells and Verne and stuff?"

She nodded.

"You're right. It would have been nice if she'd been here too, if she was into astronomy and all that caper."

He was trying to cheer her up. It didn't seem to be having the desired effect. Better change the subject.

"At least we came to Mars," Banjo looked round with his hands on his hips. Through a gap in the cliffs he saw rock-strewn sands curving up to the foothills of a mountain vaster than he'd ever seen.

"And we may come again," said the voice in his head, kinder now. He looked at her in surprise. *Fucking hell, a smile. Now there's a rarity.*

Banjo stuck his hand out. Alexandra shook it. Beyond her the drone detached the articulated tunnel from their flyer, leaving the door open. Air puffed out in a cloud.

"It's letting us get back on board," said Banjo. They made their way to the vessel. As he passed a fortress window, he caught a glimpse of bloody swirls passing across a white-blanked window and shuddered. *Poor bastards.*

Alexandra scrambled into the craft and turned around to look at him, her face unreadable. *You're not going to leave me marooned on Mars, are you?* She helped him climb up. The door slid shut. Banjo noticed that the entrance to the forward part of the ship was sealed. A hiss filled the room and his suit ablated into cellophane shreds. He sniffed - air. The partition irised open and Ekaterina stared at them, clawed hands at her side and eyes burning through her tangled hair.

Alexandra's instinct was to rush up and embrace Ekaterina. The singer's expression stopped her. For the first time she looked completely calm - a Futurist sculptor's face of glass and geometry - utterly inhuman. She watched the commissar as if she too was an unearthly creature. Banjo was uncharacteristically quiet. She'd expected the Englishman to be slavering all over the actress. He kept well back and she couldn't blame him.

"Why didn't the white fluid destroy you as it did Pavel?"

Alexandra tried to make it not sound like an accusation. Ekaterina tapped her temple very slowly.

"It protected me, of course. And now it speaks to me in here."

"Speaks to you? What's it saying?"

"It shows me visions of worlds and oceans and skies and raving creatures that dance on wings of light and asks me if I know them by name. I do. The Dola Porion, Meska, Mara and Blud. They abandoned our planet in horror at Man's cruelty, thousands upon thousands. To call on them all would take more centuries than the world has left. Pavel is in here," she smiled and pressed her hand to her breast. "And here. He speaks to me as well, begs forgiveness in that tiny, wretched voice of his." Her smile was horrible to see. *"Ekaterina I never loved her, I only ever wanted you,"* she whined in imitation of whatever she heard in her dark recesses of her transformed mind.

Was it true? Could she actually communicate with the fluid? Maybe there was still hope. Alexandra walked to the nearest observation bubble and looked at the windows of the nearby building. They were paper white.

"If you can you talk with it, ask it to go back with us to Earth to rescue the Star Tsar."

Ekaterina laughed a mad, poisonous skirl.

"Jesus Christ," muttered Banjo.

"Our planet is a pit of lies and betrayal where evil men destroy the souls of their lovers, tearing them out to bury them in fields of mud and blood and gas. Now they seek to chain the poison that dwells in the heart of every sun and use it to wipe out whole cities in the blink of an eye. They feed on children and offer them up to Moloch, casting them into the furnaces of what they laughingly call their new world. I told it everything Alexandra, everything. It shall never come to Earth and neither will any of the other creatures of light and star-joy."

She was hopelessly mad. Alexandra took her friend's wrists and looked into her eyes.

"You who guard the Star Tsar's fortress," she said to whatever might have curled itself around Ekaterina's soul. "If you really are in there and can understand me, the being that sent us here needs your help. He's dying."

"Poor sweet Alexandra."

Ekaterina stroked her cheek. Alexandra didn't know what else to do. She turned away from the remains of her last broken doll and walked to the front of the ship. The sun had set and two bright stars hovered above the distant crags. *Venus and Earth.*

"What was all that about?"

Alexandra told him. The engineer whistled.

"Finally cracked, poor lass."

"I think the voices in her head are just hers. She's not talking to the elixir, or celestial creatures, or anyone, only ghosts. We've failed. We should return to Earth."

"Perhaps we'll be able to bring the creature here so it can be cured."

"No. The reason it sent us in the first place was because it's no longer strong enough to make the journey. We have to go back and I'll contact the committee of Soviets and get them to marshal all the knowledge and skill of our savants to try and do something before it's too late."

And I'll find you, Natasha. I'll go Petrograd and find you. You must be a great scientist in the service of the proletariat by now. I've realised, after all this time, why I stopped writing to you after my row with Anton. There was one more revolution that had to happen, one more truth of my own material condition waiting to be revealed, but I was too scared to face it. I love you. Will you forgive me? If I bring all the wonders of the stars we whispered about at night in Uncle's dacha and lay them at your feet, will you forgive me? Will you love me?

"You won't make it past Moses and his lunatics on your own," said Banjo. "If that flying machine's piloting this ship to Earth we might be able to persuade it to help us as well."

Alexandra doubted it. She'd no idea how the alien would react when it found out they'd failed and that the fault lay with the idiot actor the creature had sent before him. If the Star Tsar was really dying would it resign itself to its fate? Would it believe Alexandra's offer of aid on behalf of the Soviets? Or would it use its Super Science to unleash a hellish vengeance on humanity in its last death throes?

They rose up from the surface of Mars. Banjo gave a cry and ran to the forward observation bubble, pressing his hands against the glass and craning to catch a final glimpse of the immense star rocket standing brushed-silver in the ochre dust. Alexandra knew he was watching his dreams slip away. The ship rattled and lurched, accelerating through the thin atmosphere but the engineer didn't move. Neither did Ekaterina, who was rooted to the spot, staring at the cabaret of fantastical monsters in her head. As for Alexandra, she couldn't even bear to look outside. She pulled her coat around her and sat in the corner with her knees drawn up - the same position she used to take during the endless, dead silences between the German artillery barrages. This time she couldn't lose herself in daydreams of future possibilities. Instead she stared at the inhuman geometry dancing across the opposite wall.

The lift off eventually forced her into the blue couch where she fell asleep. She dreamed of hunting for the Star Tsar in his pumice labyrinth, Ekaterina's laughter chasing her through tunnels that grew increasingly steep until she was crawling on hands and knees like a baby. She came to the centre of the maze but all she found was the dead body of Natasha, ice-eyed and swathed in alien gossamer. Beyond her, in the darkness, glowed the red eyes of Tugarin the earth dragon. *So it's true! I know what you are. We all do. You're sick in the head, Alexandra,* it growled.

I'm not, she screamed back at the demon. *I know who and what I am at last.*

She woke to find the ship in space and the planet Mars already the size of a pinhead in one of the rear-facing domes. Banjo still stood at the forward observation bubble, head lowered and arms folded. Ekaterina slept curled up on the other side of the couch. Alexandra let her rest and joined the Englishman. A blue spark glistened in the centre of the void. The sight filled her with wretched sadness.

"You know what we didn't find on Mars," said Banjo, gazing at the stars.

"Any electrical girls or six-armed monsters."

"So they're not part of the Star Tsar's gang."

Alexandra remembered the wheeled boxes and the smeared dough face staring up at her out of the mountain pit, oil-drop eyes filled with cold hunger. Neither possessed the clean, inhuman precision and delicacy of the space being's science.

Who made you?

"The Star Tsar told me that the second men, the Whites, tried to steal his knowledge to fashion weapons," she said. "Do you remember how we thought the flying machine was created by a Tsarist scientist?"

"Are you saying Russian aristos built those perambulating corpses? I see how someone might cobble one together but why? And what would it do? Hundreds of those trolling towards you across the battlefield would be a bit alarming but I doubt they'd do much damage. Besides, what science can grow a man an extra pair of arms?"

Alexandra didn't have an answer but a phrase kept rolling around inside her mind. What did the creature tell her? *They built fortresses in the mountains and changed their slaves into machines.* She'd forgotten in the wonder of their journey to Mars, but now the image of Ekaterina's brother carried down the ramp by those things - *Baba Yaga's spider children* - played itself out endlessly. They'd have no opportunity to investigate if she was to get to Petrograd in time to help the alien. Besides she wouldn't want to go into the lower levels of those mines without several hundred armed comrades at her back. Yet escaping the valley meant retracing their route through the mountain and she had a horrible suspicion that their arrival had alerted every vile abomination living in those unlit boreholes.

"If no-one's faffed about with the locomotive it'll take me two to three hours to get her up and running from cold. That's when we'll be most vulnerable. After that you can run her through the mountain at top speed and you'll squash any of those maggoty buggers flat."

"You're not coming too? I need you to drive the train."

What would the Englishman do in the valley by himself? Banjo let out a sound like a tired buffalo settling into a waterhole and continued to glower at the cosmos.

"Do you think Madam's right? Do you think the universe hates us because of all that misery and bloodshed and horror? Are we unworthy to go out there?" he gestured at the stars.

"Unworthy before whom? God? The universe? We killed God, and the universe doesn't care. We have to make our own worth now. Ekaterina talks to her own madness, no-one else."

The engineer sniffed.

"I hope you're right."

They spent the next two days wrapped in their own thoughts. The actress was so silent that once or twice Alexandra thought her dead. Ekaterina's eyes looked at nothing though her lips moved. It seemed like she was having conversations with someone - perhaps those gossamer spirits of the cosmos she'd told them about. At least she wasn't hissing through anyone's collected works anymore. She didn't even seem interested in the Star Tsar's cocaine.

Alexandra constantly ran through their brief adventure on Mars, trying to understand what she could have done differently. If she'd been fast enough to get between Ekaterina and Pavel she might have prevented their death struggle. But the creature's intelligent elixir had already decided they were a threat. It must have seen the actor murder Galina. How did he do it? Did he entice her outside into the copper and rust desert and rip the membrane from her face so she suffocated? Why? The fool had fallen in love with the girl. Why kill her? The commissar had met her once or twice and she was unremarkable - another ingénue seduced by promises of revolutionary freedom and art. What horrors did Pavel see on his way to the Red Planet? In the mines? In Kirill's village and the space creature's citadel? *Pascal says infinite spaces send us mad so let's go mad together, Alexandra!* Natasha's voice burst into her memory like an arctic wave and she gasped. The window was empty and full of light. Looking out at the ocean of stars, she longed to spread her arms and soar. In that second the dream came back to her and the words she'd yelled at Tugarin. *I know who and what I am at last.*

Alexandra stared out at space for half an hour before gathering the courage to speak.

"Your Aunt..."

"Auntie Jessie and her friend Constance? What about her?"

"Why do you keep saying 'friend' like that?"

Banjo laughed.

"Well, she was a very special friend, if you get my drift."

The stars rotated as the ship changed course.

"They were lovers? And nobody minded?"

"Jessie was the black sheep of the family. It's funny with Quakers. On the one hand they're all for suffrage and the equality of men and women and all that. Then next second they're banging on about godliness and sin, well my lot were anyway. Jessie told them all to fuck off and shacked up with her fancy lass in a flat in Headingley. The Bohemian set there don't give a monkey's who does what to whom. Why do you ask?"

"Nothing. It doesn't matter."

"Ah, right. I see. Well, I've nothing against the Abominable Practices of the Greeks myself. Condemn buggery and that's half the navy and nine tenths of the Colonial Civil Service gone. Love is love as far as I'm concerned, though until the world turns you'll need to be discrete."

She felt her ears go red.

"I wasn't talking about myself!"

"Didn't say you were. But don't end up like my mate Walter. He was a clerk in the Customs Services in Jaipur who spent most of his spare time romping his way through the local menfolk. Wrote an epic poem about it called *The Buggeriad*. Silly bastard had two hundred copies privately printed in Calcutta and one accidentally turned up on some nabob's desk in the Colonial Office. That was the end of Walter. I suppose it's easier to hide with lasses."

"No-one should have to hide. The Soviet Government has abolished the cruel laws of the Tsarists and the prejudices of the church and in our new world all forms of sexual love are equal, noble and cherished."

"Glad to hear it. Auntie Jessie and Florence would be pleased."

But will Natasha? I never said anything to her because I didn't understand, but now I do. A terrible fear settled on her heart. *What if she hates me too, like Anton? How much of this new universe must I give to her to make her love me?*

They returned to Earth. The ship's entry into the thicker

atmosphere of their own world was a vicious, gut-churning affair of fire, screaming metal and an endless bone-grinding pressure, finishing with an unholy bang flashing white around the nose of the craft. When the punishing deceleration had stopped and they were flying smoothly again, Alexandra went to the window. The ship drifted down over Russia, returning across the eastern seaboard. She spotted Sakhalin in an iceberg-flecked sea but Vladivostok was too far south. In less than an hour they'd passed over the Yablonoi Mountains and she recognised the valley of the Old Believers. Her hands were shaking. She interlaced her fingers to try to get them to stop. *Now I have to tell the Star Tsar we've failed.*

"It wasn't your fault." Banjo scowled down at her. "I'll come with you when you face this thing."

"Thank you," and she meant it.

"Hold out your hand."

The Englishman dropped a red stone into her palm. He tossed another into the air and caught it.

"Souvenirs from Mars until we go back. We *are* going back, by the way, whatever happens."

The commissar laughed and pocketed the rock. The vessel coasted into the cave and the door opened.

The second they stepped outside Ekaterina fell to her knees and dabbed at the white line stretching across the cavern. She sobbed.

"Dead."

The temperature plummeted and shadows filled the hangar. Alexandra forced herself to look down. The strand had yellowed. She touched it and the surface flaked away to reveal what looked like iron filings underneath. *Tiny machines with their own thoughts.*

She followed the thread across the floor and into a passageway. It angled hither and thither through the pumice labyrinth until she came to the circular chamber. The stench made her stagger back, grabbing the edge of the archway for support.

"Jesus Christ, what a stink," Banjo turned to be noisily sick against the wall. Something black, as big as a cow and multi-jointed lay in the centre of the room, unmoving. "What the fuck is that monstrosity?"

"The Star Tsar." Alexandra could barely bring herself to look at it.

"It's so pretty," wailed Ekaterina.

Crying stopped, the singer wafted past them and stood beside the creature. The fog covering the ceiling had fallen with the alien and the last curls dissipated through the tatters of her dress. Alexandra looked beyond her mad friend and saw the white figure still sitting with its hands on its knees. Summoning up her courage she sidled around the edge of the room to stand before it. The body was cracked and yellow up to the chest but the skin above glistened, moving in sluggish ripples.

"You failed." The voice filled the mountain.

"The man you sent before was mad for love and murdered his companion. Your essence saw this act as a threat." She pointed at Ekaterina. "When she met him they fought and unleashed its anger. The powder you gave her consumed her mind. Why? We're not strong enough to control the powers you force on us."

She stopped herself. What was the point of blaming the Star Tsar for humanity's weakness?

"The new soul she thrives on is pure and clarified to help her peer beyond into the mysteries of other worlds," said the avatar.

"It drove her mad and your white fluid has locked itself in your citadel on Mars, ready to kill anything that goes near. We barely escaped with our lives."

The alien had no answer.

"I can journey to Petrograd and return with our greatest scientists to help you," said Alexandra.

"It's too late. I am already dead. This voice is just the echo of my mind, encased in engines that also fade."

Alexandra sank to her knees.

"What's it saying?" Banjo stood beside her. The commissar didn't know how to answer. *You came to nurture humanity with your Super Science and we failed you.*

"You have power over what is left of my dominion inside this mountain. Use it," the voice creaked into brittle silence.

"To do what?"

But the Star Tsar was nothing more than a cellophane-cracked dummy.

"Let's go back to Mars," said Banjo.

"What?"

"Let's go back to Mars, now, and get on that big spaceship and explore the universe - the three of us."

Alexandra got to her feet and looked at Ekaterina who stood next to the corpse of the Star Tsar, staring off into the distance, hands spasming in claws.

"Lady Macbeth'll be alright - won't you fair one?"

Her face twitched to peer at Banjo, hawk eyes filled with alien intelligence that tracked him from under her fringe.

"Its powers are ours now," she whispered.

"There you go. We'll tell that flying machine to open up the rocket and take us out there." He pointed at the ceiling.

"No," said Alexandra.

"What do you mean no?"

"We have to bring this knowledge to the savants of our age. There is so much they can learn. Just understanding the way it farmed the food for the Old Believers will help our scientists solve the terrible famines of the world and create a new healthy Soviet man."

"You're a stuck record," thundered the engineer. "It's all bollocks. Do you seriously think this'll be used for the betterment of common folk like you and me? They'll take it off you, put a bullet through your skull for your pains and turn it into bigger and more horrible weapons. Didn't the war teach you anything?"

"I won't believe that. I can't believe that. Soviet man..."

"Soviet man can kiss my arse. Alexandra, come with me to the stars. Princess, you too."

"Banjo, if you're worried about your safety as an enemy of the Soviet Union I give you my word I will do all in my power to guarantee you safe passage and forgiveness for your crimes so you can eventually go back to England."

"Eventually go back to England?! The entire fucking universe awaits us you cowardly turd."

He rubbed his hands over his beard and through his hair, and gave a huge sigh.

"Oh what's the point? I'm going into space."

Banjo stamped out of the chamber. Alexandra struggled to control her own temper. She turned to her childhood friend.

"Ekaterina, we need to return to Petrograd."

The singer didn't even acknowledge her existence. Instead the actress danced back and forth in front of the white seated figure like a courtesan trying to charm an eastern prince. Sick at heart, Alexandra left the chamber and stumbled through the labyrinth into a succession of stone corridors that sloped downward.

She passed through chambers she'd never seen before. Some were unlit caverns with the suggestion of heavy and intricate machinery. Others were still lit by a flickering radiance. One room was full of long couches and man-sized vertical tubes of cloudy liquid in which she glimpsed dead shadows. Another had a floor of slots, each holding a glass square the size of her hand. She picked one out and held it up to the light. It showed a faint image of an ice plain with a city of black spires. She assumed it was a photograph until the skeletal creatures in the foreground strode urgently towards her and she almost dropped it. She recovered enough to tuck the slab into her coat. *This'll be your proof, Natasha.*

After an age of wandering she came to the passageway leading to the church. Voices murmured as she peered around a corner. Three men with torches waited at the far end of the corridor.

CHAPTER SEVENTEEN

Hands pulled her backwards and clamped over her mouth.

"You wander out there and you'll be killed. Moses'll burn you at the stake and eat you."

"I have to try. Anyway, didn't you say you were going back to Mars?"

"Fat chance of that. The pilot's disappeared and so has Madam. And besides I don't leave friends behind, even a fat-headed communist like you. You need me to fire up the locomotive for a start but then you're on your own, lass."

"If we can make it there."

"This can't be the only route out of this place," said Banjo. "When Ekaterina danced off laughing she was babbling about endless rooms and tunnels and God knows what. She seems to know her way about. Perhaps that space cocaine poured a map into her head. She gave me the slip in two minutes flat. Track her down and she might find us another path."

Banjo pulled Alexandra back along the tunnel. She reckoned that other exits would be on the same level but where to start? The citadel was a labyrinth of cold rock, brushed metal and that strange pumice. For all she knew the configuration of the passageways was still changing, even though the Star Tsar was dead. They returned to the flying machine workshop and a thought struck her.

"If we get the sentinel that piloted the etheric flyer to Mars to carry all three of us past the Old Believers and over the mountain, we'll also have proof for Petrograd."

"Sorry, that's taking me and Ekaterina back to the Red Planet. I'm not risking having it blown out of the sky by Captain Bastard-features or pulled to bits by your Bolshie egg-heads."

Alexandra geared herself up for another argument but saw by the Englishman's expression he'd made his mind up. The commissar had no weapons and no way of taking her companions or the sentinel hostage.

"If can you make this bugger work, he's yours," Banjo said, gesturing at the tank with the second tentacled flyer floating in its bath of milk. The elixir still seemed to be active, billowing sluggishly under the crystal lid. Maybe the tank's mechanism protected it. Alexandra had no way of knowing and no idea how to get the machine operational.

Frustrated by her helplessness and the Englishman's pig-headed obsession with going back into space, she left the workshop. Banjo trailed after. There was no sign of Ekaterina, though once she heard the other woman's laughter echoing through the fortress from a distant vault. She called out but there was only silence and she wondered if she'd imagined it.

Two hours searching found no other route outside so they descended into a warren underground. Eventually they came to a room filled with more glass vats rising out of pits in the ground. They stretched in rows under a curved ceiling. At first Alexandra panicked, thinking something moved overhead. *The Star Tsar's come back to life and is crawling above, ready to punish us.* When she risked a glance upwards, she saw only patterns - black coils and curlicues oozing over dark grey stone. Signs? Words? Instructions?

"This looks familiar," Banjo stood by a tube. It was filled with amber liquid. Motes glittered in the half-light. "I reckon it's that piss from the wheeled cabinets. This is what they pickled the poor buggers in."

"You think the Tsarists came here? Made their monsters in

these rooms?"

"They might still be here. We could be right in the middle of those bastards' lair. I wish Madam hadn't lost her pistol on Mars. It was the only weapon we had."

"No, not here. The Star Tsar said Whites took his science to make slaves into machines. Whatever this is, they stole it and carried it off somewhere else - the mines."

They crept the length of the vault, finding nothing but more cylinders, all filled with the preservative. Tubes and wires ran from the lids, merging with the gold filigree in the floors and walls, but there were none of the lights or shapes they'd seen elsewhere in the complex. *This hasn't been used for ages*. Further on, the passageway angled back and forth, passing more caverns of artefacts whose purpose they could only guess at. *This whole network of chambers is a mould for our new technological age*. But she couldn't shake the Cossack's murder out of her mind or the image of the creatures abducting Viktor. *Slaves into machines*.

"I reckon there's a tunnel from here to the other mountain," said Banjo. "If the Whites had been trundling back and forth through the village and the valley, we'd have seen more signs. I can't imagine they'd be trooping monsters and machinery through that church."

The Englishman had a point, though if Father Kirill was in league with the Tsarists he wouldn't have boasted about it to a Bolshevik. On the other hand, tunnels would make it easier if they hadn't been sealed after the break between the enemy and the space being.

They picked up the pace, moving further and further down through the citadel, boots tapping echoes through the labyrinth no matter how softly they walked. *We must be hundreds of feet underground by now*. After a while Alexandra noticed the blue haze covering the walls and floor turn patchy and they increasingly walked through stretches of corridor swamped in grainy dusk. At the next bend Banjo stopped and studied the metal panels.

"Someone's been shooting in here," he pointed at a couple of shining ricochet scars. As they carried on Alexandra noticed more on either side and underfoot. They coincided with the absence of light, as if the bullets had killed whatever generated the blue radiance wherever they struck. At last they came to a long vault. She spotted a scrap of cloth and a heap of spent cartridges just by the archway, picked them up and turned them over in her hand. Banjo took one of the cases and held it to the light.

"That's from a Mosin-Nagant rifle."

Alexandra flipped the grey material over to find half a badge still attached.

"Czech Corps officer."

"I saw some of those buggers on the train to Ikayungri," said Banjo.

"They headed east with the *Orlik* armoured train. After they handed it over to the Japanese I thought they'd all escaped via Vladivostok. Why'd they return?"

"Don't ask me."

"The Tsarists and their allies were in here, the ones that tried to steal the Star Tsar's science. Did they confront it in these vaults first before the battle moved back to the valley on the other side of the mountain?"

"Doesn't look like much fighting happened here," said Banjo.

Alexandra stepped out into the cave. It was empty but when she walked closer to the nearest wall she saw the blue light had been torn away by arcing splashes of soot laced with countless scratches.

"You're wrong. There was a vicious struggle but it didn't do much damage. These plates are tougher than rock," she said.

The end of the cavern was sealed by an immense valve identical to the one in the tunnel leading from the church. Alexandra hunted for a mechanism, finally locating a spherical hollow in a wall panel. She knelt down to peer closer. The inside was criss-crossed with delicate orange lines. Not wanting to have her hand taken off at the wrist by some infernal interplanetary trap she tossed a cartridge case into the hole. Nothing happened. Banjo stood behind her with his arms folded and an expectant grin on his face.

"Go on then," he said, unhelpfully. Alexandra closed her eyes and reached inside. With an oily hiss the door slid back into the wall.

"Jesus Christ Almighty."

They stared down a long tunnel hewn out of the rock. This was human work - the granite hacked and chipped by picks and drills, punctuated here and there by the remains of dynamite bores. A storm lantern hung from a hook so the commissar lifted it down. It was half full of oil. All they needed was a match. She turned just as the door rolled across the archway, sealing her outside and Banjo within.

He's locked me out. The bastard's abandoned me.

She was about to hammer on the metal and yell curses at the traitorous shit when the valve opened again. The engineer stood next to the control.

"Just testing - in case we get chased back in here."

Alexandra managed to calm down enough to ask if the man had any matches. To her surprise Banjo tossed her a box.

"Nicked them from the train. Can't fire up a locomotive without lucifers."

"Can we go now?"

The Englishman gestured along the corridor.

"Ladies first."

"Right. For heaven's sake keep quiet. And don't do anything ridiculous before telling me first."

The man looked ready to launch into another of his childish tirades but in the end he pursed his lips and nodded at Alexandra knowingly. In the man's lexicon of stupidity that expression probably meant something but the commissar had neither the patience nor the interest to find out.

"We may well meet creatures who I believe have been tortured into monstrous shapes by evil Tsarist science," she thought she ought to add.

"Oh Jesus Christ, you're not thinking of liberating them too are you? Can we just get you on the train so I can go into space? If you want to introduce a bunch of horrors to communism, do it without me when you come back from Petrograd with your deranged mates."

To be honest, the commissar had no intention of going anywhere near either the electrical men or the six-limbed creatures. Alexandra had reconciled herself to Viktor's death and there was too much nightmare in those mines to make her want to linger. It'd take her all her courage and wit to get through the warren of pits and tunnels. At first she'd wanted to find out what really hid under the mountains, but now, here, in the rough-hewn water-dripping passageway, armed with only a flickering oil lamp, all thoughts of heroics fled.

"Don't look so sloughened. Here we go, eh? You and me," Banjo thumped her affectionately on the shoulder, making her stagger. "A pair of Yorkshire fists and a pompous windbag bluestocking to bore the enemy to death. They'll melt away."

Alexandra breathed deeply, cleared her mind and set off without bothering to reply. Not wanting to linger, they jogged over fallen rubble. A mile in and the tunnel dwindled to a point at both ends, although ahead in the distance she could see lamplight etching orange rings in the pipe. Despite his initial enthusiasm Banjo had begun making comments like "We could be exploring Mars or walking through alien forests under triple suns instead of pissing around down here." The commissar lost patience.

"Will you stop shouting nonsense in my ear? This is serious."

"Eh up," answered his companion, nodding ahead.

Movement flickered against the distant glow.

"Now see what you've done with all your gassing," hissed Banjo.

Alexandra blew out the lamp. They pressed themselves against the wall and waited, hoping they wouldn't be seen against the darkness behind. Nothing stirred. *Perhaps it was just a fall of dust or stones against the light.*

Another quarter mile and side tunnels appeared. That wasn't good. Anything could emerge into the passage behind them and they'd be cut off. Alexandra stopped to listen. Still nothing. After a hundred yards the corridor dissolved into a cluttered labyrinth of uneven crawlspaces, ginnels and fallen rock. After worming their way in the cold and damp for what felt like ages they emerged down a slope made from shattered boulders into a wider vault. As soon as they reached the bottom Banjo pulled her into the shadows.

Six cabinets rolled past on thick-tired bicycle wheels, their preservative-filled boxes glowing a dull orange, spattered with brighter searchlight rays from lights in the bases. Five men and one woman - her hair dancing back and forth like a tide-pool anemone. *Are they really alive?* It was impossible to tell if their eyes were open. The faces were just sun-fringed silhouettes in a constellation of floating scraps. Even so she sensed intelligence in the ordered way they followed each other across the uneven ground.

They trundled past. After they'd gone Banjo and Alexandra stepped out to watch them recede into the distance, squares of gold leaf shrinking against the night.

"What the hell are they? Half man, half machine?" asked Banjo.

Alexandra remembered the broken creature found by Aminev.

"Our enemy created them. The Tsarist savants stole the Star Tsar' secrets, learned how to combine a human being with such a device and used them to fashion an army of monsters, here and in the underground warrens at Ikayungri."

"Jesus." Banjo shuddered. "You Russians are mad."

Alexandra remembered the happy hero of her play. *Comrade Machine Man, you're real, machine and human as one, but they made you into something vile.*

"What about the Great White Apes? There's nothing machine-like about those buggers."

Alexandra had no idea. She made her way around the edge of the vault, keeping to the tumbled shadows in case any more of those abominations rolled up. She didn't even want to think about bumping into the four-armed spiders down here. But this was their kingdom too and if the Whites had been defeated and driven away, who was their king?

"Let's go back to Mars eh? Or we'll fight our way past Moses and his lot. At least they're human. I could brain a good dozen with that baptismal font for starters."

She ignored the Englishman. No matter how much the crushing abyss around them pressed on her soul, she wanted to find out what had happened, why and if there was any way to put things right. *There's another malignant intelligence at work here. Who are you?*

Banjo gave up attempts at persuasion. In silent agreement the two of them followed the tunnel, hugging the darkness and moving in the opposite direction to the creatures. Eventually Alexandra entered a circular chamber. Cubes the size of bread loaves littered the floor. They glowed with a yellow phosphorescence and she guessed they'd been hacked out of the mountain depths and brought here for light. She was a quarter of the way round the edge when her companion swore. Alexandra looked back to see the Englishman had blundered into a pit up to his waist. The engineer scrambled out.

"What is it?"

"Some kind of hole. It doesn't half stink."

Banjo hunkered down and bent his head to the side.

"It's the entrance to a tunnel under the floor."

"There's another here," Alexandra stood next to a pipe slanting into the ground. There were gouges in the dirt on the inside of the lip.

"And over here. They're all over the shop. This place is like a giant cheese."

Artillery thundered in the commissar's heart. *White maggots.* She stared at Banjo and saw her own fear echoed in the man's open-mouthed look of petrified stupidity.

"Burrows," he said.

She hurried across the vault towards the three exits at the other end. Any would do, just to get out of that room. Banjo muttered and huffed close behind. It was the first time she'd heard the man pray.

They ended up in the leftmost tunnel. It sloped upwards, which was some consolation. Alexandra padded swiftly along, fighting the urge to run in case the noise attracted the dwellers in this obscene, porous world. A few yards in she caught the sound of grunting and rustling. The passageway they'd chosen was dark, the cave behind a pale yellow circle. Alexandra paused, summoning all her courage to turn and look down the corridor. In the weird half-light a shape moved at the entrance of a hole. A pair of arms emerged, then another, as if an embracing couple wriggled their way out. But there all humanity stopped because the shadow only had one head and the body shuddered with the busy twitchings of a wasp emerging from a rotten peach. It stood up. More movement and a second appeared next to it, then a third.

Alexandra and Banjo backed away as quickly as the darkness and the uneven floor allowed. The creatures hadn't seen them, though judging by the dancing shadows in the yellow light more were squirming out of the ground. The entrance shrank to the size of a kopek and they were past a curve in the tunnel. Never mind the noise - they broke into a desperate run. More patches of phosphorescent rock lit their way and once or twice they passed mine lamps swinging from hooks in the ceiling, their cancerous flames staining the grubby glass blue.

After two more corners Alexandra calmed down enough to stop and risk a glance behind. Nothing - the tunnel looked empty. Either the multi-limbed men still brooded in their cave or they'd gone in the other direction.

"You said three hours to get the train ready to move."

Banjo exhaled a couple of oaths.

"I can try to do it quicker but it might damage the valves or blow up the whole locomotive. Once I start we'll just have to hope we don't attract attention to ourselves."

"Don't attract attention to ourselves? With a steam engine hissing and smoking away on top of those monsters' lair?"

"What do you suggest?"

Alexandra seethed. This was hopeless. She hated to admit it but the oaf might have been right when he said they should have gone back, but now they had those mutants between them and the Star Tsar's mountain fortress. There was no choice but to carry on, even though she'd no clue in which direction. They should aim for tunnels leading upwards but for all she knew they could just as easily take them into the centre of this foul realm.

"We need to find weapons," she told the Englishman. "If the Whites were shooting down here, they might have left some of their rifles and ammunition."

The corridor bellied out and she found himself stumbling over railway sleepers. *This is more like it - we're in the mine.* Half a mile further on they emerged into the corner of a hall filled with unused machinery.

"Steelworks." Banjo pointed at crucibles suspended from chains and empty furnaces with gaping mouths.

They crept from shadow to shadow, past piles of clinker and ore. Gantries once ran across the gulf above but had collapsed, leaving their rusted skeletons to heave over the machinery like antediluvian monsters trying to claw their way out of tar pits.

"It's another factory created by the Whites but what were they making?" asked Alexandra.

"Not trains. Not down here."

Beyond the abandoned furnaces they came to a cluster of workbenches with rusty lathes and fused clumps of metal that once were tools. A brick archway led to a second workshop.

"Now you're talking," Banjo held up what looked like machine gun parts.

"Why create weapons here?"

"Secret munitions factories are not that odd, are they?"

"But here? Why not in Ikayungri? There's no reason to hide any of this."

A few luminescent globes lay scattered on benches and the floor. When Alexandra placed her hand on one it was warm to the touch.

"Star Tsar science?" asked Banjo

"Perhaps."

The Englishman paused, picked up a crucible and shook it.

"Are you sure this is just a gold mine?"

He showed the commissar yellow stones at the bottom of the bowl.

"I don't recognise it. Do you?" asked Alexandra.

Banjo shrugged.

"No idea. They were using it when they made these guns. Wonder what it's for."

Alexandra pocketed a lump. Another question for Natasha, if she ever got to Petrograd. *I will. I will find you. I swear.*

The room was the first in a series of low-ceilinged workshops with more tables covered in gun parts. They were clearly left-over scraps and there was no sign of any finished weapons. They found another passageway sloping upwards, carrying the cart track to the upper levels. It joined a crossroads that looked more recent and she started to hope.

"Can you hear that?" asked Banjo.

A deep throbbing sound and a breeze on her cheek, bringing a sour cocktail of copper, electricity and chemicals. Fifty yards to their left the railway led into a cavern lit in reds and yellows. More machines rose up to the ceiling and their heat rolled out of the archway in treacle surges.

"Behind us!" hissed her companion.

Alexandra looked past the man but saw nothing. At the same moment the track in the cross tunnel rattled. A flare in the machine cavern illuminated an alcove in the wall opposite, barely larger than a shadow. She dashed across the railway and squeezed in sideways, relieved to find it went deep into the rock. She glanced back, expecting Banjo, but the idiot hadn't followed and in the glare from the furnaces she couldn't make out if he was still in the other passage.

The rumbling grew louder and a wagon carrying three armoured-car-sized spheres coated in yellow dust ground past. Six multi-limbed creatures pushed the cart along, their grey skins glistening with mucus. A stench of decay billowed around the commissar and she retched, even as a wheeled electrical man jounced after the slaves. She got ready run back to help Banjo but more four-armed men boiled out of the tunnel from the monsters' warren. Stay here and she'd be discovered. Alexandra squeezed further into the cleft. It opened onto a flight of stairs spiralling up through the rock. A mutant shadow unrolled at her feet so she hurried on, taking the steps two at a time, trying not to cry out in fear. At last she emerged into a wide room full of scrap, rubbish and the stink of sweat and shit.

"Hello Comrade."

CHAPTER EIGHTEEN

A second's hesitation and the daft cow had run off without him. Not only that, but his way was now blocked by a train of horrors pushing their own equally bizarre equipage. And those walking worms from the nest they'd stumbled through were coming up fast on his arse, with a wheeled specimen as well, leading them along as if it'd decided to take the dogs for a stroll. The circus had definitely come to town.

Long practice in the ironworks had taught Banjo how to be invisible so he flattened himself against the side, scooping up dirt to plaster on his face and holding his breath. The passageway was wide enough and the walls a jumble of rock with plenty of shadows. Maybe they'd smell him, but given the overpowering reek of sweat, shit and rot that preceded them, he doubted it. The cabinet trundled past, sunken profile nodding in the cloudy liquid. Half a dozen of the white creatures followed. He couldn't make out much detail in the gloom and didn't particularly want to. They moved with slow, clumsy movements, like sleepwalkers or the shuffling gassed stumbling over battlefields in desperate search of help or death.

It was his first time in proximity to the shapes who'd haunted him since he spotted them on the periphery of the Ikayungri works. Great White Apes he'd called them, but that gave them identity where none existed. Giant monstrous gorillas he could have coped with, tigers, sharks, beasts from other worlds, anything, but not this. He wasn't a coward, having faced down horrors other men would blanch at, so why did he push back against the wet granite as if trying to force himself through the rock? Was it the half-glimpsed membranous skin, swollen and riddled with black pores? The idiot faces with their torn sack eyes and mouths? Even the hints he caught in the darkness made him want to flinch away or scream himself hoarse. They were painted on top of nothing - an utter emptiness that pressed up against reality, threatening to burst into the tunnel like a rupturing boil. Death, decay and rot, and beyond it the void.

The monsters joined the rest of the parade and he allowed himself to sag down the wall in exhausted fear. The carnival stumbled to a halt and while he gathered up the fragments of his thoughts he managed to study the engines rising out of the thickening mob. He struggled to make sense of the mechanisms though one looked like it might be a bulbous weapon. In the golden light he saw scintillating globes speared on crystal sticks with wires and pipes spiralling down on either side. This cart ran on thick rubber treads, dusted with a yellow powder that reminded him of the rocks he'd found in the crucible. As the crowd briefly shuffled apart, he noticed the double-headed eagle of Imperial Russia picked out on an obsidian shield. *Alexandra was right. Those mad Tsarists built all this. Are they preparing a legion of horrors to take the country back from the Reds?*

Banjo had no chance of following the commissar. An army stood between him and the other side of the corridor. He'd have to retrace his steps and try to find another path, hopefully without meeting any more of those vile buggers en-route. A hundred yards down the passageway he came across a branch tunnel. It rose up into a narrow chimney, but he managed to wriggle his way up and grab hold of a ledge above his head. He hauled himself into a second conduit. Further along a single beam of yellow light dropped from a fissure in the wall.

It opens onto that cavern they were heading for.

The crack was only a couple of inches wide but enough to

realise he was looking at the centre of the lair. The air was filled with a roiling haze that turned everything into muted silhouettes, but he recognised clusters of cylinders, spheres and valves as big as houses. They arced lightning, bouncing it off the scorched granite ceiling to disappear into the pit below. It resembled the inside of a bomb, a ticking clock of destruction waiting to chime the final second. Above the crackling hum he heard the ever-present rustling of those unholy workers. In his imagination he saw them maggot-swarming over the floor and walls, crawling up the vats and tanks in endless motion. The idea sent him hurrying along the vent to a set of steps that dropped down into a rough-hewn tunnel. He had to stoop and after several turns realised he'd completely lost his sense of direction. Banjo found a single illuminated globe wedged between a fallen rock and the wall. He picked it up to light his way ahead. It was that or blunder through total darkness.

He hoped the passage would re-join the main tunnel later on or he'd find another route to take him after Alexandra. Of course anyone with any sense would return to the Star Tsar's mountain and leave the arrogant prat to her fate but then Mother had always told him he was the stupid one in the family. Besides, abandoning the Red down here would engender all sorts of future nightmares. No thanks - he had enough of those stacked up already.

Plodding on he tried to make sense of this warren. So the Whites had poached alien science and were using it to manufacture a vengeful hoard of six-limbed beings and trundling electrical cabinets with men and women trapped inside. Disgust and horror apart he struggled to see how either would stand up to artillery, machine guns and tanks, unless those weapons harnessed powers that rendered any defence useless. He'd no doubt there was some link between this pit and the labyrinth under the factories. For all he knew this was merely a fraction of the mutant army and the rest were creeping around under the engine sheds and furnaces of Ikayungri, waiting for a signal.

The tunnel joined a larger brick-lined corridor with shining globes hanging from the ceiling. This was more like it and after a quick check to make sure it was deserted, he stepped down to find himself splashing through ankle-high mud. Further on he came to an iron door set in the rock face - a watertight ship's hatch. He tried to open it but the wheel wouldn't budge - *locked or rusted shut.* There was a porthole in the upper half but no light on the other side. Holding his own sphere up had no effect. The thick glass was too grubby, with what appeared to be finger trails through the muck on the inside. He pressed his ear to the metal, but all was silent.

The valve was the first of several, stretching away on both sides. When he shone his light into the next sealed chamber, he could just make out a dim outline. Someone sitting on a bench? *This place is a prison.* But if it was a person in there it didn't move and a foul stink seeped out despite the tight seal. It grew stronger as he stole along the passage until he eventually found a lit cell. He peered through the smeared glass and jerked back. The room was full of too many memories. *Butchery and mud and gas, screaming mouths drowning in seas of blood.* It might have been open but all he wanted to do was get as far away as possible. *Why have they packed it into cauldrons and let it rot? To feed those monsters?* The pipes and dials made him think of a brewery. He put his hands on his knees and bent double, trying hard not to be sick.

Banjo hurried past the rest of the doors until the tunnel jack-knifed right into a storeroom with open-topped vats on either side, crammed together so they filled the hall. Steps led up to gangways between the metal barrels which stood over ten feet tall and, by his reckoning, a good five yards in diameter. It was the only way onward but he hesitated. The stench had ebbed, replaced by a peculiar vinegary smell drifting out of the containers. He dreaded what he might find swilling around in those giant scarred and crusted buckets. But what options did he have? He cat-stepped softly up the stairs and peered over the edge of the nearest.

Empty, though a wet ring glistened halfway up the inside and he spotted scraps of what looked like rubber stuck to the metal.

He crept along the platform - all the others were the same - until he came to the last two. He dug his fingernails into his palms and tried to force his heart to slow down. The vats were full of dark liquid in which white eels as thick as a man's leg writhed ceaselessly over one other. No, not eels. These things had multiple arms and flat bodies. They reminded him of the buckets of live squid he'd seen for sale in the morning market in Hakodate but a hundred times bigger.

A smeared face slid over the top of the mass and he jumped back with a stifled cry. He waited, expecting one of the creatures to heave itself out of the vat. After a while he looked again. It had vanished, churned into the mix by the endless squirming tentacles. *This is where they make those bastards. They're grown in these jars like tadpoles.* So much for Alexandra's romantic nonsense about the Star Tsar's science ushering in a new utopia. He'd tried to tell the lass that it'd all end up being used for more terror, more bloodshed and grim misery. And here was proof - dark evil suited to foul pits and shadow labyrinths filled with deranged monsters and rooms bulging with the hacked remnants of corpses.

Banjo heard a noise from the passageway ahead. He wouldn't have time to return to the corridor so he slipped over the side of the gangway and down between two tubs. The corroded metal felt warm - a putrid heat that made him want to shrink away. Crouching down in the darkness he saw a cabinet roll into the vault, followed by six synthetics pushing a mine cart. The wheeled machine stopped at the last vat and delicate dentist drill arms waved complex patterns in the air.

Machinery grumbled into life and an overhead crane crawled forward, dipped a hook into the barrel and pulled out a bundle of greasy rags. It unravelled into the cut-out of a four-armed man. *It's a skin, without stuff in it to make it move.* To Banjo's horror the limbs flopped and wriggled slowly. *Yet it's alive.* The hoist unceremoniously dumped the pelt into the truck and the box and its attendants set off the way they'd come, the cart's wheels rattling over the grating. *So now they'll pump it full of something to turn it into one of those shuffling horrors.* The Yorkshireman's curiosity was up and he toyed with the idea of following to see what was going to happen next. Then he remembered those fermentation canisters in the locked room, the ones swilling in knee-deep putrefaction. He could already guess the main ingredient of this foul alchemy, though Christ knew how they turned it into a functioning slave.

He forced himself to wait an hour. Nothing returned so he pressed on. The gantry ran through more caverns with more vats, but all were empty and silent, caked with the crusted residue of ancient chemicals and scraps of shrivelled tissue. This was built to make an army but only two tubs still functioned.

Beyond the last hall the walkway dropped down into a storeroom and for the first time since getting blackjacked in the Vladivostok brothel his luck turned. Half a dozen open-topped crates were stacked with guns, though of a design he'd never seen before. The barrels swelled into three spheres like boiled eggs speared on a chopstick. It resembled a miniature version of that cannon with the Romanov crest he'd seen pushed along the tunnel by the friends of Hieronymus Bosch.

He lifted one up to the light. The workmanship looked crude and the mechanism rusty but there appeared to be enough grease in the chamber. He worked the breech and nothing jammed so he hunted around for ammunition. Another box held hundred-round drums but only two were loaded, stuffed with yellow-tipped bullets. He picked one out. Odd looking thing, like a Dum-Dum, but the tip was warm. Banjo remembered the rocks in the crucible - some kind of explosive?

He loaded up the weapon and drew the bolt. On the side of the rifle he found a dial set to three. Guessing it was the number of rounds per trigger he left it as is, just to make sure anything he shot at would get a decent volley. Until he knew how it handled he wasn't going to waste them. Besides he'd always found that single, carefully placed bullets were far more effective than hosing the works like an Ilkley flapper with her first bottle of champagne. Now let the buggers come. At least he could give good account of himself. He stuffed the second magazine into his tunic and set off.

Banjo had worked out that as long as he kept more or less level and in a spiral, he'd eventually end up back at the crossroads where Alexandra disappeared. He reckoned he was circumnavigating that main chamber, and all these rooms and hallways were storerooms, cells and laboratories servicing the diabolical machinery in the centre. He also realised that time was running out if he was going to rescue the wretched communist, though the pillock had probably already been eaten, stuffed into a cabinet or minced up in one of those brewing tubs in the mutant factory. He picked up the pace, turned a corner and found himself face to face with a glowing box on wheels, standing in a cascade of filthy water from a chimney shaft above.

He hefted the machine gun and was about to shoot when he realised the creature was alone. It was also two yards away, which meant that firing exploding bullets at the thing might not be the brightest idea. He'd no idea how powerful those yellow-tipped rounds were.

It looked like a man inside, his head slumped on his chest. The hidden light illuminating the preservative flickered, the mechanical arms juddering in time. *It's broken.* He shouldered the weapon and stepped closer, trying to make out more details of the poor bastard. He wiped the water from the glass with his sleeve, sniffed a drop and tasted it. Fresh - had to be from an underground stream. He peered at the corpse. A soldier, probably an officer judging by the fine walrus moustache. Heavy brows hid the eyes. Tangled dark hair had been bleached into a patchy brown by long exposure to the chemicals and teased out into a nimbus that filled the top third of the box.

Banjo realised the hybrid wasn't a threat but something made him pause. *Wretched devil.* No doubt the bits they'd hacked away from this mutilated doll had been tossed into those retorts he'd seen on the other side of the locked valves, the ones stewing up the brew they used to fill the slaves. He checked the tunnel beyond the cabinet just to make sure none of those multi-armed fuckers were trudging towards him. Nothing, and nothing behind either.

He hunkered down and examined the case, cursing himself for sentimental idiocy all the while. *Number 402*. There was an access door with a butterfly key in the side. He muttered an apology to the creature, like an embarrassed nurse giving a rating the once over for the clap, opened the hatch and looked inside. *There's your problem, matey.* A loose wire sparked at the bottom of the box, beneath a multi-coloured cluster of globes, tubes, flasks, and what looked like the guts of an alarm clock complete with dial and hour hand. He picked it up between finger and thumb and fastened its crocodile clip to the empty terminal above. It must have been the right one because the light steadied and the arms stopped twitching.

Banjo stood up and nearly yelled out. The dead officer stared at him from cracked-mud eyes singularly devoid of gratitude. His act of charity might have been a bloody idiotic mistake after all. Now what? Was there some way of getting through to this thing? Perhaps he could force it to lead him to Alexandra. He couldn't speak Russian but if this creature was once a Tsarist aristo it probably understood French.

"Bonjour," he tried. Did the monster have mechanical ears? After waiting in vain for a reaction he tapped on the glass. One of the articulated arms reached across and clicked back a rhythm on the wooden cabinet. *Morse code?* There was no mistaking the words. *We shall purge the world of you filth in a storm of atomic fire.*

"Charming, you ungrateful shit."

Reflected movement in the tank made him spin round. The biggest six-limbed man he'd ever seen squeezed down the tunnel towards him. It had to be all of fifteen feet tall, crouching down as it pulled itself along with four sausage hands. Mucus-coated skin bulged and slithered against the rock. Gobbets of dark matter fell from the being's mouth and eyes as if it was freshly baked and a sloppy cook had stuffed too much of that putrid mince into its body.

A metal claw clamped his arm but he shook it off, hefting the gun to his shoulder. *Atomic fire?* The thought stopped him letting rip in this confined space. The officer juddered upright, blocking his route past. He looked up at the hole in the ceiling. *Is that the bottom of a ladder?* He put one foot on the electrical man's frame and jumped. The extra vigour from the Star Tsar food boosted him into the chimney. He grabbed an iron rung. It started to bend, so he yanked himself further up, reaching for the next, terrified that any second now a corpse fist would close over his ankle.

He scrambled up the pipe. The cleats were sturdier here, hammered deep into the rock. After a few seconds he realised no-one had torn his leg off. Banjo risked a glance down. The creature hadn't followed him. A shape moved in the passage, a fretful shadow interspersed with glimpses of mottled skin. *It's like a cat that's lost a mouse, trying to sniff the poor thing out.* It must have seen him scramble up the funnel. He'd been silhouetted against the glow in the officer's cabinet. Besides, wouldn't the machine man hybrid tell his monstrous pal where the Englishman had gone? As if reading his mind, the mutant rammed its head into the chimney, staring up at him with those ragged pit eyes. Without thinking he unslung the gun, aimed downward and pulled the trigger.

The shot was nothing more than a quiet cough. A black puddle plopped open in the monster's forehead and just as quickly closed again. *Oh for fuck's sake.* The weapon was about as useful as a catapult with perished elastic. He tried to untangle the strap it so he could at least hurl it down at the beast, but it caught in his tunic so he turned and climbed as fast as he could. His pursuer would have a bugger of a job squeezing after him but he knew the boneless horror would give it a go.

His fingers just touched the edge of the pipe where it bellied out into a second chamber when the mountain spat him upwards in a column of bright yellow vapour. He thudded against the ceiling and tumbled onto the floor beside the hole, the wet rock smacking all sense out of him. He smelt burnt rubber, and crisp flakes of orange-smouldering tissue fluttered down around him. Banjo's chin felt warm. His beard was on fire. He patted it out and sat up, every muscle and bone screaming.

He crawled to the well and looked down. Far below he saw a cherry red disc which he assumed was the floor of the tunnel. It faded back through the spectrum to dark grey. The heat pulsed up the shaft in waves, the skin on his cheeks crisping tight like sunburn. *Bugger me sideways, that was molten rock!* He pulled the drum magazine free and examined the bullets again. *Atomic fire.* But surely any force capable of slagging granite would have incinerated everything for half a mile around, including him, turning the tunnels into colossal blowtorches.

Part of him toyed with the idea of firing off another slug just to see what would happen, but last time the packed offal body of a giant horror had dampened the eruption. With its barbecued remains plastering the rock for a hundred yards on all sides he didn't want to risk letting a second unrestrained inferno kick off. Anyway - what smashing luck! Now he had something to protect himself. Even if the kerfuffle alerted more monsters he stood a much better chance of making it out of here. Come to think of it he wasn't sure if there'd been an explosion at all. Surely his ears should be ringing?

He couldn't go back down. Although the rock had stopped glowing, he felt the heat. A second chimney lofted from the ceiling and more iron cleats in the chamber wall let him spider his way up. Banjo climbed in the darkness, squeezing past jagged outcrops and cursing with the frustration. He was heading further and further away from wherever Alexandra had ended up. It was highly unlikely the Red bugger still lived but the thought of the wee lass being hacked apart and stuffed into one of those glass cases drove him on.

At last when his enhanced strength was fading, and he had to pause at each step to rest his cramped fingers and aching shoulders, the engineer emerged into an alcove set in a long tunnel of wet rock. Damp air flowed across his face, free of the endless sluggish chemical rot that had clung to him ever since they'd left the Star Tsar's lair. After checking for enemies he eased out into the main passageway and realised he was standing next to a wide gauge railway line. Ice coloured light kicked off the rock fifty yards to his right and as he stepped over the rails and sleepers he spotted the train he'd stolen from Aminev, abandoned and framed by a ring of watery sky from the Old Believers' valley beyond.

It took him all his remaining self-control not to sprint towards it, yelling happily all the while. He checked back and forth, stealing as quietly as he could through the shadows. Nothing - all those monsters must still be hiding deep below. Why weren't they up here? And where was Moses and his rabid mates? All he heard was the wind over the stones.

The locomotive was just as they'd left it when Ekaterina shot her brother so he climbed aboard. If he stoked the beast ready to fire that should speed things up. The most dangerous part would be waiting for enough steam. He reckoned he'd need to survive three hours, hoping nothing turned up. If they did, well he had his atomic machine gun. It took him no time at all to get the cabin prepared. The only thing remaining was to light her up and hunker down. *Free at last. Through the mountain, out into the world.* There was Aminev and his Red army to deal with but at least they'd be human. He looked at the engine, set it in reverse and tapped a few dials. *Go on then, start her up you idiot.* After a further ten minutes of random pottering, during which he opened the firebox door four times to toss another lump of wood inside, he jumped down onto the tracks.

"Damn you to hell you pompous Red turd," he grumbled and set off back towards the tunnels, gun braced at his hip.

CHAPTER NINETEEN

The voice sounded right next to her ear - an urgent, sweaty whisper, and yet it came from the shadows at the end of the room. As her eyes grew accustomed to the darkness, Alexandra realised she was in another workshop filled with countless benches scored with gouges and cracks. In the sputtering light of a lamp hanging from a single hook she saw beakers, retorts, crucibles, weighing scales of stone, brass and iron, bottles of countless shapes and sizes intermingled with what appeared to be a carpenter's tools - saws, chisels, hammers and hand-drills. Every surface glimmered with a greasy stickiness that made her want to shrink in on herself. The reek was so overpowering she had to breathe through her mouth to stop herself being sick. It was hard to tell but she guessed the walls were peppered with more arches opening into night-black tunnels leading deeper into the mountain

"Leave her. She's our guest."

Alexandra turned to see the six-limbed creature that had followed her up the stairs, so close now she could touch it. She staggered back, bumping up against the edge of a workbench. The voice giggled.

"Don't be frightened, my dear. He won't harm you. He is unthinking - lumpen in all senses of the word."

The mutant looked as if it was made out of grey cellophane

stretched over brown clay, the face designed by a bored child amusing itself by poking odd holes for eyes, smaller ones for a nose and a ragged trench for a mouth. The commissar couldn't make out any actual eyeballs and wondered if it was blind.

"It sees atomic rays in the same way we see light. Its vision is clearer than yours or mine in these poisoned tunnels. How is my old friend the being from space?"

She let the owner of the voice read her silence however he wished. The voice rambled on regardless.

"The specimens I've made of late are not as good as the first ones. I grow tired and forgetful. I'm no longer sure of the technique, the right proportions, the correct blend of essences. The machines I borrowed are failing, the knives and saws blunted from overuse. I need his help once more, though we had a small disagreement and his angels of death are ever watchful. I hoped he would forgive me. Do you think he will?"

"Who are you? Show yourself." The man wasn't an Old Believer from Father Kirill's village. He spoke with the easy accent of a drunk Petrograd aristocrat.

The shadows at the far end of the room coalesced into a mountain of flesh wrapped in sackcloth. A dome head sat on top and two eyes watched her from deep, grime-scored sphincters of fat. The mouth was that of a four-year old girl, but the bare shoulders and arms were covered in coarse black hairs matted with dirt and sweat.

"You do not catch me at my best." The figure wobbled forward on bare feet swollen into pale loaves of flesh. "Once I fed with the greatest, dined on *Selle de Chevreuil Grand Veneur* and *Duchesse à la Régence* as I argued the case against God with the Tsarina's Holy Fool Grigori Yefimovich. I was at the Mariyinsky Palace the night after Pyotr Arkadyevich was shot, you know. A glum, tedious affair, that banquet, all sparkle and wit gone. I saw the future clearly in Tsar Nikolai's eyes, even though he was blind to it himself. You were stupid fools to kill Prime Minister Stolypin. He was a reformer and a realist, not a childish dreamer chasing after the impossible as he treads filth across the corpses of the great.

Now, because of your great revolution I am forced to make my own food from whatever scraps and chemicals are left over. It is a poor diet."

The man leaned against a bench, wheezing and gasping despite only having tottered a few steps.

"Sergei Bakolov at your service."

He attempted a grotesque bow, as if greeting a guest at a soirée.

Bakolov? Even if this wretch had dined with the Tsar in Kiev, the name meant nothing. He could be any one of a thousand court officials, though he seemed to have adopted the mantle of a savant. Alexandra had never heard of a scientist called Bakolov.

"How many of you are here?"

Another chuckle.

"Oh, we are legion."

So, one man and a thousand monsters.

"When the Whites fled they left you behind."

Bakolov stared at the bench, pulling out splinters with cracked midnight nails.

"Ingrates, all of them. They had no patience," he murmured to his fingers. "They whined that the atomic rays in this place would be the death of them, even as I promised them enhanced life. If they'd waited and trusted, your armies would not have defeated us so readily. The science in these mountains is enough for one man to snuff out your world in the blink of an eye."

The man's voice rose to a petulant crescendo as he sank to his knees, clearly exhausted. His lower body disappeared under the carpet of fat hanging out from under his vest, so he resembled nothing more than a human pudding sitting on the filthy ground.

"If they'd waited."

He sounded close to tears. Bakolov rubbed his face with his hands and frowned past Alexandra.

"What is it?"

With a lurch of fear the commissar realised the six-limbed creature was pointing at her coat.

"You've got something in your pocket," said the White in the sing-song voice mad Efrosinya had used to frighten her when Father wasn't around. "What are you hiding?"

Alexandra pulled out the yellow fragments and let them roll across her palm.

"Oh. Oh dear," chuckled Bakolov. "Looks like you've no choice then."

Dread made it difficult to concentrate. She tipped the stones onto the bench and wiped her hand on her coat without thinking.

"Pitchblende. Atomic ore, refined using the science from the space creature. Sadly, it started to kill you as soon as you stole it. Weeks, perhaps only days. You'll already be weakened. You have pains in your joints, no? Do you taste blood yet? Your hair will fall out and you'll rot inside. In fact I'm surprised you made it this far. Some of the soldiers were dead within hours. You communists are clearly built of sterner stuff."

Bakolov giggled again. Alexandra had never felt better in her life but decided to keep it to herself.

"So why aren't you sick?" she asked.

"The chemicals from space protect me. They fortify my body, like those superstitious idiots in the valley. If you've eaten any of the manna from heaven then I suppose you're protected too, but after you've become one of us it won't matter anyway."

"Why would I become one of you? The workers won, you lost. There's a need for savants to build our new world. If you understand the wonders here you can help your fellows transform humanity. Come with me to Petrograd and I'll ensure you're given a fair hearing."

Bakolov laughed.

"I admire your courage, Comrade. Even here you give speeches. What's your name?"

"I am Commissar Alexandra Lobachevsky of the People's Commissariat for Education."

"Education," the man gave a sad laugh. "I thank you for your kind offer, Comrade Commissar. Poor Bakolov will never leave this realm now but his science shall indeed come to your world. I promise you that."

Alexandra sensed more creatures entering the room. Shapes moved behind the alchemist - some six-limbed, others grubby cabinets on wheels with silhouettes in faintly glowing liquid.

"You were wrong to tarnish us - to see us as the enemy," Bakolov continued. "Not all Whites were the corrupt worshippers of that imbecile Nikolai and his medieval fantasies. We also recognised and understood the revolutionary potential of man and looked to science to forge that perfection - to lift those noble Russians with the clarity of vision and the strength of will above the herd. We wanted to liberate the worthy so they could build a new age."

"We?"

At first she'd assumed the scientist was alone, a crippled maniac struggling to survive among the remnants of experiments he no longer understood. The man's fretful boasting and whining self-pity made it clear that she was the first human he'd spoken to in a long time. But Alexandra sensed a history of others - shadowy cabals formed out of the cruelty and desperation in the last months of the *ancien régime.*

Bakolov, lost in his theme, ignored the question.

"I shall free us. There will be no more slaves and no more workers. With the learning and wisdom from beyond the stars I can create the Hands we need for all our labour - to work in our factories and to march upon our enemies with new wondrous weapons."

The commissar looked at the figures standing behind the Tsarist like grotesque dolls moulded out of flour and water. In among them she spotted more luminous boxes. White eyes in still-living corpses watched her through dirt-flecked preservative. She remembered the Star Tsar's vault of cylinders - the pure clarity of a future science centuries away from this squalid alchemy. *What did you think you were doing when you handed over your knowledge to Bakolov? Did you have a hand in the design of these monstrosities crowding in around us? To what end? How could a creature of Super Science believe that butchered cripples in glass boxes and animated grotesques were a step towards the perfection of man?*

"Hands and Minds. Labourers and clerks who will take over the menial tasks that enslave us and free you and me to become gods."

Curiosity overcoming fear, Alexandra walked towards one of the cabinets. To her surprise, the six-limbed humans shuffled aside. She knelt and examined the mutilated torso on the other side of the glass. A thin face with a moustache and beard stared back, skin rendered yellow and porous by the liquid. The grey-mustard jacket had the insignia of the Czech Legion on its sleeve.

"Not all of them made it to Vladivostok," said Bakolov. "Some refused to abandon the *Orlik*, their beloved armoured train."

That wasn't right.

"It ended up in Harbin - the Chinese have the rail ironclad now," said Alexandra.

"Wherever the *Orlik* is, it doesn't matter. We have the means to make new engines of destruction that will turn man's mighty steam fortresses into so much slag and ash."

Contempt made Alexandra bold. She tapped the glass in front of her. The spindly mechanical arms protruding from the wooden case twitched. Cracked clay eyes flickered as if the ruined soldier was searching for the source of the noise.

"And is this how you'll make the legions of warriors and slaves for your new world of perfect men? Hacked bodies in aquarium tanks and bloated toys designed by imbecile children?"

Alexandra noticed a movement to her right. Another figure in another cabinet, the number *539* bright and shiny on newly polished Bakelite. All her anger disappeared in a second, and a horrible, stomach-churning wave of dizziness flooded through her. Despite herself she barely managed to stifle a gasp, even though in the face of such deranged cruelty she should have guessed.

Viktor. I won't cry in front of this bastard, I won't cry.

The poet's hair waved like river grass. Both arms had been hacked off at the elbow, the muscles, sinew and bones bleached into paper-white rags. Alexandra didn't want to imagine what lay below the forest of tubes and wires coating the bottom of the tank, where it merged with the mechanism inside the hull. Thankfully, her friend's eyes were upturned so he couldn't glare at her in accusation. Only the whites showed but the mouth worked. *He's saying something.* She barely managed to lip-read one word in ten. Their import appalled her.

"It takes a while for the process to embed itself," explained the White. "Unfortunately, as the creature from beyond the stars will no longer treat with me, my chemicals and processes are tainted, cruder. I wish I was able to do more to stop the pain. Too many of them go mad with it and become useless to themselves and us. I think he'll survive though. Like I said, you communists are tougher than the arrogant fops I had to deal with in the beginning."

Alexandra stood up as slowly as she dared, fighting the urge to leap across the room and tear the bastard's throat out. Bakolov picked up a glass flask half full of the same preservative fluid swilling around what was left of Viktor.

"Mixed with opium it was once a powerful medicine but each time the side-effects grow, as you see."

The scientist drained the liquid. His face screwed up, he clasped his stomach and shat noisily, the stench rolling through the cavern.

"Forgive me. This is not how I would want to greet a guest."

Alexandra looked at Viktor, locked in an endless theatre of agony and terror.

"You would consign the workers of the world to this and have them become the slaves of a few," she said. "How can you possibly imagine that we would agree? Your vision of the future is the total opposite to mine."

"Is it? The peasants didn't take too well to revolution I hear. Many are not as enthusiastic as you think. You've seen them - bovine and stupid, hankering after Tsars even as Nikolai ground their faces into the filth or sent them off to die in the trenches. They don't want to be like you and me. They seek to become as those primitives with their church in the valley, singing gibberish to a dead god in front of their holy icons. Thanks to those morons we have to speak to the star creature in Slavonic, for God's sake. They're useless to my world and yours. They held us back, but not anymore. With our science we shall turn them to good use, awakening them to their destiny."

I'm going to die here. She was ringed by a crowd of monsters, her only escape route lay on the other side, down one of those unlit tunnels. There was no way she could get past the four-armed giants. The wheeled electrical men-machines might be easier. Perhaps she could vault over them and hope the mutants were too sluggish to stop her. It was the only way to avoid the same fate as poor Viktor. *I could have gone to the stars with my friends - a barbarian and a lunatic.* If she'd had Banjo beside her they'd have put up a good fight, maybe even won. The odds against her alone were nigh on impossible. She wondered if the brawling oaf had found a path back to the Star Tsar's lair. Bakolov would have told her if the Englishman had been captured as well.

Fatalism made her bold.

"You're a sad monster in a pit of monsters. How will you bring your vision to the world? How will you stand against the united proletariat? We won't fall for your insanity. You're mad - abandoned and dying deep within this mountain, surrounded by abortions you created in the delusion that they offer you mastery. Mastery of what? Shadows and shit. Humanity has moved on."

Bakolov chuckled.

"You've seen the power of the creature from space. He didn't only teach me how to create drones and slaves."

Spheres coated in yellow dust, pushed into a cavern filled with light, heat and noise like a sun captured underground.

"There is radium and uranium here, powerful metals with the energy of the universe encased in their atoms. The power that fires the machines and servants of the space being will give me the ability to create my own dominion, not just over our Mother Russia but the whole world."

Weapons of atomic fire.

"I'm tired," said Bakolov. "Take her away."

Before she had a chance to react flabby white fingers closed over Alexandra's arm and pulled her across the vault. She saw Bakolov's head slump into his body, making him look like melting ice-cream dropped on the pavement in summer. She struggled and fought but she was a child dragged along by an impatient adult. They entered an unlit tunnel. She stumbled and half-fell over broken rock, slamming against the walls as her captor strode on. At last they came to a heavy door opening onto a room lit by a single phosphorescent sphere tossed into a corner. The creature pushed her in, the valve slammed shut and the wheel screeched as the lock span tight.

Alexandra stood trembling, trying to marshal her thoughts into a semblance of order. *He has atomic weapons of incalculable power. He talks of an elite of savants supported by a population of monstrous slaves grown in vats or vivisected into machine hybrids, They are the ones who will be left behind after he has turned the world into a radium furnace.*

Her suspicions were right all along. The White forces had fooled the Star Tsar into handing over his knowledge and technology for Bakolov to use for weapons to wield against the Bolsheviks. When it realised its terrible mistake it fought them, driving their troops back into the mines and sealing itself in its citadel. The civil war finished just in time - the Revolutionary Army defeating Kolchak's Siberian troops before the enemy had a chance to equip itself with these new horrors. In the mopping-up afterwards the defeated survivors abandoned the alchemist in his nest, leaving him to struggle on with the memories of the space being's lessons, fashioning creatures more and more debased and monstrous as his understanding and his materials dwindled.

Can he really destroy the USSR, the world, with his radium weapons? To Alexandra the engines, forges and workshops she'd seen were dismal, broken echoes of a fool's dreams of futurity - nothing compared to the Star Tsar's laboratories here and on Mars. Half of her wanted to think that this diseased slug of a man, wallowing in his own shit and misery, posed no threat, and that his mutant servants and electrical men would die out in this wilderness. Yet the blazing cavern filled with atomic fire hinted at enough power for a madman to wipe out cities.

She paced back and forth, banging her forehead with her fists. How to stop Bakolov? She'd no doubt the Star Tsar would have ended this in a second but the alien was dead, betrayed yet again by stupid men. Moscow and Petrograd had to be alerted, Aminev brought here with every gun, bomb and armoured train he possessed to wipe this horror from Earth before it was too late.

She tried the door - no good. The only piece of furniture was a broken chair. Alexandra snapped off a leg, thinking to use it as a weapon, but tossed it away in disgust when she realised it would be futile against the creatures. Moments later the door opened. Four multi-limbed golems entered, followed by the Czech officer in his wheeled glass box.

The officer's eyes had stopped twitching. They were wide open - the pupils bleached white by the hideous chemicals in the liquid, the sclera a filthy brown. He stared at the prisoner and grinned, though whether it was in pain, anger or madness the commissar couldn't tell. Articulated arms as delicate as dental drills twitched and shuddered. Motes of dirt, clots of blood, skin and hair suspended in the fluid moved convulsively and Alexandra saw the man's chest rise and fall. *He's still attempting to breathe. Bakolov said the process takes time.* She could see it in the spasming throat, the clutching at air no longer there. The officer clung to humanity even as it leached away from him in that foul piss-coloured brew. *The Great Zoltan tapping out his fortune on Brighton Pier. A dark stranger will take you to the stars. My God, he spoke the truth.* The resemblance between that fairground toy and the ruined man shivering in front of her was grotesque. This too was a circus trick - mountebank magic. The Soviets would find no Super Science or perfect mankind here, just bloody farce.

"I'm so sorry." Alexandra wondered if the soldier heard her. Not even her worst enemy deserved such torture.

The Czech officer turned and trundled into the passageway. The creatures dragged her after him. So soon? Had Bakolov changed his mind and decided to kill her? Was she to have no choice? Too much time trying to make sense of what she'd found instead of planning her own escape.

They trudged through narrow passageways. Alexandra cried out but her shouts went unanswered. On either side tunnels flickered past. In some she noticed artillery shells standing on concrete floors flecked with yellow powder. *Radium.* It hadn't been an empty boast. This mountain was an atomic arsenal. In other chambers she spotted coiling white flesh, ragged-eyed faces grimacing at each other under pulsing phosphorescence. *I should be counting, calculating, gathering intelligence on numbers and materiel for when I get free.* But the nightmare sucking her deeper into the stone whirled away all thoughts.

At last they came to a low vault that stank of rotten flesh and a weird vinegary smell billowing from open-topped barrels. A metal slab covered in dried blood and gobbets of meat stood in the middle, flanked by two more electrical men. Alexandra begged them to let her go, pleaded with the officer in the hope her words might penetrate the glass and formaldehyde. The white creatures pushed the commissar onto the table and iron bands dug into her wrists and ankles. A electrical man in the uniform of an artillery brigade sergeant stared down at her from one side. On the other a four-armed servant picked up an axe and a rusty saw. She heard the bright *woomf* of a blow torch and by its acetylene glow spotted the heap of bodies and limbs. They were mangled in such a way as to almost make her faint. She struggled and kicked out with renewed strength, determined not to scream even as the blade descended towards her belly.

A flash of heat and steaming gobbets of flesh spilled over her. Something hit her on the hip and clattered to the floor. Simultaneously the cabinets on both sides of the table burst apart, showering Alexandra with glass and acrid liquid. A bubble of fire rolled across the ceiling, so bright that when she clamped her eyes shut she still saw it flow between the studs and teeth of granite. She smelt burning. Hands slapped her up and down. Her arms and legs were suddenly free and she was yanked into a sitting position. Banjo stood next to the slab, holding two machine guns, hair and beard soaked in fluid and gore and steam rising from the top of his head.

"Sorry about the eyebrows. They'll grow back."

CHAPTER TWENTY

Banjo dragged her splashing through vile chaos. Glowing fragments fell from the walls and ceiling. Some of them looked molten. Alexandra's mind struggled to catch up. The man unslung a machine gun from his shoulder and pushed it towards her.

"Come on, you great big girl's blouse, shape yourself. I picked up one of these for you. Found out how to get to the train and I've got a plan to stop those bastards interfering while I fire her up."

Alexandra looked down the corridor. A diseased light flickered from the door leading to the operating room but to her surprise the rest of the tunnel was empty. Surely the Englishman's shouting would bring Bakolov's legions down upon them? She stared at her hands, caked in soot and preservative. Why weren't they shaking? She'd been on the point of being sawn in half and stuffed into a wheeled aquarium. It was like watching a confusing play in a foreign language from a long way away.

"These are bloody amazing!" Banjo was waving his gun at the ceiling. The Englishman pointed at a dial above the trigger guard. "That regulates the size of the explosion. For God's sake keep it on two. Anything over five will bring the entire mountain down on our heads."

The Bolshevik gawped at the strange weapon.

"You're shooting atomic bullets."

"Oh yes, but these aren't any old atomic bullets. They're silent for a start."

The commissar assumed the bloody explosions had been ear-splitting. Now the man mentioned it she didn't remember any sound.

"Watch."

Banjo fired down the corridor. The gun gave a hiccup and a second later a ball of luminescent fire blossomed in the centre of the wall. The explosion looked very odd - like a handful of burning soap bubbles rolling through the tunnel. Where they touched the sides and ceiling clumps of molten rock dropped onto the floor.

"They're enveloped in some kind of skin that focuses the disintegration. It's how I managed to kill those murderous buggers and only singe you a bit. Mind you, that was on two, Christ knows what happens on ten."

The bubbles vanished. The last shreds of yellow flame skipped across the floor and the ceiling collapsed in a sticky heap of glowing slag. Banjo looked worried.

"Ah. Someone might have that heard that. We don't want to be hanging around. Come on."

They ran along the tunnel. It switched back and forth through the mountain, angling upwards. Just as they approached a junction an electrical cabinet rolled out of an alcove right in front of them. Alexandra glimpsed the naked torso of an old woman in liquid so filthy it looked as if she floated in a cloud of soot. She shouldered her rifle ready to shoot but Banjo put his hand over the barrel.

"Too close."

Instead he squatted down, grabbed the underside of the cabinet and heaved the machine onto its back. The glass shattered. Rancid preservative flooded across the tunnel floor. The human remains flopped and twitched amid the fragments. Alexandra tried not to look down as she leaped over and raced after her friend. At the end of the passageway Banjo turned and fired a single shot. A ball of flame swelled over the wreckage and for a second the commissar glimpsed the silhouette of a body against the flames before the bubble erupted in white fire, evaporating chemicals and blackened flesh. Movement to their left. Mutants scrambled down a wide rock staircase and loped towards them.

"Hold them off," yelled Banjo.

Almost thankful for the opportunity to focus her thoughts, Alexandra went down on one knee to steady her aim. She fired. Bright clouds shredded the advancing creatures. It seemed too easy. Now these monsters were alerted they'd arm themselves and start shooting back. Behind her came the scraping of metal on stone.

"That's it, come on."

Banjo had dragged three waist-high yellow-tipped cannon shells out of a side room and stood them upright just inside the junction. He fiddled with dials on their casing.

"If these don't bring the roof down on those bastards God knows what will."

"Are you sure you know what you're doing?"

"No. Run."

If mere bullets caused the carnage she'd already seen, the powers locked in these shells would surely flood the tunnels and kill everything. Before she could object the Englishman sprinted in the opposite direction to the mutants, who lurched towards them, seemingly oblivious to pain as their clay feet hissed on the boiling rock at the foot of the ancient staircase.

Another turn and Alexandra saw an opening to a vault dead ahead. Banjo hurled himself into the cavern, pulling the commissar close to the wall on the other side of the entrance. The ground rocked. In the darkness around them colossal shapes of iron and rust suspended in chains made from links as large as a man swung back and forth like lanterns on a sledge. A jet of membraned fire roared briefly past them, illuminating a chamber bigger than any cathedral and stacked high with machines, engines, blocks and twisted fragments of metal and rock, all of them ancient and none of them of earthly design. Alexandra crunched her eyes shut, feeling her skin crackle. When she opened them again the Englishman was patting his smouldering beard.

"I should just shave the bastard off and have done."

More rumbling from beyond the scorched entrance. *Rock falls.* Perhaps the idiot's recklessness had sealed off their pursuers and bought them more time.

The two fugitives raced across the cave. Far to their right chains finally snapped and a house-sized forge thundered to the ground, making the granite bounce under Alexandra's feet. They reached another archway with more stairs leading upwards. A dozen yards up and Banjo turned and fired into the darkness behind them. More links gave way in a scream of rust and rotting metal. Machinery crashed down, sealing the opening.

"That should keep the buggers at bay. I reckon that's the main entrance to this part of the mine. There'll be ones further on so watch out and shoot anything that tries to stop us."

Banjo led her to a shaft with a spiralling ramp. Alexandra recognised it as the path down which the mutants had carried Viktor. The sight made her sick and wretched, remembering the agonised fury in the man's eyes as they stared into hers through filthy chemicals. The silent darkness of the mountain seemed to weigh down in judgement on her soul, infinitely more horrible than the monsters they'd escaped. It was only when Alexandra reached the top of the slope and saw the watery daylight skittering over the stones and glinting off the rails that she could breathe again. They jogged to the train and the Englishman jumped on board and checked the controls.

"This might be the stupidest thing I've ever done in my life," Banjo hefted the atomic machine gun, paused and looked up at the ceiling as he ran through some lurid catalogue in his head. "One of the stupidest things."

He fired into the chamber and slammed the door shut. Alexandra heard a dull *woomf* and the locomotive shuddered. Banjo hopped to the side as tendrils of white fire briefly speared out around the hatch.

"Bugger me sideways - it worked. I'm hoping it'll speed things up again as long as none of the pipes rupture."

Alexandra clambered up beside him.

"In case we get interrupted - you'll be going backwards so once we're out of the mountain take it nice and slow. These are the brakes. This regulates the pressure. Make sure that needle doesn't go below red if you want to keep moving."

"You're still planning on going into the ether? You and Ekaterina?" Didn't the oaf realise there were more important things than his ridiculous space fantasies? After all, he'd hunted Alexandra down and rescued her when he could have just as easily escaped back to the alien's citadel. The man had a conscience when it came to his companions. She had to find a way of getting him to see his duty to all of mankind. In truth she didn't want to be the only one carrying the dreadful truth to Petrograd.

Banjo had already clambered down to check the wheels. Alexandra stepped onto the tracks. The sudden flame had rendered everything a stark silver and the after-image still lay across the darkness. The distant walls of the vault were peppered with holes. She hoped Bakolov's monstrous army were too occupied trying to repair the damage they'd caused to come after them yet. Her companion stomped back to the cab, slapping his hands together.

"All we can do is wait. Those bullets burn like buggery so we should get up a decent head in a couple of hours maximum. What happened to you after you pissed off and left me behind to deal with those slimy buggers?"

Alexandra told him about her meeting with Bakolov and the demented Tsarist savant's plans to conquer the world with atomic fire, leaving an elite to rule, kept in power by mutants and machine hybrids created from the remains of those workers allowed to live.

"That battlefield on the other side of the mines and the skirmishes underground were between the Whites and the Star Tsar's sentinels because they tried to nick its science to make armies of monsters," said Banjo. "Do you reckon your lot can stop him?"

"He threatens the world, not just the Soviets. Your British empire is in as much danger. You must come back with me and add your voice to mine. We have to tell the people the truth."

"Don't look at me. I'd be fuck-all use. People listen to you because you've got a badge on your hat and sound like you know what you're talking about, to other communists anyway. No-one ever gave a tinker's cuss about me and my opinions."

"Surely you care about the future of mankind?"

"If I go back with you and miraculously survive getting shot by Commander Bastard in Ikayungri, what do you think I can do? Wander into Lloyd-George's parlour? 'Begging your pardon, but space monsters with ray-guns are coming, according to my Red mate Alexandra who met a maniac called Bollock-off in a mountain in Siberia. If there's any poor buggers left who haven't had their arms and legs blown off at Passchendaele perhaps we could round them up and give the Great White Apes of Barsoom a bloody nose. What do you think, Taffy? King and Country eh?'"

"I have no idea what you just said."

Banjo sighed and put his hands on his hips.

"Look. I'll get you to the other side of the mountain then you're on your own. There's no place for me in your world, other than at the bottom of a lime pit with a bullet through my heart. You're a good egg, Alexandra, but you're talking to the wrong fellow. I'm no hero."

"These mines are poisonous." Alexandra hated herself for what she was about to say but she'd try anything to get the oaf to stay. The road back to Natasha suddenly seemed endless, and she didn't think she could walk it alone.

"What do you mean?"

"Radium and Uranium. That yellow powder on the bullets and in the workshops fills the air with poisonous rays. I'm sorry Banjo. We're dying already. Even if you go into space, you won't survive. Bakolov is doomed too."

"Codswallop. You said he's been drinking that preservative fluid to keep going. We've been eating the Star Tsar's food and I never felt better. If that greasy piss keeps Bollock-off alive then the stuff you and I scoffed will have us farting radium without a twinge."

Banjo slapped her on the shoulder so hard she nearly fell off the footplate.

"You worry too much."

He turned to tinker with the wheels and levers in the cab, whistling through his teeth. So much for trying to scare the oaf into cooperating.

"Eh up. I think we've got company."

Banjo cocked his machine gun. Alexandra cursed her own inattention and peered down the tunnel. Were those shapes moving in the darkness? The Englishman aimed a round at the distant ceiling. Churning clouds of sour light burned in grape clusters, illuminating pale spiders as they slid out of the mountain's pores.

She shouldered her weapon and pulled the trigger. The fireworks were impressive and she understood why the engineer was so excited. But the membranous explosions foaming throughout the cavern made it impossible to judge their effect or how many of the six-limbed worms were piling towards them. The only noise was a delicate crump as each round detonated, sounding for all the world like someone plumping a pillow. None of the mutants cried out as they were shredded into fragments of rancid charcoal. Alexandra guessed they'd destroyed the first wave of men but had no illusions. These creatures only had to bring up their own weapons from the depths and start firing back and it'd be over in seconds. The Star Tsar's food might have rendered them immune from the radium gas in the mine. It wouldn't protect them from atomic shells.

Banjo stopped shooting and frowned. Granite churned into glowing toffee slumped down from the walls and rock fragments from the void above tinked off the rails.

"If we bring the roof down it'll block our escape route."

He peered at the dials and thumped a few pipes, swearing under his breath.

"Nowhere near - we need at least another hour. Looks like we're going to have to leave her and run for it."

Impossible. Alexandra had to get through the mines and back to Petrograd.

"If you want to flee I'll fight these monsters alone."

"You can't defeat them you daft bint," Banjo pointed down the tunnel. The smoking floor and walls were covered in pale, writhing tendrils, scraps of butchered men turned into maggot puppets to hunt them down.

"We have to try."

Alexandra aimed again but a sharp blue light appeared beyond the seething mass. As she feared, Bakolov had brought up one of his infernal weapons and they had no chance. The glare intensified, outlining the monsters and scoring their shadows along the floor. Odd, the beasts scattered away as a star detached itself and drifted into a side tunnel. Flame blasted from the opening, carving smoking gouges in the crowd. Alexandra spotted an inverted cone with writhing hair silhouetted against the explosion and on top of it rode a white angel with clawed hands and blazing eyes. *It carried her over the mountain and she came in through the old battlefield entrance.*

Banjo roared in delight. The drone hurtled towards them, spitting its lethal sparks into the remnants of the mutant army. Ekaterina leaped light-footed onto the fuel stack and jumped over their heads to the cabin roof where she crouched, grinning down at them. Alexandra could have sworn her eyes actually glowed and she saw foam on her friend's chin. She must have rammed her head into a trough of Star Tsar cocaine and inhaled the lot. The singer was an interstellar demon.

"Madam," Banjo gave the word three extra syllables and twirled his hand in an extravagant bow. "It is a delight beyond ecstasy to have you among us once more and you have routed our enemies with incomparable valour."

The actress's face twitched from side to side, turning towards the commissar like an eagle eyeing up its next meal.

"The way is clear," she hissed.

A chance. Alexandra turned to the drone and shouted in Slavonic.

"Take this engine through the mountain."

The machine flew past Ekaterina and flipped upside down. Its tentacles shot out and wrapped around the boiler. The train lurched, sparks cascading up from the wheels. Cursing, Banjo released the brakes.

"What's it doing? It'll shear the bogies off and tear up the tracks."

The footplate tilted and Alexandra staggered, dropping her gun. It disappeared over the side. *Shit*.

"I don't think we're even on the tracks," she yelled grabbing onto the side to stop the wind ripping her out of the cab. Ekaterina jumped down between them and for a second Banjo put his hand around the singer's waist to steady her. The drone fired over their heads at unseen enemies and in the glowing pulse she saw the Englishman holding on to the beautiful, mad actress with one arm and brandishing an atomic rifle in the other. He looked like the happiest boy on the planet.

Bakolov's army of pitiful golems became nothing more than brief scratches of white and grey in the wind. A few smears dotted the side of the cabin when they ploughed through the survivors. Underneath the cold slipstream - the reek of iron and electricity that made her hair stand on end and put metal on her tongue - she caught flashes of decay and rot and the charred scent of destruction but they came and went in seconds. The locomotive plunged on in a race through the mountain, crossing caverns scarred with pits and trenches, some of which she vaguely recognised, others utterly unfamiliar. It was clear they were flying, the machine's alien strength sufficient to lift the entire engine and power it forward at hundreds of miles an hour.

Once in a while the drone spat more fire bullets across plains of littered rubble or up through rusted gantries to splash on glitter-seamed rock. Maybe the Tsarist madman's creatures were still trying to capture them. Alexandra never caught a glimpse and at last a pale disc rushed on them and they burst out of the tunnel, the sentinel placing their train back onto the tracks with delicate precision.

The machine lurched and juddered. For a second Alexandra feared it would derail and crash into the petrified huts. Banjo managed to stabilise it and they steamed across the battlefield. This place made terrible sense now. The struggle in this valley had been between the Star Tsar, the White army and Bakolov's creatures. Even with all his electrical hybrids and six-armed worm-men, the savant had been defeated. Among the destruction Alexandra thought she spotted slagged rock and trees, men and horses flashed instantly into charcoal - the lunatic's weapons or the sentinel's own alien cannon? Did that mean the etheric traveller's science matched the atomic fire Bakolov had harnessed? The being was dead but the secrets to defeat the Tsarist apocalypse might still be locked inside his citadel. If she got to the Supreme Soviet and Natasha in time, together they would unravel them and crush this new threat to the Revolution.

"Stop"!" Ekaterina shouted in Slavonic. The tentacles bit down and the locomotive slowed. Banjo engaged the brakes and hauled on a couple of levers. Steam billowed around them. The iron and soot smelt so sweet after the shit and vinegar reek of the mines.

"No-one's followed. You'll be safe from here on," said Banjo.

Alexandra stood on tip-toe to see the drone clamped to the boiler like a second enormous smokestack.

"This is perfect. With this flying machine in our hands no-one will doubt us. We'll be able to return and defeat Bakolov and salvage the Star Tsar's science. Ekaterina, you're a genius."

The singer stared at her. Their eyes met and Alexandra froze, appalled. There was precious little of the actress who'd sung and danced on makeshift stages in front of yelling workers, or the revolutionary brandishing Mausers above her cowering menfolk on the barricade on Nevsky Prospekt. She truly had become a cosmic firebird, hands clawed and twitching as she glowered at Alexandra's wretched humanity. Jealousy, sorrow and admiration tumbled through her, catching her off guard. Lost for words she turned to Banjo.

"If you want to make yourself useful you'll need a coal shovel," he told her. "There's one in that chest over there."

Mechanically, she opened the trunk and looked inside. Empty. "Sorry Alexandra."

Hands grabbed her ankles and flipped her upside-down into darkness. The lid slammed shut and she heard the bolt drive home.

It took a good hour of kicking before the chest popped open again. The train clacked along at a steady pace. Alexandra struggled to her feet, cursing. *That treacherous, ignorant bastard.* She dabbed her temple where she'd thumped it against the bottom of the box and hissed. There was no sign of the engineer or the actress and the drone had gone, though its tentacles had left bright grooves across the boiler. She searched the sky. Beyond the tops of the firs and birch she saw nothing but grey clouds. The Yablonoi Mountains were just thicker shadows in the distance. There should have been an inverted cone with two figures clinging onto it, rising up towards the void. She wasn't even permitted a last glimpse of her friends.

An incoherent fury swept over her. Of course she would have tried to stop them, threatened them, shouted at them, but if in the end it had all been futile they could at least have given her a proper farewell instead of just stuffing her into a box like so much rubbish. And now her companions were heading back to the mountain ready to journey to the stars. Wounded pride and loneliness replaced rage. *I'm the one who's supposed to be Earth's herald to the universe, not a drunken, whoring moron and a cocaine addict.*

She spotted a book on the floor with a bullet hole in its centre. Was this intended to be compensation for the Englishman's betrayal? This fatuous bourgeois fantasy made it ten times worse. Alexandra yanked open the fire door ready to toss the novel into the furnace.

A Princess of Mars.

She paused and leafed through the story. The Englishman had

underlined the last sentence. *I believe that they are waiting there for me, and something tells me that I shall soon know.* Underneath he'd scrawled a message in pencil - *Sory Alexandra. We need Baba Yaga to go into space. Good luk in Petrograd. I hope you and yore 'frend' Natasha are happy together. B Z H.*

"You lumpen shit."

Alexandra tucked the book back into her coat.

After a day she came to the fallen armoured train. It still lay by the side of the track. She feared the drone had damaged the rail during its first attack or her way would be blocked by wreckage. The line was clear. She caught sight of the body of the frightened Cossack Aminev had executed. He lay where he'd died, his head the colour and shape of a burst aubergine.

The next night she journeyed under a cloudless sky, looking up at the stars and hunting for the sign of any ship ascending into space, scoring the cosmos with atomic fire. Nothing. They were long gone, heading to Mars no doubt, ready to board the interstellar dreadnought. Alexandra started to read the book by the light of the firebox but after the first chapter she felt so wretched that she rolled himself up in her coat, lay on her side and listened to the mindless tick of the wheels.

I should be fired with revolutionary purpose, carrying a revelation more profound than any saint, one that will transform humanity. But all she could think of was the squalor, death and filth in Bakolov's mountain and the grotesque corpse of the Star Tsar. She knew it was Tugarin the earth dragon whispering to her, boasting that it had refashioned the universe in its own image and all her silly hopes were nothing more than bright scraps lathed from abysmal engines of war to fall and disappear in grime and gore. *This was why The Hammer never clawed his way back to the world.* It wasn't the horror that undid you in the end, it was the sheer exhaustion. She hunted for memories of Natasha but even they were lost to her.

In the morning Alexandra was wakened by shouting. She looked out to see cavalry riding towards her - Red Cossacks. They pointed guns and ordered her to stop. She remembered enough of Banjo's lessons to apply the brakes.

"I am Commissar Alexandra Lobachevsky of the People's Commissariat for Education. I order you to take me to the new commander immediately."

CHAPTER TWENTY-ONE

And so Banjo's dream came true - soaring over the mountains on a flying machine with his arm around a beautiful princess. He doubted she needed his steadying hand but the woman didn't seem to object. Ekaterina kept swaying back and forth. It would have been nice to think she was about to swoon in his arms. In truth he reckoned her lack of balance had more to do with the amount of space drugs she'd consumed.

He felt guilty about locking Alexandra in the chest. The lass had come over all fiery-eyed and Banjo realised she was all for taking the sentinel to the Reds. The engineer didn't speak Old Russian and still wasn't sure whether the machine actually understood French. He had to stop the commissar giving the thing orders he couldn't understand or countermand. At least the twit would be back with her own people now. Perhaps she'd persuade Commander Bastard-features she hadn't gone utterly insane and the Bolsheviks would march on Bollock-off's mountain lair and wipe his abominations out once and for all. He struggled to see how a crowd of piss-filled ambulatory fish tanks and French-letters stuffed with galvanised rot would stand up against a modern army, even one exhausted by eight years of war. Mind you, those atomic weapons looked devilish violent and he shuddered to imagine what they'd do to a city like Moscow or London. Not that it mattered to him anymore. He was off into outer space. It wasn't very noble or patriotic. Maybe Alexandra was right and he should be sacrificing himself for the good of all humanity. But what about that interstellar flyer standing on the desert plain of Mars, constellations shimmering across her pristine hull? *She is the ship of all ships. I'd be cracked in the head not to chance it.*

To be honest he'd miss the lass. The po-faced otter shared his love of the future even if her version seemed as devoid of fun and possibility as Mother Superior's knickers. Now this was what it was supposed to be like - adventure, great wonders, exotic places and creatures from the stars, and his own Dejah Thoris snuggled up beside him. Once the pair of them returned to space he would find her a jewelled harness to wear in some bazaar on another planet - one with leather and jingling chains and jewels to enhance her kohl-lined eyes. And a great big scimitar for himself. *Alright Banjo. You are the fool of fools if you think there's the chance of anything between you and her, but hey ho, a man must dream and fortune favours the mad.*

The sentinel swooped low over the valley of the Old Believers as if searching for something. As far as he knew the singer hadn't spoken to it so either it followed its own initiative - which was worrying - or had started to drift off course - which was worse. If its power was exhausted after the battle in the tunnels they were trapped on this miserable planet. If not he needed to find a way of getting it to obey him so he wasn't totally reliant on the whims of Madam here. It seemed to respond to him on Mars so if Banjo could steal a few moments with it alone then he'd try to parlez-vous with it again.

A rock spanged off the metal carapace and the sentinel lurched upwards. The tentacles formed a rigid fence around the top of the machine, presumably to protect its passengers and stop them tumbling off. Ekaterina stepped to the edge of the platform, holding one to peer down at the village. Banjo joined her as close as he dare. He didn't care for the oily shimmer on those scales or the ropy pulses that ran from base to tip. Damned if he was going to touch it.

He guessed the Old Believers had chucked a missile at them. For all the good the alien did them they singularly lacked gratitude. He suspected they treated it like one of the prisoner priests of ancient times, kept alive as mouth-pieces for the gods before being dragged to the top of a ziggurat to have their heart torn out by the next patsy in line. He didn't have much clue about the intricacies of the Russian Orthodox faith but was pretty sure it didn't include space monsters.

Ekaterina hissed like a cat and he thought he saw shadows scatter into the houses. Her eyes blazed fury and for a horrible second it looked as if she intended to unleash a star missile on the village. Wiping out the already-dead was one thing but laying waste to a bunch of stupid peasants seemed pointless slaughter and he'd had a belly-full of that. To his relief she merely spat in the direction of the church and gave a sharp laugh of disdain.

The ship floated around the houses in a circle, the tension passed, and the vessel hummed up the side of the mountain. For the first time Banjo realised just how massive the Star Tsar's lair really was. He spotted countless windows and openings disguised in the shadows of rocky outcrops or buried deep in clefts in the mountainside. Most of the spaces beyond lay in darkness but some still glowed with chemical lamps and energies that had outlived their master. He longed to explore - they'd only visited a fraction of it before being thrown into space - but not now. More than ever Banjo wanted to get back to Mars and on board that vast etheric flyer. But they needed to gather supplies and that would give him a few moments to scout for anything else useful or interesting. To begin with he ought to figure out what the princess was after. She'd barely exchanged words with him and the few she uttered were all mad. Most of the time she behaved like he wasn't even there.

The drone entered a new tunnel and dropped down a shaft so rapidly the woman's hair streamed up in a reverse ebony waterfall and the soles of his boots rose off the platform. The machine slowed. To his surprise they emerged in the workshop where its companion still lay in its white bath. They stepped down into the laboratory. After the filth and stench of the mines it was like falling face-down into a bank of wild violets. Just looking at the gleaming surfaces purged his mind, even if he hadn't the foggiest idea how anything worked. Ekaterina interlaced her fingers and looked about her with placid disinterest. Banjo thought he ought to get a few things straight.

"If we're returning to the planet Mars we'll need to gather supplies. Lots of them, seeing as how you intend to take me with you and all."

She stared at him.

"Take you with me?"

"Yes."

He nodded enthusiastically and tried a little louder and slower. "Take me with you." Perhaps pointing at the ceiling might help the message get through the layers of opium. "To Mars."

"Why should I do that? You are an ordinary man, an Earth creature whose soul is bound by what he sees in the moment. You are not fit to ride the space ways among the transcendent ones."

Christ Almighty.

He mastered his temper with difficulty. To be fair, standing and staring him down with magnificent contempt, her pale blue eyes burning, she presented such a strapping specimen of Trojan womanhood that he struggled to marshal his thoughts. In normal circumstances he'd have been happy to stand slack-mouthed and drooling while mashing whatever headgear he had in his fists. *Come on, young fellow-me-lad. Show her who's skipper.* At the same time, if he kept this conversation going long enough in French the sentinel might pick up a bit more. It hovered behind her and he swore it was earwigging. Those red lights on its midriff glowered at him with the keen suspicion of a chaperone. Still, with any luck the machine intelligence would gather sufficient understanding of the language for him to tell it what to do. He decided to turn the eloquence up a notch.

"Fair one. Indeed, I am nothing more than your worthless servant and although I realise your enhanced wisdom ushers you without question into the ranks of those superior intelligences and spirits that reside beyond Earth, there will also be very real and brutish perils that only a warrior such as I can protect you from."

Enhanced wisdom my arse - opium and cocaine-induced delusions more like. If she persisted in her line of argument, he might have to leave her here and go it alone if he could somehow get through to that flying thing.

Ekaterina tossed her head, put one hand on her hip and gestured at the heavens with the other.

"Very well but you will know your place in my service and do all that I command without question."

So much for equality in the new Soviet world. Scratch a Bolshie and underneath you find a frothing aristo. Surprise surprise.

Banjo gave a deep bow, presenting a leg and wiggling his hand as he imagined a Parisian gentleman might do.

"Your humble servant, madam."

She ordered him to follow. He dutifully trundled after her, the drone humming in his wake. When she turned a corner he hung back and waited until she was a good twenty yards along the passageway. He faced the sentinel - God it was bloody alarming looking up at that cluster of black tentacles, knowing it had the strength to lift a Pacific-class locomotive clear off the rails.

"*Arrêtez-vous.*"

The machine halted. He smacked his fist into his palm. *It does understand me.* Banjo didn't have time to test the extent of its vocabulary but it was a start. If he got the thing to help him gather food for the journey he'd have a chance to carry on with its lessons.

They returned to the hangar with the space flyer. He politely told the actress she might want to rest a little, what with the effort of slaughtering hundreds of abominations and all, but she ignored him and walked along the tunnel to stare up at the sky. The grainy orange light from the bloated sun faded and a few stars appeared. The sight fired him up even more and he decided not to hang around to see if the cosmic angels in Ekaterina's head were going to tell her to fling herself off the precipice. Time to work a bit more on Baba Yaga's loyalties.

"Follow me," he told it.

He and the drone wandered down a dozen levels until they came to a cavern with an indoor garden. It didn't look like the forest they'd found when they first entered the mountain but he noticed a couple of pieces of half-eaten fruit at the base of a coiled indigo tree trunk. Maybe this was the place after all. If so one of his companions had sneaked a crafty scoff on their way through. Probably the actress in search of more hellish intoxication.

"Come over here," he said in French.

The drone flew towards him.

"Pick fruit."

No response so he pantomimed with a bush covered in blue apples. That did the trick. It zipped among the trees, dropping its harvest into sacks picked up from the corner of the room. A few caverns further on he found cartons of water. Based on their trip to Mars they had enough for about three weeks. He fully intended to be banqueting as a special guest in the court of the Grand Pooh-Bah of Aldebaran long before then. He made his way back to the hangar, the sentinel following him festooned with bags like a sinister Christmas tree.

Half way along the corridor he paused. *What about Madam's space cocaine?* Did he need to find more to feed her drug habit or should he leave her with whatever remained of the original stash? Difficult to know which was worse - a happy raging dope fiend, or a raging dope fiend with the shivering hab-dabs. He supposed he'd better see if he could track down an extra supply. It might give him a bargaining point after she'd finished off the first batch. He had time. The sentinel piloted the etheric ship to Mars so taking it with him would ensure Ekaterina couldn't head off into space on her own if the fancy took hold. Might as well explore further in case he turned up anything useful for the voyage. He walked down one of the tunnels leading out of the grove and called the machine.

It dutifully hummed in pursuit, coming to rest a couple of yards in front, those evil-looking fronds waving back and forth like demon hair. Had it really learned the language just by listening in on his conversations with the actress? If so a hell of a machine mind lay inside that upside-down dunce's hat. On the other hand, since Ekaterina snorted all that jolly dust she'd kept rabbiting on about how she communed with space angels. According to Alexandra the drug had re-organised the woman's brain so she had instant access to all her own thoughts and memories and more besides. Did that mean there also existed a link between her and the creature's machines, a telepathic connection that allowed them to absorb her knowledge including her mastery of French? The white liquid powering the Star Tsar here and on Mars was made of minute flecks of metal that moved as if they had intelligence. Was the alien cocaine the same? Had she spent the last few days hosing the chambers of her skull with microscopic engines that not only thought for themselves but acted like radios?

Bugger me.

Not good. If he was right she had a direct telegraph line into this flying thing's inner workings. The only consolation was that she hadn't realised herself or didn't act as if she had. He decided to keep this revelation quiet and let the actress continue to order the flyer about in Old Russian. At the moment she seemed content to chase fairies through her head. If she stopped and had a think she might realise what powers really lurked inside her addled visions.

Drug factories seemed in short supply. Ages wandering along tunnels up and down revealed endless caverns walled with glass-smooth granite or jigsaw pumice. Most stood empty or contained geometric blocks. Dead machines or pieces of furniture? He had no way of knowing. The smoky light coaxed everything to abstraction, layering the world with pipe-smoke swirls. Banjo stood under a glowing panel and swept his hand through the tangerine air. Patterns and eddies shivered at the threshold of his perception.

He stopped. This room was different. The ceiling shone with a coruscating sheet of radiance, filled with patterns. It looked like some kind of movie projection. He didn't see any mechanism or tell-tale fan of light shining through the mist. Below it, ten hollow cylinders about three yards high were ranged in a circle. They'd been cut in half vertically and their curved sides faced inward. A circular plate at human head height glowed in each tube. The engineering powering this outré magic lantern show felt very much alive, a bone-grinding hum filling the air and percolating up through the soles of his boots. He didn't know if it was static or another more alien force but the hairs on his arms stood up and he swore he was being watched. But where from and what by?

He approached the nearest column and tried to make sense of the disc. It flickered with shapes too soft to understand. To get a closer look he'd have to step within the radius of the tube itself and he wasn't that stupid. Alexandra and her chums could order one of their bright-eyed cadets to stand inside for the glory of the Soviet Union if they were desperate. Banjo was happy to give it a miss.

He craned up at the ceiling again and tried to understand the pattern. Ragged green and blue shapes with a huge sine wave of darkness, all overlaid with tiny orange and red sigils interlinked by lines and a tiny script he guessed was a cosmic alphabet. It was so familiar - why? With his head flung back he rotated on the spot and nearly fell over. For a second he was in the interplanetary rocket again, staring down on Earth from space, struggling against vertigo. *There's the continents and seas and that's day and night.* Right now he floated over India. He recognised the Bengal Coast and assumed the cluster of lights on the seaboard marked Calcutta. But when he glanced westward the subcontinent shrank to the edge and line of the Shatt al-Arab bulged out in the middle of the disc. Further towards Africa and the same thing happened. Iraq crushed itself into the rim and Sicily took centre stage. It was like looking at the surface of a globe rotating as he moved his eyes. Damned clever but horribly creepy at the same time, especially as the countries at the periphery didn't disappear behind the mystic sphere but stretched out around the circle as if pulled along an alien geometry. He tore his gaze away, massaged the crick out of his neck and turned to the machine hovering inside the door.

"What do those coloured dots and lines mean?"

It wasn't going to tell him. Resisting the dizziness he looked again, navigating his way towards Siberia in fits and starts. *There we are.* An orange speck shimmered against a grey-green semi-circle of crumpled land. Two threads speared out from the marker, one heading east. He followed it to the Japanese island of Hokkaido where more motes of light danced near the volcano of Yezo Fuji.

The Star Tsar's not the only creature hiding in our world. Like his Bolshevik mate he'd assumed the alien had stranded itself by accident in these mountains centuries ago and made a home for itself among the local peasants. Looking at this map he started to wonder if there wasn't a legion of the buggers. Well if that was the case why hadn't any of the others come to lend a hand when their mate got sick?

"So, are all the sparkly lights men from the stars? Like your master?"

Still no answer. He tried to focus. As his gaze moved, so the earth swelled and receded across that monstrous geometry. *Sinkiang, the Himalayas, Bombay, Turkey, Marrakech, fucking hell there's one in the Bog of Allen in County Kildare. A Fenian space monster no less. Iceland...* Banjo struggled to breathe. He was drowning under the weight of that map as it pulsed the world at him like the devil's own heart, each beat freckled with the lair of another inhuman being. And he knew that with every gasp he sucked in more machine dust to fill his lungs and creep through interstices of his body.

He stumbled away. All the wonders and anticipation of a journey to the stars shrank into a dead bullet in his stomach. *It's the horrors of the mines,* he told himself. He couldn't take back control of his shaking hands so he begged the sentry to wait, lurched into the corridor and round a corner before slumping down against the wall. He reached instinctively into his pocket for *A Princess of Mars* before remembering he gave it to Alexandra.

What would John Carter do? Leap free with one bound, slaughter a dozen enemies with his sword, rescue the damsel from the villainous clutches of Tal Hajus and piss off back to the twin-towered city of Helium at high speed in a flyer. All those sparks on the map would be a bloody menu to him - choose what to behead or disembowel next and off you go. The slimy horror of Iceland, the tentacled triple-headed turd of Tibet. Take your pick and set to.

He rubbed his face with his hands.

That's a story, Banjo, this is real. Lurid twaddle, Mother said when she caught you reading She and Allen *in the crapper.*

Amid all the shit and misery of this world the Quaker lad had turned to the stars, to his imagination and tales of wonder and adventure - H. Rider Haggard, Abraham Merritt's *The Moon Pool*, even that wet weekend Lord Dunsany, and of course Edgar Rice Sodding Burroughs. They were all the templates for the fantasy and heroics he'd hungered after to fill his dreary childhood, convincing himself he'd be a hero one day in a cosmos that cared about nobility and would recognise simple goodness not born from a sour moral cant or blind patriotic creed. Not this universe. It had no place for ripping yarns of heroes and villains, of flyers, monsters and gorgeous princesses, no matter the fleeting resemblances. This was altogether something else - an immense cold void beyond understanding.

We blithering idiots thought the Star Tsar was us but nobler and cleverer.

But what if he wasn't? What if he was worse, far darker, truly alien and unknowable - a terrifying cipher in a whirling chaos, a dark ocean across which this little planet drifted like a rotting life raft, its idiot crew convinced their wisdom encompassed all possibility? *What did the Chinese say about us British? Toads at the bottom of a well looking up at the circle of stars above their heads and thinking it was all of creation. Now what? Go or stay?*

Alexandra would have an answer. Her mind was built for this machine world. No doubt she'd spout some bollocks about Destiny and making friends with the Soviets of other planets and be daft enough to believe it. *Get a grip and see this through.*

"Come here,"

The sentinel floated out into the tunnel.

"Help me up."

A tentacle wrapped around his wrist and eased him to his feet.

"Let's be off to Mars."

He didn't have a choice. A thousand miles on either side filled with enemies. The stars it was and if there were unmentionable horrors beyond comprehension waiting to tear him to pieces he'd be the first man on Earth to have the privilege. That had to count for something.

He made his way back to the hangar. The drone tossed the bags of supplies into the ship, flipped over on its side and slotted itself into the hull. Ekaterina stood by the forward window, her hands like eagle claws rigid at her sides and a couple of empty tins lying at her feet. She'd slung the remaining atomic machine gun over her shoulder.

"We're ready - time to set sail," Banjo said.

No response. He noticed the foam on her lips and eyes rolled up into her head. *How much more of that bloody powder has she snorted?* No point trying to get through now. Wait for her to come down and then have a proper talk, just to let her know what was what and who stood where. Banjo spotted the last magazine for his atomic machine gun sitting on a box. There were a few bullets left inside so he went to fetch it. The hatch slammed shut behind with a deafening clang and the space ship roared down the tunnel and up into the grey sky, the shock wave knocking him flat onto his back.

CHAPTER TWENTY-TWO

The cavalry accompanied her to the ironworks. A couple of miles out from Ikayungri more Cossacks came to meet the train. A man in overalls rode among them. He cantered alongside and jumped from his saddle into the cab while another grabbed his horse. He nodded to Alexandra and took over the controls, working with crisp precision. Clearly he wasn't one of the peasant engineers Aminev despaired of. He knew exactly what he was doing. The new commander must have poached him from Chita or further down the line.

"Where are you from?"

But though she shouted above the racket, the newcomer ignored her. Instead, the man leaned out to get a view of the tracks, operating the controls without looking as he brought the locomotive to a halt.

"Why have we stopped out here?" she asked.

They were several hundred yards from the complex. Still no reply, so the commissar pushed past in irritation and climbed down beside the track. She felt her mouth drop open.

The biggest armoured train she'd ever seen blocked the line, a fortress of green iron cutting a sharp hole in the overcast sky. It bore two main turrets studded with pipes, vents, rifle slots, snorkels and periscopes. They each carried a pair of battleship guns that had to be eight-inchers at least. A smaller conning tower sat in the middle. Even matched beside the Star Tsar's wonders this was impressive, in the same way an ornate medieval mace would look next to a Maxim - a brute lump of thuggery rendered into steel art and vicious abstraction. Alexandra walked away from the rails to get a better view. A second single-turreted ironclad rested further down the track, separated from the leading carriage by eight infantry wagons, all fitted with gun ports.

At first she guessed that a new contingent of mechanics had managed to finish the armoured trains the Whites had left behind. Ignoring the offer of a ride from a Cossack officer she approached the behemoth. The cavalry thundered off towards the warehouses and factories. At least they didn't see her as a prisoner but she'd hoped they'd take her straight to the commander. Her mission was of the utmost urgency yet she couldn't shake the fascination of the monster rearing up before her. She noticed a plaque under the first turret.

The Orlik. That's impossible.

The most powerful armoured rail cruiser ever made, built by the Tsarists to crush the Revolution and driven by the renegade Czech Legion across the length of Russia as they tried to escape to the east coast. She'd thought they sold it to the Japanese and later it had ended up in the hands of some Manchurian warlord operating out of Harbin. So how was it here and, more importantly, why? Judging by the bright paint on the turrets and the gleaming steel cannon it had undergone a serious refit designed to match it against the greatest and most potent of foes. Was that why it was in an abandoned White foundry in the middle of nowhere? Did her comrades plan to use it to attack the Star Tsar's sentinel? If that was the case this wasn't merely an outpost being scavenged by the Soviets for forgotten machinery and parts any more. Someone very high up in the government had sanctioned this, maybe even Comrade Stalin himself.

Using it to fight against the sentinels would be futile. The burning stars would rip it to shreds in seconds. However it might help her stop Bakolov or at least get through the mines to the citadel so the Red Army could capture the alien's science and turn it against the maniac and his vile legions. It would be risky. Even with those battleship guns she didn't know how long it'd stand up to the alchemist's atomic fire.

A couple of trucks jounced over the muddy ground, spitting out clouds of diesel smoke. They pulled up alongside the dreadnought. Workers clambered out and started to pass what looked like lead sheets up to the turrets where more engineers popped open the hatches to receive the plating. Tearing herself away, Alexandra hurried past the train towards the warehouses.

She heard her name shouted out and turned to see Aminev walking along the train's roof between the gun towers. The commander was in shirt-sleeves and smoking his pipe. He scrambled down the side with an agility that belied his age, put his hands on his hips and looked her up and down. The officer gave a lizard smile of disbelief. *The last time I saw you was under a wagon blown apart by the sentinel's ray gun,* she thought.

"Comrade Commissar as I live and breathe. We thought you were dead. Where are the others?"

It took a moment for Alexandra to snap out of her surprise. *And how on earth did you get away?* she almost asked, but that could wait.

"I'm the only one left."

"What the hell happened?"

"It's a long story, I need to make a full report, urgently, to you and you alone."

Aminev fished a dirty rag out of his back pocket and wiped his hands.

"Very well. Are you hungry? Get some food down you and a surgeon to check you over and then we'll talk. Are we in any immediate danger?"

"Not that I know of but I have to speak to you right now. We can't delay. The future of mankind is at stake. After I've explained everything I'll need to get to Petrograd as fast as I can."

Aminev studied her for a few seconds before whistling to a Cossack officer who rode over.

"Take fifty men up the line and post pickets."

"You've got the *Orlik* here."

The commander followed Alexandra's gaze.

"We call it the *Zaamurets* now. I prefer its old name. We'll have it painted on before we go."

"I thought it was in China."

"We took it back from those fucking monkeys. It's spent the last six months being upgraded in Vladivostok and we're just putting the finishing touches here. I finally persuaded those bastards down the line to let me have some proper mechanics. What happened to your English pet? Dead as well?"

"Why is it here? Where's it going?"

Aminev chuckled and slapped her on the back.

"I'll get some food brought over so you can eat while we talk."

Aminev guided her through the complex to his office. On the way the commissar noticed more of the new mechanics working the machinery, scrambling through the factory gantries or standing in knots consulting plans and ledgers, locked in earnest discussion. The peasants she'd seen when they first arrived had disappeared. This was more like a proper military camp instead of a scavenging outpost. The commander had even treated himself to a bigger stove, burning sharply against the cold in the middle of the room. A man in a trench coat and cap stood in front of it with his back to the door, fists clasped behind him. He turned when they entered and Alexandra found herself staring at Cousin Anton.

I know what you are. We all do. You're sick in the head, Alexandra.

"Alexandra!"

Her childhood friend whipped off his hat and flung his arms wide with a crazy grin. Before she had a chance to draw breath he hugged her. She lost all sense, all reference, the world collapsing in on her memories of her comrades, her broken dolls, Natasha. Despite her Star Tsar strength she barely had the energy to push him away. He laughed, as if the moment was merely awkward.

"Look at the state of you, How long has it been? Six years? Seven? My God!"

He paused and put his hand on Alexandra's shoulder.

"Alexandra! What is it?"

All she could do was shake her head and try to breathe her heart down.

"She's clearly been through hell. Give her room," said Aminev.

The commander pulled open a drawer and tossed a bottle to Anton who passed it over. The vodka was cripplingly awful, even by Red Army standards, but it helped her find her voice. *You are a commissar and the herald of a new age. Nothing else matters.*

"Viktor, Pavel and The Hammer are dead. All the actors on *A Bolshevik Forever!* were murdered by Old Believers living in the mountains."

"What about Ekaterina? Is she alive?"

A sergeant came in with a steaming pot of porridge, followed by a camp surgeon who yanked Alexandra's eyelid down, listened to her chest, mumbled something around his cigarette, shrugged and left. Alexandra, floundering for purchase, tried the food. It tasted strange, as if the Star Tsar's fruit had rendered all others bitter. She remembered Bakolov boasting about the radium poisoning yet felt no different. *I'm changed. I am a new woman. I know what I am.* Everything was distant. This life, once so familiar, cold and leached of colour like a faded photographic plate. *A photographic plate.*

She almost dropped the billy can. Reaching into her coat pocket she pulled out the tablet she'd taken from the archive in the Star Tsar's mountain and held it up to the light. Nothing. The moving figures in their strange landscape had vanished. She turned the slab of crystal this way and that. *It's lost its power. I have no proof left other than my own words.*

The flare of Aminev's match snapped her back into the present. She turned to face the commander so she wouldn't have to look at Anton.

"What I'm about to tell you sounds completely insane, unbelievable. Every word is true. You must understand that the Soviets, the Revolution, the world itself, stands on the edge of a new age. What we decide next, here, in this office, shall send us plummeting into destruction that'll make eight years of war look like a child's game, or will carry us soaring to the stars."

"Good heavens, how dramatic!" said Anton. She ignored him.

Aminev put his boots on the desk, plaited his fingers over his stomach and fixed her with his basilisk gaze.

"Go on."

She told them everything from the moment the sentinel attacked the train. Neither man said a word or showed any reaction, although the commander's eyebrow went up when Alexandra described their voyage to Mars. Sometime later Yohzin entered with a stack of reports but Aminev bellowed at him to get the fuck out and shut the door behind him. It sounded like the poor fool fell down the stairs in his desperation to get away.

As she talked an odd suspicion came over her. By any standards the tale she told was utterly preposterous. She was babbling like a moon-struck simpleton or deluded drug addict yet both men looked deadly serious, even when they should have been roaring with laughter. In the end she explained about Bakolov's legion of horrors and her own escape from the mountains. In the silence that followed Aminev and Anton exchanged glances.

"Sergei Andreivich Bakolov." Anton rubbed his chin as he watched the flames twitch in the stove.

"You know the name? He said he was some great scientist who'd dined with the Tsar."

"Scientist might be a bit of an exaggeration. He was well connected - an illegitimate grandson of the old Grand Duke Michael Nikolayevich, lingering at court - one of the many mice hiding in the linen cupboard like fortune's fools. They finally booted him off on a geological expedition just before the war, which is how he ended up here. Bakolov showed some propensity for the earth sciences. He wrote a ridiculous paper on the Tunguska explosion which was laughed out of Petrograd and he ended up printing himself. *Visitors from Space* he called it."

It was hard to keep the curdled anger of so many years from bubbling over. Alexandra tried to keep her voice even.

"How come you know so much about this?"

"Like you I was a Commissar in the People's Commissariat for Education. How come you don't?", replied Anton.

Was?

He gave her that mocking half-grin of old, his charcoal eyes glowing in the firelight. He winked.

"You don't believe me," said Alexandra.

Aminev pulled his feet off the desk and tapped out his pipe against the chair leg, exhaling very slowly. Alexandra turned to him.

"Comrade Commander, I must go to Petrograd. The Star Tsar has science in its lair that will transform us. We stand at the edge of a new dawn yet this monster Bakolov seeks to destroy everything, to turn his weapons of atomic fire on mankind. We'll order the finest scientists to come here immediately and study the creature's knowledge so we can defeat the foul bastard."

She realised she was up on her feet, pacing back and forth, beating her fist against her palm as the visions washed over her.

"We can build our own etheric craft - a space flyer. If we get our greatest savants in Petrograd University to study the Star Tsar's machines it should be easy. And with our own ship we too can go to Mars and perhaps from there we can make contact with the denizens of other words, other Soviets so that we can take our rightful place in the future. We must leave immediately. If you need more physical proof then let's return to the Star Tsar's lair with the *Orlik* to protect us from that Tsarist bastard."

"Why do you want to go to Petrograd and not Moscow?" asked Anton. *You smug shit. You know why.* She could have killed him there and then.

"I think we already have the proof we need," said the commander.

Alexandra stared at Aminev. *Of course.* In her enthusiasm she'd forgotten about the officer's electrical girl.

"That? It's not enough. Bakolov's creatures are grotesque human experiments performed by a maniac with little grasp of what the Star Tsar taught him. He uses foul essences and materials, corrupt fluids that are a pitiful imitation of what lies within the creature's citadel. We need to show the real..."

"We've found another one, alive, with several of its servants - those four-armed creatures that chased you through the mines," said Aminev.

"Another machine man hybrid? Where?"

"I finally persuaded my men to search the cellars properly. The ones that survived found it deep within the tunnels."

"Survived? There was a battle?"

For the first time Aminev laughed out loud.

"Not exactly. I had to hang three of the snivelling cowards *pour encourager les autres*."

He twisted a piece of paper and used it to light a second pipeful from the stove. Alexandra remembered the crazed cavalryman. *His forehead popped open like an egg moments before the drone tore the world apart.*

Anton slapped her on the shoulder, making her jump.

"Come, let me show you. Then we can decide if it's enough for Petrograd or Moscow, and what to do next."

Aminev nodded.

"Glad to have you back safe and well, Comrade Commissar."

Somehow Alexandra found herself climbing down the outside gantry behind Anton. *Any second now he'll turn on me again. Once we're out of earshot.* Her cousin jumped down the last few steps, whistling through his teeth, before turning to smile up at her as if they'd never been anything other than childhood friends.

"You've been a stranger too long Alexandra."

"The Revolution's pulled us all apart." She tried not to sound too guarded, too desperate to ask the question. There was no need.

"Mother and Father are well and I'm sure they'd love to see you again. Natasha too, though she lives far away now. She never finished her studies. Instead the great scientist fell in love with a party activist and they headed off to Kurgan to help set up the collectives there. He hunts kulaks and she stays at home to look after their son, Anton. My little namesake is one year old already.

God, Alexandra, how the years have passed. You really should write to her. She'd be so happy to hear from you after all this time."

Alexandra stopped and stared at the wet mud between her boots. Silence poured into her arms and legs, filled her torso and swelled up through her chest, neck and head. She became dark, cold water drawn from sunless seas far beneath this Siberian patch of dirt and iron.

"Alexandra?"

There's one more broken doll I was supposed to mend but I forgot about her. But now the damage is so deep it's better to let Comrade Commissar Alexandra Lobachevsky crumble into nothing.

"Are you alright?"

"Yes, yes of course."

"You went into the radium mines and breathed the air and touched the ore. Are you sure you're ok?"

"Never better."

Anton laughed.

"Alexandra you always were such a dreamer. Aminev said that Pavel performed our play *Man of the Future!* Fancy that. I'd almost forgotten it. What a load of childish nonsense it was. We won't write plays about the men of the future anymore, we *are* the men of the future."

Foreheads touching as we bent over the script.

They walked through a factory transformed into a thundering machine of sparks, crucibles, ovens, smelters, milling tools and lathes. More of the new engineers directed workers on gantries and platforms, shouting up through the smoke. With every step Alexandra forced her battered self back into a semblance of life.

"Iron Felix sent you?" she heard herself ask. "He won't be happy to hear his cousin has fled into space."

"I'm GPU now."

That brought her up short.

"You're Cheka? Secret police?"

Anton grinned and guided her by the elbow down a passageway towards a set of double doors leading to the cellars.

"The proper term is State Political Directorate. The Cheka were dissolved last year, remember?"

"Why on earth did you become one of the secret police?"

Anton stopped and turned to face her, his face sombre in the half-light.

"Things are changing Alexandra. Comrade Stalin brings the directives from Vladimir Ilyich these days. It's clear who's in the ascendant. You're better off away from Moscow and Petrograd. We all are. When Comrade Lenin dies everyone will have to be on their guard and prepare to fight even harder for the Revolution, with clarity and without remorse. How well do you know Stalin?"

"I was with him in England. What's there to say? He's a Georgian - a poet. His essays are clumsy but have clarity and passion. Ekaterina knew him better than I from their bank-robbing days. Is Vladimir Ilyich really so ill?"

A thought speared through Alexandra's head, making her gasp. In a second all the pain and regret scrabbled to the edge of her mind.

"The Star Tsar's food! It'll cure Comrade Lenin. We can avoid the crisis, have proof for the government and demonstrate our power to the world."

Anton dragged the door open.

"We'll take the train back to the mountain. Tonight," said Alexandra. "With a squad of soldiers we can get past Bakolov's monsters and raid the Old Believer's gardens before anyone realises we're there."

They descended steps into the basement.

"Yes let's do that," Anton took down a storm lantern from a hook and lit it. "As soon as we've finished here Commander Aminev can fix up a train and a crack squad to get us back to the valley."

"Tonight?"

He gave another easy laugh.

"Tonight."

I don't need more proof of Bakolov's evil. Get me on a train away from here, away from you, and back into the mountains where I can finally do some good.

"I brought you down here because there's things you and I should talk about, but not in front of Aminev," said Anton.

At last. Let's hear it again. Spit in my face and tell me I'm sick in the head, how happy you are that Natasha was nothing but the sad dream of the perverted bitch who jilted you.

"Go on."

But the newly-minted secret policeman said nothing, putting his finger to his lips and winking.

They didn't really need the lantern because the commander's men had set lamps in the corridors and rooms. A few uniformed guards sat or stood in bare concrete chambers. Some smoked and chatted, saluting when the two commissars passed, but most just stared at their boots or hands. The shadows were full of uneasy fear. God only knew what Commander Aminev had threatened to get them down here.

"We found where the Whites held that flying machine," Anton was saying. "The idiots imprisoned it here and then somehow transferred it to the train. Maybe Bakolov discovered a way to control it, but not for long, and it broke free."

After switching back and forth through tunnels that grew narrower and rough-hewn they stepped into a cavern. Alexandra hadn't been paying attention and it was a shock to find out how far they'd come.

"How big are these cellars?"

Anton lifted the light. Its reflection glinted off wet rock and steel in the blackness. The rest of the vault was just a storm cloud of shapes in grainy murk.

"It looks like the enemy converted an underground cave network stretching for miles in all directions. No idea how they did it. It's a mighty piece of engineering. The men won't go far. They claim the lowest passageways lead directly to Hell and they can hear the shrieking of tormented souls. Some of the workings look ancient, and they're odd. The geometry's all wrong."

"Must have been the Star Tsar. He came here too - that'd be nigh on four hundred years ago."

"Older. These are much older. I haven't spent a whole lot of time down here. It looks as though your man from space found this already built and sealed the passages for some reason. There are plugs deeper down fashioned from a strange marble, melted and reset like wax. Explosives won't shift it. We plan to open them again once we've mapped the upper levels. This one runs for miles with tunnels on all sides. Some head towards the forest."

It made sense. This was how the hybrids and mutants ended up in the factories. There was a way to Bakolov's lair underground. Why were his monsters coming here? What were they looking for? As far as the commissar knew there was nothing in the foundries and engine sheds that came anywhere near the Star Tsar's science.

Alexandra took a step forward and a wooden tablet skittered across the concrete. The Virgin Mary's bruised eyes stared into hers with tragic reproach. Her companion picked up the icon, laughed and tossed it into the darkness.

"The Tsarist lunatic used them to placate the herd, kidding them the power of the saints would keep their Baba Yaga at bay."

Alexandra spotted a pit with its half-circle hatches flung aside. Deep scratches criss-crossed the underside of the metal and grooves and scorch marks scored the walls. She knelt down to take a closer look.

"The sentinel could have broken out of here with ease. I saw it pick up a locomotive and carry it through the mountain."

It waited until the Whites' armoured train carried it nearer to its home before making its escape.

"Come on Alexandra," Anton nudged her with his toe.

They crossed the cavern and entered a passage with a pair of guards at the end, standing on either side of a door. They looked pleadingly at the two commissars, desperate to be relieved. Alexandra paused as the horribly familiar stench of rot, chemicals and shit drifted into the tunnel. Anton sniffed and grimaced.

"Stinks, doesn't it?"

"Bakolov's mutants are nothing but skins filled with rotting flesh given life by microscopic machines."

"God."

Anton pulled out the commander's bottle of vodka and took a swig before passing it around. One soldier was almost sobbing as the secret policeman finally prized it out of his fingers.

Alexandra stepped up to the door and peered through the grill. Despite having seen the creatures before she still jerked back. A cabinet sat in the middle of the room on its thick bicycle wheels. This one was very much alive. The preservative looked clear - an early version perhaps, before the deranged Tsarist began to forget how to use the alien's science.

"She was pretty in life," her cousin murmured in her ear, his voice full of insinuations.

A young woman's naked torso, her face gaunt and eyes blazing. Articulated arms thrashed back and forth with none of the convulsive twitching she'd seen in the mines.

Number 110.

She stood in the middle of an invisible square and at each corner a four-armed monster faced them, greasy skin rippling in the light cast by the chemicals inside the tank.

"Can they get through?

Anton patted his coat pocket.

"I have the key."

That wouldn't be much use. Those bastards could rip the door off its hinges if they wanted to. So why didn't they?

"Have you tried communicating with them?" asked Alexandra.

"They don't respond."

"Try Slavonic."

Her friend gestured for Alexandra to go ahead and she shouted 'Come forwards' through the grill. None of the prisoners moved but the woman fixed her with burning eyes and mouthed something again and again.

Help us kill him.

CHAPTER TWENTY-THREE

There was very little he could hurl around. Most of the Star Tsar's equipment was too heavy, although he managed to shatter a crate against the wall and shove two empty cylinders over the edge of the cave mouth. They bounced off the rock face below, triggering a minor landslide. With one hand to steady himself and oblivious to the drop beneath his feet, he peered up into the clouds, searching for any sign of the space flyer. Maybe she'd relent and come back. *Miserable, ungrateful, coke-sniffing opium-eating harridan. I hope that happy powder makes your fucking head explode.*

Alright, he'd made a complete blithering idiot of himself by trying to act all la-di-da on the off chance he might at least get a squeeze of a tit but nothing he'd said or done warranted this betrayal. Had it? *Seriously, Banjo Zeal-for-the-Lord Hawkridge, what is your problem with women? Flash of an ankle and you turn into a dribbling simpleton. What in all of the good Lord's creation did you expect would happen? A Bolshevik Russian aristocrat would really hop into the hay with a thick, hairy Yorkshireman just because he bellowed romantic stupidities and had beefier forearms that her anaemic Bolshie chums? And you impersonated a bloody Frenchman, for God's sake. How low can a man stoop?*

He kicked a few dents into a metal box until his foot began to hurt. It didn't give him any consolation so he wandered back into the hangar and sat down on the floor, chewing one of the alien's blue apples and trying to work out what to do next. *Now then lad, you've always fallen down the toilet and crawled out covered in gold. Remember that time when you tried to smuggle the King of Siam's mad catamite across the border into Tonkin as a favour to the Dutch and ended up a tree surrounded by tigers? They were still ravenous after finishing off the fat twerp, silk pants and all. This isn't any different.* At times like this the flyweight in his head inevitably counterbalanced the blue devils in the end. Once his fury had worn off there was no point in brooding. Nevertheless, the thought of the stars denied brought another stream of incandescent oaths in several languages.

"She called you a silver-tongued barbarian for fuck's sake!"

He could imagine the supercilious *told-you-so* look on Alexandra's smug otter fizzog. Good thing the pompous arse wasn't here or she'd be following those empty tanks down the mountainside.

Now what?

There was nothing stopping him staying here in the Star Tsar's lair. He had enough food to keep him alive and plenty of wonders to amuse. Presumably if Alexandra had persuaded her Red chums she hadn't gone stark staring bonkers they'd all eventually turn up here. That wasn't promising. The little communist seemed to think she could put in a good word for him. If the Englishman's previous experiences were anything to go by it would be men like Aminev who called the shots. Those sour-faced bastards would have no qualms about putting a bullet in Banjo's head and chucking him off the top of this mountain.

He needed something to protect himself - a weapon, whether he was planning to stay or leave. That frothing Bedlamite had taken the mad Tsarist's machine gun with her though she'd left the bullets behind. He tapped out the magazine he'd stupidly gone to fetch. Six rounds. No use unless he was thinking of chucking them at his assailants.

Or he might have a go at escaping. The Agit-Train was down in the valley and from what he remembered it was in working order, providing none of those religious maniacs had interfered with it since they fled into the mountain. The difficulty would be sneaking past them in the other direction. Apart from the tunnel to Bollock-off's lair the only exit was through their very own church and when Alexandra tried to creep out that way they'd found Moses had posted a guard on the door. Even if he made it through the village he'd be back to a three hour wait for the locomotive to gather up enough steam while fending off any buggers who fancied their chances with the coal shovel. The constipated simpletons were armed and if the monsters from the mines rolled up he'd have atomic guns to contend with as well. This time there'd be no reinforcements flying out of the clouds to carve his path through with a heat ray. *What an utter bloody shower.*

Huffing, wheezing and grumbling to make a point to the universe, he picked himself off the floor and retraced his steps to the drone workshop. First he examined the disassembled guards hanging from the ceiling, their parts strewn in piles under each one. *Nope, no clue.* He wouldn't know where to start. The cabinet with the dormant sentinel still hummed and lights winked along the side. He peered through the cover at the machine.

"Right you bastard, let's see if you'll wake up and dance for Daddy."

For all he knew pressing stuff might make it blow up. What choice did he have? *How would an engineer of Super Science from beyond the stars get this to work? Come on man, think.* The lid was fashioned from some odd crystal that made everything inside scintillate with unholy clarity. There had to be a way of activating the bloody thing. He jabbed the glowing symbols at high speed. The hum rose to a whine and the cabinet flooded with pulsing yellow light. It had *I'm about to explode and take you and the mountain with me* written all over it.

"Fuck. Fuck. Fuck."

He hammered the sarcophagus as hard as he could and everything switched off, the noise fading to a whisper before cutting out completely.

Brilliant. You've knackered it.

He hunted around the room but all he found were more dead machines and boxes. The tank with the drone didn't seem connected to any power source. Refusing to give up all hope, he tried commanding it to wake up in French and then shouting the few random words of Russian he'd picked up. Nothing happened. Hopeless - he'd have to defend himself with his own bare hands unless he could find sufficient bits and bobs to cobble together a weapon. A pipe thin and strong enough might make a passable mace. He gave the box another truculent kick and limped out of the workshop.

Exploration was rapidly becoming tiresome. He discovered rows of vats which he recognised from the pits in the mines. His heart jumped until he realised these were empty. They were also a lot cleaner and well-tended than the filthy barrels Bollock-off used to grow his synthetics. *So this was where the cracked bastard learned the trade?* What in God's name did the alien think he was doing? Helping mankind better itself? *Christ, no wonder it gave up and died. We base fuckers broke its heart.*

More rooms full of cylinders of pale lemon liquid. Star Tsar piss - the stuff poured into the cabinets to keep those butchered nothings alive. Interesting. The White alchemist would give his left testicle to get his greasy paws on these if he was running out of ideas and materials. So why not come back for a top-up now he had all those atomic cannon and an army of gibbering things?

Because he doesn't know the man from the stars is dead and he's still terrified of him.

A wide ramp led up to the next level. After an hour wandering through more cavernous vaults, some rough-hewn, some resembling the insides of polished cubes and spheres, he found a room that looked useful. Sloping benches covered in flickering lights jutted from three walls at waist height and in front of each was an open-topped box filled with the same blue sand as on the ship. This was more like it - a control centre. Banjo eased his bottom into one, feeling the familiar grainy motion as it settled to his shape.

Squares flickered on the surface before him and he leaned over for a closer look. Moving pictures showing different scenes - the inside of a tunnel, the valley beyond, even the interior of the church. Moses himself stood with his head bowed in front of the iconostasis, no doubt muttering arcane curses intended to bring the wrath of the Almighty on their heads. *This isn't a film. It's like the map of the world in the ceiling - these images show what's happening right now.* It had to be some kind of visual radio. He'd heard rumours of two Frenchmen transmitting the alphabet via a modified Braun tube before the war but these were as crisp as living paintings. *Incredible.*

He pressed a few coloured shapes and the scene changed to a view above the village looking towards the mine entrance. A line of white figures emerged out of the mountain. It headed across the fields in the direction of the houses, joined by more creatures from the woods on the left. A thread of smoke rose up from the tree-tops. *The buggers have fired up the actor's train.* That might be a way out if he chose to take it. He turned back to the growing crowd. Great White Apes. At least a hundred. He spotted several bulbous atomic cannon jostling along among the monsters. *Oh shit.* Pressing more squares returned him to the edge of the settlement where groups of peasants assembled at the end of the street, facing the oncoming horde with clubs. The mutants stopped and a giant as big as the one Banjo killed in the tunnels came scrambling forwards on hands and feet like a spider. He could just make out a grotesquely fat man sitting in a howdah on the creature's back. *So that's Bollock-off. He's finally going to war.*

Anton tugged on her sleeve.

"Come on, time to go if you want to set off for the Old Believer's valley tonight."

"Wait."

Kill him? Kill who? Bakolov?

"What is it?"

"She's talking to me."

"For God's sake, Alexandra. It's a monster. They tried to saw in you in half to turn you into one of them. Are you serious about getting this magic food for Comrade Lenin or not?"

The soldier who'd swigged a third of the vodka fell to his knees and scrabbled at Alexandra's coat.

"Burn them, Comrade Commissar, burn the demons and set us free of this evil."

Anton laughed and handed the man the rest of the bottle.

"Compliments of Comrade Stalin. Just make sure you're sober when Commander Aminev finds you or he'll have you swinging from the ceiling like your brother. Come on Alexandra, we're wasting time here."

Her friend was right. As tantalising as the girl's words had been, there were more important matters to attend to. She followed Anton back through the cavern.

"If I didn't mistake what she said, Bakolov's creatures may be ready to turn against him in vengeance for the tortures he's inflicted on them. The villain is not as secure as he thinks. I don't know how many of the bastards we killed when we flew through the tunnels but now might be the time to strike. The four-armed mutants follow orders. They can't think for themselves but the poor wretches in those tanks can. If his knowledge has faded then his hold over them is wavering. I saw the torment in Viktor's face. He's still human, Anton, still human."

Alexandra stopped, reaching out to the wall to steady herself as tiredness flooded her mind, bringing with it an aching sadness. Her vision blurred as she struggled for breath. Anton put a hand on her shoulder. He looked genuinely concerned. *Am I wrong about you? Was it nothing but a simple argument all those years ago when our passions were everything? Were those words of yours - the ones that have haunted me down the years - the mere thoughtless anger of a jilted boy?*

"Hey, what's this? It wasn't your fault the others died. You were always our voice of reason, Alexandra, you're not to blame for anything."

She managed a nod, forcing her sorrow into a knot of anger before straightening up and looking round. The tunnel didn't look familiar.

"Are you lost?"

Anton gave her a grin.

"No I'm not lost It's this way."

It seemed as if they'd walked for ages, doubling down corridors and past endless empty rooms lit by lanterns set on the floor. At one point she swore they'd actually gone deeper. They stopped at a crossroads and Anton looked along the passageways. Alexandra was getting tired and impatient and suspected her friend was playing games. The policeman pointed at a fan of light across the stone.

"In there."

"What for?"

They stepped inside. The door shut behind and Alexandra found herself standing in front of a noose hanging from the ceiling. A cracked chair covered in concrete dust sat underneath. In the corner Yohzin stood leafing through a ledger next to a bored guard, his lips moving as he read the words.

"What's this? Why are have you brought me here?"

The adjutant stared at her with the empty expression of a man spotting someone he didn't want to meet in a crowd. Alexandra looked at the rope again, the inside of the room. It was like seeing a grainy photograph in a newspaper.

"I'm not interested in watching another of Aminev's cruel executions, if that's what we're doing."

Was the commander trying to intimidate her as well? Anger billowed up - the arrogant bastard, treating her like those morons in the factory, easily cowed by boneheaded violence. Something poked her behind the ear. Alexandra turned round to see her cousin pointing a Mauser at her face. The man still had the same exasperated smile he'd always had, even when they played together as kids.

"Stop joking around. It's not funny Anton. We need to get a train ready to return to the valley like you said. Why are we wasting time with this?"

She pushed the gun barrel away without thinking.

"The revolutionary war has to continue," Anton gave a lazy

shrug. "The fight against the enemies of the people will never end, ever."

Enemies of the people? Realisation dawned and it was so absurd she laughed out loud.

"Enemy? Me? What ridiculous nonsense. Oh come on Anton, we have no time for this foolishness."

Hands seized hers and pulled them behind. A rope wrapped around her wrists half a dozen times. It had turned so cold in there, the shadows deepened to black while the light bouncing of the damp concrete walls shimmered into an evil silver. All her thoughts fell apart and she stared at them, struggling to understand how she could pick them up again and fit them into sense.

"Don't you realise? I bring news of wonders that'll transform us all," she said. "I walked on Mars itself, felt its dust under my boots and watched our sun set in a strange sky. I saw a starship the size of a cathedral waiting to take Soviet man to the eternal community of worlds. Our society will be reborn. We can change everything."

"What if we don't want to change everything?"

We?

"Iron Felix sent us here to find Pavel."

"Iron Felix sent you here to die on Comrade Stalin's orders. Well, not quite. Not you specifically. You're not that important," Anton waggled his head as he acknowledged his exaggeration. "You're a class enemy, Alexandra. Artists, dreamers, malcontents and madmen babbling of perfect futures in order to make the workers unhappy with the present. Drug addicts. Sexual perverts," he winked at her. "You were supposed to perish in exile, lose yourself in this vast wilderness, be eaten by bears. I don't know. But instead you come charging out of the mountains talking of 'wonders'. We won't have that - our world is too fragile. It simply will not do."

He pointed at the chair with the Mauser.

"Up you get. Don't worry. Commander Aminev's an amateur, but the GPU know how to make this quick. I'll just yank on your feet and it'll be over in seconds."

She couldn't help but laugh and something in her voice made Anton turn pale.

"This isn't anything to do with Stalin or class enemies. This is just your spite."

"What are you talking about?"

"He tried to kiss me," she explained to Yohzin. "And I told him to get lost. He said he loved me so much and when I refused he spat in my face and told me I was mentally ill because of my feelings for his sister."

Now Anton laughed.

"You seriously think I came all the way here to snuff out your pitiful life because you dumped me all those years ago? I don't give a shit about you or that silly girl who thought she was in love with Natasha."

"I LOVED HER!" screamed Alexandra. She forgot her wrists were tied when she went to slap Anton but the rope snapped easily. Ignoring the Mauser, she hit her cousin, shrieking all the while. Bone crumpled under her palm and the secret policeman flew across the room to land in a heap, the side of his skull crushed like a paper bag, blood and teeth leaking from his mouth.

Alexandra stared at her fingers. *Star Tsar strength.* A rifle bolt clicked behind her. She turned as the guard lifted his gun, grabbed it out of his hands without thinking and thumped the man in the face with the stock. The soldier's skull caved in, brains splashing against the rough wall. Yohzin fell to his knees, arms over his head and whimpering.

"Please Comrade, please..."

Alexandra hoisted him up by the neck, holding the wretch at arm's length so his feet were a good six inches off the ground, his boots dripping piss. She twisted her wrist a fraction. Bones clicked against her palm and Yohzin's body went slack. She threw the corpse across the room. It collided with the wall like a sack of wet washing.

Silence.

She picked up the ledger, wiped the blood off with her sleeve, and glanced down the list. Unfamiliar names. No, wait.

Ekaterina Leonovna Rusanov - Class Enemy and Drug Addict,
Viktor Leonovitch Rusanov - Class Enemy and Drug Addict,
Pavel Mikhailovich Gusev - Class Enemy,
Ivan Ivanovitch Mosalev - Class Enemy and German Spy,
...even The Hammer. We're all here.
Alexandra Sergeyevna Lobachevsky - Class Enemy and Sexual Deviant.

And after another five pages she found the signature and typed below it - *Felix Edmundovich Dzerzhinsky.*

Alexandra.

Father's voice in her mind.

I've sent old Efrosinya Nikolayevna away. She was sick in the head and I never should have let her frighten you with her silly tales, my little one. Come to my study. I want to show you something.

Heavy goggles clamped her face.

This is magnesium, Alexandra. This is science. Watch how it burns away the darkness with light and reason. Nothing can withstand it, not even Tugarin the earth dragon. Science will burn away all the ignorance and cruelty that binds us to the base earth so your soul can fly among the stars.

Breathing filled the room like an ocean scraping back and forth over sand beneath a black sun. *How can that be? I've just killed everyone else.* Of course - Tugarin was here with her and now came the sound of its heart, a drum pounding in the roots of the mountain as the beast hunted for her soul. She laughed. *You stupid monster. I have none, at long last I realise that. I'm already dead. I gave my soul to Mother Russia and she burned it at Smorgon and scattered the ashes over the barricades on Nevsky Prospect. I gave my love to another woman and she never knew.* Alexandra clenched her fist and held it up to the light. *The Star Tsar blessed me with the strength of a bear and the power to resist atomic rays and yet I have neither a soul nor love.* One yank on the rope and the hook in the ceiling broke free in a shower of stones and dust.

Anton's head was a mess. There was nothing of her cousin left in that broken doll's face or crushed eyes. She pocketed the

Mauser and listened. All had faded to silence again, Tugarin had slunk back to its lair on the border of Hell. No shouting or running feet. The walls down here were thick so the sound of fighting wouldn't have carried far. Aminev wanted this execution hidden from the rest of the camp. The death of a commissar would raise too many questions.

Betrayal. Banjo was right. They don't care about the future, the possibilities of Super Science. They want endless revolution because they know they will pass from history once it's over. She missed the oaf with his ridiculous, childish pronouncements on life, women and the world. The Englishman really was God's own fool, blundering through truth while everyone else crept in and out of lies.

Alexandra shook herself. *Now what?* Part of her wanted nothing more than to go back to the foundries, find Aminev and tear the cruel bastard limb from limb. She longed to burn the world to the ground, squat down and piss on the embers. But what would that achieve? Besides, even with her new powers she wouldn't stand a chance in the ironworks. She didn't know who else was in on Iron Felix's treachery. The second they spotted her they'd realise she'd escaped. Star Tsar medicine wouldn't save her from bullets.

I'm trapped.

Or was she? Alexandra reached into Anton's pocket and pulled out a key.

'Help us kill him,' she said.

Alexandra opened the cell door, stepped outside and closed it behind her. At first it was a struggle to remember the route Anton had used but at long last she came to the cavern of the sentinel's pit and the corridor with the guards at the end. Aminev's vodka had done the trick. Both sat on the floor, legs out, nodding into their chests. If the commander found them like this the bastard would probably shoot them on the spot. Alexandra knelt down, her hand poised over the biggest one's throat. *What did Anton say? The GPU know how to make this quick.* She shook the guard awake. If the man was in on the conspiracy she'd recognise it in his eyes and kill him, otherwise the commissar didn't want two more corpses to her name. All she saw was the same pleading look for release as before.

"I'm sorry Comrade, Please don't tell Commander Aminev we fell asleep."

"I won't. He's summoned you and there's a relief detail on its way. I'll keep watch until they arrive. Make your report. If I were you I'd get rid of that vodka stink before you speak with him. Onions will do it."

The soldier nodded, eyes full of pathetic gratitude, and dragged his companion to his feet. Good. The cretins would no doubt spend half an hour chewing raw onion before daring to go anywhere near the officer. That would buy her time. Just in case, she reminded them of the way out, sending them down the wrong route. They staggered into the darkness.

Alexandra summoned up her courage and opened the door. The woman and her four monstrous guardians were in the same position as before, her head bowed. It jerked upright like a marionette's when she stepped inside the cell. The cart rolled forwards and the monsters clenched their fists.

"Stop," tried Alexandra in Slavonic.

To her surprise the girl halted. The commissar knelt down to eye level. *Anton was right. You were once beautiful but now you are nothing more than a dream of death.*

The butchered woman mouthed the words again.

Kill him for me.

Licking her fingertip Alexandra wrote *Take me to Bakolov and I will*, backwards in the dust coating the glass. The girl's eyes flickered as she read the sentence and her lips pulled back over dagger teeth in a cruel grin. The commissar rubbed out the script, smeared more dirt on the tank and added *Through the secret ways*.

The cabinet juddered towards her. She stepped aside and it rolled into the corridor. Three of the four-armed mutants joined it outside, gathering around the cart.

She's communicating with them.

A hand fell on her shoulder. She looked up into the ragged face of the mutant. Busy movement seethed in its mouth and eye sockets as its putrid flesh shifted and flexed under the control of the Star Tsar's essences. She'd made a dreadful mistake, it was going rip her apart. Instead it pushed Alexandra forwards. She followed the others as they loped into the cavern, angling left to enter a rough-hewn passageway she hadn't spotted before. Half a dozen turns and there were no more lamps, only the amber glow from the cabinet's preservative to light their way.

CHAPTER TWENTY-FOUR

Bollock-off and his cohorts were heading in Banjo's direction. Fighting the Old Believers was one thing but standing against an army of atomic-weaponed monsters with an improvised mace would only end in tears. He hammered on the lights in front of him and the view switched to the tunnel leading from the church into the Star Tsar's lair. *Shit, it's wide open.* He banged the console at random. A few distant clangs echoed throughout the fortress followed by a muffled explosion somewhere upstairs and the grating of rock on rock close by. At last the huge circular wheel rolled across the passageway.

There was still the tunnel from the bottom of the mountain to the mines. Running from panel to panel Banjo spotted a screen showing him the littered corridor he and Alexandra had walked along. Odd - it was empty. Surely the buggers would head straight down it if they wanted to get inside. He found the coloured light corresponding to the one that closed off the church passage and pressed it. The door shut. More searching located another three suspicious looking access corridors which he also sealed.

Only then did he notice a breeze playing across his face. Puzzled he traced the source to an archway concealed behind an upright disc set next to the wall. *I must have opened that just now.* He walked through it to stand on a balcony a mile above the valley floor.

The soft mist distorted everything. Even though he was far away, standing on the edge of a bowl covered in a pale sky and ringed by the blue ghosts of mountains, he discovered that looking closely at one point for a few seconds magnified his vision. It was like hurtling through space towards the valley. The first time, when he focussed on the mine entrance, the illusion was so complete he threw his hands up, convinced he was about to smash against the rocks. After realising he was still on the ledge and unharmed he calmed down.

It's the same trick as in the map room. It turns the air itself into a telescope. Bloody clever.

When he turned to the village again it was as if he floated just yards above the rooftops. White creatures dragged away the corpses of Old Believers. Some still lived, struggling violently against their captors. A man lashed out in mad fury until they pulled his legs apart like a wishbone. The air amplified the sound as well and Banjo heard the man's pelvis shatter and his accompanying shrieks. Fire blossomed from several roofs. Sickened he looked away. There was no chance he'd ever get past those monsters without a proper weapon. He was stuck until the Red Army turned up. *Alexandra's mates had better come prepared if they want to hold their own against this lot.*

With nothing left to do but wait he wandered back down towards the drone room, thinking he might have another go at waking the machine. As he passed the entrance to one of the Star Tsar's gardens a bullet smacked into the wall a foot above his head.

What the buggery?

It was Moses himself, lurching at him through the golden haze, his face covered in soot and blood and his beard clotted with gore. *The bastard must have sneaked in before I shut the door.* He held a Mauser, arm as stiff as a ramrod, clearly never having fired a pistol in his life. He pulled the trigger again and the automatic kicked upwards, sending another round thudding into the wall behind Banjo.

"Stop firing you cretin. I'm on your side!" He yelled again in French. No bloody use. This moron only knew how to grunt in Caveman Russian. At least it looked like the bastard was by himself. The coward had left his flock to be slaughtered by monsters.

The priest pointed at Banjo with his free hand, head flung back and eyes boggling, and started to bellow something apocalyptic, no doubt involving hot coals, pitchforks and sulphurous boils. He finished his diatribe and fired a third time, managing to control his aim sufficiently to send the bullet zinging past Banjo's ear. *Bugger this.* Banjo launched himself at the refugee, grabbing his wrist just as the Mauser went off again, deafening him. The man fought hard. The Star Tsar's food had left them evenly matched and the engineer's grip loosened as the Russian struggled to bring the weapon to bear. He smacked the git as hard as he could on the nose with his forehead. An immensely satisfying crunch and warm blood spurted over his face but the stubborn cunt still wouldn't drop the gun. He tried to remember any of the tricks that little Jap fellow in Ayabe taught him, hooking his foot behind the man's ankle and throwing his weight to one side. All he succeeded in doing was bringing the pair of them crashing to the floor, locked in a squirming death struggle. Moses kneed him in the balls. In the second before the agony kicked in he bared his teeth, fully prepared to chew the fucker's head off.

Something grabbed him round the waist and yanked him into the air. Adrenaline and terror blanked the pain from his groin when he saw the metal tentacle. Another one had the Old Believer in the same grip while the third had plucked the Mauser from the hierophant's hand and was holding it out of reach of either with a very human attitude of fastidious distaste.

His attacker stared at the sentinel in fear. Of course - it was attracted by gunfire like its mate when it attacked the train. Any second now the bastard would snap out of it and start ordering the thing about in Slavonic. Banjo would be completely fucked.

"He's the enemy, destroy him," he bellowed in French.

The priest's expression was almost comical as he gawped at

the Englishman and then back at the drone. More tentacles shot out - an explosion of blood and body parts and the Father Kirill's head sailed past, mouth open in an O of surprise.

They trudged in silence through the darkness. Alexandra's feet stumbled over rough concrete and every so often they had to make their way past heaps of fallen timber and masonry. She had the impression of a chain of halls, each one larger than the last, suggesting they were heading deeper. The glow from 110's cabinet barely shifted the gloom but once or twice she fancied the walls were peppered with holes like a catacomb.

Pursuers would have lost themselves in this maze by now. As the churning rage and fear subsided, and the dark monotony of stumbling through a lightless world ate away at her, Alexandra's mind looped through the last few hours like a broken zoetrope. *Hitting Anton. I loved her. Hitting Anton. Stays at home to look after their son. Hitting Anton. Class Enemy and Sexual Deviant. Hitting Anton. I loved her.*

Iron Felix sent us to Siberia to die. If the wilderness didn't finish us off then Aminev would have obliged with a few bullets or Anton with his noose. You're such an idiot, a child. Did you really think that all those visions of freedom and love were true? That all the promises we told each other in our poems and plays and pamphlets would be honoured? How long did it last? Five years at most? And now the door grinds shut on hope. Class Enemy and Sexual Deviant. Bohemian art, drug-taking, bourgeois frivolity, reading H. G. Wells, speaking French, falling in love with another woman - how many excuses did they need? Ekaterina's links to Felix never meant anything. Christ - that might even have made it worse. Make an example of her to prove how the bonds of family mean nothing in the workers' struggle. Dzerzhinsky had spent his lifetime whittling his soul to the sharpest edge in the service of Lenin and Trotsky - another pass of the knife and there they all were, discarded shreds on the floor of history. *There's another bastard, too. One who brings the orders from dying Vladimir Ilyich. Our old friend Iosef Vissarionovich. Comrade Stalin.*

A bullet to the back of the head. That's all it needed. So why bring Anton out here? Did he really come all the way to Ikayungri to hang the girl who pushed him away when he tried to kiss her? Alexandra stopped as a sick, horrible realisation flooded over her. *He's here to make a pact with the scientist, turn Bakolov's monstrous experiments to the service of the USSR as weapons of war.*

Her hands fell to her sides and she lurched to a halt, unable to move onward. The glow of the cabinet faded and she realised the monsters had entered the mouth of another corridor. Looking around, Alexandra detected movement in the air - a breeze that carried with it the scent of pine and melted snow. As the orange light vanished a faint blue radiance filled the cavern. Moonlight, though she couldn't see any opening in the massive rock dome. Half-built colonnades and arches punctuated the vault, the wreckage of engines intended for the mines perhaps. *I'm standing in the tomb of a long-dead civilisation. All purpose fled, leaving nothing but a remorseless and indifferent world. What do I do? Where do I find hope and love again?*

Mars. In a red desert hundreds of millions of miles away stood a silver interstellar craft. *There's hope in other futures. Ours is not the only one. If I perish, different men on different worlds will rise up in my place.* Alexandra realised at last what she needed to do - kill Bakolov and destroy the mines and the Star Tsar's citadel. At least that would put a stop his Super Science being used for cruelty and destruction.

A distant square of light marked out her escort. They'd stopped and when she approached she saw them standing next to a torpedo-shaped frame on wheels. It rested on a set of tracks leading into the darkness. The structure was the size of a railroad car. She heard a dull humming from a pyramid of spheres at the front and felt warmth emanating from their tarnished copper skin. The creatures climbed on board, two picking up the cabinet and placing it in the centre of the platform. A monster reached down and pulled Alexandra into the air like a mother hoisting a child out of her tantrum, depositing her at the back. The vehicle lurched forwards, gathering speed. So this was how they moved between the mountains and the foundries - along a secret railway powered by more unholy engines.

At last Alexandra saw a ragged shape which turned into an exit at the end of a rubble-strewn ravine. It was still before sunrise and the stars were out. A half-moon hung low above the trees. The mountains cut paper-hole shapes out of the landscape. The car clattered into the gully, weaving from side to side past a stream rushing down its centre. Ahead, a waterfall tumbled down the cliff face and next to it stood another mine entrance with rusted rails leading into the darkness. Once inside the wagon glided to a halt at a set of buffers.

They continued on foot, eventually finding another set of tracks. Moments later Alexandra's boots kicked aside broken icons. They passed the shattered barrier between the workings and the realm of the Old Believers. Soon they'd come to the spiral ramp leading down into Bakolov's lair. To her surprise her escort didn't turn down a side passage but kept heading towards the valley.

Dawn rose and the Star Tsar's citadel built a powder blue wedge in the sky. Three columns of black smoke rose through the seething mist, two from the woods to their right and one from the foot of the mountain. *The village is on fire.* It was hard to tell at this distance but it looked like every single house was burning.

Now she understood why they'd brought her here. *Bakolov attacked the settlement because he wants to get inside the mountain.* That meant the White scientist had left his pit and was somewhere ahead of them, in the valley. Would that make it easier to kill him? They followed the rails, the giants walking on either side while the hybrid bobbed along on her rubber-tyred wheels. Two corpses lay in the grass. As they got closer Alexandra recognised Old Believers reduced to so much burnt meat and charcoal bone. *So that's what atomic bullets do to a human being. That's what Aminev plans to turn upon his own comrades.* More bodies further on, and next to them the shattered case of a machine man. Number 110 trundled over to her fallen comrade and pulled something out of the grass. An atomic pistol - Mauser-sized but with the now-familiar spheres along the barrel. She thrust it at Alexandra who took it and stuffed it out of sight in her tunic. Getting close enough to shoot the maniac was a hopeless task, but it was her only choice.

She looked at the carnage around her. What had emboldened the Tsarist to attack Father Kirill and his people? Why didn't he fear the sentinel or the star being anymore? He must have found out the creature was dead and the remaining drone had journeyed into space with Banjo and Ekaterina. *Am I too late?* The Old Believers wouldn't have stood a chance against atomic guns yet judging by the bodies they'd given a good enough account of themselves.

They followed the railway line into the forest and Alexandra spotted the Agit-Train ahead. Smoke rose from its stack and two cabinets directed half a dozen synthetics passing yellow-tipped shells hand to hand and stowing them in the carriages. It looked like they planned to use it as a supply train for a final assault. A wild idea crept across the fringes of her mind. *These tracks end just in front of the church door. If I hit it fast enough and detonate that ammunition it'll seal the main entrance to the fortress.* Kill Bakolov and Aminev would replace him. A chaos of atomic fire would slag the entire cliff face. Perhaps that was enough to seal the mountain forever. She'd have to find a way of surviving the explosion so she could get inside and wreck what was left of the Star Tsar's science. And then there were the mines to destroy. It was hopeless and insane but the more damage she could do, the greater the chance of stopping this madness.

Alexandra guessed her escorts were following the railway to their master, who was no doubt down in the village glorying in victory. As they trundled past she saw the locomotive cab was empty and the pressure gauge high. Before any of them could react she climbed up into the cabin and slipped the brake. A mutant scrambled after her but she picked up a shovel and smacked it in the chest. It fell back as the locomotive began to move, painfully slow at first. Luckily the creatures were just as sluggish. Another one appeared on top of the coal. Alexandra fired the atomic pistol and a burning sphere enveloped its head.

The monster overbalanced and disappeared.

The village hove into view, most of it covered in smoke. The church lay straight ahead. She guessed the Old Believers had barricaded it to block the entrance but it wouldn't delay Bakolov for long. Creatures scattered on all sides. Alexandra was moving too fast to see if the White scientist was among them.

Too late to change her mind. Yet some instinct made Alexandra slam on the brake just as the train smacked into the facade. She dropped to her knees as the locomotive bucked and lurched, sheets of sparks slicing the chaos on either side. Fragments of flaming wood thundered off metal as the machine shrieked to a halt, jack-knifing when the momentum of the carriages behind pushed it into the mountain.

Alexandra leaped from the cab and hurled herself at the iconostasis even as the engine slid after her on its side. Somehow she managed to land on her feet and keep running, even though she that knew any second now she'd be incinerated in a wave of atomic fire. A crash and a rumble and she looked back to see the roof collapse. The shells hadn't detonated, even though several had tumbled after her into the tunnel. *I failed*.

She staggered along the corridor until she came to a dead-end. Half a dozen bodies lay in the tunnel, charred corpses mangled by more radium bullets. Bakolov had captured the Star Tsar's lair. He was in there now, plundering the secrets. Smoke and grit enveloped her in a choking fist. The wall ahead rolled to one side. Without wondering how, she stumbled through and it closed behind her. *Bakolov*. She had to find Bakolov and kill him. But where was her gun? She'd lost it in the crash. With her bare hands she'd rip the bastard's heart out and hold it up in triumph to the stars. Something lifted her off her feet. She struggled to fight the monster but God's voice roared forth from the darkness.

"Alexandra, you outrageous pillock. How in the name of fuck-buggery did you end up back here?"

The Bolshevik staggered away with her mouth open. She looked in a bad way - covered in mud and dried blood and smoking slightly, and there was something in her eyes Banjo hadn't seen before. The hissing spark of revolutionary joy had disappeared and he didn't like the look of its replacement. If he wasn't mistaken, sick hatred hovered behind those dilated pupils. As much as he wanted to give the daft lass a great big hug, for the first time in his life the pompous little tart actually scared him.

"Did you just drive the Agit-Train into the church? How in hell did you survive that?"

"It was supposed to blow up and bring the mountain down. The wagons were full of atomic shells. I thought the impact would make them explode."

"Wouldn't work. You need to set their detonators first."

Alexandra went briefly cross-eyed and staggered, the crash catching up with her. She blinked and looked at Banjo as if she was seeing him for the first time.

"You were going to the stars. Is Ekaterina...?"

"Don't mention that cocaine addled bitch to me! Princess my scabby arse. After making the effort to be all gentlemanly and keeping my hands off her derrière, despite endless protestations from the old man, the bloody woman only goes off without me."

"What? Ekaterina's gone to Mars by herself?"

"Taken the ship and the sentinel - lock, stock and barrel. She inhaled half a ton of space cocaine and that was it. A dope fiend out of her mind on fairy dust is hurtling through the cosmos while we fine pair are stuck on earth. Ingrate. That's bloody Russian women for you, you're all a bunch of total and utter..."

Alexandra held her hand up. She still lurched back and forth like a drunk in a swell.

"Wait a second. She took the ship and the drone? So we're trapped in here with no weapons?"

"Yep. You and I are not going to the stars after all. I'm glad you're back though, it's bloody miserable here on my own. I had a brief visit from Moses but he's now lying in bits upstairs. Lucky I was on hand to let you in."

The woman snapped rigid as a statue, staring into some private hell a foot in front of her face. She was actually hissing -

like an enraged cobra in a trench coat.

"What's up? What happened?"

"You were right. My government betrayed me. We weren't sent to search for Pavel, they exiled us out here to die as enemies of the Revolution. The Red Terror."

"The what?"

"A war against saboteurs, counter-revolutionaries, class traitors, sexual deviants. It is now that the people's struggle is at its most vulnerable. We need to be unsparing, iron-willed and without mercy if the workers will triumph. But that's it Banjo..."

Alexandra turned her haunted gaze on him.

"The Revolution can't be allowed to succeed because it has to be eternal. It's an end in itself. If you or I dream of a better world of Super Science, of peace, of glorious labour under new suns, that makes visionaries like us enemies of the workers." Her eyes filled with tears and her voice cracked. "And they say that because I was in love with Natasha I'm mentally ill, a sexual deviant, sick with an incurable bourgeois disease, so I must be killed."

"What a load of total and utter bollocks. The bastards. Still, never mind eh?"

Alexandra's mouth dropped open.

"I don't think you realise just how..."

"Well of course it's a kick in the tits, I appreciate that, but there's no point mithering on about it."

"My whole life was dedicated to the Revolution," squeaked Alexandra, ears turning red. "You can't just shrug it off. It's not a joke."

"Look, when madam buggered off I was in a blue funk like you. I faced dying in this shitty country of yours sans pint, sans pie and sans fucks. But I'm never one for moping so I thought I'd have a poke around and guess what I found?"

"You haven't understood a thing I've said, have you? This is infinitely more important than your failure to have sexual congress with Ekaterina."

God the pillock was hard work. As pleased as he was to see

her, he'd forgotten what a tedious nag she could be. To forestall another lecture he turned and whistled. The second drone hummed around the corner and stopped in front of them.

"Ta-dah! I figured out how to open the box."

Alexandra's eyes seemed to fill half her face - no mean feat without her glasses. He decided against speaking to the machine in French, especially as the runt's fire was definitely back on and a little too crazy-looking for the engineer's liking. There was no telling what the daft bint might do next.

"There's more."

He took his friend to the balcony overlooking the valley. The village still burned and the train crash had strewn the remains of the church all over the square. White shapes moved here and there.

"After that lunatic flew off I stood here and watched all those horrors and cabinets swarm out of the mountain yonder. I reckoned they'd come along the tunnels too so I shut them down remotely. There was a big barney. Those religious pillocks put up a good fight but Bollock-off's atomic rifles made short work of them. Lucky for you they'd fired up the train."

"You closed off the passages to the mines from here?"

Banjo led Alexandra to the control room and showed her.

"Those doors are several feet thick and moulded out of some alloy from outer space. The cabinets shot atomic bullets at them, but they won't budge. Funnily enough the corridor we used to escape is empty. The fight between Bollock-off and the Star Tsar must have scared them away. The good news is we could live in here for years. But with matey-boy," he jerked his thumb at the sentinel hovering at the back of the room, "We don't need to. We hop aboard and get it to fly us over the mountains to freedom."

"We can't leave."

"Eh?"

The Bolshevik spoke in Russian and all the machine's tentacles stood vertically upright.

"Christ, what did you say to it?

"I wanted to know if it could wipe out everything in this

citadel, it said yes."

She asked it another question - same response.

"But it would destroy itself in the process."

Oh for God's sake. Why am I not surprised?

Banjo sighed the sigh of ages, feeling like a collapsing Zeppelin. And the bugger had the temerity to look all disappointed because he wasn't jumping up and down and clapping his hands with happiness.

"Wonderful," he said in the flattest voice he could manage. Alexandra rubbed it in by coming over all Sunday school teacher.

"Commander Aminev and the others will come here and use this science for evil ends. They'll make a pact with Bakolov or steal his processes to enslave the workers of the world and turn them into synthetics ruled over by a cruel dominion of hard-souled men. We have to stop them."

"Do we, indeed? And how do you propose to manage that?"

"Why, by blowing up this mountain and the mines, of course. We can't let anyone get their hands on any of this."

"You're serious, aren't you?"

Alexandra nodded and gave him a grin filled with deranged visions.

CHAPTER TWENTY-FIVE

"You could wipe out Bollock-off's lair by detonating his ammunition but you'd unleash an explosion which would flood the mines with atomic fire. It'd be suicide."

Banjo knew as soon as he opened his mouth it was exactly the wrong thing to say. The insane glow in Alexandra's eyes turned incandescent.

"Why don't we send the sentinel in there to blow it up?" he suggested, even though he'd planned to use the drone as their route out of this place. Logic told him to pack the twerp off to cheerfully martyr herself and then tell the machine to take him to Mandalay or Timbuktu or wherever, so why was he offering to help? *You soft fool.* Alexandra shook her head.

"We need it to destroy this citadel as well. With your engineering skill it'd make more sense for you to go into Bakolov's lair while I stay here and supervise the sentinel."

Banjo's laugh died in his throat. *Bugger me, she's deadly serious.*

"I realise it is a great thing to ask of you, my friend." The earnest pillock even had the temerity to point at the ceiling as if she was lecturing the workers. "But we absolutely cannot let the Star Tsar's Super Science, or that Tsarist bastard's arsenal, fall into the hands of men such as Aminev or Stalin."

"So you want me to go into that bloody monster's pit again and blow it and myself up while you stay here and bring this place down around your ears like Samson in the temple?"

Alexandra patted him on the arm with a nod and a grin.

"Fuck off! I'm not doing it."

The smile vanished.

"But you must. We have to do this. For the sake of all mankind."

"Mankind can kiss my arse. Come with me."

Before the Bolshevik had a chance to protest Banjo led her up through the mountain to the room with the map of the world. Fighting down the vertigo and fear from his first encounter with its bizarre geometry, he gestured at the lines and dots.

"Earth, right? There, there and there. Hokkaido, Tibet, Belgian Congo, Marrakech, Iceland, even Ireland. They're all over the place. Space beings, monsters, ancient mysteries, Atlantis, the lost bloody continent of bloody Mu, probably. Matey-boy here was just one. Blowing this mountain up won't stop anything. Next week some Frog philosopher might stumble across the Grand Poo-Bah of Neptune taking his regular constitutional in Agadir and Monsieur Poincaré gets his mitts on atomic weapons, or they end up in the hands of the Empress of Ethiopia. It's too late. We can't prevent it."

Alexandra's mouth worked like a fish's. At last she managed to speak, though she sounded as if she was being strangled.

"If these show the location of more space beings why haven't they made themselves known to us? And why didn't they come to the aid of the Star Tsar?"

Banjo hazarded a guess.

"I don't think they were his mates. I reckon this is a catalogue of wonders it knew about. There wasn't any communication between them."

"This doesn't change anything. We still must destroy Bakolov's experiments. Aminev is on the verge of grasping his secrets and turning them into the service of Comrade Stalin." Alexandra gestured at the map. "We'll have to pray these others stay hidden."

For crying out loud. Banjo calmed himself down with a massive effort of will, realising he sounded like a dying steam engine.

"Listen. One of those other places might have an interplanetary flyer which means that you and me, and metal-man here, can escape from this planet and journey to the stars. We'll explore the universe and rescue princesses from monsters and villains. You'll do science and I'll roger temple maidens."

"Those are childish fantasies from your silly book. Mere stories."

Banjo jabbed a finger at the ceiling.

"They don't look like mere stories to me. That's real, Alexandra. We can go. And if the bastards who shat on you and shat on me want to wipe themselves out in a sea of atomic destruction, guess what? I don't fucking care."

"That's a lie. You do care. I've seen in your deeds that you possess nobility and bravery, and you're not just an ignorant, lumpen, fat-headed and abusive shit with no manners whatsoever."

"I give up, what's the use? Go and blow up Bollock-off's den if you must but count me out."

He stomped out of the chamber, not trusting himself to hang around. He whistled and fortunately the drone buzzed after. At least Alexandra wouldn't be able to tell it to blow everything up while it stayed with him. In truth, he was all for ordering it to carry him as far away as possible, but something held him back. *Bloody conscience. When the hell did you grow one of those?* He found the control room and plonked himself down in a tub of blue sand. *Don't kid yourself. You've always had it. That sodding otter knows exactly which guilt button to poke. She's worse than Mother.*

"Why is there a lone electrical man in the tunnel?"

Alexandra stood beside him, pointing at a screen. Banjo heaved to his feet and had a look. Odd. Bollock-off's monsters were still avoiding the passageway, except for a single cabinet shuffling back and forth outside the door like an old codger desperate for the toilet.

"Can you make this picture bigger?"

"Dunno."

The engineer poked a few coloured squares and the image vanished. He swore and hit things in a temper until it re-appeared.

"No, why?"

"What's the number on the creature's case?"

Banjo squinted

"539."

"It's Viktor."

"What?"

"Viktor. How do we get him inside? If you open that door we can trap him and reseal the tunnel."

"Why would you want to do that?"

The memory of a clock ticking away in the bowels of a pickled White officer popped into his head.

"Alexandra you're a genius!"

He slapped his hand on the controls and the valve rolled aside. Viktor froze. Alexandra muttered something in Russian that sounded like a prayer. Slowly the cabinet trundled through the door.

"Got him." Banjo sealed the corridor behind the hybrid.

"They cling onto their old life in the beginning," Alexandra told him as they ran down through the mountain with the sentinel humming in their wake. "They are desperate for release until despair takes over and they turn into machines. Bakolov drugs their preservative fluid with opium to dull their minds and make them more receptive but Viktor was already an addict and hardened to its effects. We may be able to get through to him still."

They found the butchered remains of the man standing inside the door. Ekaterina's brother stared at them with tragic eyes. For a second Banjo wondered if he had a weapon and had returned to claim his revenge on those who abandoned him.

He just wants to get better, poor bastard. How's that going to work?

"Does Viktor know Morse code? The one I found when we got separated did."

"Morse code?" Alexandra stared at him, light flaring in her eyes. "Of course. We all learned it in the service of the

Revolution."

The figure grinned, the mouth nothing more than a ragged hole. *They must have smashed his teeth out when they changed him.* It jabbered, the poet shaking his head, stirring up the pale liquid so that scraps of skin and hair eddied back and forth. The cabinet jerked to and fro and the dentist drill arms spasmed.

"Morse code or not, the poor bastard's gone doolally. Great. I thought he could help but the sod's no good to us if all he's going to do is stand there and have a fit. Best put him out of his misery."

He looked around for something to smash the machine but Alexandra stopped him.

"What was your plan?" she asked.

Maybe it was worth a go.

"Can you calm him down?"

Banjo studied the ruined face. It mouthed a word he recognised - *Ekaterina.*

"Is there any more of that cocaine left?" said Alexandra.

"There might be a tub upstairs. You going to coke him up? But it only affects her."

"Ekaterina and Viktor are brother and sister. Do you remember when she cut her hand on the white fluid? The creature must have analysed her blood and fashioned the opiate to match it. It might work for him too. It's worth a try."

"So he won't only be mad, he'll be mad and drug crazed. Brilliant!"

"Just see if you can find some, will you?" Alexandra knelt and wiped at the glass with her sleeve. Metal arms whipped the air on either side of her face. She didn't flinch.

Officious arse. Resisting the over-powering urge to tell the lass to away and boil her head, Banjo clumped up to the hangar, fearing he might have tossed the last of the drug down the mountain in his fit of pique when the ungrateful termagant abandoned him on Earth. He made sure the sentinel came with him, still not trusting Alexandra with it on her own. Luckily he found a tin wedged between a dead console and the wall. He unscrewed the lid, rubbed a finger-full on his gums and stared at the ceiling. Nothing at all - about as exciting as chalk.

When he arrived back at the sealed doorway the Bolshevik was tapping on the glass with her nail. The machine limbs had stopped moving.

"You were right - I can talk to him in Morse."

"And?"

"Viktor wants to die. He's in pain and torment. I'm barely able to get through to him. His soul hovers on the edge of insanity and seeks only oblivion."

"Perfect! Here you go."

"Have you no compassion?"

"For a dope-addled Bolshevik? Of course. Lots."

He handed the drug over. The commissar glared at him, opened the tin, sniffed and shrugged, clearly as unaffected as the engineer.

"The Star Tsar's powder re-arranged Ekaterina's mind, fed on her madness but touched her with glorious inspiration and understanding. With the enhanced insight and wisdom it brings it may help us persuade Viktor to our cause."

"Jesus Christ, you're all as bad as each other. Do you ever stop speechifying? Come on then, how are we going to get it inside bugalugs here bearing in mind he doesn't breathe anymore and can't sniff underwater?"

Alexandra examined the top of the cabinet. Banjo looked over her shoulder and saw a circular plug with a raised edge. The Russian unscrewed it. When she lifted it up the stench of rancid flesh pickled in formaldehyde made Banjo gag. His companion took a handful of cocaine and held her fist over the opening so it trickled through her fingers. *She's feeding him like a goldfish.*

Alexandra swished the liquid around. The powder descended in clouds towards Viktor's head. He blinked and twitched.

"It took about three days for Ekaterina to recover. All we can do is wait and hope this works more swiftly. What was your plan?"

Banjo stared in dismay at the crippled poet. The poor bastard shook his head faster and faster, until the whole contraption juddered on its rubber wheels.

"He's got a clock in him. When I opened up the White soldier I saw it. It's part of their machine guts and probably regulates cycles - sleeping, recharging, pissing, that kind of thing. If we get our hands on one of those atomic shells I'll wire the detonator so the fuse is as long as we like - hours even - enough to plant the bomb into the magazine inside the mines and then escape. Viktor'll know the route. If he's desperate to die it's a way out for him and you can wreck his arms in case he has second thoughts."

"There's ammunition in the tunnel from the wrecked train. When it collapsed behind me I saw shells scattered over the floor."

Leaving Ekaterina's brother to shudder through the effects of the cocaine they returned to the control room. Banjo checked the passage leading from the church and Alexandra was right. A handful of shells lay strewn among the rubble on this side of the cave-in. They were small, 3-inchers by the look of them, but even the smallest atomic rounds melted walls on their lowest setting. He reckoned he could fix one of these buggers to trigger a big enough chain reaction to obliterate the warren, if Viktor planted it in that cavern with all those glowing engines he'd spotted when looking for Alexandra.

"It'd be safer to send in the sentinel to fetch them." The commissar pointed at the drone hovering in the shadows behind.

"Not sure that's a good idea. It doesn't seem to like weapons much. They kick off its defences and it might destroy them. That tunnel's sealed for the time being but we'd better be quick. It won't take Bollock-off long to re-open it. I'll go. You keep an eye on Viktor."

When the door rolled aside whirlpools of dust danced through the tunnel, bringing the scent of fire and broken iron. All was utterly silent save for the occasional trickle of stones and dirt from the cave-in. Banjo had no idea how Alexandra had survived the crash and it was a miracle the Agit-Train's boiler hadn't exploded. Judging by the stillness the creatures on the other side weren't clearing away the debris. Odd. With the Old Believers out of the way what was stopping them trying to get into the Star Tsar's fortress?

Of the six rounds only two had intact detonators. Maybe he could have rigged the others also but without knowing exactly how they worked he didn't want to risk it. Back up in the control room he discovered why the mutants weren't bothering with the church.

"Now we know why Viktor's corridor was empty." His companion pointed at the screen showing the view in front of the mines. Banjo's heart dropped into his boots with a leaden thud. Without a word he went onto the balcony for a better look. Alexandra joined him, pushing her cap to the back of her head and blowing air out like a suffocating whale.

"It's Bakolov's entire army. At least it means the mines'll be empty. You shouldn't have much problem getting to the centre."

A seething bed of maggots covered the fields beyond the village. Lines of figures emerged from the edge of the forest and the entrance in the distant mountains where the railway disappeared into the workings. In the soft golden light Banjo saw the occasional glint as of sun reflected from glass or copper. Hybrid machine men clustered around the maniac's artillery, directing the mutants. A black shape came after, trailing smoke. Another train. Alexandra shook his head, expression dark.

"Aminev. He's here."

"Are they going to fight each other?"

The engine towed half a dozen ordinary wagons into the daylight, followed by an immense shadow topped and tailed with two turrets that had to be at least ten yards high. Banjo gawped at the beast. *Where the hell did that come from?* None of the armoured trains in the factories came anywhere close.

"It's the *Orlik*," said Alexandra.

"The what?"

"The biggest and most powerful armoured train ever. White engineers built it and the Czech Legion rode her eastwards when they tried to escape. I thought it had disappeared, but Aminev told me they'd got it back and refitted it."

"Refitted it?" Banjo struggled to understand how the titan even moved, let alone grind its slow way towards the writhing crowds on the other side of the valley. "It's bloody monstrous. Those are naval dreadnought guns."

"Do you think they can breach the Star Tsar's doors?"

He managed a weak laugh.

"I don't they need to bother with the doors. They'll just pound holes in the rock itself. Aminev is in cahoots with Bollock-off. Is that what you're saying?"

The armoured train rolled across the fields, synthetic men stepping off the tracks to let it through.

"I was stupid not to realise it from the beginning when he showed me his electrical girl. He was testing me out, seeing how I'd react. He wanted me to join them, as Anton did. They must have realised I couldn't betray the future - my vision of a Soviet future - for their eternal revolution. They decided to eliminate me instead. They were in contact with Bakolov long before I turned up."

"It's not your fault. You're too good-hearted for this scum. Don't blame yourself for not being as big a cunt as Commander Bastard or mad fatso down there."

Alexandra stared through her boots into an abyss only she saw.

"I believed the liberation of the workers was a step towards a utopia of Super Science. I, or my descendants, would cast off the brutality of the foul years that began this century and take our rightful place among the spaceways. In this dawn we would all be free to live and love as we chose. I was an idiot. Just as the soon as the door was opened, Anton, Iron Felix and Stalin forced it shut again."

The last thing he needed was a Bolshevik in a blue funk. Banjo slapped his hands together and gave his biggest winning grin.

"Well let's make sure we stop 'em eh? Blow up the mines and this fortress and everyone'll be trapped here. But best not to hang about. Those guns'll begin shelling the mountain soon and bombs don't explode by themselves."

The train slowed to a halt at the edge of the village. Behind it two wagons exited the warren on thick rubber wheels, pulled by synthetic giants crawling on all fours. Each flatbed carried what looked like an enormous atomic cannon, trumpet-muzzled with clustered metal spheres.

"Why do they need conventional explosives if they have guns that can slag rock?" mused Banjo.

But Alexandra had already left the room. He followed her back to the chamber where Viktor waited. The commissar was silent for a few moments, staring at the broken poet who had either died or fallen asleep.

"Once you gave me your word as an Englishman you wouldn't try and escape and the next day you broke it. I understand why. You wanted to live. This time you must be truthful and honest with me. If I don't return do you promise to stay here and destroy the Star Tsar's domain to ensure that neither Commander Aminev nor Bakolov get their hands on its Super Science?"

Banjo wasn't going to argue. He put one hand on his heart and held the other up with two fingers together.

"Scout's honour."

That seemed to satisfy the mug. God only understood why. Banjo had no intention of letting the insufferable wart immolate herself in the tunnels. Alexandra knelt and tapped on the glass. No response.

"We killed him. Bloody stupid idea coking him up in the first place. It would have been nice to bring him along. He'd know the best way through the maze and if anyone turned up he could pretend you were his prisoner. We can still use his clock though."

"You're right." Alexandra stood up. "It's hopeless. I'll have to chance it alone."

An articulated arm shot out and snagged on the Bolshevik's coat, pulling her back down to eye-level. The other tapped on the glass. Viktor's eyes were wide open, the whites already rotted to a greasy ochre. Banjo recognised Morse but the words were in Russian.

"What's he say?"

His friend listened, piecing together the meaning.

"Ekaterina has gone to the stars."

"How does he know?"

Alexandra tapped out a few sentences and the singer's brother replied. The commissar's face was a picture.

"He says she sleeps in a mighty ship on its way to a dark planet."

"Can you get him to speak in French so I understand?"

The commissar switched languages.

Viktor, how do you know? she asked the poet.

She speaks to me.

Right now?

The halls of my mind awaken to knowledge, understanding. Through the long corridors of time Ekaterina calls my name though her voice is faint.

"It's that bloody space cocaine. He's either hallucinating or the little machines up his nose are talking to the ones in his sister's head over millions of miles."

Ekaterina won't come back. Won't mend me. The science is here but I have no arms to operate it. I cannot use it. Help me, Alexandra. I am in such pain.

Viktor we have little time. Take me to Bakolov's weapon factory deep in the mines. We have to stop him or he'll turn us all into slaves and feed on our souls like he fed on yours.

Banjo heard a faint boom in the distance

"It's started. That's the train's guns. Maybe they're saving the atomic cannon for later," he said "We need to get this bomb rigged and the pair of you through that door."

My old friend, you and I together. Let's go back into the mines and stop this evil once and for all.

Ekaterina, help me. What should I do?

Banjo had no idea how long the cocaine would delay the actor's descent into monstrosity. Perhaps it had stopped it altogether but there was still no way to save the man. Even if the wherewithal was in the Star Tsar's citadel neither he nor Alexandra had the slightest notion where to search. Was the poor bastard really talking to his sister? Were their minds speaking to each other across the vast chasm of space via the cosmic cocaine or was it merely a sad fantasy he clung to?

Ekaterina says I must go with you. She will never see me again. She says farewell.

"Thank Christ for that," said Banjo. "Give me your coat Alexandra, and I'll need the wire out of one of his arms."

The commissar stood up, bog-eyed and unsteady on her feet. Banjo needed to take advantage of the moment. Trying not to look into the poet's eyes he unhooked the panel at the base of the tank and located the clock. It only took him a few minutes to link it to a detonator. He hung the yellow-tipped shell on the cripple's back in a makeshift sling fashioned from the lass's torn-up coat. Viktor didn't even budge when Banjo stripped a length of copper thread from the hybrid's limb, leaving it dangling uselessly against the cabinet.

"I've set the timer for forty minutes. As soon as you switch the detonator here," he pointed at the shell. "It'll start. You'll have to run but I don't want to risk a longer fuse in case anything happens. The more we leave it the greater the chance of someone finding Viktor and realising what's going on. We'll have to trust that he stays on our side. Once you're in the centre of Bollock-off's lair wreck his wheels so he can't piss off if he changes his mind."

We go, now, Alexandra tapped on the glass.

Banjo stuck his hand out.

"Good luck. Make sure you come back. If anything goes wrong it's been a pleasure."

"And you will destroy this fortress if I don't return within two hours?"

So much for fond farewells, distrustful twit.

"Yes, of course. I promise." He tried not to sound too exasperated.

They shook hands.

"I'm not one for long goodbyes so fuck off."

The valve rolled open and the empty corridor stretched into the distance. Good. The way was clear. Viktor trundled forwards, wheels bouncing over fragments of rubble, the makeshift bomb rattling against the glass. Alexandra followed him, turning once to look back and raise her hand in farewell as the door slid across the entrance. Banjo wanted to say something else but couldn't think what. He stood and stared at the hatch for what felt like ages. Part of him wanted to open it, grab the dozy lass and get the flying drone to take them far from this mess. At last he turned on his heel and went back to the control room to watch the siege unfold, and to try a little experiment of his own with the rest of the shells.

CHAPTER TWENTY-SIX

Viktor rolled along the corridor. *Do you really want to help me after I forsook you in the tunnels? Or do you plan on betraying me to Bakolov?* wondered Alexandra. She was unarmed, though at a push she reckoned she could use the shell to stave in the glass tank and the mechanism keeping her friend alive. *Banjo said I'd still be able to set the clock if he's dead.* Sense told her to kill the creature now and carry on with the bomb by herself. Wasn't that what the new men and women were supposed to do, these creatures of eternal revolution, warriors of a never-ending struggle? Anton would have had no qualms about murdering another old comrade. *I'm not like you even if I crushed your head with one blow.*

Viktor turned down an unlit side tunnel. The darkness cascaded over Alexandra's eyes like cloth. She stumbled after the hybrid, trying to trace the rough-hewn walls where the faint radiance from the preservative fell. *These are old tunnels.* The passage opened onto a ledge that ran alongside a chasm. A cold wind from deep within the roots of the mountain poured over the edge, carrying the scent of wet rock and lichen. Her guide stopped, head slumped. Alexandra cursed. *I should have brought more cocaine. I put a handful into the water, more than Ekaterina ever consumed in one go.* Perhaps the chemicals in the fluid hampered its effects. The remaining good arm tapped on the glass, the

Morse echoing through the lightless caverns.

If I take you to Bakolov he'll repair me.

You can't be made whole again, Viktor. They destroyed your body.

If I tarry long enough Ekaterina may come back one day. She will mend me. I need only wait.

Alexandra fought the rising panic. She sensed the desperation in the staccato beat of metal on glass, the yearning to escape from formaldehyde and copper agony.

Is that what she says, that she'll return?

My sister is far from us now, soaring with the endless ones on the star winds. Their singing grows louder while her voice grows so faint. I ask her time and time again to come back. It's hard to hear the answer. It could be yes, it could be no.

Viktor stopped tapping, turned away and rolled to the edge of the cliff. Alexandra froze, waiting for the man to throw himself off. She wondered whether to make a grab, knowing the weight of the machine would carry them both into the gulf. After an endless silence the actor swivelled round and continued on his way. It was then Alexandra realised she'd stopped breathing. The granite-tainted air roared back into her lungs.

They came to a row of rusting bridges and crossed one. It creaked and shifted under her boots. She wondered how deep and how far this complex went into the mountain. *Is it like the caverns under Ikayungri, built ages before the Tsarist scientist came here?*

At last they entered a corridor filled with warm light from lanterns. Alexandra heard the thud of machinery ahead. After creeping through the silent darkness for so long she welcomed the sound, even though it was deep in the enemy's warren. Viktor stopped by an arch. The commissar looked beyond into the glowing cavern packed with atomic machines towering up to the crumpled rock ceiling. She struggled to understand how they worked with their spiralling cords of piping, glass, and encased energies bouncing from orb to steel flask to orb. Chains of fretful electricity played across the immense casings. A few synthetics stood motionless in front of the engines like acolytes at an altar.

She didn't see any other machine men hybrids.

Is this the main power centre? she asked.

Yes.

Before she had a chance to set the detonator the butchered poet rolled into the vault. Alexandra swore and hung back, thinking she'd be seen.

Red Army soldiers have come down here, Viktor's faint Morse signals came back to her through the warm haze. *They will think you're one of them.*

Red Army? Aminev's troops are in this pit already? Maybe she looked like just another guard to the monsters but her old Soviet comrades would recognise her as an intruder in a flash.

She had no choice but to follow the cabinet as it rolled along. Alexandra sensed empty eyes and grey dough faces turned towards her. Nothing moved or called for them to stop. They made their way among the towering machinery like bugs in a radio, past more engines and through a second set of arches into a cavern filled with shells, casings, barrels, flasks and containers. *At last. Destroy this and we'll ignite a fire that'll fill the mountain.* She knelt down to start the detonator's countdown.

"Comrade Commissar?"

A human voice made her turn around. Three Red guards with pointed rifles at her head.

"Come with us."

Viktor had vanished among the stacks of ammunition and there'd been no time to set the fuse.

As they escorted Alexandra up through the mines she saw more of Aminev's infantry carrying boxes and pieces of machinery to the upper levels and the railway tunnel. Once in a while she spotted a four-armed synthetic or a cabinet on wheels. Whenever they crossed paths with these creatures the guards paused or gave them a wide berth. She remembered the sheer terror of the idiots guarding Electrical Girl 110 and wondered what the commander had promised or threatened his men with to force them down here. Should she try to reason with the soldiers, appeal to their comradeship and humanity? Why bother? The world in which hope mattered was long gone, replaced by this foul, monstrous hell. Viktor told her to kill Bakolov and then vanished without giving her a chance to start the fuse. What remained? The commissar might get a chance at the madman but what good would that do? The diseased maniac's time was past. He was already handing his legacy over to the Soviets. Anyway Alexandra doubted she'd come anywhere near the man. As soon as Aminev clapped eyes on her she was dead.

They came to the railway line and walked along it towards the valley. As they emerged into the warm light Alexandra realised how large Bakolov's synthetic army really was. There had to be at least a couple of thousand in a ragged crowd, swelling in size as it approached the village. She remembered Banjo comparing the mountain to a giant cheese and managed a smile. *The maggots have all been tapped out.* The Englishman had promised to destroy the Star Tsar's citadel. Maybe she'd trusted the idiot too much yet something told her the oaf wouldn't just fly away and abandon the alien's wonders to the enemy. Would he actually blow everything up? She was still prepared to be surprised by the mad fool.

Alexandra didn't see any discipline in the monstrous horde. They were more like a mass of pilgrims converging on the ruined church in search of relics and redemption than a functioning army. Here and there she spotted the brass spheres of bulbous atomic cannon or the honeycomb tubes of stranger-looking weapons. The guards closed ranks around her and she noticed the drawn horror in their eyes as they tried to ignore the creatures on either side.

The *Orlik* loomed ahead. Despite its horse wagons Alexandra couldn't see any cavalry, although she heard a few frightened whinnies. *They're keeping them away from the mutants for fear they'll panic and stampede. Whose bright idea was it to bring Cossacks here? Surely they're not going try and charge the fortress.* The rest of Aminev's soldiers stood in a ring around the land ironclad. She estimated there were a couple of hundred. Half the guns pointed at the sky but the others were aimed at the mutated crowds. *So the truce between Aminev and Bakolov isn't so secure after all.*

The cannon on the dreadnought opened up, the noise a physical punch in her gut that nearly brought Alexandra to her knees. The ground buckled as the entire train concertinaed backwards. A handful of men dropped their guns and clapped their hands to their ears until a sergeant bellowed at them to pick their fucking weapons up. The shells hit the church and it disappeared in explosions. Wood and rubble leaped hundreds of metres into the air. Flashbacks to the trenches almost had Alexandra crawling under the nearest wagon to escape the rain of mud, gore and shit her memory told her would follow. Instead the barrage stopped and a hatch in the conning turret popped open. A man in shirt sleeves with a cap on the back of his head and a pipe in his mouth climbed out and studied the target through binoculars. He jumped down onto the walkway between the turrets and shouted to someone on the other side.

Aminev. Now's your chance to kill him and Bakolov.

Alexandra's alien-enhanced strength would give her a brief advantage. If she wrested one of those guns from the soldiers she'd have time to put a bullet through the cruel bastard's face and cut down the scientist if he was here. It'd be better if she got her hands on an atomic machine gun but she didn't see any. It was too late - her escort were pushing her up onto the train. She scrambled over the rough iron to where the commander was talking to the White scientist. Bakolov sat on a howdah perched on the back of a giant who rested on all six limbs like a white crab. He reminded the commissar of an obese child squatting in a filthy play-pit. The stench of shit and chemicals made her head swim.

"An aura surrounds the mountain and protects it from my atomic fire," the lunatic whined. All immediate thoughts of killing him left Alexandra's mind. *His guns are useless against the fortress?*

"Your weapons can defend us against the space creature's flying machines if there's any remaining." Aminev's voice was full of tired contempt. "The *Orlik* will pound through the rock and then we'll get the sappers in."

He turned and gave Alexandra a disarming grin that looked so bizarrely genuine she didn't know how to react.

"Well here's the commissar who killed three men with her bare hands, freed your monsters and escaped back to the fortress of her friend the space creature. Tell me, can we speak with your beings from other worlds? Will they make a deal?"

"Kill the bitch," shrieked Bakolov. "She's dangerous. Kill her before she does more harm."

"You won't overcome the defences," Alexandra bluffed. "The Star Tsar's guards will destroy you."

"Perhaps. Comrade Bakolov here says there's little left in that mountain that can hurt us. Apparently the flying machine that attacked our train in the forest was old and damaged, though it gave a good account of itself. It hasn't appeared again, despite all this. Didn't you say it flew into space with your actress friend?"

He took Alexandra's elbow and led her to the conning tower, out of earshot of the alchemist.

"Christ, that Tsarist cunt stinks."

Bakolov's spider creature crept away. Alexandra said nothing, waiting for the commander to pull out his gun and shoot her. Instead Aminev knocked his pipe on the side of the turret and refilled it, striking a match on the sole of his boot and puffing away until they were wreathed in smoke.

"That's better," he gestured at the hatch. "Come and see."

When Alexandra hesitated the officer span her round and pushed her in the small of the back. Depending on how many crew were inside she might have a chance to kill them all and Aminev without the rest of the soldiers realising. She climbed into the belly of the *Orlik* and the commander closed the hatch behind them. They stood in a low corridor flanked with walls of ice. It was freezing. To her surprise they were the only ones in this part of the train. The others must be manning the guns. *He must know I can slaughter him in seconds. What's he playing at?*

"Bakolov had us turn this into a giant refrigerator with lead walls. Not sure why. He wants to replace the steam engine with an atomic machine of his own and apparently he needs all this to make it work. I'm not going to execute you, if that's what you're thinking. I like you, Comrade Lobachevsky. You're a good woman at heart and you understand all this. I was against your execution, even when your friend Comrade Commissar Poltzin threatened me with all sorts of party shit. When I heard you killed him and escaped - well, it cheered me to be honest, even if you cost me a couple of men. And now we have a chance for a proper talk in private. Just you and me."

Alexandra looked around. *He's going to power the Orlik with atomic fire?*

"You know what Bakolov is planning, don't you?" she said. "He wants to turn the proletariat into synthetic slaves in his vats and stick men like you and I in glass tanks on wheels to serve his new race of scientific masters."

Aminev grinned and shrugged.

"I can see that might appeal to some."

"We have to stop this, Comrade Aminev. It's evil - madness turning science and learning into more destruction and more machines of war. If we follow this lunatic's path it will take us straight back to the trenches and all the scientific engines of the new age shall be nothing but altars to Moloch - the cruel gods of old consuming our children in their furnaces and forges."

The officer gave her a tired smile.

"He hasn't got a path, whatever he thinks. No-one has, neither forwards nor backwards. There's no progress towards a higher purpose, a final liberation of man, only order and disorder. Your realm of Super Science won't create a workers' utopia. It'll serve whoever is the strongest, whoever has the clarity of soul and the strength of will to fashion an image of destiny for weaker men to cling to. That's what we need, not fantasies of endless revolution. Someone needs to wipe the world clean of misery and suffering and start anew, master humanity's future so that gods and goddesses shall walk the earth again."

Aminev rested his hand against the ice-wall.

"Gods and goddesses?" said Alexandra.

He means us.

Alexandra recognised the fire of a prophet in the man's lizard eyes and it threw her. Aminev of all men? It was insane. *When is this endless parade of maniacs hankering after the space being's powers going to end?* Standing in his uniform, with polished boots and bristle head, the commander still looked nothing more than a brutal career soldier, a well-organised and efficient thug. Yet his quiet voice was as a prophet's calling on the Tsar to fashion Moscow as the third Rome and conquer the world in the name of Christ Pantokrator. The shadows crowded in.

"Gods. Goddesses, like yourself," said Aminev. "Isn't that what you are now after eating the fruit from beyond the stars? Bakolov's sad beasts and his filthy Tsarist chaos are a means to an end, our end, nothing more."

A silence fell on the train as the aeons of deep time and vast reaches of interstellar space crowded into that metal box, waiting for Alexandra's answer. Aminev leaned back, folded his arms and grinned through his pipe smoke, as if they were friends setting the world to rights over vodka.

"Open the mountain and I'll kill Bakolov, and then we'll be lords of the Earth. We'll arm the *Orlik* with atomic weapons and use your star beast's technology to make it fly. Imagine, Alexandra, you and I voyaging above the clouds, dropping fire and judgement on those who would stand in the way of hope and progress. You want to build interplanetary ships to conquer space? Let's do it and no-one will stop us, neither Tsars nor Soviets nor Kings nor Emperors. Your creature understood. He kept the Old Believers like dumb cattle, stewing in their superstition and peasant ignorance. Great science is no measure of goodness. We learned that in the war. Up there in etheric space it's the same as down here - cruelty and struggle and dominion."

He saw the horror in Alexandra's eyes.

"Oh come on. You used the Star Tsar's powers to shatter your friend's skull, stove in the face of a guard, and break Yohzin's neck."

"Out of self-preservation."

Aminev shrugged and smiled as if he'd won the argument.

"Me too. Self-preservation with the strength of the new science, for all humanity. Hello?"

He reached up and opened the hatch. Outside the men were shouting.

"Well, well. Baba Yaga returns." The commander leaned out and studied the sky with binoculars. Alexandra peered out through an observation slit in the base of the turret, knowing full well what she'd see.

The stupid fool.

A speck emerged from a portal high in the rock face. The gunners on the *Orlik* traversed their weapons and ripples of movement spread out among the crowd of synthetics as the barrels of the atomic cannon drew a bead on the sentinel. He was supposed to destroy the citadel but instead the cretin had ordered the flying machine to attack the army.

"Let's see if Bakolov's guns work," muttered Aminev.

As the drone descended, jagged lines of electricity speared up towards the creature. They hit it head-on. Alexandra waited for the fragments to fall out of the sky but instead the rays splashed off an invisible barrier. More bolts joined the first and where they met she spotted an egg of light glowing white, then blue.

Bakolov said an aura shields the mountain from atomic fire. The flying machine has it too.

Firing stopped and the sentinel spiralled up towards the clouds, unharmed. What was that sitting on top, surrounded by the writhing tentacles?

I don't believe it. The stupid idiot's actually riding the thing.

"Baba Yaga!" shouted a soldier. A single gunshot followed.

"Any more fucking cowards care to comment?" bellowed an officer.

"Pathetic," grumbled Aminev. "So much for that Tsarist bastard's super weapons. Can you stop the thing?"

Before Alexandra could answer the atomic cannon started again, joined by a crackle of small arms.

"What's it doing? Why won't it shoot back at us?" said the commander. She had no idea. Dancing around in the sky drawing fire was probably part of the Englishman's plan but what he hoped to achieve was beyond her. Unless...

The fool knows I'm in the Orlik. He must have seen me arrive on the viewing screens and wants to rescue me.

"What the...?" said Aminev and the universe exploded.

It was like being on the interplanetary flyer when the gravity turned off. Alexandra floated into the centre of the wagon as all the observation slits filled with fire. She clamped her eyes shut but nothing happened. She still saw everything in stark black and white - ink drawings on sheets of endless howling chaos - each dial, lever, rivet and seam so bright they bored silhouettes through her head.

The world came back and she fell to the floor, splashing in water with her arms over her face as she felt the hairs on the backs of her hands crisp. *All the ice melted in a second.* From outside came the sound of a mountain collapsing mingled with a single vast shriek of pain and fear. Shells cascaded around her. The *Orlik* lay on its side, filled with choking steam and smoke. Alexandra clawed her way into the conning tower and grabbed onto Aminev's legs. They collapsed. The commander's top half had disappeared, leaving a hard crust sealing his hacked waist out of which trailed a cloud of cooked intestines.

The dreadnought shuddered and rolled upside down, iron spine shearing in staccato explosions. Coated in dust and oil and barely able to see, Alexandra fell into the turret, knee-deep in filthy slush. Another clang had her gripping the sides of her head to stop it bursting, just as the tower was wrenched away from the rest of the machine. She watched the twisted ironclad disappear into boiling clouds below. Nothing made sense. Was she floating in the air? Had the explosion tossed the entire armoured train into the sky? But Alexandra wasn't falling. Instead she rattled around the upturned conning tower like an egg in a bowl and it felt as if the whole assembly was accelerating upwards. She scrambled to her feet, holding her arms out to steady herself. Her hands were red, as if she'd got out of a steaming bath. Bracing herself against one of the wall struts, she reached up to grab the lip and peered over the edge onto Hell itself.

The forest and fields were a burning wasteland filled with charred corpses and littered here and there with oily fires. The train lay in pieces next to the track. The second armoured carriage looked half-melted. *How did I survive?* She turned to Bakolov's mountain, trying pick out detail through the endless churning soot and ember-soaked mist.

Smoking trenches miles long fanned out from every entrance, as if the cliff face had sprouted titanic blow-torches. Boiling slag ringed each hole, semi-molten rock dropping in red toffee strands into the steaming mud. A piece of the mountainside broke free and rolled down in an avalanche, sealing the main archway. The world shuddered with the impact and the inverted tower bucked, almost sending her sprawling to the bottom.

Viktor did it. He detonated the armoury and destroyed Bakolov's lair. Somehow the ruined poet had managed to set the detonator himself and trigger a holocaust of atomic fire to sweep through the mines, coring out the very peak itself.

Alexandra turned to look at the Star Tsar's citadel. Hill-sized scars caused by boulders hurled from the other mountain covered the cliff above the church. Otherwise it looked intact. The village had been flattened. Alexandra spotted tiny figures staggering back and forth. Mutants? Aminev's soldiers? It was impossible to recognise those bloody clusters of twigs lurching through the flames.

Banjo.

She clambered down into the turret. The hatch where Aminev had been standing was still open and all the water had drained away. Alexandra lay against the dome's inner surface and poked her head out. The flying sentry was directly below, its upright tentacles rigid, holding the conning tower above it. In the middle of the cluster stood the Englishman, clutching onto one limb and peering between the others. The man looked up, spotted her, gave a big grin and waved. Alexandra tried to call down but her voice was a dusty croak.

"We have to go back. We have to destroy the Star Tsar's

citadel."

She gestured frantically at the mountain receding behind them. Banjo nodded, grinned a bit more and flashed her the thumbs up. She shouted again but the engineer tapped his ear, shook his head and shrugged. No amount of pointing got through. It was obvious the man knew exactly what she wanted but was deliberately ignoring her. Alexandra called to the drone itself in Slavonic but the wind carried her words away. Peaks hurtled past on both sides. *The bastard's running off and taking me with him.*

She toyed with the idea of climbing down but they were speeding up and the increasing hurricane would snatch her off the second she tried. They were beyond the mountains now and the sun was setting to her right. *We're flying south.* Night came. Exhausted and with no options left she closed the hatch, rolled herself up in her coat and fell asleep.

Alexandra woke as the turret touched the ground with a gentle bump and tilted over onto its side. As she staggered to her feet she spotted Banjo and the sentinel conferring twenty yards off. The landscape looked completely alien. A flat line separating dark earth and pale sky, punctuated by the silhouettes of man and machine. Had they somehow ended up back on Mars? No, the gravity was too high. They were still on Earth, but where? The Englishman was saying something and gesturing into the distance.

"We have to go back, we have to go back now!" Alexandra called out. She staggered towards the pair just as the sentinel lifted into the air and sped away. Banjo picked up one of two sacks and held it out to her.

"Before you go off on a bloody to-do I told it to fly home and destroy the Star Tsar's den. At least I think I did."

"You don't speak Slavonic."

"No but it understands French as well."

"French?"

"I taught it French. Well, maybe it also got some from the radio cocaine inside Ekaterina's head."

"You're a total lunatic," yelled Alexandra. "What were you doing taking on Bakolov's army with the flying machine?"

Banjo pulled a pair of apples out of his bag, plonked one in her hand and bit into the other, ruminating at the dawn.

"I couldn't understand why Bollock-off didn't melt his way in with his cannon so I set off two of the looney's radium bullets inside the lair. The whole mountain's covered in some kind of ray protecting it against atomic fire as was the sentinel. When I saw you imprisoned in the train it was Banjo to the rescue. You can say thank you anytime. I'm not proud."

Alexandra looked around.

"Where are we?

"Border between Mongolia and China. I noticed a railway line somewhere that-a-way. And there's a bunch of characters not far off with horses. Shape yourself. We're still alive and I have a taste for new wonders."

He heaved his sack over his shoulder and set off southward, whistling through his teeth. Alexandra stared after, trying to decide whether or not to murder him. *If I do that I'll have no-one. Everybody else abandoned me.* She scanned the horizon but the drone had disappeared. Would it go back and destroy itself and the Star Tsar's Super Science? It was a lot more trustworthy than that idiot swaggering across the desert like he owned the world. But what could she do? Run after it? They were hundreds of miles away, if not a thousand. She stared at the apple in her hand until Banjo was a dot on the horizon. Eventually she stuffed it into her pocket and staggered away from the last fragment of the *Orlik*.

Marrakech, French Morocco, September 1924.

The endless chain of men and women stumbled back and forth under a bleached sky full of acid sunlight and choking dust. Moroccans, French, Spanish, once in a while an American or two in sweat-stained suits clutching battered cases as they threaded through the alleyways beneath the window. She'd seen her friends among them.

Broken dolls all.

The scouring sand recast their desiccated flesh into porcelain and cellulose, cracked and broken as they shuffled past, eyes full of reproach. Ekaterina, The Hammer, Anton, Viktor, Pavel, even Aminev, sloppily stuck back together so his guts flapped out of the back of his pants. That made her chuckle.

The second bottle of cheap Cognac was almost empty. These days getting drunk by mid-morning was a long, brutal affair. She fought a losing battle against Super Science - the star creatures inside her that turned her into a god and rendered alcohol impotent. She laughed into the splintered table top. Most days Commander Aminev's goddess walked the Earth in piss-stained khaki with the mother of all hangovers.

Alexandra was a dead soul, drifting through the fragments of all her hopes. The Soviet Union - her Soviet Union - was no more, had never even existed. All the hope and possibility, the new-forged fellowship of men and women, the freedom to love whoever she wished and be loved in turn without fear or judgement - all taken away, and when the Star Tsar offered her a chance to touch the stars she'd said no. Once or twice Alexandra had tried to kill herself but something stopped her. Probably it was because she was nothing more than a pathetic coward in the end. She'd located an opium den in one of the Marrakech slums but the Star Tsar's food had made her immune to the drug. All she found were the tag ends of dreams in which she ran through a mountain rotten with tunnels and filled with maggots as big as men. They all had her own face, slack jawed and stupid as they lectured her on dialectical materialism.

Instead she sat day after day in the ramshackle apartment and tried to drink herself into oblivion. Somehow Banjo made enough money for the two of them. Christ only knew what he was up to. She couldn't understand why the Englishman hadn't abandoned her. Instead he pestered Alexandra to go on expeditions to curio shops, libraries and, once or twice, the remains of ancient observatories in the desert. She always refused and the man patted her on the shoulder and said maybe next time. If she'd been in the Englishman's shoes she'd have left ages ago.

A book thumped onto the table, jarring her out of a doze. She read the title upside down.

The Gods of Mars by Edgar Rice Burroughs.

"At last. I've been hunting for this one for years. I'd heard it was out but it was a bugger getting hold of a copy, what with the war and all. You can borrow it after. I got you this to be going on with. It's exactly the kind of pompous blather you like."

Another book landed beside the first.

Ralph 124C 41+ by Hugo Gernsback.

"Ralph one to foresee - get it? Foresee the future? Oh, never mind. Anyway..."

Banjo pushed a newspaper across the table, tapping a column with his finger.

"Listen to this. A glass maker's been murdered. Apparently the poor bugger had been fashioning a lens as big as a church door. It was for a special client who they say was in league with a giant demon whose lair is deep inside the Atlas Mountains. His family found his gutted body stamped flat in the middle of a load of footprints that are five times human size. The police gave up, claiming it's a bizarre crime of passion. Sounds like adventure and excitement to me. What do you think?"

Alexandra pushed the paper to one side and opened the book.

The stars shone with a brilliancy never seen from Earth.

"A lens as big as a church door? What for?" she managed to ask.

"I don't bloody know, do I? But I'm itching to find out."

"They haven't come for me." Alexandra slopped out another measure of brandy but before she could grab it Banjo moved the tumbler and bottle out of reach.

"Who? Your Bolshevik mates? They're still in a tizzy after matey-boy Lenin died, aren't they? I doubt very much there's hordes of Red spies hunting you down. They'd have found you by now seen as how you've been sitting at the window in plain view pissed as a fart and lamenting to the heavens for the last three months."

He tapped the paper again.

"What do you say?"

Endless chain of men and women against a bleached sheet sky. Broken dolls all. But her friends had vanished. There was only her and Banjo left. Alexandra put the novel in her pocket and staggered upright, peering down into the street.

One to foresee the future.

She just about managed a nod.

THE END

Extract from *Slaves of Titan*…

Banjo and Alexandra swung back and forth over a bottomless pit in the depths of the Atlas Mountains, each dangling by the ankles from their own steel chain. The little Russian pillock was still unconscious, arms hanging down, hands flapping as if she was trying to conduct Satan's orchestra, which no doubt lay a thousand miles below at the bottom of the shaft, tuning up. Once in a while they'd bump together. Their captors had arranged it so the two companions' heads were at the same level and whenever they met their skulls smacked like conkers.

A tunnel above admitted light into the volcanic chimney, which was otherwise sealed by a hill-sized boulder. The miserable trickle from the diseased stars outside ping-ponged off a few crystal seams, but other than that it was a featureless rock throat. Not a whiff of sulphur or brimstone from the darkness below, just the eternal leaden notes of granite, quartz and grit.

You have read your Mr Jules Verne, have you not, Signor Banjo? the bastard had asked as his chums tied them up. The sleeping gas wore off faster with the engineer, but he hadn't time to muster enough strength to fight back, otherwise Prince Mincing Shit and a few more of his flunkies would be heading core-ward. *This truly does lead to the centre of the Earth. I would keep still, very very still. If your chains break, you will fall for days.*

Alexandra shuddered, arms flailing. Banjo wondered if she was waking up, but the Russian merely grunted and flopped back into unconsciousness. *She's not fondling the lass in her sleep, is she? Has she no sense of place?*

While he oscillated gently to and fro, feet growing numb, he supposed there was an odd poetic justice to all this. He'd first met the canting lunatic after being captured in an iron works in the middle of Siberia eighteen months ago. At the tag end of the Civil War, the Soviet army drove the last of the international troops out of a slush, shrapnel and soot-coated dump called Ikayungri, leaving him trapped behind in an immense factory. The Reds had strung him up by his ankles in a shed and were getting ready to cut his bollocks off with rusty shears to add to their stew, and then push the rest of him into a furnace. It was only when Alexandra had heard him swearing at his captors in English that the commissar intervened and saved his life.

Because they shared a love of scientific romances, the mad bint had got it into her head to convert Banjo to communism. That hadn't lasted, but they'd stuck together and now dangled upside down side by side in a right perilous do. At least this time his beard was shorter, so he could see what was going on, which was bugger all. It was also a damn sight hotter here than in Siberia. Big blobs of stinging sweat trickled out of his cheek whiskers and into his eyes. He felt like one of those hams they sold in Barcelona markets, strung up on a hook and dripping endless mucky grease into a foil bucket. He was also starting to feel the urge to piss and no matter the gymnastics it'd be bound to go everywhere.

Enough of this.

What their captors didn't know was that, during their sojourn in the village of the Star Tsar, the pair had consumed several bowls of alien food filled with tiny machines that now scampered up and down their bloodstreams, conferring boosted strength. Alexandra, being a weedy bookworm, would be easy to carry. If Banjo jackknifed he might be able to grab his own chain and use his knees and one hand to pull himself up while hauling the comatose Red after him. Halfway was close enough to the entrance for him to swing back and forth until their momentum carried them into the tunnel. All he'd have to do then was wrestle free of their chains and Bob's your uncle.

He wriggled around to face his friend and reached out to grab her. At that moment the idiot flailed out at her dream enemies and smacked Banjo in the mouth, sending him into a corkscrew spin. The Englishman swore long and violently as he pendulumed to and fro. He lunged once more and caught the woman's trouser leg. This was proving a lot harder than anticipated. Every movement sent the pair of them oscillating in the semi-darkness. Their manacles chafed and twisted together and rust fell into his eyes and up his nose. If the links got tangled, they wouldn't be going anywhere.

Banjo reached up to ease the two chains apart. Alexandra's loosened around her ankles and she began to slip. The engineer bellowed and grabbed wildly for the woman's belt, but only succeeded in pushing himself away. One of the Red's feet slipped out, and the lass hung from the other like a wonky cross. As she swung back Banjo reached upwards to grab the chain in an attempt to loop it tighter. He'd underestimated his strength. Far above the piton holding the links to the ceiling snapped, the metal rattled past his fingertips, and Alexandra, still unconscious, fell into the bottomless darkness.

Slaves of Titan, Book 2 in the Banjo and Alexandra series, will be published late 2023...

John Guy Collick was born in Yorkshire, England. When he was 10 years old his grandfather gave him a copy of *A Princess of Mars* by Edgar Rice Burroughs, and from then on he was hooked on science fiction and fantasy. He worked for Scotland Yard before moving to Japan for ten years to lecture in literature and philosophy. Now he works as a consultant in education and technology. He spends much of his time giving presentations at conferences around the world on transhumanism and the impact of ICT on society, the individual and the classroom. *The Star Tsar* is his fifth novel and the first volume in the *Banjo and Alexandra* series.

John Guy Collick lives in Hampshire, England.

Website: https://johnguycollick.substack.com

Other books by John Guy Collick

Thumb

Ragged Claws

AntiHelix

Dark Feathered Hearts

Shakespeare, Cinema and Society